THIS LIFE AND THE NEXT

ASTRONOMICAL LOVE SERIES
BOOK 1

K. ILLER

First edition January 2024

Book Cover by Kim Giller

Editing and Formatting by Vanessa Mena, Dark Queens Author Services

Ebook ISBN: 979-8-9897308-0-3

Paperback ISBN: 979-8-9897308-2-7

Hardcover ISBN: 979-8-9897308-1-0

To those of us that wear our heart on our sleeve, want a love that transcends all time, makes us reach for the stars, and to have a man that fucks us like his dirty little whore.

———·★·

To all of us survivors. Some of the wounds they inflicted upon us will be there until our dying breath. It's okay to stumble and fall. To truly break under the weight of the effects their imprints left on us. But never forget, we fight until we think we have nothing left. And while they cower behind their masks and rituals to get through their miserable existence, we will always be the ones that come out on top. This is our story. This is our moment. Repeat after me.
"I fucking survived and I fucking win."
Now say it again, and on every dark day that feels like it will smother us into submission.

THIS LIFE AND THE NEXT SPOTIFY PLAYLIST

Listen to the full playlist here: https://open.spotify.com/ playlist/3shybyw83fJcBazBuL0cXN?si=jEBGh4jUTimkRBw4Pb b2_A

ITALIAN TO ENGLISH TRANSLATIONS:

Amissa Stella - Lost Star
    vaffanculo - go fuck yourself
    madre - mother
    nonna - grandmother
    porca puttana - pig whore
    cazzo - damn / fuck
    dio mio - oh my god
    bastardo - bastard
    che cazzo state facendo, idioti? - what the fuck are you idiots doing?
    idiota - idiot
    scusa, capo - sorry, boss
    mia figlia - my daughter
    dimenticare - to forget
    bellissima - extremely beautiful / most beautiful
    amore - love

TRIGGER WARNINGS

Off page rape, body horror, on and off page sexual assault, body modifications, off page child abuse, dead bodies & body parts, violence, dismemberment, death, eyeball trauma, off page self-harm, genital mutilation, physical assault, needles, bodily waste: such as vomit, feces or urine, mutilation, nudity, physical injuries, blood, scars, drug use, death of a friend, drug trafficking, death of a parent & guardian, tobacco and marijuana use, asphyxia, strangulation & suffocation, slut-shaming, blackmail, abandonment, captivity & confinement, off page cheating (not between main character's), disappearance of a loved one, domestic abuse & violence, electrocution, emotional abuse, explosions, infidelity, arson, intimate partner abuse & violence, garroting, addiction, gun violence, alcoholism, kidnapping, anxiety & anxiety attacks, knife and ax violence, depression, murder, gambling addiction, attempted murder, hallucinations, torture, intrusive thoughts, vitriolage, acute Obsessive-Compulsive Disorder, mentions of piquerism, phobias, profanity, Post Traumatic Stress Disorder, sexually explicit scenes, sleep disorders, breath play, substance addiction, primal/prey play, alcohol consumption & abuse, brief mentions of religion, drug abuse, religious criticism, drugging (fentanyl and flumazenil), off page amputation, blood & gore depiction, impact play

BEFORE YOU BEGIN READING

The following prologue contains depictions of domestic violence. There is no SA in this scene but it is violent. If you're not comfortable with this, please skip the prologue and start on Chapter 1.

PROLOGUE

DEVIL DOESN'T BARGAIN

3 MONTHS AGO

Nova

This isn't the life I want. I haven't for a long time. I've been lying here for what feels like hours. The pain from the blooming bruise on my cheek makes me wince as I wipe away my tears. Behind me, I can hear my soon-to-be ex-boyfriend finally start to snore. I was wondering how long it would take for the drugs and alcohol to knock him out. I've wanted to escape him for a long time, but I could never find the motivation. How did I become this person? Before him, I always said I would never let a man control me or put his hands on me. Yet here I am, bloodied and bruised from another torture session with him.

I've put up with his bullshit for far too long, and I'm fucking done. With him passed out hard, tonight is the perfect night to leave. Another saving grace. He was too fucked up to tamper with my car like he usually does. I have been preparing for this for a while and packed everything I need in the trunk of my unlocked car. All I have to do is grab my shoes, keys, and phone.

Taking a deep breath, the searing pain from my ribs at the motion almost makes me pass out. Squeezing my eyes shut tight, I barely hold back the hiss of pain. Letting out a shaky breath, I slide out of the bed. I feel for my keys between the mattress and the box spring. I hold them as tight as possible so they don't make any noise. Pocketing my phone, I tip-toe around the bed. This feels almost impossible, trying to monitor both him and my steps so I don't run into anything or trip. Unable to stop myself, I look over my shoulder at the door to make sure he's still there. Breathing a small sigh of relief, I put my keys in my pocket and grab my Converse. Sliding them both on, I decide against tying them right now. As quietly as I can, I unlock the deadbolt and knob lock. Gripping the door knob tight with my left hand, and placing my right palm against the door, I brace myself to escape. As soon as I manage to crack the door, he grabs my hair and slams my head into it. "Ah fuck!" *Oh god, what do I do? Fuck, fuck, fuck. Stay calm, Nova. Focus and figure a way out.*

"Where the fuck do you think you're going, you little fucking bitch? Hmm? Are you running out to go fuck someone like the cum guzzling slut you are?"

I attempt to shake my head, unable to move with his grip on my hair. "No Frankie, I wouldn't do that. You know I wouldn't. I wanted to go outside for a smoke, that's all. I swear." He releases my hair and spins me around, pushing me up against the door with his body. I grimace at the feeling of his cock brushing against me. Of course he's hard, he always is when he's hurting me. Looking up into his eyes, I can see that his pupils are so blown they're almost completely black. When his eyes get like that, the demon is here to seek and destroy. I put my palms up and place them on his chest to placate him. "I promise, Frankie, it was just for a smoke. Why don't we go back to bed huh?" I slide my hand down his chest until it rests over his cock and give it a quick stroke, "Don't you wanna take me to bed?"

He thrusts his cock into my stroking hand, "Mmm. That's right, you little cum guzzling gutter slut." I flinch at his words.

As much as I'm used to them, they still hurt. Releasing my hold on his cock, I push a little against his chest.

"Come on, lead the way, babe." He turns and walks through the dining room heading to the kitchen. I frantically look around for anything I can use as a weapon. My eyes fall on the toaster that's on the counter. Grabbing ahold of it and yanking as hard as I can to unplug it, I lift it above my head and bring it down on the back of his head.

Frankie stumbles and yells, "WHAT THE FUCK BITCH?!" He spins around and I clip him on the head again with the toaster. I throw all my weight forward and tackle him to the ground. The toaster is pinned between us so I rear my head back and throw it forward onto his nose. I shuffle as fast as I can to get up. Doing so unpins our hands and he brings his up, gripping my throat. I can barely breathe. Bringing my hands up, I start tearing at the flesh of his hands and wrists. I release my hold on him and jab him in the eyes with my thumbs. Pushing as hard as I can, I get him to release his hold on my neck. When he lifts his hands to get my thumbs out of his eyes, I move my hands and grab the toaster again. I hit him with it in the jaw, drop the toaster, and begin throwing wild punches anywhere I can hit. I hit him enough times that he stops deflecting my hits. Scrambling back as fast as I can, I pull myself up with the help of the counter. Keeping an eye on him and looking for a better weapon, he starts to get up off the floor. I see a pot on the breakfast counter and grab it by the handle. Holding it out towards him, "Stay right there, Frankie. Please, just let me go."

He lets out a dark laugh, "Let you go? I told you before, bitch. The only way I'll ever let you go is the day I kill you. Looks like that will be tonight." He starts marching towards me, so I lift the pot over my head and run towards him. Swinging, the pot hits him in the head once to the left side, then the right. I hit hard enough that he stumbles back and looks dazed. I can't risk stopping now, so I lift the pot in the air again and bring it down on top of his head over and over again. After the fifth hit, he falls to the floor.

Panting from the exertion, I take a step back with the pot still raised in the air. I can't waste this chance, I need to leave now. I continue backing out of the kitchen towards the front door. I bring the pot down to my right side and check my hoodie pocket for my keys and phone. I don't know how, but they stayed in my pocket. *Thank fuck for that, I need every ounce of luck I can get.* Ripping the door open, I shove through the screen door and run down the porch ramp to my old beat-up Civic. I hop in slamming the door shut behind me. *This would be a great time for automatic locks.* I lock the driver's door and then lean over, locking the passenger door. Not wasting any time, I jam the keys in the ignition and turn the car on. Flying down the driveway, I speed out of the neighborhood. I drive to the nearest gas station and park. Hopping out of the car, I slam the door shut and run into the gas station. Last second, I put my head down and lean down to tie my shoes while covering my face with my hair. I probably look like I stumbled out of a horror movie set. I grab two energy drinks and head for the counter. Still keeping my head down, I ask the clerk, "Hey could I please get two packs of Marlboro Smooth 100s and a lighter?"

The clerk doesn't make any move to get what I asked for. "Hey miss, umm, is everything okay?" Looking up I catch the look of shock on the older lady's face. She lets out a small gasp, "Oh my god, dear. What happened?"

I shake my head and let out a nervous chuckle, "Rough night, that's all. Umm, I don't wanna be rude, but I'm really in a hurry." She searches my face for a moment, then nods and grabs my cigarettes and lighter. Ringing everything up, I pay her as she bags it up. "Thank you, have a good night." I turn and start walking towards the doors.

"You sure you don't need me to call anyone?"

I look over my shoulder and smile, "Thank you, but I'm okay. I'm free from this life, now onto the next." She gives me a small smile and nods.

I push through the doors and run back to the car. Hopping in, I toss everything on the passenger seat and pull my phone out. I pick one of my many favorite **FUCK FRANKIE** songs on my favorite music app. The sound of *We Are Never Ever Getting Back Together* by *Taylor Swift* fills my car. I toss my phone on the passenger seat and turn the volume knob all the way up. I crack open my energy drink and take a long drink from it. Fishing around in the bag, I grab one of the packs of smokes and pull them out. Patting them against my hand, I tear off the cellophane and wrapper. I crank the window lever to roll my window down a little and light my cigarette. I exhale the smoke and whisper, "You are Nova Skye Hart, and no one will ever control your mind, body, or heart again."

"I was heartbroken, scared, I had a lot of anxiety, I was worried, I felt weak, and I had no idea how I was ever going to come up with the strength. But I just closed my eyes and took a blind leap. I knew I had to get out of there." ~ Casey

CHAPTER 1
DON'T FEAR THE REAPER

Nova

I gasp and jolt up in a panic, gripping my chest and panting. I ping-pong my eyes around in the darkness, searching for the threat. I jump out of bed and reach for the bat hidden under my bed. Gripping it tight, I grab my phone from the nightstand. I shakily bring the phone to life and unlock it. I turn on the flashlight and point it around the room, illuminating it. I take deep breaths to get my breathing under control. I have to know. Is he here, or was it another nightmare? *Fuck, please let it be a nightmare.* I look under the bed, finding nothing there. I search my entire room, holding the bat at the ready. I check every corner of the room. I stop in front of the closet, grab the handle the best I can with the bat in hand and rip the door open. I bounce the flashlight around the inside of the closet and hit my clothes with the bat just to be sure. The scrape of the hangers on the bar makes me grimace. I step back when the only sounds surrounding me are my panted breaths and the creak of my clothes on their hangers. I turn myself sideways as I enter the bathroom to make sure I can be ready for anything from any direction. The bat starts to slip from my clammy hands. I grip it tight until my knuckles turn white and ache. I swing the bat as hard as I can and it clinks against the wall, echoing in the tiny space. *Empty.*

Okay, Nova, just check the rest of the apartment. You won't find him and everything will be okay. Heading into my living room, I search every corner and behind my couch. My small kitchen is empty as well. Turning towards the French doors hiding my washer and dryer, I tip-toe over and rip the doors open. I take in a shaky breath. Okay, just a nightmare. I walk over to my door and double-check my locks. Knob, deadbolt, chain, all locked. *Good.* I point the flashlight at the mini alarm connected to my door and see it's still switched on. A sigh of relief escapes me when I've made sure that every window is locked, wood blocks in place, and mini alarms are all switched on. Knowing that I'll never get back to sleep, I head to the kitchen and start a pot of coffee. After I put my bat away, I turn my flashlight off and note the time. 4:49 AM, *great.* I slept for maybe 2 hours. "Typical," I groan out in frustration. Since sleep isn't happening, I might as well get my workday started. I open the drawer in my night-stand and pull out my laptop and charger. Glancing at my collection of knives and pepper spray, I grab one of each and put them in my pocket. After putting my laptop on the couch, I head back to the kitchen to check on the progress of my coffee and grab my cigarettes and lighter. I switch the mini alarm to the chime position, unlock all three locks, and take out my can of pepper spray. It's ready to go before I step outside. I leave the door open a crack and sit on my patio chair. I position myself perfectly in a corner so nobody can come up behind me and I can see everything... more like anyone who approaches me. I put the pepper spray on my little patio table and grab my pack of cigarettes out of my pocket. Pulling one out of the pack, I place the cigarette between my lips and light it. I take a deep inhale of the smoke and lay my head back, tossing the lighter on the table as well.

Oh, Nova, you replaced one hell for another. Fuck it, I can live with that. This version of hell is still far better than the one before. I'll remain hyperaware and vigilant forever just to avoid being his torture toy again. Closing my eyes, I conjure up the image of the captivating green eyes that visit me in my dreams. I smile at the image, wishing I could dream more about those green eyes rather than the nightmares of Frankie. Finishing up my smoke, I grab everything and head inside. Locking up again, I head to my room and grab the wooden box on my dresser. Bringing it out to the living room, I put it down on the table and pull one of my joints and lighter out. Lighting it, I walk to the kitchen and grab my coffee so I can start my work-from-home job.

———➤

I sit back and yawn while rubbing my eyes, pulling off my headphones that are blaring *(Don't Fear) The Reaper* by *Blue Oyster Cult*. Looking at the time, I've been working for just about 7 hours. *Thank fuck for being an online assistant where I get to choose my hours.* This company was my lighthouse on a stormy night. After weeks of driving around and slumming it in motels on the last bit of money I had, a job offer from them came in. Resume power words for the win. I didn't even know the town of La Grande existed and had to look it up. Small town life and far from Frankie sounded perfect to me. After excitedly responding to them that I most definitely would be taking the job, I may have jumped and danced around my motel room. We won't discuss the laughter and tears that joined the party.

I shut everything down and place the laptop on my side table. Stretching out, I sigh as various joints pop from long hours of hovering over my laptop.

Grabbing a *Monster*, I decide to hop in the shower. I chuckle as I take my black shirt with a skeleton throwing up the okay sign saying, 'NEVER BETTER' from the drawer. I shut the top two drawers to avoid hitting my head on them... for the thou-

9

sandth time. My clothes are thrown on the bed as I open my closet to search for one of my hooded black and red flannels. I grab that and a pair of black Converse from my shoe organizer and kick the door shut. Turning on my speaker, I open *Spotify* on my phone, scroll through my songs and pick *Rewrite the Stars* by *Zac Efron* and *Zendaya*, maxing out the volume.

I grab my *Monster* and finish the last of it, tossing the can in the garbage. I crouch down and open the sink cupboard, shuffling through my little container of shower steamers. Picking the caramel apple one, I toss it in the container in my shower and turn on the water. I avoid my gaze in the mirror and turn away to pull off my hoodie and sleep shorts. I step into the shower to wash my hair with my cinnamon apple shampoo and conditioner. Grabbing my razor and shea butter shaving cream, I shave my armpits and legs. Shaving a little too fast, I wince and hiss at the slice to my knee. I look down and watch as the blood slowly pools to the surface and drips down my leg. A door slamming outside startles me, making my heart pound and my stomach roll with unease. I take a deep breath and sit on the floor of the shower under the water spray. Shaking my head, I fold my arms over my knees and put my head down. *Jesus Nova, get a fucking grip*. Having enough of my stupid freak out, I get up, shut the water off, and step out of the shower.

I grab my towel from the rack, and rub it through my hair. Wrapping the towel around my body, I head to my room to get dressed. *I need to go hang out at my favorite spot so I can chill out.* After getting dressed I walk back to the bathroom and throw my towel in the hamper. I pocket my phone and head back to my room, making sure to turn off my speaker. Grabbing my wallet out of my nightstand, I grab a can of pepper spray, connect the keyring to my belt loop, and slide one of my knives into my pocket. I head over to my closet and grab my Harry Potter backpack, tossing my wallet inside and zipping it up.

I throw the backpack over my shoulder and head to the front door. Grabbing my smokes and lighter, pocketing them in the breast pocket, I head out the door and lock up. With the warmth of the sunshine on my skin, I roll up the sleeves of my hooded flannel. It may seem ridiculous to wear this in late spring, but the weather is unpredictable in Eastern Oregon. I unlock the door, toss my backpack on the passenger side floor and drop in, quickly locking the door.

Opening *Spotify*, I pick *Give* by *Sleep Token* and turn the volume and bass up to max level. The vibrations of the bass running through my body bring a sense of comfort. Tossing my phone on the passenger seat, I crack open my window and reach into my left breast pocket for a cigarette. By the time I'm pulling out of the parking lot, *Give* is done playing and I'm now jamming out to *Enter Sandman* by *Metallica*. Drumming the steering wheel and screaming the lyrics, I reach the amazing bookstore here in town where I work part-time. I search for a parking spot and pull in.

"We all struggle to make sense of our own minds... We all battle with demons that nobody else can see." ~Renata Suzuki

CHAPTER 2
EMERALD EYES

Nova

Swan & Scribe. My home away from home. I love everything about this bookstore. The place is huge. I mean, don't get me wrong, small and quaint bookstores are great, but this place is pure magic. Multiple areas for people to lounge and read, places to play games and chat, and a fucking coffee bar! I mean, seriously, it doesn't get any better than that. Looking around, I spot the owner, Vanessa, heading back to the register.

She looks up just as I approach and smiles, "Hey, Nova girl. It's your day off. Are you on a mission for something new and spicy, or just here to hang out?"

Leaning my hip against the counter so I can talk to her and still be aware of my surroundings, I let her know, "Oh you know me, V. I'm always here to hang out while on the hunt for something new and spicy. Is The Horde here today? They'll give me shit if they find out I was here and didn't grace them with my presence." I chuckle at the absurdness of it. *Who the hell gives a shit if I say hi or not? Fuck. That's Frankie talking. Knock it off, Nova.* Shaking my head at the thought, I look up at Vanessa and catch her looking at me with concern. Feeling uneasy that she caught on to my wariness, I wave her off and she lets me know that The Horde is here.

Pushing myself off the counter, I tap it with my hand, "Welp, better go get my caffeine fix and go see them. When slacker hours hit, join us."

As I'm walking away I hear her grumble under her breath, "Slacker hours, my ass." Chuckling at the statement, I head towards the coffee bar.

Once I reach the counter, I order an iced caramel coffee- *extra, extra* caramel of course, and an apple crumble muffin. While waiting for my order, I take the seat that lets me sit with my back to the walls. Bouncing my knee up and down while drumming my fingers on the tabletop, I look around the bookstore. While waiting, I daydream of the green eyes I see in my dreams. I don't even know who they belong to, but they bring me a sense of calm I've never felt before. They've never felt like a stranger to me, more like a missing puzzle piece. It reminds me of that song *IDK You Yet,* when they sing about, *"How can you miss someone you've never met? 'Cause I need you now, but I don't know you yet."* Every time I see those green eyes or think about how much I miss them, I always think of that song. I'm snapped out of my thoughts when the barista calls my name. Getting up, I walk over and grab my drink and muffin. Smiling, I hold up my drink, nodding my head and thanking them.

Weaving in and out of book aisles, I head towards the back of the store to find The Horde. They usually hang out back here so they can bullshit and play games. Considering I only see and talk to them here, I feel pretty close to the tight-knit group. When I first met them I told myself not to get too close and build friendships, because who knows how long I would actually be able to stick around La Grande. They weren't having any of that shit and took me under their wing immediately. When you think of usual cliques, this group would never fit the mold. It's a collective of people with different styles, interests and beliefs. You would think it doesn't work but it does and they're a family in every way. Speaking of family behavior, I can already hear the group bickering. I turn the corner and see the group loud and animated.

"I can't believe they let a bunch of fucking heathens up in this bitch!" At my words, they all look up and immediately greet me, and shuffle around to make room for me to sit down. Noticing the space they've given me, it shows yet again, I'm one of them. They all made sure to give me the seat with my back against the corner. Letting out a nervous chuckle, I push back the skin-crawling feeling of being known far too well. I ask what they're all bickering about, and as usual they all start answering at the same time. "You guys, one at a time, holy fuck. Information overload."

Viking, which is a totally fitting name for the dude, begins telling me that they're scoping out their *Pokémon* cards and deciding who has the best ones. I sip on my coffee and eat my muffin while watching the chaos unfold. Finishing up my snack, I grab the garbage, standing up to leave. Everybody stops what they're doing and looks up at me.

"Anyone ever told y'all it's creepy as shit when you do that?" Tilting my head towards the garbage, "I'm gonna go look for my book porn, y'all."

As I start walking away, I feel a pull on my sleeve. Turning to look I see that it's Jade. Furrowing my brow, "Uh, hey Jade, what's up?"

She smiles up at me, "It's funny how we all end up exactly where we're supposed to be, isn't it?"

Chuckling, "Uh, I mean I guess. Not quite sure I've had my moment yet though."

She tilts her head squinting at me, "You'll see, hunny. Your happiness is right around the corner. I know it." I'm tempted to tell her nothing works out for me, but something stops me at that moment.

"I..." My heart slightly pounds and I suck in a breath. The strangest feeling washes over me, like something is shifting. *What the fuck?* I shake my head at the feeling. "Maybe."

Lifting my drink in cheers, "Here's fucking hoping, huh?" She releases her hold on my sleeve and nods, slowly walking back to the group.

Tossing my garbage, I head over to spice land to scope out my next read. Rubbing my chest, I pull at my clothes as I walk. The feeling from before still hasn't left me, and I can't pinpoint what it is. While searching through the books I grab a mafia romance that looks intriguing. As I'm reading the synopsis, I can hear two guys whisper-shouting.

"How much longer are we going to be here for, Dori?"

"I told you not to fucking call me that, you asshole. And I don't know, maybe I'll make you wait for an exponential amount of time."

"Really? Just cuz you're a genius doesn't mean you need to throw random ass big words in your sentences. Makes you sound like a... pretentious douchebag."

"Look at you, Reese's Pieces. You used a big word yourself. Did it hurt your brain?"

"Oh, ha-ha. And don't call me Reese's Pieces."

"Listen, if you can call me Dori, I can call you Reese's Pieces."

Quietly laughing at the two, I go back to reading about the book. Deciding the book I'm holding will be good, I scan the shelves for another. As I'm searching through the various books, my heart starts to race. I bring my hand to my chest, book included, in a failed attempt to calm my racing heart. *What the fuck is going on? Fuck it, I'll just get this book and get back to The Horde.*

I quickly turn and immediately stop in my tracks just before running into two men. Quickly averting my eyes from them, "Uh, fuck. Sorry about that, lemme just get outta your way."

"No need to apologize. You don't need to leave on our

account." I freeze at the man's words. Looking up in the direction the kind voice came from, I see a tall man with slicked-back, wavy brown hair. He smiles at me when our eyes connect. *Is it possible for someone to look like a badass and a cute little puppy all in one?* He's all tatted up, wearing a black button-up, the first three buttons undone, showing a portion of a Baphomet tattoo, and black, torn skinny jeans. The kind face is what screams golden retriever though. *Words Nova, use them.*

"Umm… no, no, I'm not leaving because of you two. I just wanted to get back to my friends." Looking over at the other man, I note his brown work boots, black jeans, *Led Zeppelin* shirt - *ha nice*, black and red flannel and tattoos peeking out of his shirt collar. As if he feels my eyes on him, he looks up and our eyes widen at the same time as we sharply inhale. *Green. Green eyes. **THE** fucking green eyes that I see every time I dream. This isn't possible, is it?* We stand there staring at each other for who knows how long until a throat clears. Our heads shoot up in the direction of the noise and see his friend standing there looking back and forth between the two of us.

"Heh, are you guys okay? I've been trying to get your attention for a minute now. Do you guys know each other or… ?"

Shaking my head yes and then no, he lifts a brow at the conflicting motion. "No, I… no, we don't know each other. I mean, I don't think we do…"

Turning towards the man, he's still looking at me as if he's trying to figure it out as well. "Umm, do we know each other? I feel like… Like…"

"Like we do know each other? Yeah, same. I just… I can't figure it out." Running his fingers through his light brown hair, he shakes his head and squeezes his eyes shut. I can't explain it, but all I want to do is reach out to him. Apparently, my body is really on board with this idea as I see my hand start to reach out toward him. I freeze, curling my fingers in my hand I squeeze until my nails indent my skin. Taking a step back, he snaps his eyes open at the movement.

"Wait, where are you going?" He puts his hand up to his

chest, "I'm Rhys," he then points to his friend, "This is my best friend Dorian."

Dorian raises his hand in a cute little wave, "Hiiii. What's your name?"

I let out a laugh when I realized how fitting their goofy nicknames for each other were. I start to answer but another big laugh comes out of me. *Oh no, here we go.* I lean forward bracing the book and my hands on my knees as I continue chuckling. A small snort escapes me and I leap up with wide eyes covering my mouth. Rhys and Dorian are both smirking. Pointing at both of them, I clear my throat and rein in the giggles, "Not a fucking word. That didn't happen. I just... I heard you two earlier, and now I understand the silly names and it really made me laugh. Reese's Pieces for Rhys and Dori for Dorian. That's fucking amazing. Anyways," clearing my throat, I take a deep breath and compose myself, "sorry. My name is Nova."

Rhys quickly reaches his hand out and I slightly flinch at the movement. A look of concern crosses his face and he drops his hand. I step forward and grab his hand immediately. The goal was to shake his hand but the moment our hands touched, a tingle zips up my arm and a rush of calm washes over me. I sigh in contentment at a feeling that I thought was only possible when I dreamt of his green eyes. They're definitely the eyes I've been seeing this whole time.

"Hey guys, there's a really excited-looking lady behind you. Purple and green hair, ringing any bells?" My head shoots up at his words, realizing he's talking about Jade. Without releasing our hold on each other, Rhys and I both turn our heads to look at Jade.

She has the biggest smile on her face and nods, "I told you hunny. Right around the corner." Looking between the two of us she adds, "Finally home."

She begins walking backward, "The fuck is that supposed to mean, Jade?"

"You'll see. Don't forget to come see everyone before you

leave." Nodding my head in agreement she turns and walks away. *I need to go, why can't I let go of his hand?*

"I really should get back to everyone. It was really nice meeting both of you." *Move, Nova. Move your fucking feet.*

Rhys nods his head at me, not releasing my hand either. "Okay, do you think I could maybe get your number before you go?"

I must take too long to answer because he lets out a nervous chuckle, running his fingers through his hair. *Jesus, Nova, focus!* A crashing noise in the direction of the coffee bar makes me jolt. I step back, quickly releasing his hand. The moment is broken and just then I remember that I can't let myself be trapped again. I can't trust my feelings or body's reaction to this man. To any man. I learned that the hard way, and I refuse to ever allow it to happen again. Wrapping my arms tightly around myself, I let out the breath I was holding and look up at Rhys. Our eyes meet, and I can see the concern there, but along with that, the realization that I'm going to deny him. Shaking my head, I take another step back from him and whisper, "I-I can't. I'm so sorry." Quickly turning away, I head back towards The Horde.

From behind me, he yells, "I'll wait."

Halting my movements, I stand there frozen at his words. *Wait? He'll wait? For what? I'm not important enough for someone to wait for.* Turning back towards him I say, "Don't bother. It's not worth the wait... *I'm* not worth the wait." He looks stunned by my response and opens his mouth.

Before he can say anything, I quickly turn and bump into a bookshelf, "Fuck!" Correcting my movements, I hurry back to the group.

By the time I reach the group, my heart is pounding and I can feel the beads of sweat at my temple. As soon as I close in on the table they all look in my direction. Not wanting to see their looks of concern and confusion, or answer any questions I look down at the floor while rounding the table to my chair. Picking up my backpack, I throw my book in and pull my keys out.

At the end of the table, I hear Rader first. "Hey Nova, is everything okay?"

Not trusting my voice, I shake my head no, then realize that's not the right answer and nod yes. Zipping up my backpack, I scoot the chair in and accidentally slam it into the table from the force. I grimace at the noise and put my hands up in apology.

Viking is the next to ask a question, and I'm not even surprised by it, "Did he hurt you? The guy Jade said you were talking to?" Looking up and meeting his eyes, I shake my head no. He nods his head and looks away. The great thing about him is he knows to show he's there and then let me be the one to reach out when I'm ready to talk.

As I walk away I hear Jade say, "Why would you ask that? You know he wouldn't hurt her. We all do."

What the fuck is that supposed to mean? Not important. I need to get the fuck out of here. Rushing towards the front I catch V's eyes and her look of concern. Shaking my head no at her as well, I rush through the doors. Looking in every direction, I see that everything looks clear. Rushing to my car, I hop in and with shaky hands turn the key in the ignition. Grabbing my phone, I scroll through my music. Unable to focus on picking a song myself, I smash my finger against the screen to hit shuffle. Missing the first time it sets me off and I start smashing my finger against the screen continuously and gritting my teeth. "FUCKING SHUFFLE, BITCH!" Finally, my finger hits directly on shuffle and *Emerald Eyes* by *Anson Seabra* blares through the speakers. Exhaling a choppy breath, I slam my head against the headrest.

The closer to home I get, the worse I'm feeling. The dark thoughts are pouring in and I just want them to shut the fuck up. The most peace I've felt in months happened while meeting a complete stranger. *How fucked up is that?* I can't even trust it. Trust him. Trust myself. Anyone.

Pulling into my parking spot, I shut the car off and grab everything. Looking around the area, I see that it's clear and hop out, locking my car. Picking up the pace, I head up my walkway and unlock my door. Shoving through the door, my door alarm chirps. I slam it shut behind me, lock all the bolts and switch the alarm to continuous beeping. Sliding my hand from the alarm, I brace my hands and head against the door. The slam of my neighbor's door makes me jump away from mine. Dropping my keys on my end table by the door, I head to my room and toss my backpack on the bed. The adrenaline is wearing off and a wave of exhaustion hits me. My knees buckle and I drop to my bed. I take deep breaths while bracing my head in my hands. Unable to sit still, my right knee starts bouncing, jabbing my hand against my head over and over. Not able to stand the way that feels any longer, I jump up from the bed. The apartment is quiet, but my thoughts are screaming. *Music. I need music.* Grabbing my headphones from my nightstand, I turn them on and put them over my head. I grab my phone from my pocket and scroll through the songs. The sound of my pounding heart and heavy breathing echoes in the confines of the headphones. I see a song that will get my body moving and distract me from the storm of dark thoughts invading my mind. Hitting play, *Don't Stop Believin'* by *Journey* starts blasting through the headphones. *Perfect.* I sigh as my body turns to butter, melting away the edgy, dark feelings. Sliding my jacket off, I toss it on the bed and dance out of my room humming along. Heading to my kitchen I pull a *Monster* out of the fridge, crack it open and drink half of it.

I turn to my fridge and start searching for dinner. The options are limited. *Shit. I need to go shopping. Soon.* Deciding on grilled cheese, I pull everything out, kick the door shut and put it all on the counter by the stove. I grab a skillet out of the cabinet, put it on the burner and flip the knob to medium. Waiting for the skillet to heat up, I prep my sandwiches. Heading to my room, I grab my laptop and charger to bring them out to the living room.

Setting it up on the coffee table, I start it up and open up my work email. *Might as well see if there's any work to be done.*

A food ad pops up on the side of the screen, jolting me into action. "Shit! Food!" Running back to the kitchen, I throw my sandwiches in the skillet. At the first sizzle, I deeply inhale the aroma. I put everything away in the fridge while I wait to flip them. Hopping up on the counter by the sink, I lean back against the cupboards and watch my sandwiches. I kick my feet against the counter, humming along to the music that's playing a personal concert just for me. Sliding off the counter, I grab a spatula and flip my sandwiches. Fuck yeah, golden. *Ophelia* by *The Lumineers* starts playing and I immediately start belting out the song, using the spatula as my own personal microphone. Humming some of the words, I grab a plate down and flip the sandwich on it. Taking a deep breath, preparing for the next part of the song, I put everything into this shit like I'm trying out for *American Idol*. Turning the burner off, I move the skillet to the back burner and toss the spatula in the sink. Grabbing my plate I head over to the living room and plop down on my couch. Putting the plate on the seat next to me I grab my laptop and put it on my lap. Opening up my secured work email, **VEGA ALTAIR** with its Summer Triangle constellation logo pops up on the top of the screen. After loading, a new email pings in the inbox. Clicking on it, the email loads with the information needed to complete my tasks. After collecting price quotes on hotels and rental cars, I move on to the task of inventory. Blowing a raspberry, I go over the list so I can start making the necessary orders. Don't get me wrong, part of me really loves making this list, I get to pretend I'm making a silly shopping list. But then there's the part where I have to pay attention to the stupid numbers. *Eww.* Not to mention the fact that the lists can get really weird. It's like a mix of the funny memes of someone buying odd items for sex, and then the horror memes of someone buying serial killer toys. Wrapping up the final task and my food, I shut everything down and head outside for a smoke.

. . .

Sitting in my chair, I lean back and lay my head against the building. My thoughts drift to the *literal* man of my dreams. I don't understand how it's even possible, but I would never forget those eyes I see in every dream. In another life, I would've gladly given him my number. Hell, I would've spent the whole day with him if he asked. The problem is, this isn't another life, I'm living this one. The life where I'm better off alone. It's safer alone. The heat of the cherry burning too close to my fingers snaps me out of my thoughts. Putting my cigarette out, I head back inside and lock up, resetting the alarm. A bath sounds amazing right about now, so I head to my room to put my stuff away and pick out a fresh hoodie and sleep shorts. Picking up the wooden box from my dresser, I head to the bathroom. I pull out a joint and light it along with all of my apple pie candles. The smoke and scent of the candles fill the air around me and I take in a deep breath through my nose. Smiling at the smell, I walk over to my tub and turn the knob for hot water all the way on and give the cold knob a small turn. Checking the temperature, I quickly pull my hand back and hiss from the burn. "Fuck!" My hand has a slight pink tinge from the temperature. Turning the cold knob a little further over, I give it time to readjust. I pull up a piano playlist for some relaxing music. Hitting my joint a few times, I put it down on the edge of the sink and strip out of my clothes as I turn away from the mirror. I lean over the tub and check the temperature. *Ahhh, perfect.* I drop a bath bomb in and grab my joint as I step in the tub. It's not as hot as when I first tested it, but the heat is still noticeable. Sitting down, I lay my arms down against the sides of the tub and take a deep breath, inhaling the cedar and vanilla fragrance. Finishing my joint, I dab it in the water to put it out and lay it down on the edge of the tub. Leaning my head against the wall I close my eyes and am instantly met with beautiful, emerald eyes. It may not be safe to give him a chance to destroy me, but it doesn't hurt to think about him. Remembering his tousled, light brown hair and panty-melting smile, my breath hitches at the throb in my clit and my tightening nipples. Picturing our meeting, I scan down his body. The tattoos peeking out of the collar of his shirt, his badass *Zeppelin* shirt, his flannel that he pulled off far better than anyone I've ever seen. Probably the bulging muscles and hint of tattoos made it work so well. Running my fingers down my chest, my nipple peaks as I graze it. With my hand I slide down, reaching between my thighs. An image of Rhys eating my pussy like a starved man has me rubbing my clit in circles. Rolling and pinching my left nipple at the same time, the image morphs to me being on my knees for him. *I'm gripping his hips tight as he holds on to my head while he face fucks me. He's pounding his cock in and out of my mouth and we're both moaning. Drool is running down my chin all the way to my tits.*

He growls when I moan, looking down at me he smiles. 'Look at you taking my cock so well. Fuck, you feel good, baby.'

Wanting to feel him deeper, I push forward until the head of his cock is sitting just past the entrance of my throat. 'Oh fuck. Fuck, that's good.' Reaching down, he grips my throat and groans, 'Holy shit. I can feel my cock in your throat. Fuck, that's good.' Keeping his hold on me, he makes short thrusts. Releasing a hand from his hip, I roll his balls in my hand and suck harder on his cock. He pulls back and groans from the suction I'm keeping around him, my tongue piercing dragging across the pulsing vein that runs the length of his cock. With just the tip in my mouth, I flick my tongue across the slit. He thrusts forward with one hand on my throat and the other on the back of my head, shoving his cock further down. Tears are running down my face and I gag, making my throat massage the head of his cock. 'Oh fuuuuuuuu-uck.' Spurt after spurt of cum hits my throat. When he pulls himself back I can feel a shot of cum hit the back of my tongue and then the middle. Once his cock is out of my mouth, I look up at him and stick my tongue out showing him the last two spurts of cum. My failed orgasm brings me back from the fantasy. I slam my hands down in the water, splashing it over the edge of the tub. *Dammit! Every fucking time.*

I unplug the tub and then turn on the water. Once it's the

perfect temperature, I pull the shower lever up to wash off all the bubbles. After rinsing off, I hop out of the tub and wrap a towel around myself. Blowing out my candles, I grab the ends of the towel and dry my hands off. Picking up my phone, I head to my room to get dressed. Tossing my phone on the wireless charger on my nightstand, I finish drying my body off and wring out my wet hair. I put on my sleep shorts and then my hoodie. Picking up my towel, I take it to the hamper in the bathroom, my frustrations making me throw it harder than necessary. Starting to shift my eyes to the mirror, I bring them back forward just as fast. *Nope, we're not playing that game tonight.* Jumping in bed, I check my phone and notice the notifications from The Horde group chat and open it up.

> JADE: Hey, hun. How are you doing? Do you need anything?

> MRS. VALOUR: Yeah, just let us know if you need anything, or need company...

> VIKING: She'll get back to us when she's ready. Like they said, Nova, let us know if you need anything.

> ME: I'm alive. I'm fine. Thank you. I don't need anything. I was just doing some work stuff and took a bath. I'm going to bed now.

> JADE: Ok.

> RADER: Ok.

> MRS. VALOUR: Ok.

> MUGGZY: Ok.

Locking the phone, I toss it back on the wireless charger and close my eyes. The quiet takes over and I contemplate turning my tv on. Rolling over, I grip onto my pillow and blankets, whis-pering into them, "Please no nightmares tonight. Please, please, please."

"Those eyes of yours could swallow stars, galaxies, and universes. What hope did I ever have?" ~Love and Space Dust

CHAPTER 3
OUT OF MY LEAGUE

Rhys

Watching Nova walk away was the hardest thing I've ever had to do. I can't quite figure out why, seeing how I dealt with so much shit with my parents. Hell, even in my line of work, you would think at least any of those situations would be more difficult. But no, this beautiful woman I just met is consuming my thoughts, and there's an ache in my chest. I rub my fist in circles over it, as if that will make it go away.

There's a smack to my right arm, jolting me from my thoughts. Snapping my head to the right, I glare at Dorian. I swing my arm and smack the back of my hand against his chest. "Oomph, oww."

Dorian puts his hand to his chest, rubbing the spot I smacked. "Don't hit me unless you want the favor returned."

Dorian moves so he's facing me, "I was just trying to get your attention," pointing his finger at me and walking backward he adds, "don't be a dick."

Making a face, I use noises to mock his words. "Neh, neh, neh, nehhhhh. Your face is a dick." At the same time, we mirror each other with double middle fingers raised. I chuckle at our antics when the sight of Nova rushing by catches my attention. My feet start moving in her direction, but a hand on my chest stops me. Scrunching my brow, I look down, following the arm attached to it.

I see Dorian with an awkward half-smile. "Give her time, Rhys." When I nod my head, he pats my chest twice, and walks off. Following him, we pass a group of people at a table. A few look up and exchange nods with Dorian. They nod my way and with a clipped nod in return, I attempt a friendly smile. As soon as they look away, the fake smile drops and I speed up to catch Dorian.

I quietly ask him, "Uhhh, do you know them? If so, you might want to tell them I didn't mean to give them my resting bitch face, but they caught me off guard."

Dorian shakes his head and lets out an exasperated sigh, "Rhys, it's common courtesy to be cordial to people, especially when they acknowledge your existence. Now, let's get back to the warehouse. I got a notification about a lead."

With a slight bow of his head at one of the employees he walks out. I clap my hands and rub them together, "That's what the fuck I'm talking about. Let's roll."

<hr />

Once we walk through the warehouse doors, we head straight for the makeshift conference room with screens across one wall and what can only be best described as a giant murder mystery board in the corner. I walk to the end of the table, hop up and grab my smokes. Dorian grabs the remote and the click of a button changes everything shown on the screens. Looking through the various images, my eyes catch the top right corner where there's a surveillance feed showing the front of the *Amissa Stella Asylum*. The remaining screens show photos of different targets and their families, deals, and trips they make. Along with that, there are records of questionable online purchases. After clicking a few buttons, everything fades away except for one picture and correlating information on the target. Looking at it, I can tell this version was made specifically for me. Dorian looks at all of the information, while all I need are the basics and if they deserve to be snuffed out by my demons.

"I know you like your dossier as simplified as possible, so I didn't add this tidbit of information. Ricci here has been dealing at the same place every night. He shows up at *B & G's Pub & Grill* at 11:30 PM on the dot, exits the building at 1:30 AM, goes to his car, and hangs out in the alley behind the pub until 4 AM."

Tilting my head away from Dorian, I blow out a puff of smoke while listening and a thought comes to mind. "What kind of foot traffic are we looking at?"

"Do you want the average, a visual, or both?" Pointing up at the screen I tell him, "Throw the average out at me and show me a sped-up version of the footage. See if I catch anything unusual."

Lifting the remote to the screens, Dorian clicks a few buttons and has the video from the back alley rolling. "Ricci is out there for two and a half hours every night. The amount of foot traffic at that time is anywhere between 5-10 people. Of that-"

Pulling my cigarette from my mouth, I quickly blow the smoke from my mouth and smash the cigarette in the ashtray. I cut Dorian's sentence off, "For the love of everything, man, please just spit out a number. Do I look like a book of Sudoku? No. No, I do not. Which means I don't want or need a bunch of numbers thrown at me. We really need to find you a nerdy minion so you guys can just ping-pong facts off each other." Dorian mock glares at me, rolls his lips in to hold back a laugh and flips me the double bird.

Throwing my hands up and making a scared face, I say, "Easy there, Highlander, you're gonna take an eye out with those finger swords. Now throw that number out, smarty pants."

Keeping his fingers up, he lifts one fist, "One," lifting the other fist he says, "two." I push off the table and he knows I'm going to tackle his ass if he doesn't just spit it out. He backs away laughing.

"Okay, okay. You're so easy to rile up. Seven. The average is seven people walk through the alley."

Taking another step towards him, he shakes his head and audibly gulps, "Ya know, brother, you are way behind on your self-defense lessons. We should fix that." Lunging towards him, he yelps and twists around to run.

"I don't wanna work on self-defense training, Rhys! We have work to d- oomph!" Tackling him to the ground, I crouch down just above his back and place my hands against his head.

I look down and laugh, he's panting and his face is red, "You and I both know I can't get out of this. Can we maybe come back to self-defense training another day? You know, when you don't have a target to go after."

Ruffling his hair, I lift myself off him and stand up with my hand outstretched, "I feel like you're trying to be sneaky with your words here, seeing how I always have a target to go after. Nice try, Dor."

Rolling over to his back, he crosses his arms over his chest, "Yeah, I'm so not taking your hand. You don't trust my words, and I don't trust that you'll help me. Go get your gear ready, ya big oaf."

Walking backward, I nod my head, "I'll go get my shit ready; you order us food. We have a little while longer 'til I have to head out."

His eyes light up and he gives me a goofy smile, "Burritos the size of our heads, yes?"

Pointing finger guns at him, I say, "Absofuckinlutely, brother."

29

Leaving the room, I head across the warehouse to our armory. It took us a while to get it this nice, but I'm proud of it. Every wall has a display of weapons and gear. Along the back wall are various handguns, shotguns, sniper rifles, and my dream toy: the grenade launcher. I've yet to use the sexy machinery, but one day I will. The wall to the right is filled with every type of knives you can think of: filet knives, butcher knives, machetes, bowie knives, meat cleavers, and scalpels. There's a slight chill in the air when I step in. I feel my skin tighten as the hairs on my arms stand on end.

Tossing my canvas duffle on the supply island in the center of the room, I fill it with various guns, knives, rope, ammunition, handcuffs, and zip-ties.

I place my jacket next to the duffle and walk over to the left wall with armored gear and boots. Grabbing a pair of steel-toed boots, I toss them on the bench, the thud echoing around the quiet space. I grab a bulletproof vest from the wall, pull it on and strap it tight. Dropping down to the bench, I untie my Carolina work boots and pull them off, tossing them under the bench with a thud. I grab my steel-toed boots and slide them both on, pulling up the hems of my jeans and lacing them up tight.

I pull out my ankle knife holster with two magazine pouches from the drawer filled with holsters and sheaths in the supply island. I open the drawer with various magazines and grab each one I need for my holster. Tossing everything on the island, I put the rest in the pouches of my vest. Putting the holster, magazines, and my knife down, I lift my pant leg and strap the holster to my ankle. I slide the knife in and add the magazines to the holster. I put on one of my plain, black baseball caps off the wall and walk back to the supply island, throw the duffle bag over my shoulder with a huff, and head to the conference room.

After finishing our dinner, Dorian slides over the black zip-up case with a syringe of Fentanyl inside.

Holding it up, I say, "As much as I love a good fight, this is helpful for a quick grip and dip."

Smirking at my wordplay, Dorian rolls his eyes, "For someone with a lot to say about my choice in verbiage, you sure do have a propensity to speak in a rather unique way."

I throw my garbage at his face but he smacks it away and laughs, "Dorian, I swear to fuck, if you weren't family, I'd be forced to punch you in the mouth for the shit that comes out of it."

Dorian brings out the puppy eyes and puts his palm to his chest, "Hurtful, Rhys. You wound me. Please leave before the first teardrop falls."

Pocketing the black case, I walk away, "Yeah, yeah, don't go dehydrating yourself with those waterworks."

———————★.

Pulling into the alley, I shut my truck off and unbuckle before I call Dorian.

"Are you ready to apologize for the tears you caused?"

Chuckling at his question, I shake my head as if he can see me, "Nahhh, not yet. I'm checking to see if anything important popped up on surveillance while I drove here. And to remind you to do your job and wipe footage after I leave, of course."

Biting my lip to hide my laughter, Dorian's hysterical voice bleeds through the phone, "What?! When have I ever forgotten to do my job?! NEVER! That's when!"

Throwing my head back, I guffaw, unable to hold it in any longer, "Now look who's easy to rile up. Just text me a yes or no with the answer on surveillance. It's time to start my sing and sting."

Dorian groans at my words, and I smile, "Dude, can't you just say you need to get in the zone or something?"

"Pfft, no. Where's the fun in that? Come on, dude, it's clever. I'm going to *sing* while doing a *sting* operation. We're done speaking until you learn to appreciate my finesse for words."

As I go to hang up, I hear Dorian shout over the line, "You too, asshole!" I pull out my earbuds from the glove box and put the left one in. Connecting it to my phone, I scroll through and find my sing and sting song *Choke* by *I DON'T KNOW HOW BUT THEY FOUND ME*. Pressing play, I see it's 1:15 AM and toss my phone. Drumming on the steering wheel and singing along, I keep an eye on the door to the alley. Adrenaline spikes through me as I wait, taking me higher than any drug ever could. After a short while, the door swings open and Lorenzo Ricci walks out. 1:30 on the dot. Smacking the steering wheel hard enough that I feel the vibrating sting through my hand, I shake it out. *Showtime.*

I scan the area for anyone and find nothing. Pulling the black case out of my pocket, I pull out the syringe and carefully pocket it. I push the door open and hop out, the gravel crunching beneath my boots. Walking along the side of my truck, I see Ricci heading towards his car. Staying aware of my surroundings, I follow behind him. His steps falter, and he tilts his head. He knows I'm behind him. Reaching the hood of his car, he does a slow and dramatic turn and sits back against the hood with a creak from the weight and crosses his arms. He gives me his best, 'don't fuck with me look.' *Jokes on him, that shit doesn't faze me.* The hunt has started and he'll soon realize I'm the predator and he's the prey, not the other way around.

When I stop in front of him he glares up at me, and in a heavy Italian accent says, "You don't look like my usual customers, get the fuck out of here."

Letting out a small, dark laugh I say, "For someone so dumb, that was a pretty smart observation there." In a quick movement, I rear my head back and slam it against his face, while simultaneously stomping my boot on top of his foot, holding him in place. He falls backwards against the hood of his car at an awkward angle with my hold on his foot.

Bringing his hands up to his forehead, he shouts, "*CAZZO!*" I yank him up by his v-neck, the force of the pull making him fly forward. Releasing my hold on him, I step aside as he falls forward. I kick the back of his right knee, bringing him down to the ground. Before he's fully hit the ground, I thrust my boot into his back and push him down the rest of the way. He's shouting at me in Italian and scraping his fingernails across the asphalt. Dropping down to a kneel, my boot scrapes across his back and my knee slams into the back of his head.

I pull out the syringe and take the cap off with my teeth, spitting it to the ground. "You might want to hold still for this."

"Wha-ahhhhh!" Stabbing the needle in the side of his neck, I push the plunger down, injecting the Fentanyl. He attempts to bring his hand up to the spot, but since I'm bringing more of my weight down on him; he's unable to do so. His body wants to fight the drug, so he continues flailing his arms in front of him, looking like he's trying to swim across the alley. His movements slow down, so I lift off of his back. I bend down and take a deep breath. Scrunching my nose when the smell of his cologne hits me, I stand up and suck in fresh air.

"God, what brand is that? I'm leaving a bad review on that shit. You should be ashamed of yourself."

I hold my breath, grab his ankles and spin us around. I start dragging him towards my truck. He's slurring more Italian at me, I'm sure cussing me out in every way possible. Once I reach my truck, I drop his feet and open the window and tailgate. When I lean down to pick him up, I see that he's knocked out. The door to the alley swings open with a loud squeak and smacks against the brick wall.

Gritting my teeth, I grip the nape of my neck whispering under my breath, "Fuck."

"Hey man, uh, is everything okay over there?"

Standing up, I wave my hand, "Yeah, my buddy here had a little too much to drink. He said he was going to take a piss and decided passing out would be more fun." With a lopsided smile, I thrust my arms out and shrug.

The guy walks over and says, "Here, let me help you get him loaded up."

"Oh, shit yeah, that would be great. I'm just putting him back here so he can stretch out. Plus, easy clean up if he spews like a volcano."

The guy laughs at my words, grips Ricci under his armpits as I grab his feet. "One, two, three," grunting as we lift him, we bring him down to the floor of the truck and push him further back. After I've made sure his feet are out of the way, I lift the tailgate and shut the window with a click.

Lightly slapping the guy's shoulder, I tell him, "Thanks, man, that would've taken forever on my own. Have a good one."

Nodding his head, he walks backward, "Yeah, no problem." Rounding my truck, I open the door and hop in.

Once seated, I let out a long exhale, "Woooooo, fuck, that was close."

Backing the truck up to the bay door, I look in my mirror and see it slowly rising. When there's enough clearance, I back up until I'm in the warehouse. Looking ahead so I can put the truck in park, I see Dorian pushing the button to shut the bay door, and he gives me a half-salute.

I hop out of my truck after grabbing my phone and look at Dorian, "Hey man, can you bring me one of the rolling tables?" He nods and hurries off to grab one. Walking to the back of my truck, I open the window and tailgate. Reaching in, I slide my duffle bag to the edge of the tailgate. I turn towards Dorian when I hear the squeaking wheels behind me. He rests the end of the table against the tailgate and walks around. Each of us grabs a foot, and we pull Ricci forward to get him on the table. Grabbing the strap of my duffle, I toss it over my head and across my chest as I head towards my playroom with the table. The only sound is the wheels squeaking and echoing off the hall walls.

Crossing the threshold, the drastic change in temperature has me involuntarily shivering. I kick the door shut behind me. The wheels squeak as I push the table over to the chair. I put down the locks on the wheels to keep them in place. Grabbing Ricci under his armpits, I drag him off the table, his shoes scraping against the tabletop. Once his legs hit the edge of the table, the weight makes his feet plummet and smack the floor. Briefly dragging him across the concrete floor, I toss him on the chair. He hunches forward, and when I press against his chest, his back strikes the chair and he remains still. Only his head touches his chest now. I drop my duffel on the table and push it over to the side. After I've pulled out a roll of duct tape, I walk up to Ricci and tie his right wrist to the arm of the chair with the tape. Ripping the tape away from the roll with my teeth, I spit out remnants of the torn tape and I wrap the remaining length around his wrist. Twisting the tape around his other wrist and both ankles, I decide to place some around his chest and the back of the chair. While he's still knocked out, I pull my weapons out of the bag and lay them across the table top. After the bag has been emptied, I toss it to the floor, and lean against the table. I wipe the sweat from my brow and light a cigarette.

Pulling my phone out of my pocket, I connect it to the Bluetooth speaker and open my music app to pick a song for playtime. Scrolling through, my thumb halts when I see *Ocean Eyes* by *Billie Eilish*. My mind immediately goes to the beautiful Nova. If I close my eyes, it's as if she's right in front of me. Reddish brown hair framing her beautiful face, those mesmerizing blue eyes, her full lips, rocking a hilarious shirt and a hooded flannel that matched mine. Don't get me wrong, everything about the way she looks is fucking perfection, but there was something about her presence that felt like... home.

A groan to my left pulls me from my thoughts. Looking over, I see him slightly moving his head side to side. Scrolling one last time through my songs, I click play on DAYWALKER by *Machine Gun Kelly* and *CORPSE*.

The hanging hose swings lightly in the cold air, my spine tingling with excitement at what's to come. I pull the hose down and squeeze the lever back, shooting a stream of freezing cold water. Seconds after the water soaks Ricci, he gasps and attempts to scream. The water goes in his wide open mouth and he starts choking and garbling out nonsense. Letting go of the lever, the water stops and the hose retracts above my head with a clank. Droplets from the hose fall over me and I take a few steps towards him in silence. Ricci looks up, blinking away the water and shaking his body the best he can, trying to get out of the tape's hold. "WHAT THE FUCK?!" Standing before him, I wait for his vision to fully clear. I see the moment it clicks for him, and his eyes widen, "YOU! What the fuck is going on?!"

Chuffing out a laugh, I smirk and look down. I look back at him while clicking my tongue, "Wellllll, that is a great question... Lorenzo Ricci. I have the same exact question about *Amissa Stella*." Registering the words, there's a flicker in his eyes. If I blinked, I would've missed it.

Gritting his teeth he snaps, "I don't know what the fuck you're talking about."

With an unamused laugh, I shake my head, "We're going to start this off with a cliché torture line. Ready? To earn yourself a quick death, I'm going to ask you questions, and you're going to answer them. If you don't, then your death will be slow and painful. The choice is yours. Choose wisely."

I can see a vein pulsing in his temple and his face getting red, "FUCK. YOU!"

Grimacing at his words, "Blech, no thank you. Guess you're choosing the hard way." I saunter up to the table and grab a scalpel and hammer. Spinning back towards him, I notice he's wiggling around trying to loosen the tape. "I don't suggest that. You may be able to break through the tape, but the drug still has

36

you weak. You will not win a fight against me." He pauses when he sees the scalpel and hammer in my hands.

"Wh-what the fuck a-are you going to do with those?!" He stammers.

Holding them in front of me, I flick my wrists showing them off, "Aww, these ol' things. Nothing, if you answer my questions." I give him my brightest smile and shrug, "What do ya say, Ricci, wanna play?"

He spits at me but I sidestep away from it and he yells, "You're a sick fuck!"

My brow furrows as I look down at my choice of weapons, "We haven't even started yet. Please hold all reviews and ratings until the end of the ride. Now, let's start with a really simple question. What is your name?"

Rolling his eyes at me, he purses his lips and in a low voice says, "You already know my name. Next question."

Making an obnoxious buzzer noise, I hold the hammer to my face like a microphone, "Oh, I am so sorry, but I know for a fact your name isn't *You Already Know My Name*. Yikes, first question and you're already giving wrong answers." Tsking, I shake my head and step towards him.

The glint of the light reflecting against the scalpel in my left hand hits my eyes. I place the tip of the blade between the nail and nail bed of his left pinky. His hand flexes and I look up at him, "I wouldn't move if I were you, you'll only make it worse." Holding the blade in place, I lift the hammer and aim it towards the end of the scalpel. "And a one," bringing the hammer forward I barely tap the scalpel and Ricci shuts his eyes tight and hisses, "and a two," *tap*, "and a," bringing the hammer all the way back, I swing it forward and shout, "THREE!" Smashing the hammer against the scalpel, it tears through the top of his nail bed and shoots through the nail, ripping it off.

I chuckle at his blood-curdling scream. Bending down, I pick up the nail that fell to the floor, "Aww, you dropped this, buddy," putting it down the collar of his shirt and I pat his chest.

Sweat is pouring down his face and he pants, "Lorenzo Ricci, my name is Lorenzo Ricci."

Letting out a whoosh of air I say, "Ooo, I am so sorry, but your chance to answer that question is over. On to the next one. What is your job at *Amissa Stella*?"

He scoffs at my question, "You know the answer to that too."

I place the scalpel between his nail and the nail bed of his ring finger. "I gotta say, you really suck at this game. For future reference, let's just assume I already know every answer, but I want you to answer it as if I don't." The swing of the hammer against the scalpel slices through the nail. Blood spurts out and drips down his finger, hitting the floor. Scooping up the fallen nail, I toss that in the front of his shirt with the other one. His body shudders uncontrollably and he glares up at me.

"I won't tell you a fucking thing about that place. Do your fucking worst."

Grunting, I nod my head at him, "Oh, I plan on it. You'll soon find out, just like everyone else," I pause and give him the craziest smile I can and whisper, "I'm the thing that monsters have nightmares about." Stomping on the button that controls the chair, it starts leaning back and he jolts from the sudden movement. Once he's reclined, I toss the hammer and scalpel on the table. They slightly bounce and clang, making the other weapons shift. A mini torch lighter and a meat cleaver are my next choices and without preamble, I walk over to Ricci and cut the remaining fingers off of his left hand. He screams with every chop of his fingers. Blood spurts out of his hand at every point of torn flesh and bone. The fingers all fall and roll on the floor below. The flick of my lighter interrupts his whimpering as the flame bursts to life and I cauterize his hand. Smoke and the pungent scent of burning flesh drifts up and hits my nose. His scream is a half sob that dies down as he loses consciousness.

An idea pops in my head and I smile. Dropping the lighter and meat cleaver on the table, I head over to the small row of lockers against the wall. Opening one, I pull out a jumpsuit that Dorian says is made of PTFE. I zip myself into one, making sure everything is secured. The thick face mask from the locker presses hard against my mouth as I pull the string behind my head. Pulling the hood up that is attached to it, I tighten it around my head and tie it off. I still need a face shield and gloves, this is going to be messy. I find the ones made from PTFE and slide them on. Stretching my fingers out in the gloves, I smack the locker door shut. I find the gold mine in the next locker and pull out a gallon sized glass jar. Carrying it over to the table, I place it down gently and twist it so the label with big, bold letters is facing him.

Stepping below the hanging hose, I pull it down and start spraying Ricci in the face. His gasps and chokes are the only sound in the room as he shakes his head. Releasing the hose, I wait until I have his attention. His eyes squint as he tries to clear his eyes to look at me. "Good morning, princess. Ready for our steaming hot tea party?" Arching his brow, he opens his mouth to speak, but stops when I tilt my head towards the glass jug.

His eyes follow the tilt of my head, and he whimpers, shaking his head back and forth, "No, no, no, please no. Please, don't do this."

Looking down at the label, I smile and turn my head back to him, "Yeahhhh, sulfuric acid. It's gonna make you nice and toasty," clicking my tongue, "guess you should've just answered my questions in the beginning."

Twisting the top off of it, I pick it up by the handle with my right hand and hold my left hand on the bottom of it. He shrieks in horror when I pretend to stumble and tilt the jug to allow a few drops to fall on top of his thighs. He looks down at his legs and squeals as he watches the acid drops burn through his dress pants and the surface layer of skin. "DIO MIO! DIO MIO! NO, NO, NO!"

Tilting the jug further, I pour the acid over his thighs, the steady stream burning through his clothes and skin faster. His screams turn into chokes and gasps as the fumes from the acid and burning flesh mix together and burn his mouth and throat. I pour it all over his stomach and up to his chest.

Looking him in the eye while he continues to choke, scream and cry, I yell over him and say, "YOU MIGHT WANT TO HOLD YOUR BREATH FOR THIS NEXT PART!" Lifting the jug away from his chest, I raise it over the top of his head. He looks absolutely terrified.

Looking him dead in the eye I say, "I told you I was the fucking nightmare." Tipping it all the way over, I watch as the remaining acid pours over his head and down his face. His hair starts falling away in clumps and smoke is drifting up in the air. Every bit of skin the acid has touched looks like swirls and spots of pink, red and white. Areas of skin are pulling apart from each other creating dips, grooves and holes in his skin. His screams die down, but I can see his chest still moving, so I know he's only passed out.

My beautiful Tiffany blue 1911 pistol sits on the table, where I go to pick it up and flick the safety off, pulling back the slide to check the chamber. When I see a round locked and loaded, I release the slide, snapping it back in place. I level the gun straight at his head and kick his foot. He lets out a half groan, half whimper and I kick him again. His chest heaves with sobs as he snaps his head up. When I see I have as much of his attention as I'm going to get, I put my finger on the trigger and say, "See you in hell, bitch."

I watch as the bullet enters the center of his forehead and his head snaps back. A perfect circle is left in the center with a drip of blood pouring straight down his face. Walking over to the door, I smack the intercom button with my elbow.

The intercom crackles and Dorian's voice pours through, "Ready?"

"Ready."

"Okay, I'll be right there."

I let go of the intercom button and glance at the material of the jumpsuit I'm wearing, "Oh shit." Smashing the button again,

I yell, "DORIAN! Wait! As soon as you walk in you need to put that PTFE shit on before you go near Ricci."

The intercom crackles again and Dorian says, "10-4, good buddy, I'm on my way." Rolling my eyes, I let go of the button and walk back to the table.

As soon as he walks through the door Dorian looks over and grimaces, "Blech." He puts all his gear on before walking over. "Dude, you didn't even start chopping a little to get the process started?"

Looking back at Ricci, I dramatically point my arms down to the floor, "Excuse me? Chopped fingers, right there. Plus, this is good practice for you."

"Me? What do you mean by good practice for me? I'm just the tech guy that helps make sure everything goes according to plan."

Spreading my arms out wide, I say, "Someday, this will all be yours."

Shaking his head, he counters, "Not funny. Not even a little bit. Let's get this done and over with, I need to attempt to get at least two seconds of sleep before my shift."

Jumping into action, I mumble, "Shit, you're right. My bad, brother."

"The aim of torture is to destroy a person as a human being, to destroy their identity and soul. It is more evil than murder..." ~Inge Genefke

CHAPTER 4
NOT TO BE DRAMATIC

Nova

Don't. Move. A. Muscle. Nova. Just keep your eyes shut and you'll fall asleep again, bringing you right back to your very hot, very wet dream. Great, now I have to pee. Just a little lo- my phone buzzing on the nightstand snaps me completely out of the moment. Growling in frustration, I grab my other pillow and toss it over my face, "SON OF A BITCH!"

Still holding both sides of the pillow, I push and pull the ends, like I'm aggressively playing an accordion. As soon as I hear my phone buzz again, I toss my pillow to the floor. I've apparently morphed from a 25-year-old woman to a 2-year-old toddler, as I start thrashing in my bed and kicking my feet in a full blown tantrum. My phone buzzes a third time and I straighten out my whole body, locking it in place.

"FINE! Fucking fine!" I toss my blankets off me and throw them as if they've wronged me. Jumping off of my bed, I grab my phone and unlock it, seeing three messages from V.

Taking a selfie with my crazy bedhead, winking with my tongue out and a middle finger up I send it to her in response. I toss my phone on the bed and start my zombie walk to the kitchen to grab a *Monster*. My phone goes off while I'm grabbing my clothes for the day. Chuckling, I leave it be until after my shower. I already know it's V responding to my picture. Rushing through my shower, I hop out and throw my clothes on. I open my closet to grab my backpack and an oversized *Sleep Token* hoodie. I laugh when I see V responded with a middle finger emoji , putting my phone in my pocket while grabbing a hair tie to throw my hair up in a messy bun. Shoving my smokes and lighter in my pocket, I grab my keys and unlock my door before setting my alarm to chime when the door opens.

I walk through the doors at *Swan & Scribe* and head straight for the counter. Going around, I sit on the stool behind it and see V passing by a bookshelf. She's holding a ridiculously high stack of books and looking around the store as if she just robbed a bank. When she gets close enough, I can see that they're all astronomy books. Rolling my lips in to hold my laughter back, she glares at the expression on my face. Reaching the counter she gently puts them down with a grunt.

Clearing my throat, I look from the books to her again,

43

"Question, astronomy enthusiast. Are we going to let your customers enjoy these books, or are you hoarding them all for yourself?"

She whips her head around, making her dark curls bounce with the movement. Gasping, she brings her hand to her chest, "Bite your tongue, heathen. These are all mine, everybody else can use a search engine like they always do."

Placing her hand on top of the stack of books like they're a precious child, she says lovingly, "They deserve to be loved and cherished, not tarnished by aggressive and grubby hands. Have you seen how college students handle these types of books for studying?" She gives a full body shudder, and slices her hand in the air, "Monsters. All of them. *These. Are. Mine.*"

Standing up next to her, I pat the countertop twice, "No worries, V. I feel the same way when I see the lonely housewives touching my spicy books with their... sticky fingers. Fucking eww."

V grimaces at my words, "I don't even want to think about that. SUBJECT CHANGE! Let's talk about the elephant in the room, Nova girl."

Immediately knowing that she's referring to my meeting and running away situation with Rhys, my face heats up from embarrassment. I look behind her and widen my eyes, making a face of horror. "Oh my fuck, you're not going to believe this, but there's some hooligans tarnishing your astronomy books!"

Glaring at me, her eye twitches and she purses her lips. It's taking everything in her not to turn and look and she grits out, "I'm not falling for that shit. *Now. Spill.*"

Groaning, I flop down on the stool behind me, throw my hands up and slap them down on my thighs. "What is there to say, V? I'm not trying to be dramatic here, but come on. Do you know how fucked up it is to meet someone that looks that fucking good," mumbling under my breath I add in, "and smells fucking delicious."

I go quiet, and she rolls her hand around telling me to

continue, "It's just, how do I explain it without sounding fucking crazy? He felt like home."

She shakes her head and says, "That doesn't sound crazy, Nova."

Holding my hand up to stop her, "It's not just that, it's…" Taking a deep breath I take the plunge and tell her about his eyes, "his eyes. They are the same eyes that I've been seeing in my dreams for what feels like forever. It's not just dreams though, I've seen them so much there, that even if I close my eyes, they pop up behind my eyelids like a fucking movie. It doesn't make sense." Shaking my head, I add, "It doesn't matter, because I can't have him. I can't trust myself to make that decision after what happened with Frankie. That piece of shit gets his fucking wish. I'll always be alone, because I'll never know anyone's true intentions with me until it's too late." Feeling flayed open and vulnerable, I hop off of the stool and whisper, "I'm going to go grab a coffee and get to work."

After ordering my coffee, I sit down at the corner table and wait for it to be ready. My mind drifts to when I was sitting here earlier waiting for my drink and all I could think about were the mystery green eyes. *How is it possible that I was thinking about those green eyes and the song I Don't Know You Yet popped up in my head and then BAM! I met Rhys?* Rolling my eyes at my thoughts, I look over just in time to see the barista at the end of the counter. Holding my drink up in the air to show me it's ready, I stand up and head to the counter. I thank them as I grab my drink and head to the back room. Excited for my drink, I start sucking it down. The caramel hits my taste buds and I smile around the straw. Wincing, I rip the straw out of my mouth and put the cup on a shelf. Gripping my head, I scrunch my eyebrows, "Urgh, fucking brain freeze."

I briefly rub my temples to push the throbbing pain away. I drop my hands and get to work and open each box and scan the items so they're added to the system's inventory. I roll a dolly over to the boxes and start loading them up: historical, autobiographies, nonfiction, and science books. Tilting the dolly back by the handle, I walk by the shelf and scoop up my drink as I go. V waves me over when I pass the front counter, dolly in tow. She pulls a box flap back, looks at the books and clicks her tongue.

"Let me guess, you're saving your dirty books for last so you can check them out on your break?"

Squinting my eyes at her accusation, I let out an exasperated sigh, "Obviously. I have to look at them before," holding my hands up and wiggling my fingers, I whisper, "sticky fingers."

Laughing at my words, she nods, "Fair enough, why don't you just leave that up here and keep it away from the goods?" she says, gesturing at the coffee in my hands.

Bringing my drink close to my chest like I'm protecting it, I say, "For shame, V! I would never leave my precious caffeine unattended. Anything could happen to it, no thank you." Wrapping my lips around the straw, I suck the last of my drink down. V narrows her eyes at me as I continue sucking through the obnoxious sound of the straw sucking air. Smacking my lips, "Ahhhh. Problem solved." Walking behind the counter, I toss the cup in the trash can.

Striking a ridiculous pose, I wave down at my body, "Think I can blend in with the brainiacs back there?"

She looks at my outfit and makes a funny face, "Let's see," tapping her chin she continues, "an oversized band hoodie, black shorts, black knee socks, and chucks. I'm gonna say no, you won't blend in, but you'll sure have the virgins drooling showing off them knees of yours."

I knock my knees together, "Mmm, so scandalous," pretending to flip my hair over my shoulder, I look at her and add, "excuse me, while I go corrupt those innocent virgins."

After I've finished up with the first three boxes, I head over to the science section and start adding those books to the shelves. Faint voices get closer and more clear, making me freeze.

"Do you even need these books? Don't you know everything, genius?"

Holy fuck. Is it really him, or am I just imagining things? With shaky hands, I put the book where it belongs before I drop it. Frantically looking around for a place to hide, I realize there's nowhere for me to go.

Dropping my head to the shelf, I mumble under my breath, "Fuck my life."

"First off, I'm doing this research for you, because we both know you're not going to do the required reading. Second, quit acting like I'm holding you back from the reason you're really here. You can easily go through with your plan while I grab the books I need."

Plan? What fucking plan? I can't see him. He can't see me. I need to get the fuck out of here. In a moment of panic, I spin towards the dolly faster than I intended to, making me trip and start to fall. I reach out for the first thing I can in an attempt to catch myself, which of course is the dolly that won't help me. When I grab a hold of it, my weight and the momentum of my fall pushes it backwards and I yelp. The final box of books on it flies up from the movement and smacks me in my knees. Knowing there's no stopping this disaster, I slam my eyes shut and brace myself for the fall. Crashing down, the wind is knocked out of me from my chest smacking the dolly. The box of books is somehow stuck between my knees, while my legs are splayed out behind me.

Wheezing, I speak to the floor, "Owww."

I can hear feet stomping behind me, "Holy shit! Are you okay?" *Kill me now.*

"Miss, do we need to call 911? Is it okay if we help move you?"

Still having trouble breathing properly, I groan, "Hello, Dorian. No 911 please."

With panicked voices, they drop to their knees, "NOVA?!"

"I'd wave, but I really don't want to move right now. Not unless it's to a black hole that can make me disappear."

Keeping my eyes to the floor I see tousled, brown hair come

into view. There's just enough space between the dolly and the floor that Rhys can fit his head through it. The moment his face comes into view I squeeze my eyes shut.

I feel his breath on my face as he whispers, "I think it's my lucky day, I just caught a falling star."

Opening my eyes, I glare at him, "Technically, you didn't catch me, you were here to *catch* the aftermath."

Smiling brightly at me, he huffs out a laugh, and then slowly his smile falls and he whispers, "Are you okay? Will you please let me move you, Nova?"

In a panic I shake my head no, the pain in my whole body makes me stop, grimacing I whimper, "No, thank you."

"Do you not want me to move you because it hurts too much, or because you're embarrassed?"

Pouting, I look away and whisper, "Both."

The way he tilts his head while he scans my face is intimidating and sexy. *Fuck. It's so much hotter seeing the stare in person rather than reading about a book boyfriend doing it. If I wasn't down already, I would've swooned just now.*

"Please don't be embarrassed. I hate that you're hurting right now, but I promise to be gentle, little star."

My heart's pounding out of my chest, my stomach is fluttering and my pussy is drooling like a bitch in heat. I attempt to clench my thighs but the box between my legs prevents it. Rhys slides out from under the dolly and I feel the box slowly moved away from my legs.

Quickly closing my legs together the best I can, I wince from the pain. "Alright, sweetheart, I'm going to roll you towards me, okay?"

Flinching at the feel of his big hand on my calf, I clear my throat and say, "Y-yeah, I'm ready." My skin feels like it's on fire as he gently squeezes my calf. He slides his hand across my legs and wraps his arm around both. He then moves his hand over my side and across the front of my hoodie with his other hand.

I jump at the feel of his hands and he freezes, "I'm sorry, I promise I'm not doing anything other than helping you."

Nodding my head as if he can see it, I croak, "I know."

I feel him grip the front of my hoodie as he starts counting, "One, two, three." In one swift movement, he has me rolled over and in his arms, cradled to his chest.

"Let me see those beautiful blues, sweetheart."

Slowly opening my eyes, I'm met with concerned green ones. "There she is."

I grab a strand of hair that's fallen across his forehead and gently twist it, "Your hair grows fast."

Smiling at my words, he says, "Technically yes, but right now it just looks that way cuz I didn't use a lot of product to keep it pushed away from my face." Releasing my hold on his hair, I slowly caress my hand down his cheek. I'm not sure which one of us moved first, but we're a breath away from each other now.

"OH MY GOD, NOVA GIRL!" Gasping, I pull away quickly and look up at V, rushing towards us with Dorian behind her with a guilty look on his face. I attempt to pull myself out of Rhys' arms and his hold tightens around me.

V drops down to the floor, "Holy shit, are you okay? Dorian found me and told me what happened. Do you need to go to the hospital? What the fuck am I saying? Of course you need to go to the hospital."

Grabbing her phone from her back pocket she starts unlocking it. I put my hand over the screen and she looks up at me, "Wha-"

Shaking my head at her, "No, V. You don't need to call 911. Believe me, I know quite well when my injuries mean a hospital visit. This isn't one of those times, I promise."

Pocketing her phone again, she looks me up and down, "Fine. But you're taking the rest of the day off," pointing her finger at me, she adds, "I don't want to hear it, Nova Skye. You will go home, soak in the tub and rest."

Bowing my head, I look up and see Dorian step forward. "Umm, Rhys, I think we should give Nova a ride home. I really don't think it's a good idea for her to be driving after a fall like that."

"What? No," I say at the same time Rhys says, "Absolutely, I agree."

Looking up at him, he's already looking at me with a serious look on his face, "I'm not risking it, Nova."

The thought of being without my car if I need it to escape makes my chest tighten and I start to panic, "What about my car? I can't leave my car here. I can't be without my car, Rhys. Seriously, I can't."

His hand is cradling my face while his thumb caresses my cheek, "Shh, shh, it's okay. Breathe for me, little star. We won't leave your car here, I promise. Dorian can follow behind us in your car, is that okay?"

Taking a deep breath, I slowly exhale out of my nose and shake my head, "Yeah, okay, that's fair. I'm sorry."

Smirking down at me he says, "Don't be sorry, just be a good girl and listen."

Clenching my thighs and biting my lip to hold back the whimper my mouth would like to unleash, I look at him with wide eyes.

V whispers, "Holy shit."

I glare at her, hoping that's enough silent communication to get her to shut her pie hole. Bringing her hand up to her mouth, she quietly giggles. With little effort, Rhys is able to hold onto me and stand up.

Shocked with how easily he did that, I gape at him, "What the actual fuck? Either you're a superhero with super strength, or you're used to just carrying bodies around."

Snorting at my words he says, "I'm not a superhero, little star."

Slapping his chest at his joke, I laugh, "Lead the way, body snatcher."

V and Dorian walk on either side of us, "As soon as you take your pain meds I want a check-in text, and another one after you wake up."

Tilting my head back to look at her, I do a mock salute, "Ma'am, yes, ma'am."

Glaring at me she says, "You may be hurt already, but I'll still throw my chancla at you."

Sticking my tongue out at her, I say, "I may be injured, but I'll still karate chop that bitch away from me."

Snorting, she rolls her eyes and then they widen, "Hold up, I have some pain meds you can take. Hopefully if you take some now, they'll have kicked in by the time you're home and you can just pass out for a bit."

Rhys stops in front of the counter and I watch V grab my backpack from the floor and put it on the counter. She shuffles things around her own bag and pulls out a pill bottle. Opening it, she pulls one out, twists the top on and puts it in the front pocket of my backpack. She cracks open one of my Monsters from the mini fridge and hands the can and the pill to me. "Stick with the one until you know how you'll react to them. Please take care of yourself." Handing my backpack and keys to Dorian, she waves and walks away.

Once outside, he carries me towards a beautiful K5. I couldn't tell you the year, but I do know what it is, and this thing is magnificent. Exclaiming in wonderment, "Wowwww, she's fucking beautiful. What's her name? And don't tell me she doesn't have a name, cuz I won't believe you for a second."

"Little star, this is my Beauty. Beauty, this is my little star."

The feeling that takes over from hearing the endearment again has me blushing. Squeaking out, I say, "F-itting," clearing my throat, I try again, "fitting. Umm, ready to go?"

Grabbing the handle, he opens the door just enough, leans back and kicks it the rest of the way open. Placing me in the seat, he reaches up and grabs the seatbelt pulling it across the front of me slowly. His hands caress the tops of my thighs and I shiver from the fleeting touch. I can feel his stubble scrape against my cheek as he leans forward to click the buckle in place. Pulling back slowly, he stops when we're face to face, our noses almost touching, our breaths dancing together. Repeating the stare from earlier, I do the same to him.

When our eyes connect again, he whispers, "I'll wait." He looks down to make sure I'm all the way in the truck and gently shuts the door. Rounding the truck, he hops in on his side and starts it up. I can feel his eyes on me, but his words have my body frozen, and my heart on the path of melting.

My vision starts to blur and I feel an intense rush in my body, followed by complete stillness. *Damn, that shit works fast. My tolerance must be non-existent these days. I feel so good though.* Rolling my head to the side, I smile at Rhys.

Giggling, I slur out the first thing that comes to mind, "Alllll thee, thrrrreeee, brurry Rhys' are hottttt."

He chuckles at my words and I faintly hear him say, "Thank you, sweetheart. You're pretty hot yourself." I smile at his words and close my eyes. Drifting off, I faintly hear him singing *My Heart I Surrender* by *I Prevail*.

"Sometimes we fall down because there is something down there we're supposed to find." ~Unknown

CHAPTER 5
READY OR NOT

RHYS

Before we get to Nova's place, she's passed out in the seat next to me. Pulling into her parking lot, I wait for Dorian to pull in. Looking over I see that she passed out with her head turned in my direction and I can't help but smile. A piece of her hair has fallen in her face, so I gently push it back behind her ear. There's a light tap at my window and I turn to see Dorian standing there.

Pulling my key from the ignition, I put them in my pocket before quietly opening my door, "Hey man, I'm going to need you to call V at the bookstore and ask her which apartment is Nova's. She's also going to need to send someone from The Horde to be here with her when she wakes up. As much as I want it to be me, she might wake up disoriented from the pain meds, and I don't want her to freak out if she doesn't remember how she got home and just have me hovering over her."

Dorian makes a sour face, "Ooo, yeah that would not be good," pulling his phone out of his pocket he calls V and puts it on speakerphone.

After a few rings, V picks up, "*Swan & Scribe*, this is Vanessa, how may I help you?"

Leaning forward a little, Dorian puts his phone closer to my face, "Hey V, Rhys and Dorian here."

"Oh hey, is Nova okay, what's going on?"

"She passed out in the truck before I could ask her which apartment is hers. Also, can you please send someone from The Horde to be here with her? I figure it would be best if a more familiar face greets her when she wakes up, so I don't freak her out."

Nervously laughing, V says, "Yeahhh, that would probably not go over very well. She lives in number twelve, and yeah, lemme call one of the girls to go sit with her. Are you okay getting her in there and waiting for someone to show up?"

Nodding my head and realizing she can't see me I say, "Yeah, of course. Thanks V."

"No problem. Bye, guys."

Dorian and I both respond, "Bye," and he hangs up his phone. "I'm going to grab her bag out of her car and lock up, just a sec."

Shutting my door all the way, I round the truck and open Nova's door. *Nova's door. I like the sound of that.* I unbuckle her seatbelt and pull it away from her. I gently slide her out of the truck and into my arms. Meeting Dorian at the front of my truck, we head towards her apartment. We find it easily as Dorian searches for her house key. Third key's the charm and he gets the door unlocked and open. We both look at the door and then each other when we hear a loud chime. Dorian pushes the door open and steps aside for me to carry her in.

Dorian starts to close the door when we hear a breathless, "Hold on, hold on, waitttt for meeee." Crossing the threshold we see Nova's friend, Jade. Dorian shuts the door the rest of the way and we both glance at the door alarm with a magnet sensor at the top.

Pointing towards it, Jade turns and looks where I'm pointing, "Bad neighborhood or?"

Apprehension is written all over her face and she bites her lip, "Uh, it's not a bad neighborhood."

She quickly averts her eyes, I step forward and tilt my head in her direction, "There something we should know about?"

Looking back to me, she shakes her head and breathes out, "Sorry hun, not my story to tell. Follow me, I'll show you her room." Walking past us she adjusts her bag on her shoulder and heads down the hallway to the room at the end. Opening the door she steps in and then pops back out with her hands up, "Uh, are you good holding her a little longer? I just, uh, need to do the girl code check here."

Nodding my head she heads back in and closes the door behind her. Not even a minute later she opens the door and waves us in. As much as I want to look around and get every piece of Nova I can, it's not my place right now. Laying her down on her bed, I slide my arms out from under her and push her hair out of her face. Sitting on her bed by her feet I untie her shoes and take them off. Noticing a few cuts and scrapes on her knees, I turn towards Jade to ask about a first aid kit.

She points to her bag and says, "I have everything I need to clean it up and take care of it. You guys go on ahead and get out of here, I'll take care of her. And of course, let her know that you were a perfect knight in shining armor," she smiles wide and winks my way.

I shake my head and chuckle, "Thanks." Before standing, I look back at Nova and reach out for her leg. Just before grabbing a hold of it, I freeze and whisper, "I'll wait for you." I turn and see both Dorian and Jade watching with smiles on their faces. Clearing my throat, I roll my eyes and point at them, "Not. A. Word." Walking past them I stop just outside the door and toss over my shoulder, "Uh, thanks Jade. Dor, I'll see you at the warehouse." I can hear low murmurs from the two of them while I head towards the door. *I swear he knows all of them. Whatever, he'll tell me when he's ready.* Getting in my truck and starting it, I see Dorian running towards me.

He's panting and looking disheveled by the time he hops in, "Dude, did you forget you were my ride?"

Rolling my eyes, I say, "I'm still here aren't I? Don't pout."

Buckling up he crosses his arms over his chest and looks out the window, mumbling under his breath, "I'm not pouting."

When we get to the warehouse, I turn off the truck and open my door to hop out. Dorian's phone goes off with a notification. He shakes his phone at me, "I'll be right behind you in a second. Might have a target for you."

"Sweet." I jump out of my truck and shut the door. Reaching the doors, I bring my palm up to the handprint scanner and it beeps with a green flash and an automated voice says, "*Please proceed with retinal scan.*" I bring my eyes close to the scanner just above the handprint one. There's a clicking noise and the automated voice says, "*Please keep eyes open until you hear approved or denied.*" Keeping my eyes open wide, I hear the whirring noise of the scanner. "*Approved,*" with that the doors make a clicking noise and then buzzes, giving me the all clear to walk in. Just before I go in, I hear Dorian hopping out of my truck. Smiling with an idea, I swing the door open dramatically and start to walk in.

"Dude, wait for me!"

Turning around, I keep hold of the door and look at him, "Ooo, no can do, brother. That is a serious breach of security protocols."

Picking up his pace, he yells out, "NO IT'S NOT! As long as one of us is here, we're always able to get in without the security measures!"

Clicking my tongue, my smile grows, "I just don't think I can risk it." I quickly step back and pull the door fully shut, hearing the resounding click and buzz of the door locking.

He reaches the door with a scowl and smacks his palm against it. "Asshole!"

Cupping my ear, I say, "Huh? I can't hear you. Such a shame. Follow security protocol like a good pup, I'll meet you in the conference room."

Walking backwards, I see him bring his hands up and flip me off, "YOU'RE SUCH A DICK!" Waving at him, I tilt my head back laughing and then turn to head for the conference room.

I enter the conference room, and make my way to the chair at the end of the table. The chair creaks as I prop my legs up and cross them at the ankle on the table. I unlock my phone and call *Swan & Scribe*.

After a few rings, I can hear background noise and then, "*Swan & Scribe*, this is Vanessa, how may I help you?"

"Hey V, Rhys here."

"Oh, hey. Is everything okay with Nova? Did Jade make it there?"

Clearing my throat, I respond, "Yeah, yeah. Dorian and I just left there a little bit ago. I just had a few questions I was hoping you could answer for me."

"Yeah, of course. What's up?"

"Full disclosure? Trying to woo her here. So I was trying to see if you could tell me some likes and dislikes so I can get started on a plan here."

"Uhhhh, I mean, I can tell you some basic things, but I'm not going to go in depth or anything. Certain things really need to come from her when she's ready."

Dropping my feet from the table, I sit up, "Of course, of course. I just meant drinks, food, movies, shows. Things like that."

Dorian walks in with his hair a mess and a scowl on his face. "You're an immature prick."

Pointing at the phone to my ear, I say, "I'm having an important meeting right now. I don't appreciate YOU being such an immature prick while I have this conversation." Vanessa starts laughing and Dorian stops in his tracks, bobbing his mouth open and shut like a fish. With a guffaw, I say, "Dude, you should see your face. You definitely look like Dory now, just blub-blubbing away with your mouth. Just keep swimming, Dor, this call is important." Flipping me off, he walks over to the screens muttering under his breath. "Anyways, sorry about that, Vanessa."

Snickering, she says, "Oh no, I am fully entertained by the two of you. I almost grabbed some popcorn for the show. Anyways, basic likes for Nova. Let's see. Caffeine is *literally* her go-go juice. There will be zero functioning from her without it. Any caffeine will do, but her favorites are *Ultra Rosa Monster* and iced or blended caramel coffee, *extra, extra* caramel. Wait, are you writing this down? If not, you probably should. Not because she'll complain if you get it wrong, quite the opposite, but *I* want you to get this right, because she deserves the best. And honestly, if you're not willing to give her the best then I'm just wasting my time telling you this. I have a feeling I don't have to worry about that with you though, do I, Rhys?"

Jumping out of my chair, I scramble around the room for a pen and paper. Dorian looks at me like I'm crazy, so I make the motion with my hand for a pen. With a nod and a silent, *'ahh'*, Dorian grabs a pen and paper for me and slides it across the table. I hold up the pen as if she can see it and then shake my head at myself. "I have a pen and paper now, let me just write that down. Are you a mom or something? Cuz that was just like those caring moms on movies that properly scold their child."

With a laugh she says, "Yes, I'm a mom. So you better listen to me, and treat Nova right. Mira, m'ijo, I'll throw my chancla at you. I don't care how big and strong you are. That girl has dealt with enough in her life, far more than she ever deserved. So listen and believe when I tell you, if you end up being a cabrón, I'll hunt you down with a machete."

With wide eyes, I look up at Dorian and mouth, *'what the fuck?'* Clearing my throat and shaking my head I say, "Well, uh, thank you for my first introduction to true fear. I might have to change myself after this conversation. Also, did you call me a hoe? I can't even guess what cabrón means."

With an exasperated sigh she says, "Ay dios mío, no I didn't call you a hoe, Rhys. Here's your free foreign language lesson on things a Puerto Rican woman says to you. Mira, m'ijo, is listen here, son. Cabrón is me calling you a fucker, and before you ask, ay dios mío is oh my god. Any further lessons will cost you an astronomy book of my choosing."

Motion ahead of me catches my eye and I look up. Dorian gives me the wrap it up sign and points back at the screens. Rolling my eyes, I hold a finger up, and no, it wasn't the please hold finger. "I'm writing this down too. Anyways, so I have drinks written down. What else?"

"As far as food, it honestly depends on her mood that day. But she's also very agreeable and thankful if someone gives her food. Even if she doesn't like it, she'll take it like it's treasure. If we're talking movies and shows, she is a big fan of horror. From super cheesy, low-budget horror all the way to the most dark and depraved horror there is. I've also introduced her to anime recently and she's hooked. She hasn't watched a lot yet, since she's still new to it. So far she's really loving *Fruits Basket, Tokyo Ghoul* and she just started *Jujutsu Kaisen*. Bookwise, you will always find that girl devouring all of the dark and smutty romance." Smiling at the similarities between us, I quickly write everything down. Looking up when I hear a tapping noise, Dorian is glaring daggers at me while tapping his pen on the table.

Groaning, I tell Vanessa, "Listen, V, I appreciate this more than you know. Dorian is being impatient. Apparently we have work to do. Is there any way I can get your number so I can bounce some ideas off of you?"

"The store has caller ID, so I'll just add you to my phone now and then text you from mine. Sound good?"

"Yeah, yeah, that sounds great. Thanks again, Vanessa. Have a great day."

"You too." I fold the paper and add it with my phone to the pocket inside my jacket. Clapping my hands and rubbing them together, I shout, "All right, let's get to work. Geez ya slacker, I've been waiting forever for you."

Narrowing his eyes, he mutters, "Why do I put up with you? Honestly."

"Pfft. Because trauma brought us together, we became brothers from different mothers and you wuvvvvvvv me."

With a thin-lipped smile, he nods, "True. True and right now, not so much. Anyways, I have a target for you, so I need Rhys The Beast right now and not mushy Reese's Pieces."

Sneering at the picture that forms in my mind from his words, I say, "Dude. Fucking gross. Mushy. Reese's Pieces. Picture it. Blech."

"I was already picturing it, that's why I said it. Moving on."

Mirroring each other we lay back against our seats, pulling out my cigarettes, Dorian pulls out his *Swisher Sweets*. "Regular or happy smoke, Dorian?"

Putting his swisher in his mouth, he lights it. *Welp, that answers that.* "We can do happy-time smoking when the job is done." Grabbing the remote from the table, he points it at the screens and presses a button. Surveillance photos pop up across the screen. "All right, I obviously didn't have time to throw together your dossier, so I'm just showing you what he looks like and I'll give you the bit of info I have for you. Ready?" The change in me is instant. I morph from joking with Dorian, into the beast he said I was. With one look we know it's game time. He points to the screens, "Vincenzo DiMarco, nickname Little Vinny. He's a pusher of sorts for *Amissa Stella*. From the looks of things, he goes around town, to places like the bars and parties, searching for potential buyers. He gives them a sample of their product and a card with a number to call if they want more. He even offers it to people that seem new to the scene, ready to get them hooked on their supply and sink their claws in them. I think he sees himself more as an enforcer though, because the people that confront him about what he's doing all end up hospitalized. My guess, he acts like he's willing to talk about things and then gets them secluded and beats the shit out of them."

My jaw clicks from clenching so hard and I grit out, "Piece of shit. I'm gonna have fun with Vinny the Ninny." Smacking the table, I stand up and say, "Get eyes on him while I pack up."

Putting the last of my things in my duffle, I zip it up and hear the buzz of the intercom system and Dorian's voice summoning me. "Yo! I got eyes on him, it's a fucking miracle in this area. Hurry up!"

I throw my bag over my shoulder and run back to the conference room.

"Dude! Thank the Gods for this generation's farmers! They all have cameras set up to keep an eye on their crops, livestock and equipment. Without these, we would've never found him out here! The route he's taking just had him passing us, so he's either going to one of the lookouts, or he's taking the back roads to *Amissa Stella*."

I dial Dorian's number and the opening song to *Tokyo Ghoul* starts playing. Lifting a brow I ask, "When did you change my ringtone to that?"

"Right about the time I overheard Vanessa tell you some of Nova's favorite shows and they just happen to align with some of the shows you watch," He shakes his head and whispers, "kismet."

"I sure as fuck hope so, now answer the phone so I can leave. Keep me posted on which direction to go."

I head past the cemetery and follow the steep hill down. Ignoring the stop sign, I take the sharp right turn and start following the farm road. "Talk to me, Dorian. Any idea where he's heading?"

"Didn't we already discuss this? I have an idea of where he's going and I will tell you when he takes a turn."

"Just remember, Moody McGee, you have a long walk to wherever he stops so you can pick up his rig. At least it will give you time to think about your bad attitude."

Groaning, he says, "Dude, I totally forgot about that part. This blows donkey dick, man."

With an exaggerated gasp, I say in a horrified voice, "Why, I never heard such foul-mouthed sinner words. I am clutching my pearls as we speak, you heathen."

Snorting, he says, "Meathead!"

"Brainiac!"

"Oh shit! He turned. All right, he chose one of the lookouts. Listen very carefully, this turn is almost impossible to see. Just keep your eye out towards the left side. You'll be able to see his vehicle on the hill when you get close enough. When you make the turn, there's two ways to get to the top. If you go to the right, you're going to creep up right behind him, and if you choose the left you'll meet him face to face. Just be ready. He won't see you coming, but he'll hear you, so there's no element of surprise."

"Got it, I've got a plan. I'll see you back at the warehouse." Hanging up the phone, I toss it on the seat. Taking the last curve, I look to the left and sure as shit, I can see his vehicle on top of the hill. Slowing down, I just barely catch the turn I need. I swerve a little bit near the top of the incline, making sure I don't overcorrect with the area being so narrow.

When I get to the top, Vincenzo is leaning against his car smoking and looks over towards me. Putting my truck in park, I shut it off and pull the lever to pop my hood. Pulling at the collar of my shirt like it's bothering me, I stumble to the front of my truck and lift the hood. Propping it up, I run my hands through my hair, ruffling it as if I'm frustrated. The gravel crunches beneath his shoes as I mumble nonsense under my breath and shake my head. *BINGO.*

Once he reaches me he says, "Hey man."

Pretending that his appearance surprises me, I jump back, "Oh f-fuck man. Snuck up on me there, heh." Scratching my neck a little, I start pulling at my shirt collar again.

Narrowing his eyes at me, a slow smile creeps across his face. "You good man? Kinda looks like you're in the need for, uh, something to get you through the day. Am I right?"

Flicking my eyes back and forth, I look at him again and give a clipped nod, "Y-yeah man. Yeah. Fuck yeah. Do you have anything on you? I'll take anything, my man." When he reaches into his jacket, I brace myself. A little baggy is now between his two fingers. I grab his whole hand and grip it tight.

"Hey, what the fuck man, let go!" I can feel his bones rubbing together the more I squeeze. Pulling him towards me, he lunges forward and I headbutt him. Pain blooms in my forehead, but I shake it off. The crunch of his nose breaking makes me smile, and the blood pouring down his face makes me laugh. "What the fuck!" His free hand keeps going up and down, as if he can't decide if he should cover his bloody nose, or reach out to fight back. Bringing my left leg behind his right, I simultaneously release the hold of his hand and shove against his chest. Throwing his arms out, he shouts, flying backwards as the momentum tosses him over my leg. Hitting the gravel, a burst of dust flies all around him and he quickly starts choking and coughing., I stand over him and look down.

"I just can't taint a beautiful view like this, I think it's best I take you to my playroom."

"Wha-" Bringing my foot up, I slam it down against his head. *Thank fuck for shit kickers.* Walking behind his head, I bend down and grab him under the armpits and drag him to the back of my truck. Letting him go, he hits the ground with a thud. Popping open the window and dropping the tailgate, I look down and try to decide the best way to get him up there. Shrugging, I step on both of his feet, grab hold of his jacket and pull hard. When his upper body is high enough off the ground, I lean forward and toss his upper half over my shoulder with a grunt. I lift to my full height and turn towards the truck. Throwing my weight forward, I toss him off of my shoulder. His head smacks off of the roof of the truck and then hits the truck bed. Hissing in, I say, "That's gonna leave a mark." His legs are dangling out of the truck, so I shove them back until they clear the tailgate. Shutting the back of the truck, I run to the driver's side and heave myself in.

Putting the truck in reverse, I back down the hill and turn towards the other opening. I shift to drive and head on out. I dial and he answers on the second ring. "Hello?"

"Hey man, I'm feeling generous, be ready to go when I get there so I can give you a lift to his car." Mumbling under his breath he says, "So generous," and hangs up.

After dropping Dorian off to take care of Vincenzo's car, I sped back to the warehouse and back up to the bay door before hopping out. Following the handprint scan and retinal scan, the bay door starts opening. Getting back in my truck, I keep an eye on my mirrors and back into the warehouse. Pushing the button to close the bay door, I walk over to one of the gurneys we have. Rolling it over to the back of my truck, I pop open the window and tailgate. Making sure to lock the gurney's wheels, I grab a hold of Vincenzo's feet and start pulling him onto the bed. Getting him situated, I shut the back of my truck, unlock the wheels and swivel the bed around. As I push him towards my playroom, his head bounces off the door with a thud. "Heh, oops." Turning the knob and opening it a little, I start pushing the bed again, using his head to push the door all the way open. I kick the door shut behind me and push the bed as close to the chair as I can manage. Locking the wheels, I toss my duffle onto my work table and unzip it. Grabbing a knife, I walk over to Vincenzo and slice the knife through his shirt, exposing his torso. Tossing the knife back on the table, I walk back over to him, grabbing a hold of him and carrying him to the chair. He hunches over slightly when I throw him down in it. Going through my duffle, I find my duct tape and start wrapping it around his wrists, ankles and torso. Unlocking the wheels of the gurney, I give it a kick so it rolls off to the side. Turning on my speaker, I scroll through my music choices. Deciding on *Ready or*

Not by *sKitz Kraven*, I click play and the music starts playing through the speaker.

Putting my phone down on the work table, I crack my neck and shake out my shoulders. I walk over to the hanging hose and pull it down. I aim it towards Vincenzo and start spraying him with the frigid water. After a few moments, his head shoots up and he starts gasping and choking on the water. Releasing the nozzle, the water stops and I release my hold of the hose as it pulls back above my head. Vincenzo continues coughing and spitting, wiggling around as if that will release him from his bindings.

"WHAT THE FUCK IS THIS?! WHO THE FUCK ARE YOU?! I'LL FUCKING KILL YOU!"

Chuckling at his words, I say, "Big talk coming from the guy bound to a chair."

"Big talk coming from the guy that will only fight me while I'm tied up! Fucking bitch boy!"

Stopping in front of him, I lean forward until I'm in his face, "I thought I would make things unfair like you do with all those innocent people you put in the hospital. Don't get pissy cuz I'm taking a page outta your book." Spit lands on my face and I shut my eyes, sneering. I wipe the spit off of my face, my eyes darken as I open them.

Slapping him across the face with his spit, I smile and say, "Who's the bitch boy now?"

Walking back to my work table, I search through my bag for my brass knuckles. Pulling them out, I turn towards Vincenzo and his eyes widen.

"Like them? My favorite part is the spikes. I can remove them completely, or move them around in different spots, it's amazing. So let's play a game. I'm going to remove all of the spikes for now. I'm going to ask you a question and you're going to answer. If you don't, then I add a spike to hit you with. Sound good?"

"No, it doesn't fucking sound good, you fucking psycho!"

Shrugging at him, I say, "Is it supposed to hurt my feelings when you call me names? Please stop wasting your breath talking nonsense. I'd prefer your answers to my questions."

Unscrewing all of the spikes, I pocket them all and slide the brass knuckles over my fingers and squeeze, feeling the metal grind against the bones in my hand. "Alright, first question. It's a really easy one, my favorite one to really get the party started. What is your name?"

Gritting his teeth he says, "Fuck. You." Shaking my head, I put my hand in my pocket and grab one of the spikes. Pulling it out I start twisting it in place.

"Vincenzo, Vincenzo, Vincenzo. The easiest question of all and you're already fucking up. We both know the correct answer is Vincenzo DiMarco. Hell, I would've even taken Little Vinny as an answer," looking down towards his crotch and back up to his eyes, I add, "makes sense. Wittle Vinny has to overcompensate with his big attitude."

I slam the brass knuckles against his hand, the spike pushing through his skin. The moment it hits his hand, he starts screaming, "You fucking piece of shit!"

Pulling the spike out there's a little resistance, so I pull harder.

Once it pops back out blood starts pouring from the wound in his hand. "Alright, next question. Try not to fuck up this time. What do you do for *Amissa Stella*?"

"You do realize, family or not, they will fucking kill me if I tell you anything!"

Rolling my eyes I tell him, "Dude! *I'm* going to fucking kill you. So you might as well start fucking talking. Why does nobody understand how this works? You talking equals quicker and less painful death. You pretend you're taking a vow of silence, and your death takes longer and is more painful. What. Do. You. Do. For. *Amissa. Stella*?" Rolling his lips inward, he shakes his head no and looks away. Pulling another spike out of my pocket and twisting it in place, I slam the brass knuckles down onto his other hand.

"Fuck you! Fuck you! Fuck youuuuuu!"

Ignoring his outburst, an idea hits and I walk to the table and toss the brass knuckles down. Picking up my phone, I start a text conversation with Vanessa.

> ME: Hey V, an idea just popped in my head and I need to run it by you.

> V: What plan would that be?

> ME: I was thinking about the things you said she likes, and I was wondering if I could set something up at the store on a day you guys are closed. I'm thinking maybe bring her favorite drinks, lay out some of those books she loves and just let her read while I hang out with her. And then if you guys have some sort of projector there, I can set up my laptop to play horror movies and anime. What do ya think?

"Since your phone is more important, can you just let me go now?"

Looking over at him, I scrunch up my face, "Dude, you're the one who decided to shut down and look away. If you're willing to talk, then sure I'll put my phone away. 'Til then, I'll get to you when I'm damn good and ready." My phone buzzes in my hand and I look down.

> V: Holy shit, that's a great idea! I fucking love it! Absolutely, we can make that happen. We're closed on Sundays and Mondays, so your best bet will be this Sunday. That only gives you under a week to get everything ready. Is that enough time? I can have the projector and screen all set up for you, and I'll grab a bunch of books for you to lay out however you want.

ME: Fuckin' sweet. Thanks V. Does Nova have a key? What time do you want to meet there so I can set everything up and wait for her. I figure you can ask her if she can do something at the store for you and I can surprise her.

V: As much as I would love to do it that way, that's not a good idea. You can't surprise Nova like that. I'll figure out how to get her there, and you can meet me there at 10 A.M. to set it all up. Sound good?

ME: Perfect. Thanks again, V.

Dropping my phone back down, I pick up the brass knuckles and slide them back on. Turning towards Vincenzo, I ask my next question.

"All right, next question. What is *Amissa Stella* up to besides the drugs?"

"Do what you have to do, I'm not telling you a fucking thing." Grabbing the last three spikes from my pocket, I screw them all in place. Rearing back, I bring my fist across his face, sinking four out of the five spikes in across his cheek, which makes him scream. Blood and tears mix together as they drip down his face.

Holding them in place, I look him dead in the eye and say, "Scream louder, I fucking love it." Without pulling the spikes out, I rip my hand down hard pulling the spikes through his flesh. "I'd say this wouldn't be happening if you would've just answered my questions, but honestly you're owed a good ass whoopin' after all the shit you did to those innocent people." His sobs get louder, and snot starts mixing with the blood and tears. The scent of urine hits my nostrils and I curl my lip in disgust.

"Please don't shit too, you're already leaking out of enough holes."

"Pleaseeee! I'm sorry, I'm sorry. I don't know anything! I swear!"

Done listening to him, I punch him in the face repeatedly. Bone is crunching and blood is splattering across my fist, clothes and face. His once loud sobs quickly morph to muffled whimpers and then garbles. His face is no longer recognizable. There's blood everywhere, some areas sunken in and a few others swelling. Since his head is shaved, I can't grab his hair, so I slam my palm against his forehead pushing him back and then punch the spikes through his throat. I hear a blood-filled wheeze escape him and that's his final breath.

Unsure how long I've been here for and if Dorian is back yet, I start the process of cutting up and disposing of Vincenzo's body. *Is it twisted that all I can think of is my surprise for Nova while cutting up a dead body? Probably, but darkness consumes us all in strange ways.*

"By failing to prepare, you are preparing to fail." ~Benjamin Franklin

CHAPTER 6
REFLECTIONS

NOVA

What do you do when you have walls made of adamantium built around your heart, but some 6 foot tall, green-eyed sex on legs man is finding a way to break them down? He said he was willing to wait for me, even though I told him I wasn't worth it. I didn't realize that meant he was going to actually put in work while waiting. Let's just recap the shit this man has been up to for the past week.

On Wednesday, my bruised and pain-filled self hobbled into the store to find a bright green gift bag with a beautiful orchid next to it at the front counter. V looked like the cat that caught the canary, and even did a little Vanna White action showcasing the bag and flower to me. I pick up the orchid to smell it and smile. "I wish I knew what kind it was, it's fucking beautiful."

Putting her phone in my face, a picture of the flower with a description is on the screen. "I looked it up, I had to know too. I didn't even know galaxy orchids were a thing. Cool, right?"

Nodding my head, I look inside the bag and find an Ultra Rosa Monster with a note that said, '*A Monster to help you defeat the day's obstacles.'* There was a bottle of ibuprofen with a note that said, *'To help take away the pain, even though I wish I could be the one to do it.'* At the bottom of the bag was another note that read, *'Meet me at the coffee bar at lunchtime.'*

Lunchtime rolled around and I went to the coffee bar. I know the note said he would be there, but I didn't believe it. Sure enough, there he was, standing by the counter with that damn sexy ass smirk. He bought me lunch and we sat down with The Horde and ate the meal without exchanging a word with each other. Once we were finished, he got up from the table, placed his hand on it and leaned down to catch my eye.

When our eyes connected, he said, "I'll wait," and then he just sauntered away.

On Thursday, I walk in and yet again find V showcasing more gifts from Rhys. "Before you ask, this flower is a royal blue lily." Cracking open the Monster he left me, I take a drink and then pick up the flower and smell it. A smile slips out and V jabs her finger towards my face, "Ha! Caught you! That, my friend, is a smile. A real one."

Rolling my eyes, I flip her off. Putting the drink down, I add the flower to my Monster can vase that I "made" yesterday. Picking up the note, it says, *'Hope to meet you at the coffee bar for lunch.'* Putting the note down, I look up at V and she's still smiling.

"What did you do, V?"

Putting her hand up to her chest, she gasps, "Me? He's doing all the work here. All I did was answer a few *very* basic questions. I promise you I didn't tell him anything major. Certain things are up to you to tell him if you choose to."

Lunchtime rolled around and I headed that way, with not as much hesitation as I should have. We ordered lunch and again went and sat down with The Horde. We talked a little bit, but I had the feeling he already knew the answers to the questions he was asking. *Damn you, V.* He again stood up, leaned into me and said, "I'll wait."

Opening the door to *Swan & Scribe* on Friday, I again find V excited behind the counter, bouncing on her toes.

"Look how pretty it is!"

Pointing down to the counter over and over, I follow the direction and see an amazing galaxy colored vase with a galaxy orchid and royal blue lily in it. Next to it is a Monster, a note and a pack of *Marlboro Smooth 100s*. Running my fingers along the vase, I breathe out, "This thing is stupid pretty." Nodding down to the smokes, I add, "I take it that was another thing you told him?"

Making a zipper motion across her lips, she grabs the flowers from my Monster vase and adds them to the galaxy one. Rolling my eyes, I pick up the note next to the vase. '*This galaxy wasn't complete until it was joined with the most beautiful star of all. I hope to see you at the coffee bar.*' Meeting him at the coffee bar, he smiles my way and a "thank you" falls from my lips for the gifts.

His smile grows and he says, "Anything for my little star."

A blush creeps across my face and I look down. His finger gently touches the bottom of my chin and he pushes up. Following the movement I look at him. "You don't have to hide from me, sweetheart."

We head over to The Horde's designated table after grabbing our lunch and sit down. As usual, everyone briefly goes silent when we sit down and then they get back to their conversations. Rhys and I join in here and there, and we both get a glimpse at each other's lives while chatting with everyone. Standing up, he leans towards me and brushes a piece of hair behind my ear, looks me in the eye and says, "I'll wait." After saying his good-byes to everyone, he heads out.

On Saturday, I notice the amount of flowers in the vase has at least tripled. Heading over to the counter, V slides her hand across the counter and moves it back. There on the counter is a lighter with a galaxy design , which has an extendable arm with a roach clip connected to it. I immediately check it out, "Holy shit, I've always wanted one of these! These things are fucking badass." Putting it in my pocket, I grab the note that's next to the vase. *'I hope this doesn't change your mind about lunch, but my puppy will be with me.'*

Furrowing my brows, I look up at V. "Uhh, since when do you allow animals in here that aren't of the service variety?"

Putting her hands up, she tilts her head to the side, "I uh, have work to do. See ya later, Nova girl."

Raspberrying at her, I say, "Hoarding astronomy books isn't work, *Vanessa!*"

Heading to the coffee bar at lunch, I'm ready to see this cute puppy he mentioned. Approaching the counter, I see Rhys there with his friend Dorian. Looking around both of them, I look back at Rhys and lift a brow, "Uh, where's your puppy?"

Dorian chimes in with a question of his own, "Puppy? You don't have a puppy."

Throwing his thumb over his shoulder towards Dorian, he smiles and says, "The one yappin' away is my puppy."

Snorting a laugh, I cover my mouth. Dorian shoves Rhys' shoulder and it turns into an arm slapping and jostling match. "Ayo, Rocky one and two, let's order lunch."

They immediately stop and nod their heads at me, "Yes, Nova." Looking between the two of them, they act as if that was completely normal.

"Do you guys always mirror each other like that? I can't decide if it was creepy or cool."

They both shrug, "It tends to happen when you spend a lot of time with someone over the years," Rhys says.

Dorian pipes in and says, "There's actually studies that have been done on people that have known each other for an interminable amount of time-"

Rhys puts his hand against Dorian's chest, "Dude. Breathe. Your word vomit is making a mess."

Grabbing our lunch, the three of us head toward The Horde's

table. Everyone greets us and we sit down, joining in on the conversations. Rhys and Dorian mesh so well with the group, it's as if they've been with us all since the beginning. When lunch is finished, they both stand and Dorian starts saying his goodbyes to everyone.

Looking over at me he says, "It was really good seeing you again, Nova. I hope to do it again soon."

Smiling and nodding, I say, "Yeah, that would be great, Dorian."

Standing up, Rhys blocks my view of Dorian and leans in. *I swear every time he does this he gets closer.* Bringing his hand up, he places his finger to my forehead and gently pokes it, the move reminds me of my shows and I slightly gasp. He looks deeply in my eyes and says, "I'll wait."

———————✦

After leaving the store, I head home and lay on my bed while listening to music and smoking a joint. My phone buzzes on the nightstand, and I roll over to pick it up. Seeing the text from V, I narrow my eyes. Instead of texting back, I decide to call her.

She picks up after the first ring and says, "Don't be mad at me."

"Your text said that already. Spill."

"RhyshasplansforyouandIhelped."

Sitting up abruptly, I say, "What did you do?"

"You already know he had some questions and I answered them, hence all the gifts that were spot on. During that talk he came up with an idea, a fucking sweet one, might I add. So I agreed that I would help him set it all up. At first he wanted it to be a complete surprise, like I tell you I needed your help at the store and he would surprise you. I told him that was off the table though and that I would tell you what was going on. I know you're scared, I know you have your walls up, but please, please give this man a chance. You know I have your back and will protect you fiercely, but I think this would be really good for you. I think he's really good for you. Or at least I think he will be." Finishing her rant she takes a deep breath and I remain silent thinking it over. "Nova?"

"Yeah, I'm still here. I just…I don't know what to do, V."

Letting out an exasperated sigh she grumbles out, "Ay dios, I just told you what you need to do. Listen, I already threatened the guy, and you know I'll follow through. I think you'll have an amazing time with everything he has planned out. Plus, selfish me really needs you to do this so I can live vicariously through you. Cuz lemme tell ya girl, if a man was pulling out all the stops like this for me, hoooo-weee, I'd fall to my knees for that man. If you know what I mean."

Snorting, I say, "Yeah, V. I know what ya mean. Jeezus," groaning I add, "fiiiiiine. I'll go, okay? Where am I going and when do I need to be there?"

V squeals out loud and I yank the phone from my ear, "Jesus fuck, V. I need my ears for my fucking jam sessions, bitch hole."

"Sorry, sorry. I'm just so excited for you. Okay, it's tomorrow at the store. I'll text you when you should head that way."

"Ugh, fine." Hanging up the phone before she can respond, I take a long puff of my joint and then put it out in the ashtray on my nightstand. Walking around the apartment, I make sure everything is locked up and all the window alarms and door alarm are set. Heading back to my room, I throw myself face first onto my bed and snuggle into my pillow.

Waking up the next day, I grab myself a Monster and start the hunt for what to wear today. I brace my hands on the top of my dresser and hang my head. *Why are you making this such a big deal, Nova? Just pick a fucking outfit. You change yourself for no one.*

I shove off the dresser and start shuffling through my clothes. Rifling through my underwear drawer, repeating *no, maybe, no* in my head, has me feeling like the *Grinch* getting ready for the

Whoville party. A wave of nausea hits and I take a deep breath, willing it to stop. Annoyed with myself, I grab a random pair of panties and bra, tossing them on the bed. I look through my shirts and grab my Kyo and Tohru *Fruits Basket* shirt. Yanking out a pair of torn up black jeans from my pants drawer, I shove it shut and throw those on the bed. Walking over to my closet, I open it and grab my black leather jacket with a built in gray hood and my black and gray Converse. Kicking the door shut, I drop them on top of everything else. *It would be great if I knew what fucking time I needed to be there.* Shaking my head, I walk to my bathroom and grab one of my caramel apple shower steamers from under the sink. Tossing it in its holder, I turn on the shower and run to my room for my phone. I hit one of my random playlists to play on my speaker and *Landslide* by *Fleetwood Mac* starts playing. Taking my clothes off, I toss them in the hamper and step in the shower. I use my shampoo bottle as a microphone to sing obnoxiously loud along with the song. *Good thing my neighbor is old and can't hear for shit. They would not be pleased with this performance.* Halfway through shaving *everything*, I shake my head. *I cannot believe I'm shaving for this man right now.* Standing under the water, I close my eyes and attempt to calm myself down. As usual, my brain refuses to listen and starts listing pros and cons to this whole plan. Finishing up my shower, I hop out and grab my towel, wrapping it around me. My cinnamon and honey body butter makes my skin smell heavenly as I rub it along my arms and legs. Opening my drawer, I pick up my pheromone roll-on and twist the cap off. Applying it to my wrists, behind my ears and down my neck, I then rub my wrists together. Putting the cap back on, I toss it in the drawer and close it. I wrap my towel tightly around me and hold it close, rubbing my fingers along the fuzzy material. Getting to my room, I dry off my body and then twist my towel around my hair. After getting dressed, I ruffle the towel through my hair and scrunch it up with mousse to give it a little bit of waves before tossing the towel in the hamper. Washing the residue off of my hands, I head to my kitchen to finish my *Monster*. My phone goes off and I immediately know it's V with her customized ringtone of her shouting, 'BOOKS!'.

Laughing at the ringtone, I pull my phone from my pocket and answer it. "Sup, book lady?"

"Hey, Nova girl. Please, please tell me you're ready?!" With each word her excitement builds and I slightly pull the phone from my ear.

Clearing my throat I shout into the phone, "VOLUME CHECK, PLEASE! And yes, I'm ready. Can I head on over now?"

"Okay, oww. Point taken. It's not my fault you're not showing the proper amount of enthusiasm here. I have to project the enthusiasm of two people here. Anywayssss, pull the thong out of your asshole, Miss Grumps-A-Lot and get here."

"That description right there is the exact reason I don't wear the full service flossers. I'm sorry, I'm just freaking out here a little bit. This could really fucking blow up in my face, V."

I hear murmuring in the background and some shuffling. After a few seconds, V gets back on the line, "Sorry, I needed to say this next part without extra ears. Anyways, I understand you're scared, but we're all here for you. Yes, there's always the chance that something could go wrong, but what if you miss out on the chance on what you truly deserve? I mean... what if this is destiny and you're trying to give it a big fuck you? I don't really recommend that by the way, so please, I'm begging you, give the guy a chance. A real one, not just show up here and go through the motions. I mean keep your mind and your heart open. Don't you always say expect the worst, but hope for the best? Let's just forget about the worst for a moment and hope for once. Manifest this shit, bitch."

Snorting at her pep talk, I nod, "Okay."

"Ahem, excuse me? A little louder please, put some fucking gusto in that shit."

"OKAY!!!"

"Ouch."

"Don't even fucking cry about it, you know I can be loud. You asked for that shit. No, no, you demanded that fucking shit. You reap what you sow and all that jazz. Alright, I'm outta here. You still gonna be there or not?"

"Psh, you already know I'll still be here. I have to see your reaction to this. The man worked hard, girl."

———————⋆.

When I walk through the doors, I immediately freeze at what lays before me. There's a trail of flower petals, that I'm guessing are from the type of flowers he gave me all week. On either side of the trail are electric tealight candles. A flash of light snaps me out of my stupor and I look in the direction it came from.

Blinking the haze away I see V behind the counter with her phone up and smiling. "Gotcha, bitch!"

Flipping her off, I walk over to the counter, "You know I hate pictures. Fucking rude," taking a deep breath and looking around, I whisper, "I guess I just follow the trail, huh?"

Nodding her head excitedly she says, "You're going to love it. We set everything up in one of the hideaway nookie rooms, I mean the hideaway book nook."

"Cute, real fucking cute, V. I'm gonna," clicking my tongue and tilting my head towards the trail I head that way. Following the trail up the stairs, I stop just outside the door with my hand frozen above the door handle. Wiping my sweaty palms across my jeans, I count to three in my head while taking a deep breath and grasp the door handle tightly. Pushing the door in, I step inside and look around. *Holy fuck, and I thought the trail was beautiful.* The door shuts louder than expected, making me cringe and Rhys turns around from the pillows he's setting up. He stands there silent as I take in all the work he's done. There's "floating" paper lanterns hanging all around the room, fluffy

18

blankets and pillows everywhere, more flower petals, a projector screen with a slideshow of anime and horror film pictures, a jackpot of smut books laid out and my *Monsters* on a table off to the side.

With every item I look at, my nerves seem to melt away, being replaced with stronger emotions. I can feel tears pool in my eyes and I immediately look up to the ceiling, refusing to blink and let them fall.

"Shit. That is not the reaction I was going for. Fuck, I fucked up, didn't I?"

Refusing to voice my answer for fear of my voice cracking, I slowly shake my head no towards the ceiling. Clearing my throat, I attempt to speak and my voice cracks, "I-" clearing my throat again, I take a deep breath through my nose and slowly exhale through my mouth.

With a broken voice that would match mine if I spoke, Rhys says, "Please look at me, little star."

Slowly lowering my head, I look at him and the look on his face shatters the last bit of control I have on my own emotions. Gasping a sob, I cover my mouth and the tears start to fall, "I-I'm s-sorry, fuck, please don't be mad."

Rushing over, he throws his arms around me. His left arm wraps around my lower back pulling me against him, and his right hand is cradling my head against his chest. "Shh, shh. I'm not mad at all, little star. I'm just really worried I fucked this up. I didn't mean to make you upset, I really thought you would love this." He starts rubbing the back of my head to soothe me and I sniffle.

With a small voice, I croak, "I doooo. Nobody's ever done anything like this for me before and it just really took me off guard. I promise. Thank you so much. Please don't be mad."

"Hey, hey, why do you keep saying that? I'm not mad, I promise."

Lifting my head, I rest my chin against his chest and look at him. His eyes connect with mine and everything disappears. An intense sense of déjà vu hits me, and instead of finding myself fearful of it, I feel nothing but peace. *I think this is what home is supposed to feel like.* Slowly everything goes back to normal and we're surrounded by everything in the book nook again. His eyes flick back and forth between my eyes and down to my mouth.

Leaning forward, he's just a breath away and he whispers, "I'll wait." Slowly releasing his hold on me, he steps back and tilts his head towards everything laid out. "So, V told me some of the things you like. It's up to you what you want to do first, either scope out the books and pick one to read in peace, or we can watch a horror film or anime and talk if you want. Or... or we could just watch it, we don't have to talk if you don't want to."

Rubbing his palms down his jeans he looks around and back at me with hope shining in his eyes.

"I'd really like to watch something with you. But I'll have to make a note in my phone of all these books, so I know to look at them again on Tuesday."

Biting his lip he looks away, bringing his hand up he scratches the back of his head. "Uh, about that. You don't actually have to do that, because I bought all of these for you so you could take home whatever you didn't read today."

My eyes widen from the shock and I choke, "Wait, what?"

Throwing my hands out towards the piles of books all over, "You bought all of these?! No, no, no. You didn't have to do that, you don't have to buy me things, Rhys. Believe me, I'm so thankful for it and really appreciate the gesture, but that's a lot of money."

"Can I ask you a question, Nova?" Swallowing the lump in my throat, I nod. "Do you not want the gifts, or do you feel like there's strings with accepting my gifts?"

'Don't be such an ungrateful little bitch, Sweet Cheeks. Quit crying about the beatings you fucking earn. The gifts should make up for it, right? RIGHT?!'

Shaking myself from the memory, I whisper, "Accepting gifts allows bad things to happen."

"What do you mean, sweetheart?"

Fuck, now or never. Taking a deep breath, I look up at him. "Can we sit for this? I just… I guess if I'm supposed to be trying and be open with you, then I should probably lay some shit out on the table right here and now. Let you know what you're getting into here."

Walking past him, I throw myself down on a pile of pillows and grab the closest blanket, holding it close. Fidgeting with the ends of it, I close my eyes and start telling him about Frankie. Without going into full detail, I tell him how Frankie abused me in every way imaginable, how gifts meant I needed to be appreciative and accepting of my punishments for my "wrong-doings" throughout the day. I told him how I put up with the abuse for years, thinking it was exactly what I deserved. Being abused in various forms is all I've ever known.

When he asked me what I meant by that, I told him about the abuse and assaults from a family member. How my parents chose that person over me. How neglectful they were growing up. Over the years, multiple men had assaulted me, or at least tried to, but I fought harder this time. I was bigger, stronger. I wasn't a little child anymore.

"So you see, I've been trained my whole life to believe I'm worthless and deserve any abuse and neglect I'm served." Opening my arms wide, I put on a big, fake smile, "Still think I'm a fucking catch?"

Crawling over to me, he puts his palms on my cheeks, wiping away the tears I didn't realize were falling. "I caught myself a falling star, and I'll gladly hold on tightly until I burn to ash. And when my soul is carried into the next life, I'll fucking burn for you all over again, just to be with you for as long as I can."

"How the fuck is a girl supposed to follow that up?"

Shaking his head, he laughs, "I can think of one way. Question?"

"Answer."

"Tell me the wait is over."

Without a second thought, I whisper out, "Ye-"

My words are cut off by his lips against mine, both moaning into the kiss. Grabbing a hold of the front of his shirt, I pull him closer. *Home.* He slowly pulls back from the kiss and I whimper at the loss. With his forehead pressed against mine, he dives in and pecks my lips three times. "What do you want to watch, little star?"

Slowly opening my eyes to look at him, I roll my eyes, "You expect me to think after that?"

"First off, there's only one time I want to see those pretty eyes rolling, and this isn't one of them. Keep it up and I'll spank your ass, Nova. Second... Okay, I don't really have a second other than will you please pick something for us to watch."

"I hope you know that wasn't the threat you thought it was. What are my options, boss man?"

Licking his bottom lip, I follow the movement, "Eyes up here, sweetheart." My eyes snap up and glare at him for being caught. "If you want a horror movie the options are endless. If you pick anime, I figured we could watch one of your favorites. V said you like *Fruits Basket, Tokyo Ghoul* and *Jujutsu Kaisen*. Not gonna lie, I like those also. One of them actually happens to be my favorite."

"That one! I want to watch your favorite one."

"You don't even know which one it is, are you sure?"

I shrug, "I love all three of those, so I'm down for any of them, but I have a pretty good guess as to which one is your favorite."

Sitting back on his heels, he smirks, "Is that so? Well, by all means, I'll close my eyes and you start the one you think is my favorite. Deal?"

I jump up, "Fucking deal!" Walking over to the laptop, I hear him chuckling behind me at my enthusiasm. Scrolling through the options, I find my pick and look over to Rhys. "Cover your eyes."

"My eyes are already closed, though."

"I don't care. Chop, chop! Cover them beauties."

Smiling, he shakes his head and brings his hands over his eyes, "Better?"

"Better."

As the opening song for *Tokyo Ghoul* starts playing, he whips his head in my direction and opens his eyes with a look of shock. "How the fuck did you guess?!"

Shrugging, I say, "Darkness consumes us all in strange ways." If this was a cartoon his eyes would have popped all the way out of his head.

"Did you... did you just... what the fuck?!"

My brows scrunch and I ask, "Uh, are you having a stroke or something?" His mouth opens and closes. Kneeling down next to him, I turn his face towards me. "Are you okay, ghoulie?"

The look of shock is replaced with a beaming smile, "Say it again."

Twisting my mouth to the side, I lift my brow, "Uh, say what again? Are you okay?"

His smile grows further and he shakes his head no, "Uh-uh, after that."

Realization dawns on me and I ask, "Ghoulie?"

His eyes light up, "I love it, little star."

I shrug as I feel a blush creeping up my cheeks, "You love *Tokyo Ghoul*, so I figure that makes you my green-eyed ghoul."

He turns me in his lap and spreading his legs, he pulls me to his chest. Laying my head back on his shoulder, I turn my head towards the screen to watch the show.

After a few hours of watching the show and talking here and there about our lives, Rhys lets me into his world like I did and recants his past with his parents. I could hear the tightness in his voice as he tells me they weren't physically abusive to him, but they'd go through extremes of verbal abuse or complete neglect. He tells me how he met Dorian in the 6th grade and how they bonded over having parents that didn't give a shit about them. They call themselves 'brothers from different mothers', and even though I'm just getting to know him, it warms my heart that they had each other. There's a twinge in my heart at the thought that I wish we found each other sooner so we could've all bonded over our traumas. Rhys puts all the pillows and blankets off to the side, and puts my books in a duffle bag.

Bringing everything downstairs, Rhys walks me to my car and helps me put the duffle in it. After shutting the trunk, he walks over to me, grabbing my hips and pinning me in place against the car.

Tilting his head, he says, "Two questions."

Mirroring his head tilt, I reply, "Two answers."

"Can we do this again, hopefully sooner rather than later? And please tell me I've earned the right to have your number so I can talk to you when we can't see each other?"

Pursing my lips, I tilt my head back and forth, "Hmmmm…"

Apparently I take too long to answer because he starts tickling my sides. Throwing my head back and wiggling around I laugh, "No, no, pleaseeeee, I'm sorryyyyyy, noooooo. No more, ghoulie, pleaseeeee."

He finally stops and I'm panting, "That. Was. Not. Nice."

"You're killing me here, little star. Let me hear the words."

I try to catch my breath but I respond, "Yes and yes."

I'm suddenly lifted in the air, making me gasp and squeal. Rhys is spinning me in circles, yelling to the sky, "SHE SAID YES! WOOOOO!"

"Put me down, Rhys!"

"Not a chance, sweetheart. As of right now, this is number two on my list of the best days of my life."

"What's number one on the list?" I ask.

Brushing his lips against mine, he whispers, "Meeting you."

I move forward and give him a quick kiss. Wiggling around to get down, he reluctantly slides me down his body and I feel every ridge of his muscles. I bite my lip to hold back a moan.

With my free hand, I make the grabby hand motion towards him for his phone. Rhys grabs his phone and hands it to me with a smirk. Typing my number in his phone, I save my name as 'Bookstore Nova'. Looking up at Rhys' laugh, I ask, "What's so funny there, chuckles?"

He waves off my words, "I'm only laughing because you added 'Bookstore' to your name. Believe me, it's not necessary. I won't forget who you are, Nova." He types away on his phone and then turns it towards me. I glance over to see he's changed it to 'My Little Star'.

Walking backwards, I almost trip over myself. Rhys starts to come towards me to help me but I shake my head, "No, no, I got it. I'm always clumsy. I, uh, I'll see ya around. Bye, ghoulie." Turning quickly, I open my car door and hop in.

When I pull into the parking lot, my phone buzzes with a notification. I can't help the blushing smile that forms when I see that it's a text from Rhys.

> UNKNOWN: I hope to see you soon, little star - Rhys.

His contact name is immediately added as 'GHOULIE'. I hop out of my car and head to my apartment. Once inside, I lock up and turn the alarm to full alert. I drop down on my couch and order a pizza and a drink. While I wait on my order, I head to my room, change into my pajamas and decide to do a load of laundry. I lean down and light the candle that's on the coffee table in the living room. The name of the candle, 'Smells Like Your Book Boyfriend' always makes me chuckle.

Running back to my room, I grab a can of pepper spray and one of my knives. After disabling the alarm and unlocking all the locks, I step outside to smoke. My thoughts go from his mesmerizing green eyes to something far less innocent. *Would he be like all of my book boyfriends? Treat me with care while we're out and about, but fuck me like a whore when it's just the two of us? Shivering at the thought, I think about the way he ran his fingers through his hair. I would love to be the one to run my fingers through it, or grip it tight while he's between my legs eating my pussy like a starved man. Whoa, where the fuck did that come from? Chill out Nova, fuck.* I'm completely startled when I hear the sound of footsteps on gravel. Seeing that it's my delivery driver, I stand up and put my cigarette out in the ashtray.

After paying for the pizza, I head inside and lock up. I open the pizza box, placing it on the table next to the *Cherry Coke. Yes. Extra, extra cheese.* I don't care what anyone says, sometimes it's nice to just have a regular ol' cheese pizza. Grabbing my remote, I turn my tv on and play my favorite movie, *'Love, Rosie'.* I'm in the middle of the movie when I hear my phone go off. Wiping away another fallen tear from this damn movie, I swipe my phone off of my coffee table. It's a message from Rhys and a huge smile appears on my face. No, I absolutely did not do a little happy dance. Deciding I want him to have his own notification sound, I change his to *Green Eyes* by *JOSEPH.*

GHOULIE: Hi little star *

ME: Hello to you too, Reese's Pieces. ha

GHOULIE: Ugh, I'm gonna kill Dori for saying that around you. I can't believe you remember that. Anyways, what are you up to tonight, beautiful?

ME: Haha, I'm so glad I heard it. I think I might make it your contact name actually :P

ME: I'm just watching a movie, what are you doing?

GHOULIE: Don't even think about making that my contact name, sweetheart.

GHOULIE: What movie are you watching?

ME: You know, telling me not to just makes me want to even more. Maybe I need to know your full name to see if I can pick the perfect contact name, hmm.

ME: Don't fucking laugh, I'll fight you. But I'm watching Love, Rosie... it's my favorite.

GHOULIE: You not wanting to listen makes me think you just want me to spank that ass til it's red and tattooed with my handprint.

GHOULIE: I don't even know what that movie is, but I wouldn't make fun of you for it, sweetheart. I'm guessing by your reaction that means it's a chick flick?

Holy fuck, did he just say he would spank me?! Way to make a girl start thinking of every way you'll dick her down.

ME: I don't know what you're talking about, Reese's Pieces. I would never provoke you to do such a thing.

ME: And yes, it is a chick flick. I watch all different types of movies, not just chick flicks.

GHOULIE: I know for a fact you've just earned yourself a red ass. Here, you asked for my full name to pick a better contact name. My name is all yours, little star ;)

GHOULIE: Rhys Alexander Slater.

GHOULIE: Any chance I get to know your full name now?

ME: Oh. I love your name. Hmm, nickname options from that. Let's see. I think your options will be Reese's Pieces or... Masturbator Slater hahaha.

ME: Nova Skye Hart.

GHOULIE: Oh yeah, you definitely want me to spank your ass. Also, you're a dirty girl. That nickname makes me think you're imagining me stroking my cock.

GHOULIE: Nova Skye Hart? What a perfect name for my little star.

ME: You have no proof that I'm thinking about you stroking your cock... well now I am. This is your doing!

GHOULIE: Ha! Now I know what you'll be dreaming about tonight. You need sleep, so I'm going to let you go. But, one last thing for you to think about. Dream about me worshiping your body, making you cum so hard you see galaxies behind your eyelids.

This man is going to be the death of me. I'm fucking speechless. Wiggling around, I can feel how wet I am from his words. *How does he have this effect on me already?*

GHOULIE: Did I lose ya, sweetheart?

GHOULIE: You're thinking about what I said, aren't you?

GHOULIE: Fuck, I'm so hard right now. Tell me to stop, little star. What are you doing to me?

88

ME: What if... What if I don't want you to stop, Rhys? I don't know what's happening, but I could ask you the same question. What the fuck are you doing to me?

GHOULIE: Let me call you, sweetheart. I wanna hear you call out my name, not just type it.

ME: Okay.

Green Eyes starts playing on my phone. I take in a shaky breath, *fuck, I can't believe I'm doing this.* "H-hello."

I can hear him breathing on the other end of the line. His voice is low and gravelly as he says "What are you doing, little star?"

"Just sitting here on my couch. What are you doing... Rhys?"

He groans, "Mmm, say it again, sweetheart. I knew it would sound so much sweeter coming from your lips."

My voice comes out breathy, "Rhys."

"That's a good girl. Why don't you go lay down in your bed for me."

On shaky legs I stand and head to my room. Slowly crawling in my bed, I lay back. "Okay, I'm in my bed now."

"Are you wet for me, sweetheart? Run your hand down your body and touch your pussy for me. Tell me how wet you are for me."

I whimper at his words, slowly running my hand down my body. Sliding my hand inside my panties, I run my fingers through my slit. I can feel that I'm already soaked. *God, imagine the damage this man could do being here with me.*

"I'm... I'm soaked, Rhys," I whisper.

Moving my wet fingers to my clit, I begin slowly circling it, and let out a low moan. I can hear Rhys' ragged breaths and knowing that he's touching himself too, I circle my clit faster.

Feeling bold, I ask him, "Rhys, are you hard for me?"

"Fuck yes, little star. I'm so fucking hard for you right now. I'm stroking my cock listening to you touch yourself. I wanna hear every sound from you. It's so fucking beautiful. Keep going. Put me on speaker so you can use both hands. I want you to put two fingers in your pussy while you rub your clit with your other hand."

Immediately doing as he tells me to, I place my phone on my chest and bring my hand down, placing two fingers in my pussy. I slowly pump my fingers in and out, scissoring them around. With my other hand I circle my clit again with even pressure and moan at the feeling.

"Mmm, fuck, sweetheart. I love hearing you. Fuck, Nova, keep going." I've never cum before, but I know I'm at that point where it's close. This is usually around the time when I almost reach the peak and crash back down without having an orgasm. I could fake it for him, but I feel like I can't lie to him about anything.

"Fuck. I... I really don't wanna ruin this moment we're having here Rhys, but I really need to tell you something. It's really embarrassing and is totally going to ruin this-"

"Hey, what's going on, little star? Talk to me. You can tell me anything. You're not ruining anything, and you have no reason to be embarrassed."

Taking a deep breath I speak as fast and incoherently as possible, "Ican'tcum."

"Slow down, little star. Nice and slow now, tell me."

Growling in frustration, I tell him, "I. Can't. Cum. And before you say anything, I don't just mean right now. I mean, never. I've never cum. I just can't, I don't know why. Fuck, this is embarrassing."

In a soft voice, Rhys responds to my embarrassing confession, "Nova. This isn't something to be embarrassed about. Thank you for telling me."

When I'm still silent, he continues, "Don't be embarrassed. It happens to lots of people. Let's see if we can work on that together, huh? You want me to make you cum on my cock?"

"Rhys, don't turn me on even more after I just told you I can't cum. Two can play that game, and I'll do the same and stop just before you bust a nut."

He chuckles at my statement, "Ouch! You wound me, sweetheart. Point taken. Let's make a plan and then bed for you. How does that sound?"

"I mean, I rarely sleep, but sure. What did you have in mind?"

"What do you think about me picking you up, and we go explore some of the trails around here?"

Of all moments my brain conjures a book moment being recreated. Can you say primal kink? Clearing my throat and pushing the thoughts back, "Yeah, that sounds great. Umm, just one thing. When you get here, can you please text me before you get to the door? So I'm not... surprised when you knock on the door."

"Yeah, of course. I can do that for you. I'll pick you up at noon and we'll go get some lunch and then head out to the trails. Sound good?"

"Yeah, that sounds great, Rhys."

"Alright, little star. Please try to get some sleep. I'll see you tomorrow. Goodnight, beautiful."

Smiling at his sweet words, I reply, "Goodnight, ghoul."

I end the call, roll over and squeal into my pillow. Getting out of bed, I open the wooden box on my dresser and pull out a joint, noting that I should head to the dispensary soon. While sitting on my bed smoking, my thoughts drift back to Rhys and those captivating green eyes. I can't believe I've spent so much time dreaming about these eyes only to discover they belong to a real person. Thinking of those eyes, I absentmindedly rub my right forearm. I freeze when I realize that shade of green is somewhere else... on my body. Looking down at my arm, I see the green stars splashed throughout the tattoo.

Holy. Fucking. Shit.

When I got the tattoo, I specifically chose the stars to be the color of the eyes in my dreams because it brought me peace.

Taking a long inhale of my joint, I stub it out in the ashtray and blow the smoke out. Bringing my forearm up to my chest, I hold it tightly against me. What does this mean? What the fuck is going on? I drift off still clutching my arm and I'm met with peace and calm seeing my green-eyed ghoul.

"Sometimes the most shocking surprises are also the most beautiful surprises." ~Lori Wilhite

CHAPTER 7
TWIN FLAME

Rhys

I'm already living for everything that involves my little star. It took everything out of me to end our conversation. Even more so to not go to her and make her cum. Groaning at the thought, I push my hand against my hard cock. I'm so fucking turned on that the touch of my hand makes it twitch. Right then and there, I decide I won't be cumming until my little star does and I quickly remove my hand. Sitting up against my headboard, I lean over and grab my smokes and lighter, lighting one up. Nova's blue eyes meet me as I tilt my head back and close my eyes. With the cigarette in my mouth, I bring my left hand down and rub my half-sleeve galaxy tattoo. I open my eyes to look down at it and note the blue stars throughout it. *Blue. Blue. Blue.* Looking closely at the stars, the feeling hits me like a *Mack* truck. The stars in my tattoo match Nova's eyes perfectly. After stubbing my cigarette out in the ashtray, I jump out of bed and pace, running my fingers through my hair. I've never told anyone that the reason I chose this exact shade of blue for the stars was because they belonged to the eyes in my every dream. How is it possible that ocean eyes and Nova are one and the same?

. . .

There's a knock at my bedroom door, and I open it to find Dorian standing there. Hand up in the air, mid-knock and a look of concern etched across his face. Giving him an up-nod, I ask, "What's up, Dorian?"

"I just came to ask you the same thing, man. What's wrong? And before you open your mouth to lie, just don't. I know something's going on, I can feel it, Rhys."

Taking a deep breath, I try to think of the best way to explain to him.

"Rhys, stop overthinking whatever it is and just spill."

Putting my hands up, "Okay, okay. I just... I can barely wrap my head around it, so I just don't know how you're going to wrap your head around it, too. I just got off the phone with Nova, and I was sitting here and started thinking about her and her eyes and it just snowballed from there. I thought of her eyes, looked down at my galaxy tat, and realized the stars are the same shade as her eyes. Same. Exact. Fucking. Shade. Dorian! How the fuck is that possible?"

Dorian furrows his brows, "Well, it's not entirely impossible. I mean, you love the color blue, picked a color and it just happens to be the same as her eyes. Coincidences happen every day, Rhys. This doesn't seem disconcerting at all."

Shaking my head vehemently at him, "No, you don't understand, Dor. There's a reason blue is my favorite color, and why I chose to use that for the stars. I... I have been dreaming of those eyes, *her* fucking eyes, for as long as I can remember. Long before we met, and before things got so shitty with my parents. Every dream I've ever had was of those eyes, and it brought me so much comfort. Especially on the really bad nights. *That* is why blue is my favorite color, *that* is why I chose the color for the stars on my tattoo. So I would always have a piece of comfort with me. Now, I find out that they weren't just something I made up in my head, but they belong to this amazing fucking girl I just met. A girl I've known for what, just

94

over a week? Maybe two? Yet I feel like she's been a part of me all along. That's fucking crazy, Dorian. It's not fucking possible!"

I'm still pacing back and forth, gripping the roots of my hair in frustration. I feel Dorian pulling my hands down. "Hey. Let go, man. You have every right to be a little freaked about this, but it's really not crazy. Have you ever stopped to think that maybe Nova is your soulmate? I know you don't have the spiritual beliefs that I do, Rhys, but you do believe in soulmates, don't you? Maybe they weren't dreams at all, perhaps they were memories from a previous life. Don't spiral over this. I promise you, I don't think this is a bad or freaky thing that's happening." Grabbing the *Swisher Sweet* tucked behind his ear, he holds it up in cheers. "Now, let's go roll one up and relax. Maybe put things in a better perspective."

Nodding my head in agreement, "Alright, just one blunt though. You have work in the morning and I'm meeting up with Nova for lunch and then we're gonna walk the trails."

Dorian spins around quickly and I have to step back to avoid us crashing into one another. "You're going to see Nova tomorrow? I know you want to spend time with her alone, but do you think you could both come have lunch with me? You usually do anyway, but this way I can hang out with her, too. Then you guys can go to the trails afterward."

Looking at him, he's giving me the puppy eyes that he knows works for everyone. "Listen, Fido, the puppy eyes aren't necessary. I already planned on doing that, dude. Just because I feel this connection to her, doesn't mean I'm going to kick you to the curb. I want you two close as well. Not too close though, or I'll have to beat your ass."

Dorian chuckles at my statement, "You forget you're the one that taught me how to defend myself. I know all of your moves. Anyway, Nova is a beautiful girl, but I immediately felt like a big brother wanting to protect her, so we're in the clear there." Clapping me on the shoulder, he tilts his head towards the living room. Following him to the living room, we plop down on the couch and smoke the blunt he rolls with his strawberry *Swisher Sweet.*

Sinking further into the couch, I feel Dorian poking my shoulder. When I roll my head to the side, I notice the concerned look on his face. "She seems really important to you already, Rhys. Do you think…"

"What? Do I think what, Dor?"

Taking a deep breath, he asks the question I should have known was coming. "Do you think you should tell her what we do? I'm sure you're probably concerned about what her reaction would be. But, she's your soulmate," holding his hand up to stop my next sentence, "you say maybe, I know she is. If she's your soulmate, then I don't think what we really do for a living will bother her. Surprise her, yes. But, I feel like she's maybe had a difficult life, and knowing what we do is for good, not evil… I think she would be okay with it."

Leaning forward, I put my head in my hands. "I know I should tell her man. I just don't want it to backfire. What if it scares her? What if she completely freaks and goes to the cops or something? Then what?"

I look up at him when he gets up from the couch. Looking down at me, he gives me a half smile. "I think everything will be just fine. It's better if you tell her sooner rather than later. Waiting to tell her might upset her more than just letting her know. Think on it. I'm off to bed."

I head to my room and throw myself down on my bed and pass out with a smile on my face, and visions of my little star.

The following morning I wake up to the sounds of Dorian getting ready for work. My first thought is Nova, so I grab my phone to text her.

ME: Good morning, beautiful star.

I can smell coffee already brewing as I pad out to the kitchen. Pulling my favorite black and blue splattered mug from the cupboard, I pour myself an almost overflowing amount of coffee. I lean against the counter as I take a big gulp of it, ignoring the burning sensation on my tongue and throat. Dorian looks over as he grabs his keys and gives me a salute to which I grunt in response and he heads out the door. It's a good thing he has such a wild style, or dressing up in his janitor jumpsuit would probably drive him crazy. Finishing my coffee, I drop my mug in the sink and head back to my room.

My closet is wide open as I rifle through my clothes trying to decide what to wear. *Jesus, I'm acting like a fucking chick right now. Just pick a fucking outfit, Rhys, it's not that hard.* Deciding on a black tee, blue jeans and my leather jacket, I toss it all on my bed and head to the bathroom for a shower. Thoughts of Nova have my cock rock hard. Growling in frustration, I grip the base of my cock trying to tame the fucker. I rush through my shower and when I'm done, I jump out, grab my hair pomade and quickly swipe my fingers through my hair. I head to my room and throw my clothes on. I want to smell good for her so I choose my *A*Men* cologne, which not so ironically has a star on it and I spray my neck, chest and wrists.

When I check my phone I see Nova has responded.

MY LITTLE STAR: Good morning, Reese's
Pieces :)

ME: Wow, first thing in the morning and you're
already asking for trouble. Keep that up after I
pick you up and see where that gets you ;) I
hope you slept well. I know I'm not supposed
to pick you up until noon, but I'm ready to see
you now. Is that ok? Can I come pick you up?

After pocketing my phone, I grab my keys and head out to my Chevy K5. As soon as I hop in, I start blasting *I Wanna Be Yours* by *Arctic Monkeys*. I pull out of the parking lot and head toward *Enchanted Blossoms* to pick up flowers for Nova. Luckily, being in a small town means it doesn't take long to get there.

The bells jingle above, announcing my arrival and I hear an older woman shout, "Welcome! I'll be right out in a moment!"

While waiting for her, I walk around the store checking out the various arrangements. *Pleasure* by *WARPs UP* starts playing in my pocket. Smiling at the song from her favorite show, *Fruits Basket*, I know it's my little star so I pull out my phone to check the text.

MY LITTLE STAR: I really wish you could pick
me up now, but I'm getting my work done now
so I have the rest of the day with you :(I'm
sorry.

ME: Damn. Ok. You finish up your work and I'll
be there by noon. And yes, I promise to text
that I'm there before knocking on your door.

MY LITTLE STAR: Thank you :) I'll see you at
noon.

Right as I put my phone away, I turn and see the older woman that helped me all week standing behind the counter with a smile on her face. "Hello dear, I take it by the smile on your face you're here to buy more of those flowers for your special girl?"

Walking up to the counter, I nod my head, "Yes. She loved the flowers and the vase a lot. I'm hoping you get those flowers often, cuz I plan on getting them for her for-" I pause, realizing what I was going to say, but, I nod my head loving the sound of that, "Forever."

Nova

Wrapping up my work for the day, I put my laptop away and grab a *Monster* from the fridge. Cracking it open, I take a long pull from it and set it on the counter. I check my phone and see that Rhys should be here in about a half an hour. Running to my room to get ready, I open my drawers and grab matching panties and bra, white and black striped tube socks, a *Metallica* shirt and black jean shorts. I toss them on the bed and head to my closet to grab my all black Converse and leather jacket with the built-in gray hood. Throwing those on the bed with everything else, I run and jump in the shower.

Rushing through my shower, I hop out and ruffle dry my hair with my towel. I throw my outfit on and spray myself with my *Vera Wang Princess* perfume. I chuckle at the bottle, I usually wouldn't be caught dead with something as girly as this. Running my fingers through my hair, I scrunch it up a little. I throw everything I need inside my backpack and put it by the front door. Just as I'm about to sit on my couch and wait, Rhys' ringtone starts playing. I definitely did not squeal and do a happy dance hearing it. Unlocking my phone, I see a text from him.

GHOULIE: Hi, beautiful star. I just parked. Is it okay for me to come knock on your door?

ME: Hey you. Yes, I'm ready.

I smile at the nickname and the fact that he listened to me as I approach my front door, slinging my backpack over my shoulder after making sure I put my cigarettes and lighter in my backpack's front pocket while I "patiently" wait for his arrival. Even though I'm expecting him, I still jump at the sound of his knocking. Checking the peephole just to be sure, I see him standing there. Fuck, he's hot. He looks a little nervous, rocking on his feet and running his fingers through his hair. I feel like I'm in a trance while I watch him and when he bites his lip. I wish I could be the one to do it. Deciding to put him out of his misery, I unlock the door and turn my alarm to chime. He looks up at the sound of the door and gives me a heart-stopping smile as he looks me up and down. "Wow. You look amazing, little star. Great shirt, by the way. Love *Metallica*."

Smiling at him, I wave my hand up and down towards his body. "You don't look so bad yourself, ghoulie." It's then I notice he has his hand behind his back, so I tilt my head towards his hidden hand. "Uh, what you got there, Rhys?"

He follows my line of sight and looks back at me with wide eyes. "Oh, umm, I got you something." Pulling his hand from behind his back, I see a bouquet of the same flowers he brought me throughout the week. Gasping, I smile up at him, "Oh my God, ghoulie! You didn't have to buy me more! You're the first person to give me flowers without a cost."

Handing the flowers over to me he gives me a sad smile, "You're welcome, beautiful."

"I'm going to go put them in that pretty vase real quick. Do you want to come in?"

Nodding, Rhys follows behind me. I step aside to let him through, placing the flowers on the end table and then turn and lock up the door. When I turn around, he's right there watching. Nodding towards the door he asks, "I asked Jade this question, and she said it wasn't her story to tell. So, I'll ask you. Extra cautious, or is there a reason you need all those and the alarm?"

Rocking on my feet and fiddling with my sleeves, I look down in embarrassment. Rhys places his finger under my chin and gently lifts my head. Keeping a hold of my chin, he searches my eyes. "Does it have something to do with the things you told me about your ex?"

Biting my lip, I nod, "The part I didn't tell you, is I have nightmares every single night of him finding me. So, I lock everything up, carry pepper spray and knives and I have a bat under my bed. Every time I wake from a nightmare I have to search all over and make sure he's not here. And... and... Jeezus fuck, this is not first date conversation. Well, second date I guess, since yesterday was technically our first date. Right? Or? Please fucking stop me. I can't stop rambling. You have to stop me-"

His lips cut me off mid sentence and time stops. The moment our lips touch a sense of complete calm and peace washes over me. Images start flashing in my mind. Green eyes, us holding hands, running through the woods, swimming and laughing. We both pull back from the kiss and gasp, touching our fingers to

101

our lips., "D-did you see it too? Did you feel it? What was that?" I whispered.

At every question, Rhys nods his head in agreement while searching my eyes. "I'm really starting to think that what Dorian said is true. Part of me believed him, but part of me just wasn't sure it was even possible."

Knitting my brows, I look at him trying to figure out what he's talking about. " What did Dorian say?" He looks as if he's completely lost in thought and my question didn't register. Placing my palm against his cheek, he immediately looks at me. "Rhys? Did you hear me? What did Dorian say?"

Gently holding my wrist as if to keep me holding on to him, he answers. "Last night, I discovered something that completely threw me for a loop and I talked to him about it. He said that he could feel the connection between us and that what I discovered meant we're soulmates. But is that possible? Is that even real?"

"I don't know. I mean, I would really like to believe that it's something that exists. But, what was it that you discovered?"

Taking a deep breath, he brings his forehead down on mine. "I didn't have the easiest life with my parents like I told you last night, and I needed to find some sense of comfort in my life. An escape. As far back as I can remember I would dream of the most beautiful blue eyes. Every time I saw them, I felt safe, like everything would be okay. That's the reason blue is my favorite color." Running his thumb underneath my left eye, he whispers, "These eyes. It was these eyes I saw."

Releasing his hold on me, he steps back and starts pulling his jacket off. As it slowly slides down his arms, he says, "I have this tattoo, and I made sure all the stars were that exact shade of blue, so I could always have that comfort with me wherever I go."

I gasp at the words he says, looking down at my arm. He pulls his jacket the rest of the way off and points to his right arm. Shocked, I throw my hand over my mouth and take a step back shaking my head.

"Whoa. Whoa. What's wrong, little star?"

I point to his arm. "This can't be possible. What the fuck is going on? I... you... what the fuck?!"

Stepping towards me, Rhys reaches his hand out. I retreat until my back hits the door. He holds one hand up as if to placate me and slowly approaches. "I won't hurt you like he did, Nova. I just want to get closer to you and talk about this."

He stops and waits for my approval. I nod to him and he closes the gap, pushing my hair away from my face. "Now, what's not possible, sweetheart?"

Inhaling a shaky breath and slowly letting it out, I tell him, "You know how you said you dreamt of my eyes and adding that color for the stars on your tattoo? Well, I've always dreamt of your eyes too. They were the only calm I could find in my life. I held on tight to that, to get me through everything. Especially everything with my ex. I... I'll just show you." Slowly pulling my jacket off, I hold my right arm up between us. "I wanted to carry those eyes with me everywhere too."

Gently grabbing my arm, he inspects my tattoo, a half-sleeve galaxy tattoo that matches his perfectly. The only difference is the color of our stars reflecting each other's eyes.

"No fucking way! You know what this means, right?" He voiced with a rough laugh. Caressing my arm, he looks up at me and then back down to my arm.

"That maybe... maybe, Dorian was right with what he told you last night?"

Looking up at me he smiles, placing his palms on either side of my face he says, "That. But it also means that you're mine, Nova Skye Hart. You've always been mine. Pieces are starting to come together, and I see it now. I always wondered why I spent my whole life searching the stars. I finally figured it out...I was looking for you, little star. We've been here before, sweetheart. You and I will always find our way to each other, in this life and the next."

When I look into his eyes, I can see that he means it. I can feel it, too and I know it to be true, as crazy as it seems. He leans forward, crashing his lips to mine. I grip his wrists, trying to pull him closer to me. He licks my bottom lip and gently prods at my mouth. My mouth opens slightly and he pushes his tongue forward and licks inside. I moan at the feeling of our tongues tangling, I don't want this moment to end. I can feel him everywhere and yet it's not enough as he grips my face and licks every inch of my mouth, fighting for dominance with our tongues. The kiss ends all too soon and I whine at the loss of him. He chuckles at the noise and begins kissing along my jawline and down the side of my neck, licking, sucking, nibbling on his way down. He caresses his hands down my shoulders, arms and sides. Finding my hips, he gives them a squeeze and pulls me closer to him. I can feel how hard his cock is. Something snaps in me and I no longer hold back. Grinding my pussy against his cock, he grunts at the sensation.

I feel him pause and he looks up at me. "I'm not a good man, Nova. I'm barely hanging on to my control here, and if you grind that hot little pussy of yours against me one more time, I will lose the last bit of control I'm holding on to. Do you understand me, little star?"

I bite my lip, looking at him and I can see it in his eyes the moment he realizes I'm going to push him over the edge. Placing my arms around his neck, I pull him towards me for another kiss and slowly grind my pussy against his cock. In an instant, his hands are gripping the back of my thighs and I'm lifted and wrapped around his body. I squeal from the momentum of it. Rhys chuckles, and bites my collarbone. Carrying me down the hall to the bedroom, he tosses me on the bed. I laugh at the feeling and look up at him. He's standing at the end of the bed looking down at me with a matching smile. Feeling nervous under his watchful eye, I squirm around a bit and look away.

His deep voice startles me when he commands, "Look at me, Nova. I want your eyes with me at all times. Do you understand me?"

Immediately looking at him, I bite my lip and nod.

"Words, Nova, give me your words."

A thrill runs through me and I respond, "Yes, Rhys, I understand. Eyes on you at all times."

"Good girl."

Holy fuck, did he just say that? This man could ask me to do anything and I would fucking do it just to hear him call me a good girl again.

He reaches his arm over his head and lifts his shirt completely off his body in one swift motion, tossing it to the floor. This man is a fucking work of art. The mystery of the tattoo creeping up his neck is before me. The whole thing is covering his ribs and chest, filled with multiple constellations in watercolors. He's muscular, but they don't seem to be gym muscles, more like muscles from hard labor. I want to lick every last inch of him.

Kicking his boots off, he unbuttons his jeans and I bite my lip in anticipation. He catches me looking and smirks. His jeans are slowly unzipped and he pulls them down along with his underwear. He tosses them on the floor as well and stands to his full height. My eyes go wide as I zero in on his hard cock bobbing in the air. Long, thick and uncut, I'm pretty sure it's at least ten inches and I can see veins protruding. Holy fuck, this man is going to tear me apart. He leans down, to untie my shoes and pulls them off. Each sock is slowly pulled off, tossing them to the floor. When he crawls on the bed he straddles my hips, places his fingers on the button of my shorts and looks up at me, as if to ask for permission. I nod my head at him to continue. Apparently my excitement shows because he chuckles and grabs a hold of the top of my shorts and panties and pulls them slowly down my legs. He grips my ankles and rubs soothing circles against the bone. Each ankle is kissed and then his hands are sliding up my legs, leaving a trail of kisses along the way. Gripping my thighs, he pushes against them in silent command. He pulls my thighs tightly against his hips and caresses the insides of my thighs. When he looks down at me, his eyes are shining and a puff of air escapes him. "Fuck, just look at you, little star. You're so fucking perfect. All fucking wet. Is this for me, sweetheart?"

He looks up at me expectantly and I nod, whispering, "Yes. It's all for you, Rhys."

He lets out a growl, "Fuck, I love hearing my name on your lips."

Sliding his hands up from my thighs, he reaches under the hem of my shirt and caresses my hips. My breath becomes ragged, the sensations from his touch lighting me up, sending tingles across my skin. Dragging the shirt up my stomach and past my breasts, he leans down and gently bites my right nipple through my bra. I gasp at the scrape of his teeth against my nipple, feeling the suction as he makes my nipple a hard peak. After releasing my nipple, he licks across my cleavage, leaving goosebumps across my chest and clenches his teeth around my left nipple. Unable to lay still, I tangle my fingers in his hair and grip tightly. I can't tell if I'm pushing him closer or pulling him away.

I'm losing focus, the sensations overwhelming me. I've never felt like this before, it's as if I'm having sensory overload and we've only just started. He releases my nipple and pulls my shirt up further, I slightly lift so he can pull it all the way off. After he's unclasped my bra, he slowly caresses his fingertips over my shoulders, brushing them over my collarbones. My body shivers at the contact and when he notices, he leans down and gives me a quick kiss. He slides my bra straps down, as soon as my breasts fall out of the cups he sucks in a breath and stops pulling the bra down. Groaning, he cups my breasts and buries his face between them. After kissing each one he looks up, "You're going to be the death of me, little star, and what a way to go."

Tearing the bra from me, he throws it across the room. He slides down my body until his broad shoulders are between my legs. Gripping my thighs, he leans down and swipes his tongue up my soaked slit. I jump from the sensation and push my hands against his shoulders.

He looks up at me in confusion, "What's wrong?"

Fuck, this is embarrassing. "I... nobody's ever done this before."

Looking away in embarrassment, I feel a bite on my inner thigh. Gasping at the sting, I glance at him, "What the fuck was that for?"

"What did I tell you about those eyes, Nova? Don't look away, and don't be embarrassed."

Releasing his shoulders I nod and lay back down. He settles back between my thighs, brings his lips around my clits and sucks it into his mouth. Moaning and jolting at the sensation, I can feel his shoulders shaking from laughter. Swatting at his head in annoyance, "Don't laugh at me, Rhys!"

His fingers slide up and down my slit, pausing to slowly circle my entrance with two fingers. My breath hitches when I feel him push in. Pumping his fingers in and out while sucking on my clit, I can feel myself getting more and more wet. He starts pumping faster and sucking harder, "Oh fuck, fuck, fuck. Oh, god."

My whole body is on fire and I can feel this tingling sensation working its way up my body from my toes. I feel an ache in my lower body. *Is this what it feels like to be worshiped?*

"Rhys?"

He continues without responding to me so I grip the ends of his hair and pull. "Rhys?!"

With a pop, he releases my clit, "It's okay, sweetheart, just let it happen."

"How did you know I was going to ask about that?"

"Because I can feel it, little star. I know you're close, and I know it's a first for you, so it's going to be overwhelming. Just let go, don't think about it, just let it happen."

I lay down just as he wraps his lips around my clit again. He doesn't take it slow and easy this time, immediately sucking hard on my clit and curling his fingers just right. He hits what I can only imagine is my g-spot and hits it over and over. "Oh fuck, yes. Oh, oh, Rhys. Fuck."

Squeezing my thighs tightly against his shoulders, it's as if a rubber band snaps and I let out a long moan as I feel a gush of wetness from my pussy. "Fuuuuuuuck. Rhys."

107

I melt further into the bed, a feeling of pure euphoria washing over me. I feel his lips against mine and I can taste myself on his lips, a slightly sweet and salty mix. Refocusing my eyes I can see him clearly, smiling down on me.

"You're breathtaking when you cum, sweetheart. I'll keep that image with me forever."

He grips his cock with his right hand and rubs it up and down my slit. A sigh escapes me as he circles my clit with the head of his throbbing cock. Bringing his cock down to my entrance, a slight pressure builds. He pauses with just the head inside, he releases his cock and tightly grips my hips. With an achingly slow motion, he thrusts the rest of the way in, both of us moaning at the feeling.

"Oh fuck. You're so tight, sweetheart. I don't think I'm going to last long. This is perfection. You- you are perfection."

Removing his hold on my hips, he places his hands on either side of my head. I wrap my arms around his sweat-slicked shoulders, pulling him closer. Leaning down he takes my lips in a bruising kiss and pumps in and out of me. Meeting him thrust for thrust, it goes from slow and sensual to fast and hard quickly. I bite his lip and lick across it begging for entrance. He opens his mouth and our tongues entangle, the taste of him exploding on my tongue. I can already feel the signs of my orgasm and I grip him tighter, moaning.

Pulling back from the kiss, I whisper, "I'm close, ghoulie."

After a short kiss he tells me, "Me too, sweetheart. So fucking close."

He reaches down and lightly clasps the front of my throat with his right hand. His eyes search mine for a reaction. I grip his wrist and pull, letting him know it's okay. The grip on my throat gets tighter, then his hand caresses down the side of my body until he reaches my clit. The slight pressure he uses to circle my clit makes me moan out loud. Pulling his cock almost all the way out, he pinches my clit hard while thrusting all the way in. The sensations set my orgasm off, wave after wave of pleasure making me arch my back from the intensity, "Yes, yes, yes."

He continues pumping his cock in me and just as I feel jets of his cum inside me, he pushes his cock in and holds it in place. Slowly pulling his cock out, he rolls over and lays on his back next to me. Placing his left arm under my head, he grips my shoulder with his right and pulls me towards him so I'm cradled in his arms. I roll over, laying half on top of him and he places a kiss on my head.

Teenage Dirtbag by *Wheatus* starts playing and Rhys kisses my head again, "I have to get that, it's Dorian."

Rolling off of him, I pull the sheet up and over me. Unable to look away, I stare at his ass as he goes. *Jesus, even that's magnificent. Every fucking inch of this man is perfect.* He grabs his jeans from the floor, reaching into a pocket to get his phone out. Groaning in what seems to be frustration, he tosses his phone down on his clothes and crawls in the bed, hovering over me.

Pressing his forehead against mine, he takes a deep breath, "I have bad news, little star. Worst fucking timing ever. I swear to you this isn't a brush off, but something has come up with work and I have to go. I swear I'll make it up to you, but I have no choice here, I really have to go."

My hand goes to his face and I stroke his cheek with my thumb, "Hey, it's okay. I'm not upset, I promise. I understand that things come up. I trust you," I hesitate a moment before taking a deep breath at the words I just spoke, "which is surprising for me. I don't trust easily, if at all because of what happened with my ex. But I feel like I can trust you."

Shaking my arm he whispers, "Soulmates, remember?"

A smile forms at my words and he gives me three quick kisses. Groaning, he sits back and looks down at me. He pulls down the sheet to look at me, "Just one more peek for the road."

Dropping the sheet, he winks at me and jumps off the bed to get dressed. After he's finished dressing, he looks at me and sighs, "I really hate to bring you out of this beautiful, blissful state you're in. But I know you'll be in a panic if you don't do it now. You're gonna have to get up, sweetheart, so you can lock up after I leave."

"Fuck, I can't believe I spaced. Thank you so much for telling me." Running to my closet, I pull out one of my oversized hoodies and throw it on. I turn around to see Rhys looking at me up and down. Feeling self-conscious, I cross my legs and pull down the hem of the hoodie, "Is something wrong?"

Shaking his head at me, "No, little star. I just didn't think you could find more ways to take my breath away. Even in just a hoodie you look gorgeous." Holding his hand out for me, I step forward and take it. At the door, he releases my hand and turns towards me brushing my hair back, "I'm sorry, sweetheart. I'll text you in a little bit, okay?"

Nodding my head, I lift up on my toes and give him a kiss. After he walks out I lock up and set the alarm again. Running back to my room, I jump in the bed and hug the pillow he was laying on. Best. Day. Ever.

"I feel this gravitational pull towards you, like the universe and all the galaxies had a talk and said, "yeah, it's time." ~Unknown

CHAPTER 8
LIVIN' ON BORROWED TIME

RHYS

Hopping in my *K5*, I head towards the warehouse. Leaving Nova feels like the hardest thing I've ever had to do. If it had been anything else, and I would've said fuck it and just stayed with her. But the moment I saw Dorian's text '*911 at V.A.E.*' I knew I needed to get moving. As soon as I arrive, I throw the truck in park and head inside to look for Dorian. I find him in the conference room, where I see him looking at the screens.

"What's the emergency, Dorian? Seriously, it better be good, you made me leave my girl at the worst possible time."

Turning towards me, his eyes light up and he grins, "Ohhh. I see you had a little," he begins thrusting his hips, "one on one time, ayy."

Scrunching up his face and shaking his head, he throws his hands up. "Sorry, sorry. That was not okay. I just gave myself the heebie-jeebies doing that now that I see her as a sister" I sigh as I watch Dorian dramatically shake his body in a shiver. I can't help but laugh and smack him on the side of the head.

He flinches at the motion and whines, "Owww. Deserved, but oww."

"You're right, not cool, Dor. Don't talk about Nova like that. Anyways, what's going on man? Seriously, you said 911 and to meet you here at Vega Altair, so what's up?"

Scraping his fingers through his hair and taking a deep breath, he looks all around the room and then back to me. He runs his hand in a circle over the Baphomet tattoo on his chest. Fuck, that's his tell. Whatever he has to say, it isn't good.

"So, I have a couple things to tell you. I can't tell you everything just yet, but what I can tell you... I'm really going to need you to sit down for this conversation, Rhys."

Raising a brow at him, "Are you asking me to sit so you have time to get away if I decide to punch you?"

Twisting his lips to the side and squinting his eyes he says, "Mmmm, mayyyybeee. Hopefully not, but definitely a possibility. Please, man, just take a seat. This is really important."

I shake my head and groan before walking to the head of the table and sitting down. Giving myself room, I prop my boots on the table and cross them at the ankle. "Alright, let's hear it, Dorian."

I clasp my hands against my stomach, preparing to hear the news. Dorian grabs the remote that controls the screens and looking up at me, he says, "Some information has come to light that's important for the mission, but it also concerns your personal life. In a way it always has, but even more so now."

Turning back to the screens, he lifts the remote and pushes a button. The screens fill with various surveillance photos and documents on one of my targets, Frankie Wendall. Gritting my teeth at the screens, I'm already annoyed. He's the first target in a long time I lost track of and it still pisses me off. I'll never forget my trip to Washington and discovering he had disappeared without a trace. All previous hang outs came up empty, nothing on any of his aliases and all of his usual junkie buyers had fuck all for information. There was only one connection left for him, and it was here in La Grande. *Amissa Stella*, the so-called "asylum" here in town where Dorian works part-time as a janitor. Joke's on those fuckers, he's just there to gather as much intel as possible. The place is overrun by a "corporation" that manufactures and distributes various drugs. It only makes sense that Frankie would be connected to them, being a drug addict and dealer.

"It's come to my attention that Frankie is here in town. I know you're still pissed about him getting the slip on you-"

"He didn't get the fucking slip on me, man!"

Raising his hands to placate me, Dorian says, "Listen, he got away. I know that's something you're not used to, but it happens. Now let me finish." Waving my hands to him to let him continue, he does. "Okay, so he's in town, and I know you'll want to finish the job. I think what I'm about to show you will probably be the best motivation for you to complete the job."

Clicking another button on the remote, the screens fill with surveillance photos of Nova and Frankie. *What the fuck? Almost every picture shows her with a black eye or cuts and bruises along her arms.* Throwing my legs down, I grip the edge of the table. *This is the motherfucker that hurt her.* Clicking another button, the screen fills with various hospital records. All of them "mysterious" injuries Nova suffered from. There's documentation of head trauma from blunt force object, broken arm and broken clavicle. Fuck, I think I'm going to be sick. My vision blurs and the room spins, I feel like I can't fucking breathe.

Faintly I hear something, but it sounds like a voice shouting underwater. I'm broken from the moment when ice cold water hits my face. Gasping for air, I look around. As I wipe the water from my face and blink rapidly to clear my eyes, I see Dorian in front of me.

"What the fuck did you do that for, Dorian?!"

"I'm sorry, I'm sorry. You just, you were really freaking out man, I didn't know what else to do. I was yelling your name and nothing registered for you. Are you okay?"

Gritting my teeth, "Am I okay? AM I OKAY?! No, Dorian I'm so fucking far from okay. This piece of shit was hurting Nova. This is the same piece of shit that still haunts her every fucking day and night. That's why she has those fucking locks and alarms all over her fucking apartment, so she's ready for him! Did you know that she carries protection with her at all times? That she wakes up in a panic and has to search the whole place just to make sure he didn't fucking find her? This ends now! Give me all the intel you have, I'm fucking ending him."

I get up and pace, I have to tell her what I know, what I do. Fuck, what if I lose her? Gripping the ends of my hair in frustration, I stop pacing and take a deep breath, "I have to tell her, Dor. I think... I think I need to tell her and offer the choice to be a part of it. So she knows the demon that haunts her is gone for good."

At Dorian's silence, I look in his direction to find him smiling, "What the shit are you smiling for, this whole thing fucking sucks."

"I'm smiling because I agree. I think it's the right thing to do. To tell her and offer her some peace."

The smile dropping from his face, he rubs a circle over his Baphomet tattoo again. I head back to my chair and plop down. I rest my elbows on my knees and I motion for him to continue, "Okay, what's the other thing you need to tell me. Make it snappy, I wanna start huntin' this son of a bitch."

Nodding once, he begins, "Okay, so everything we do here at *Vega Altair* just isn't possible all on my own. I needed people we could trust to help us out with everything. Intel mostly, but also people that could be there for us when we take down *Amissa Stella*. Don't get me wrong, you're strong and capable, Rhys, but there's no way you can take all of them on by yourself. As far as for me, there's only so much I can do to back you up. The group is here now and I want to introduce you, just please don't freak out when you meet them. Seeing them is going to connect some dots for you, and for Nova as well when we have to tell her."

Narrowing my eyes at him, I look from him to the door and back again. He grabs his phone out of his pocket, dials a number and places the phone to his ear, "Yeah, ready." Keeping his hand in his pocket after hanging up, he starts rocking on his heels.

Hearing voices from outside the room I stand, bracing myself for whoever it is.

Looking between The Horde and Dorian a thought occurs, "Wait a damn minute. Who did you know first, Dorian or Nova?"

Dorian looks over to me, "They knew me first, and I already know what you're thinking. Let me explain. Yes, they were planted at the bookstore to meet Nova. They were there so they could protect her, and to be a support system of sorts for her. She came here all alone and she needed people. It sounds fucked up, but they really are her friends, she's not just a job to them. Right, guys?"

Dorian looks over to them with pleading eyes while they all stay quiet. Stomping his foot in frustration, "You guys, this isn't funny, tell him the truth."

All at once they roar in laughter and Viking, a tall guy with a viking braid and long beard steps forward with his hand stretched towards me. Shaking his tight grip, he releases my hand, "I know we've already met a few times while you were hanging out with Nova, but I figure proper introductions should be made. I'm Viking-"

Cutting him off and waving my hand up towards his head, "Fitting name by the way."

Laughing at my observation, he continues, "We may have been put in place so we can protect her, but I can promise you, Nova is family to us. With that said, even though we're all on the same team here, you hurt her, I'll fucking kill you."

Nodding at him, "Good. Don't plan on it. I'm glad she has people in her corner."

Walking back to the group he puts his arm around a woman with medium length brown hair, glasses and rocking a Beatles shirt. "This is my wife, her call name is Mrs. Valour."

Waving at me she says, "Hi."

I point at her shirt, "Hey, nice shirt by the way. *Hey Jude* is my favorite."

Wrapping up my greetings, I soak up the information;

Viking, Mrs. Valour, Fish, Rader, Muggz, Mrs. Muggz, Sable, Lady Sable, Jade AKA Harp and Vanessa AKA Swan. Knowing now that they all have call names, I definitely need to know what Dorian's is.

"Hey, Dorian. There's already a fish in the group, so I take it Dori isn't your call name?" What starts off as a little chuckle morphs into a full blown belly laugh at the look on his face.

"No, asshole, it isn't Dori, but if you keep it up yours will be, Reese's Pieces. My call name is Eagle."

Taking a deep breath, I pull myself together and point at him, "I'm telling you right now, *Eagle*, the moment you fucking call me Reese's Pieces on a mission, you'll forever be Dori. And I'll kick your ass."

Fish steps in laughing, "Wow, you guys sound just like Nova and I."

His words stop me and I swivel towards him, "Excuse me? What do you mean that's how you and Nova talk?"

Dorian pats his hand on my chest, "Rhys, relax. He just means they bicker like siblings, just like we do. He's not being disrespectful to her."

Rader steps in front of Fish and puts her hand on his face pushing him back. Rolling her eyes, she looks at me and says, "No, really, the two of them are seriously like bickering siblings. They both turn into children when they sling their bullshit at each other."

Dorian nods with a smile and claps his hands together to get everyone's attention. "Alright, Rhys has to do something tough, so whoever is joining us for a chill session to calm him down, come and take a seat. Whoever wants to opt out, we'll give you a call when it's time to talk to Nova."

Rhys clears his throat, "Uh, just a sec, guys. Just know the questions aren't done. Some things aren't adding up here, but I refuse to get the answers without Nova here."

They all look at each other and back at me, some nodding and other's looking down in shame.

Sitting at the far end of the table, Dorian pulls out a peach *Swisher Sweet* and his tin of weed. He pulls a razor blade from the tin to open the swisher. Half of The Horde sits around the table while the others head out.

"Hey, Rhys." I look over and see that it's Vanessa getting my attention.

"Yeah?"

With a sad smile on her face, she looks at me and says, "I really need you to know that what Viking said is true. We really do care about Nova a lot. I just... I have a feeling this news could really upset her, and you're the only other person that is just finding this out. So if she won't hear us out, please let her know that we never wanted any of this to hurt her. Please?"

I nod at her words and then shrug, "I'll let her know what you guys told me, but whatever she feels about it is her choice. This is probably the first time in her life she can just be her own person and feel what she wants, so I'm not going to ask her to change the way she feels or act differently. Her feelings and reactions are hers and hers alone. We have to respect what comes from the news."

Looking down at the table while absentmindedly scratching the tabletop, she nods and sits back in her chair. The smell of weed gets my attention and I look over to Dorian lighting up the blunt. He picks up the remote, clicking a button and *Good Old-Fashioned Lover Boy* by *Queen* blares through the surround sound system. Passing the blunt around, I take just a few hits to take the edge off, but not enough to inhibit my driving. I have to go pick my girl up and I'm not doing that while fucked up. Pulling my phone out of my pocket, I open it to her contact name and smile.

ME: Hey, sweetheart. Are you busy right now?

MY LITTLE STAR: No, I was thinking about stopping by Swan & Scribe, but I can do that later. What's up?

ME: I was hoping I could come pick you up and bring you to my job. If you still feel up to it, I can take you over to the bookstore after. How does that sound?

MY LITTLE STAR: Yeah, that would be great. When should I be ready?

ME: Any chance you can be ready in about 20?

ME: And yes, little star. I promise to text you before coming to your door :)

MY LITTLE STAR: Yeah, I can be ready in 20, and thank you, ghoulie :)

ME: Of course, sweetheart. I'll see you soon ;)

When I look up, I see everyone watching me. Clearing my throat, I pocket my phone in my leather jacket, "Uh, what's up guys?"

In unison they tell me, "Nothing."

Glaring at them, I'm getting ready to call them out for it, but Dorian beats me to it. "You just had this look on your face, and it's nice to see that you guys make each other happy is all."

Slapping my hands on the table, I jump from my seat. "That's my cue to go. Have fun with your kumbaya, chick-flick moment. I'm gonna go get my girl."

Just as I'm almost out of the door, I hear Dorian behind me, "Don't tell her anything until you guys are here, Rhys. Don't try to do this alone, she needs to hear this from all of us. We want her to know that we really are here to protect her, not upset her."

Throwing my hand up in a dismissive wave, I continue

walking away. Once I'm in my truck, I blast *Sounds of Someday* by *Radio Company* and sing along, tapping my fingers on my steering wheel. *Please don't let this end badly.*

———————⭐

Nova

I decide to throw on the clothes I was wearing earlier. No use wasting perfectly clean clothes. My heart is pumping a little faster than usual and I realize that something feels off, but I can't put my finger on what it is. Heading to my kitchen, I grab my *Monster* from the counter and take a drink while pacing the small space. *Green Eyes* plays in my pocket. Smiling at the song, I pull the phone out of my pocket.

> GHOULIE: I'm parking now, little star 😉

I throw my backpack on before getting to the door and tap my fingers on my right thigh. I freeze at the knock on the door and take a deep breath. Turning, I check the peephole and see Rhys standing there, he looks almost… nervous. Taking care of the locks and alarm, I open the door and he looks up immediately with a smile on his face. He rushes forward and grips the back of my thighs picking me up. Squealing at the movement, I grip his shoulders tight., "Dammit, Rhys, you can't just pick me up like that outta nowhere," I giggle as I smack him lightly on the shoulder.

Rhys looks at me up and down and when he looks back up at me he gives me a sexy as sin smirk, "I mean, from where I'm standing it sure as hell looks like I can."

119

Rolling my eyes at him, "That's not what I-" I'm cut off mid sentence by his lips on mine, "oomph, mmm."

The kiss starts off sweet and slow, just our lips pressing against each other. Getting him back for picking me up suddenly and cutting off my words, I bite his lip. He groans at the feeling and walks me back against the wall. I feel his tongue on my bottom lip as he pushes it forward, swirling it around inside my mouth. Remembering that there was a reason for him to be here, I place my palm on his chest and break the kiss. He lets out a whine at the loss of my lips and I laugh, "Did you just whine?"

Putting on a fake pout, he nods. I run my fingers through his hair and smile, "Aww, you poor thing." Leaning to the side, he nuzzles his head in my neck. At first it seems sweet, until he bites my neck. "Hey!"

He looks at me with that mischievous glint in his eye, "Well, don't make fun of me. Of course I'm not a fan of losing your lips, sweetheart."

Running my thumb down his lips, I remind him, "Before we get even more distracted, wasn't there a plan here? It seemed like it was really important that you come and pick me up."

Looking away, he lets out a long breath before turning back to look at me. He leans forward until our foreheads are touching. "Rhys, you're gonna make my anxiety kick in. Please talk to me. You're worrying me," I whisper.

He slowly opens his eyes and I can see the worry, and what looks like sorrow there. "They told me to wait until everyone can talk to you, but I can't just hold on to this and not tell you. I... I can tell you that-" he pauses, blowing out a breath, "I'm going to take you to my work so I can explain what exactly it is I do for a living. The people that... I apparently work with now, have things to discuss with you as well. I knew nothing about this until just before coming to get you. I know this is vague and probably not helpful to your anxiety at all. Believe me, I'm truly sorry about that, I never want to be the cause of your pain, anxiety or fear. I just... I need to tell you something rather than nothing, so you don't feel like this is a total ambush."

My curiosity has gotten the better of me. So I pull away from him to get down. His grip on me tightens and a look of pure terror flits across his face. "Rhys, you have to let me down so we can go. Come on."

Patting his shoulder to get him moving, he releases his hold on me. As we're heading out the door, I hear him grumble under his breath, "I don't know why I can't just carry you to the truck."

Snorting at his pout, I walk out the door and lock up. Standing a few feet away, he's looking down with his right hand outstretched in a silent offering. Shaking my head and smiling, I grab his hand, interlacing our fingers. With my right hand I grip on to his elbow and snuggle in close.

As we get closer to his truck, he slows down and ends up behind me and smacks my ass. A moan slips out of me and I put my hand over my mouth, embarrassed by my reaction.

"Hmm, noted. You blush so beautifully, little star."

He opens the door, picks me up and puts me on the seat. Breathlessly I tell him, "You know, I could've climbed up here myself."

Leaning close like he's about to kiss me, he whispers, "I like my way better."

I'm so lost in his eyes, I barely register that he's pulled the seatbelt across my body and buckled me in. The click of the buckle is what captures my attention. I look down at the buckle and back up to him, "I could've done that too."

Gripping my chin, he guides me closer to him. Placing his lips to mine, he says, "I know," and closes the door. My heart is racing, and fuck saying butterflies, there's thousands of shooting stars taking flight in my stomach. This feeling is dangerous, but I'm starting to think these moments with Rhys will be worth whatever the aftermath is. He hands me his phone after starting Beauty up. Looking between him and his phone in confusion, I hold it up and shake it, "Umm, why are you handing me this?"

He glances sideways at me with a wink, "There's no password, just swipe and pick the music you want."

I open *Spotify* and start searching. As I scroll through, I ask him, "How can you not have a password on your phone? Talk about a security risk."

"I did have a password, but I decided I wanted a different one. When's your birthday, little star? I think that'll be the perfect password."

Looking at him shocked, I stumble over my words. "I... You... My birthday?" I clear my throat, "I mean, my birthday is June twelfth. When's yours?"

I find the song I want to play, but I hover my thumb over the play button waiting for his response. "My birthday is January thirtieth, sweetheart."

I give him an exaggerated pout, "I missed it. I would've gone all out, too."

He brings my hand to his lips, kissing it, "Next year, little star." Our hands come back down and he rests them on his thigh. Clicking play, the sounds of *Fall For Me* by *Sleep Token* fill the truck space. Rhys looks over at me smiling and winks, "Already there, little star, already there."

As we're pulling into the parking lot, I look at the giant warehouse before me. I see the logo and name of the business and gasp. *What the fuck?* Pulling my hand from Rhys, which he reluctantly lets go, I turn and lean my back against the door. Angrily unbuckling my seatbelt, the buckle hits the window. I can see a pinched expression on his face but he hasn't looked at me yet. I clear my throat to get him to look at me, he doesn't, so I clear my throat obnoxiously. He looks over with a sad smile on his face. I gesture toward the name and question him, "So, I take it this is part of the big discussion that will be taking place here today? Seeing how my work-from-home job just so happens to be working for *Vega Altair Enterprises*. Hmm?"

Scrunching his brows, "Uhh, there's a lot of things to be

discussed here, but I can tell you that was not one of the topics I knew about. You'll have to take that up with everyone inside."

Growling in frustration, I move from the door and push it open. I contemplate slamming the door, but Beauty didn't do this. Crossing my arms once more, I wait for Rhys to get out of the truck. He reaches out to me after approaching my side, probably to put an arm around me, but my walls are climbing up again. I walk up to the building, hearing Rhys let out a heavy sigh behind me. There's a loud buzz as we approach the doors, and he jogs around me to one of the doors. It stops me in my tracks, but I quickly look at him and walk in quietly mumbling, "Thank you."

Realizing I have no clue where I'm going, I move aside and wave my arm in front of me for Rhys to lead the way. He leads the way and we must be close because Rhys gruffly yells out, "INCOMING!"

I follow him through the door and my eyes widen with the realization of what's before me. I shake my head with a humorless laugh and grab my smokes and lighter out of my pocket. Holding them up, "We can smoke in here right? No, you know what? Fuck that, I'm smoking anyway." Angrily lighting up a cigarette, I shove the pack back in my pocket and slide my backpack off.

Everyone starts talking at once. Holding my hand up, I yell, "No, everyone can just shut the fuck up right now!" Angrily pacing, I glare over at everyone and shout, "One at a time, somebody start fucking explaining right fucking now!"

Everyone looks at each other and Jade steps forward, "Hunny, please sit down and we'll explain everything. I know this is a lot and you feel betrayed, but please take a breath and you'll get your answers." Inhaling the last of my cigarette, I hold it up in the air trying to find out where to put it. Dorian pushes an ashtray on the table with a shy smile on his face. I smash the cigarette in the ashtray until the cherry is completely extinguished. Jabbing my finger in Dorian's direction, I glare at him, "Don't aim that puppy smile at me, Dor! You're on my shit list, too." Immediately his smile falls, he clears his throat and leans back in his seat, looking ever the part of a chastised child.

I throw myself down in the first empty seat I see and look around at everyone. Rhys starts to walk towards me and I put my hand up to halt him. Waving my hand in a shoo-shoo motion I tell him, "Oh, no you don't. You can go over there with the rest of the traitors," I say as I shoo him away.

I swear I hear him whimper like a kicked dog, as he puts his head down and walks to the other side of the table. Slapping my hands down on the table, I ask again, "So. Who's going to tell me what the fuck is going on? Actually better yet, before you start," pointing around to all of them, "you fuckers know a good amount about my history, and that I don't trust easily. So please fucking explain to me why you thought it was necessary to give me some fake job to draw me in and then," I pause in a humorless laugh, "AND THEN! PRETEND TO BE MY FUCKING FRIENDS! NO! NO! NOT MY FRIENDS! MY FUCKING FAMILY!" When I finish yelling, I'm left panting and my heart is racing. At the resounding silence, I throw my hands forward, "FUCKING TALK!"

Rhys runs his hands down his face roughly, "Fuck, okay, I'll go. I'll tell you my side of everything and then they have to explain things to *both* of us. Dorian and I... or what I thought was just Dorian and I, we find the worst of the worst and I-" he pauses, "and I kill them. Depending on how bad they are, and if we need information from them, there are times that I torture and kill them. We're currently working on the biggest mission we've ever been a part of. A massive drug ring, who deal to children, parents, literally anybody, they don't care. Rumor has it they're working on their own creation, but we don't have all the details yet. Also, some of those involved in this drug ring abuse their family or their partners, sometimes it's both. I had a target a few months back that disappeared on me. Dorian informed me today that not only is he here in town, but-" he looks up at me with the most heartbreaking look I've ever seen, "fuck, little star. It's Frankie. My target is Frankie and he's here in town."

Out of everything he told me, I think this is the worst of it. Should I be more freaked out that he tortures and kills people? Probably. Knowing that they're fucked up people that deserve it, I honestly couldn't give a fuck. I can feel the panic within me rising.

Frankie is here. Frankie. Is. Here. Oh fuck. It's hot, too hot. I can't breathe, why can't I breathe?

Jumping from my chair so fast it falls back, I clutch my chest and begin frantically searching the room. The room feels like it's spinning, I can't see straight. *Fuck, get it together Nova, you need to get the fuck outta here right now.* There's a deep pressure on my chest. Oh fuck, he has me. He found me. On a panicked inhale, I notice the smell of... patchouli. On another breath, I notice coffee and caramel. The scent clicks in my brain and I realize it isn't Frankie, but my ghoulie. My arms wrap around him tightly and I place my head on his chest to hear his heartbeat. Everything comes back into focus as I come out of the fog. Lifting my head, I rest my chin on his chest and see him looking down at me, concern etched all over his face.

"There you are, sweetheart. Lost you for a minute there. You're okay, just keep breathing with me. You're safe, he's not here."

Taking a deep breath in, I slowly blow it out and nod my head. "You swear you don't know whatever it is they're about to tell me?"

His right hand goes over his heart, "I swear, little star. I just found out right before I came to pick you up. Believe me, I already got on them about doing this to you, and made sure that they weren't pretending with you. I know you've been through a lot, and I wasn't going to stand by and do nothing if they didn't actually care about you. I really think they do though, sweetheart." I grab his hand from his chest and walk towards my fallen chair. Rhys walks around me and picks it up, sits down and then opens his arms to me. I freeze for a moment and bite my lip. At my hesitation, Rhys fake pouts and opens and closes

125

his hands in a 'come here' motion. Rolling my eyes and huffing at his theatrics, I plop down on his lap. His arms wrap around my waist and he nuzzles between my neck and shoulder.

"Seeing how there's so much all of you need to tell me... well us, I'm going to ask a question and then one of you can answer. First question, why give me the jobs at *Vega Altair* and *Swan & Scribe*?"

Dorian leans forward, rubbing his Baphomet tattoo absent-mindedly. His lips twitch, torn between wanting to smile and frown all at once. "Please, don't be upset, uh, more so than you already are. Just know that these weren't fake jobs or pity jobs given to you. They were legitimate ones that we needed help with, that we knew you would enjoy, and it would bring you to us where you would be safe and free."

Vanessa takes that moment to speak up. "It's true, Nova girl, I swear. I know everyone feels the same, but I won't speak for them. As for me, I'm glad we got you here where you could be safe and protected. Plus, it's been amazing working with you and getting to know you. You're not just an employee to me, you're family and nothing will ever change that, no matter how mad you are at us."

The next to speak up is Viking, he leans forward and runs his fingers through his beard, "Listen Nova, you know us, shit, you know me. I don't sugarcoat shit, and I don't fake anything. Yes, before we knew you, other than what was on paper in front of us, you were a client to protect. That quickly changed after we all got to know you. Like Vanessa said, you're family and you're stuck with us, end of." Swiping his hand through the air in a cutting motion, he then taps his hand on the table twice, his rings tapping the wood and then leans back in his seat.

Dorian looks past me to Rhys and a weird look crosses his eyes. He nods his head then tilts it towards me. I squint at Dorian and then look over to Rhys with a furrowed brow, "Is he malfunctioning or is there something else that needs to be said?"

Kissing my shoulder three times, he looks me in the eyes and says, "I swear, I don't have any more bombs to drop on you, little star. I do have a question to ask you, but I think it should wait until after these guys explain some things to us. Is that okay with you?"

Wiping my sweaty palms on my thighs, I take a deep breath and nod. "Alright, so are you guys answering my question first, or Rhys'?

Dorian rubs his Baphomet and pulls at the collar of his shirt as if it's choking him. "Honestly, the whole explanation will answer both of your questions. But it's not really something we can give the Cliff's Notes version of. It's... a lot." I notice he's chewing his nails while he paces back and forth. He looks over, snaps his fingers and blurts, "Remember that conversation we had about, uh," a pause, his eyes darting back and forth, "you know about, you and...your tattoo and colors..."

"You can say it in front of her, we already talked about it and I'm not hiding anything from her anymore."

Placing my hands over his, I squeeze, "Yeah, what he said, Dor. I know about the soulmate's conversation."

Dorian leans over and drops his hands to his knees, "Phew, thank fuck. Okay." Standing up straight, he continues. "Okay, so I need you guys to keep an open mind, because everything interweaves." On the final word, he laces his fingers together and shakes them. "Alright, so rewind all the way to when we met as kids. Meeting, bonding over our shared trauma, becoming best friends, brothers, it wasn't random. It was... divine intervention, if you will. Obviously as a kid I had no fucking clue, I just thought hey, this is amazing, I'm meeting my best friend. Over time I'd have dreams, or what I thought was dreams. And, again, as a kid I just thought everything was normal. But sometimes things from the dreams would happen in real life. That's where my love for books and knowledge started. I wanted to learn as much as I could. I wanted to confirm the things I thought I already knew. As we grew up, I started to realize that maybe I was sent to you in a way to be like a... guide? In a sense."

I can feel Rhys' body shaking underneath me, and I turn to make sure he's okay. His reaction isn't what I expect at all. Instead of finding him shaking with rage, he has his hand over his mouth and he's shaking with uncontrollable laughter. "Uh, Dor, I think you broke him."

He moves his hand to wipe a tear from his eye, "A-are you... Are you trying to tell me that you're my very own fairy godmother, Dori?"

"Really, dude?! That's the first thing you think of? You couldn't at least say I'm more like a fairy godfather?!"

Rhys' head shoots up and he snorts, "I'm sorry, buddy, but you... you are no godfather."

"I could be."

Viking's deep voice speaks up, "As entertaining as you two are, maybe you should get to the point here, Eagle."

Dorian directs himself at Rhys again, "Of course. Fast-forwarding a bit, you know how I loved going to the bookstore to read as much as possible? I always chose the smaller one here in town. My dreams started up again and I kept seeing these random images of stars, swans, eagles, harps and books. I didn't think anything of it at first, figuring it was just a pot-induced dream. But I woke up one day and felt this deep in-your-bones type of need, to search out a different bookstore. While searching, *Swan & Scribe* popped up, so of course after my dreams, I knew it was something I needed to look into. I rushed there and when I pushed through the doors, as soon as I heard Vanessa's greeting something clicked. Our eyes met and I had a flash of recognition. It almost knocked me on my ass."

Vanessa speaks up next, "Uh, Dorian, the only reason you didn't end up on your ass was because of the doors. I swear, if he weighed more, he would've burst right through them."

Dorian glares at Vanessa's laughter, "Anyyyywayyyyys. We met, she introduced me to Jade and The Horde and everything felt like it was clicking into place. Vanessa and Jade spoke with me in great detail about their 'abilities' so to speak and the things that they see as well. Jade more so than me and Vanessa. I realized it wasn't just me having these experiences. The Horde discussed their personal security business and it seemed perfect for all of us to work together to reach our end goal. When I found Frankie as your next target, something was eating away at me to do a deep dive there. While discussing it with the group, Vanessa agreed that she had the same feeling. Like I said, Jade sees and feels a lot more than us and she was adamant the search needed to be done. Her only words were, 'you have to find her'. The things I showed you today about Nova was what I found. I knew we needed to act fast to help her-"

The swirl of emotions mixing inside me makes my stomach roll. Anger, confusion, love, appreciation, understanding. I stand abruptly, getting everyone's attention, and light up a cigarette. Taking a deep inhale, I try to get my emotions in check. Realizing they're looking at me expectantly, I stutter, "S-orry, I'm fine. I think. I... nevermind. Please continue, Dor. This is just a lot to take in. You guys knew all this time about Frankie? You guys-" gulping in air, "you guys saw some of the things he did to me? Talk about fucking embarrassing. Sorry, please continue. I really didn't mean to interrupt." I make the mistake of looking at Rhys and see him gripping the arm rests so tight his knuckles are white. His jaw is clenched so tight I can see a pop that matches his pulse.

"Care to explain why the fuck you didn't tell me about Nova, then? I could have fucking saved her! I COULD HAVE SAVED HER, DORIAN!" I close my eyes tightly, taking deep breaths to reassure myself that he's only mad at the whole situation and won't actually hurt any of us. The loud noise of his fist slamming on the table startles me, causing me to flinch. He stands up so abruptly that the chair falls back to the floor. My feet move on their own and I stop in front of him. Quickly stubbing my cigarette out in the ashtray, I place my hands on his chest and feel his heart hammering against my hand. His eyes soften when he meets my gaze. Reaching up, I push a few fallen strands of his hair back.

"I know emotions are high right now, but let's just take a breath and let him finish. Okay?" With a clipped nod, he places a tender kiss on my forehead. After picking up his chair, he sits down and pulls me in his lap. "I'm sure there's a perfectly logical explanation as to why you didn't tell Rhys about me. Right, Dor?"

"It was for the best. There was a plan. We had to stick to the plan," he confesses, head down.

Vanessa stands up and guides Dorian to a chair to sit down, giving his shoulder a light squeeze before stepping away "Listen, Dorian knew you would be too distracted with Nova to focus on the job. Not only that, but it just... wasn't time for you two to meet yet. So we devised a plan all on our own. You were to focus on Frankie and we were going to offer Nova a job. With Dorian's computer skills, he was able to track her job search and her skills. And of course, as fate would have it, her experience and skills lined up with what *Vega Altair* needed. So yes, things were sneaky and there were ulterior motives, but it was never anything nefarious. We all planned on having this discussion with you both when the time was right. Which is now." She smiles as her arms spread wide "Ta-da." Biting back a smile, I attempt a glare in her direction. She points at me, "I saw that." she makes a grabbing motion in the air and puts her hand in her pocket, "Saving that."

I reach in my pocket and pull out my hand with a finger up. "Hold up, here's something else you can save," I retort.

Her smile brightens, "Aww, there's the Nova we all know and love."

Rolling my eyes, I slap my thighs, "Okayyyyy, so I take it now we can do the Cliff's Notes version. So basically the three of you are our guides in a sense, and I'm guessing The Horde are the protectors? And we were all just destined to meet in some capacity? Does that about sum it up?"

"In a sense, yeah. I mean, there's always a bigger picture. But for this specific situation, yeah, that sums it up nicely."

Rubbing my temples, I remember that Rhys had a question of his own. I shift on his lap so I can look at him better, "So that happened. Hopefully all that's left now is that question you had for me, soooo…"

Roughly scraping his hands down his face, he groans, "What a fucking day. Anyway, you know what I do now and you know that Frankie is one of my targets. I can do it with or without you because it has to be done, sweetheart. I just… and please, I really need you to think hard about this decision. I wanted to know if you would like to be there when it happens? That way you know for sure that he's gone, and can't hurt you or haunt you any longer." he tapers off on a murmur.

"Uh, what was that?"

He quickly replies, "And if you wanted, you could help torture him as payback for everything he did to you."

Apparently I'm on information overload, because my only response is to start laughing like a lunatic. Every time I think I'm finished and can compose myself, I start laughing all over again. Tears are pouring down my face and my ribs hurt from the laughter. I finally get myself under control and catch the concerned look on everyone's faces. Rhys is rubbing my stomach in a windshield wiper motion. "Oh, Rhys, I will absofuckinlutely be going with you to torture that sick fuck. You guys may have an idea of what I went through with him, but nobody knows every single thing he did. I can't wait to give him a taste of his own medicine. You would think that little bitch cried enough all of the times I fought back. I'll make that look like child's play compared to the torture I'll be serving him with."

Everyone's faces morph from concern, to shock and then everyone starts cackling. All around the table I can hear "holy shit," "fuck yeah," "let's fucking go."

"Alright, bitches. I know y'all fucking smoked in here. Someone light up a blunt, we're going to smoke in our new circle of trust. No more bullshit. With that said, I'm demanding we have weekly family meetings as well. Cuz I'm telling you right now, if we have one more day like this where bombs are dropped left and right, I'll be having a fucking coronary" Pausing, I look around the room and twirl my hand around, "By the way, how do you guys pay for all of this? I mean, no offense, Dor, but there's no way your job pays for everything."

Everyone looks at each other, looking guilty as hell. Dorian clears his throat, "Uh. Since this is our new circle of trust, officially, we pool from outside resources. Unofficially, we steal from the rich, bad guys."

"Ha, nice. Alright, let's get this party started, fuckers." Musical chairs break out and the smokers move to our side of the table and the non-smokers stay at the other end.

Dorian takes a seat next to me, reaches in his pocket and pulls out a handful of *Swisher Sweets*. "Pick your poison, SuperNova."

Whipping my head in his direction, I smile at him, "That's a good one, Dor, I like it." I look down at the options and push the strawberry flavor towards him.

His face breaks out in a huge grin and he starts doing a happy dance in his seat, "That's my favorite one!"

Smiling at his excitement, I agree, "Perfect."

"Unity is strength... when there is teamwork and collaboration, wonderful things can be achieved."
~ Mattie Stepanek

CHAPTER 9
I WON'T BACK DOWN

Rhys

After smoking, everyone is sitting around the table bullshitting. I still have Nova in my arms and it's the best feeling ever. I'm so glad she didn't run away screaming to get away from me. Tightening my hold around her waist, I nuzzle in her hairline. I can smell her perfume, it's like fruity flowers and vanilla. *It's heaven, she's heaven.*

She whispers with a slight laugh to her voice, "Are you smelling me, ghoulie?"

I look up at her and smile, "I mean, I think it's only fair. You were smelling me earlier, little star." I'm not expecting the move, so I jolt when I feel her smack my thigh. "Heyyyy."

She squeezes my thigh once and then leaves her hand there. "Don't throw that in my face, ya big jerk. I was in a panic, it doesn't count."

Chuckling, I lightly bite her shoulder, "It's okay, sweetheart, you can smell me anytime you want."

A thought occurs to me, and I clear my throat with a frown, "Actually, not anytime. You might want to refrain from smelling me after a job. Nobody needs to smell that."

The lights start flashing continuously and pictures and surveillance footage fill the screens. At the realization of what this means, I groan. Turning over her shoulder to look at me with wide, panicked eyes, she asks, "What is that? What's going on? Is the warehouse under attack? Oh fuck, is he here?"

Rubbing my hands up and down her arms, "Hey, hey, hey. Breathe, sweetheart. I promise you, he's not here. Our emergency system is different than this okay? If it's an emergency like that the lights turn red, you'll see metal blockades go down across all the windows and an actual alarm will blare." I circle my finger in the air, "This is what it looks like when I have a job to do. The system Dorian set up alerts us when targets pop up on surveillance or security radars. I'm so sorry, little star. I want to spend my time with you, but I really need to go take care of this."

I try to read her reaction, her brows are scrunched and she's biting her lip. I whisper in her ear, "Please don't be upset with me. I'll make it up to you when I'm done." She pulls from my embrace, I reluctantly let her go.

She stands and spins so she's facing me, resting against the table. She looks down and fidgets with her jacket sleeves. Inhaling deeply, she lifts her head and I see a fire in her eyes. "I'm not upset, Rhys. I want to go with you."

Already shaking my head no at her words, she glares at me. "Really? You were so worried I was going to leave or be upset about all of this, and now I'm asking to be a part of it, and you tell me no. What the fuck, Rhys?" I attempt to grab her hands but she swipes them away and places hers on the table behind her.

Running my hand down my face and groaning, I look back up at her, "This is my job, little star. Something I've trained a long time for. Maybe if we do some training, you can join me another time. I offered to have you come along for the job with

Frankie because I think it could be healing for you and help you close that chapter of your life."

She crosses her arms and strolls past me, lighting up another cigarette. She scratches her brow, then brings the smoke to her lips and takes a drag. Pursing her lips, she slowly lets the smoke out, "You do know that I'm technically an employee here right? I'm sure everyone here does jobs outside of the norm for them. What if we compromise?"

She needs to stop being so feisty with me in front of everyone, I'm now realizing how much of a turn on it is. Refocusing on our conversation, I hear Nova yell my name. I stand up after adjusting my rock hard cock and walk over to her. Pulling her into an embrace, she gasps when she feels me hard against her. I whisper, "It's not my fault you're getting all feisty with me. I didn't even realize I liked it so much until you did it," in a dramatic voice I say, "Hold me, little star, hide my happy cock from everyone, they'll laugh at me." I start shaking from trying to hold back my laughter. She slaps my chest and loses the battle of holding her laughter back as well. *God, her smile is breathtaking, with the most adorable dimples I've ever seen.* Kissing all three, yes, three dimples, not two, I tell her, "I love these dimples, sweetheart. Tell me what this compromise is."

Looking over to Dorian, she gets his attention, "Hey Dor?"

He looks away from the screens and nods, "Yeah, SuperNova?"

Smiling at the nickname, she starts asking questions. "When he goes out on these missions, do you stay here and do surveillance, or do you ever go out into the field to do it?"

Walking over to the table, he rests against it crossing his arms and legs. "I predominantly stay here for the surveillance, but, yes, there are times that I will go out on a mission with him and survey things. I do, however, have to use the company van, due to my car being well known by the *Amissa Stella* people."

Grumbling under my breath, "There he goes again using his big brain and big words."

"You do realize it's not just my brain that's extraordinary, my hearing is as well, Reese's Pieces. Keep it up and that *will* be your call name."

Putting my hands up in false surrender and dramatically shaking, "Ooo, you got me there... *Dori*. I'll be on my best behavior...not."

Sticking my tongue out and flipping him off, he rolls his eyes and returns the gesture. Glancing back and forth between the two of us, Nova giggles, "I can see it now. Sometimes you guys are going to make me laugh with your antics, but other times it's really going to drive me up a wall."

I grab her belt loop and pull her closer to me, "Oh, you will definitely find yourself annoyed with us. Back to this compromise, little star? I'm guessing what you're getting at is that while I get a hold of my target, you will stick with Dorian, and then you would like to be with me while I take care of the target?" Holding my breath for the answer I know I'm not going to like, she nods. Slowly releasing my breath, I bring her even closer to me. I rest my chin between her neck and shoulder, I give her a quick kiss and a slight bite. "I'm really nervous about this, little star. I know you're not going to back down though, so here's the deal. I need you to listen to everything Dorian and I say, when we say it. There's no room for error or being stubborn. I need to be able to focus on what I'm doing, and in order to do that, I need to know you're going to be safe and out of harm's way. Can you do that for me, sweetheart?"

She's looking down and biting her lip, so I lean down enough that we're at eye level. Releasing her hold on her lip, she whispers, "I don't want to make a promise I can't keep. Don't get me wrong, I fully plan to do what's expected to keep you safe and focused. It's just," she pauses, "if something goes wrong, there's no way in fuck I'm just going to sit around. I will run to you, Rhys. Don't for one fucking second think I won't."

Grinning, I bring my lips to hers for a peck, and stay there to talk against them, "I guess it's a good thing I'm great at my fucking job and that won't be an issue then. Deal, little star. Seal it with a kiss for me."

Shaking her head, her lips rub against mine. She winks at me as she pulls back, "There's your kiss, Casanova. You'll get a better one depending on how this night ends."

Groaning at the dismissal, I clap my hands and look over at Dorian, "Guess that's my cue to get my shit ready. You go take care of the van and get Nova whatever she needs." Dorian nods and waves Nova over.

Walking in, I see half of the group on laptops, and the other half checking out the screens. I don't see Nova or Dorian. Getting ready to ask where she is, Fish gets my attention by waving at me and points to the screens. "Calm down, cowboy, her and Dorian are setting things up in the van."

Turning to go see her, I hear Viking behind me, "Hey, did you get everything you needed from the armory? Some of us are getting ready to head that way to put our gear together."

My face scrunches in confusion, I turn to look at him, "Uh, what do you mean put your gear together? Aren't you all staying here?"

Shaking his head, he says, "We're your backup." Holding his hands up and cutting off my next sentence, he follows up with, "We will stay out of your way, until we're absolutely needed. If anything we'll just be there for," bringing his hands up, he does air quotes, "housekeeping when you're finished. But we need to start working as a team, and all of us would feel more comfortable if you had us there to back you up, instead of Nova running into the unknown. I'm sure you would agree with that, right?"

Growling at the idea of anything happening to her, I nod.

Slapping the door frame twice, I turn and head out to the van to check on Nova and Dor's progress.

Leaning against the bay door frame, I cross my feet at the ankle and watch the two of them laugh and talk. They both have over-the-top goofy sides, and watching them now I can see that they both bring it out of each other. I quietly laugh as they both make dramatic gestures, funny faces and do different voices. Anybody else watching would think they were just goofing off, but they're taking care of shit for the mission while being over-animated about it all. Uncrossing my ankles, I start walking towards them.

In the worst British accent possible I say, "Chip, chip, cheerio, mates! It's time to get on with it." They both stop what they're doing and slowly turn towards me. Dorian bites his lip and Nova puts her hand up to her mouth. They both begin shaking in silent laughter until they double over, laughing hysterically at me. "Wow, tough crowd. Laugh it up, chuckles 1 and 2. We all set here?" Nova wipes tears from her eyes and takes a deep breath to get herself under control.

Dorian clears his throat and gestures towards the van. "We have everything all set up. I walked SuperNova through every-thing and we already have our necessary gear in here. Speaking of which." He hops in the van and comes out with two bullet-proof vests and a small black zip-up case. Handing the case to me and a vest to Nova, he puts his on and tightens the straps.

Nova pushes her vest towards me, "Wanna help a girl out here? I know you want to make sure I have it on... nice and tight." Smirking at her choice of words, I grab the vest from her and slide it over her head. I run my fingers down the side of her neck as I gently pull her hair out of the vest. Making sure every-thing is put together properly, pull her close to me to pull the straps tight. Bringing my lips to her ear, I whisper, "Nice and tight enough for you, sweetheart?"

She nods against my shoulder, where I feel her take a shuddering breath. Bringing my right hand down, I smack her ass. She swats at my chest and shouts, "Dammit, Rhys!"

Smirking, I let go of her and step back, clapping my hands. "Alright, Dorian, why don't you call everyone and tell them to get in place so we can all head out." Turning to Nova, I grip her face between my palms and search her eyes, "You swear you're ready?" Her hands rise to cover mine and she nods her head. "Okay. Please listen to everything you're told, okay? I need to know you'll be safe."

She looks down for a moment and then looks up and whispers, "Please come back to me."

Caressing under her eyes with my thumbs, I respond, "Always. Please wait for me."

She pulls me towards her for a kiss but before our lips meet she whispers, "Always."

Our lips collide and it's all tongue and teeth. We're as close as we can get, yet we're both pulling each other as if we can get closer. I hear a throat clear to the side of us, knowing it's Dorian, I lift my right hand and flip him off. Slowing the kiss down, I peck her lips three times and slowly release her. She whines at the loss of my lips, and dammit, do I feel her pain. Speaking of pain, fuck, I'm hard. Adjusting my cock, I wink at her and start to head towards my K5. I toss my duffel bag inside and lean between the door and the truck shouting over to Dorian. "Keep my girl safe, Dorian Alden!"

Saluting me, he shouts back, "Aye, aye, Captain Rhys Slater!" Shaking my head I hop in my truck and start it. When I see everyone is ready, I head to our target's location.

I see the sign for the *End of the Road Motel* up ahead. Rolling my eyes, I swear the owner must have thought it was so clever to be so literal when he picked the name. Pulling into the parking lot, I back my truck up in front of my target's door. Dorian and Nova park across the street and a few minutes after, The Horde shows up in the other company van. We might have to call it the clown van if they keep piling everybody up in that bitch. They drive past and head to the back side of the motel.

Reaching in my pocket, I pull the black case out. Inside is one syringe filled with Fentanyl. I pull the syringe out of the case, and carefully put it in my pocket, tossing the case on my seat. After getting out, I toss my duffel over my shoulder and head to the back of my truck, lifting the window and dropping the tailgate down. Turning to the target's motel door, I pound on it with my fist. I can hear the target grumble and shuffle around when he notices I blocked the peephole with my finger. As soon as he rips the door open, I grip his shirt and begin shoving him inside. His eyes widen, and in a thick Italian accent he shouts, "What the fuck? Who the fuck are you?"

"Now is not the time to talk, Davide," I respond after kicking the door shut. Rearing my head back, I thrust it forward into his nose. I hear the crack and blood begins pouring out of his nose. He has a dazed look on his face, his eyes watery and unfocused. Releasing my hold on him, he falls to the floor and barely catches himself. He glances back to the bedside table, and I know the fucker is looking for his gun. I let him think he has a chance and just stand there while he starts army crawling towards it, leaving a blood trail along the way. Shit, whoever is in charge of clean-up today is not going to be happy. I drop the duffle to the floor and slowly trail behind him. Pulling the syringe from my pocket, I pull the cap off and pocket it. Just as he begins reaching the drawer, I hover over him and jab the needle in the side of his neck and push the plunger. "So close, Davide, so very, very close."

The drug works immediately as he tries to reach for his gun, grappling for the table and missing. In seconds, he flops down against the end table. Pulling my phone out, I call Dorian. He picks up after two rings but I don't even let him speak, "Uh, Eagle? Housekeeping might want to get to work ASAP."

Hanging up the phone, I pocket it and toss the sheets from the bed to the floor. I grab the target under his arms and drag him on top of the sheets. Grunting and sweating from the effort, I drop him down. After managing to wrap him up in the sheet, I pick up my duffle and sling it over my shoulder. Cracking the door open, I scoop him up and carry him to the door. After doing this so many times, you'd think it gets old but it doesn't. The rush is always intoxicating. Sliding my foot between the door and frame to push the door open further, I quickly peek around. I don't see anyone of concern, so I step forward and toss him in the back of my truck. Shutting the tailgate and window, I turn back and shut the motel door. Once in my truck, I open my duffel and then reach in my pocket carefully for the empty syringe and cap. Throwing it all back in the black case, I zip that up and toss it in my bag. I pull up my music on the phone and start playing *Voices In My Head* by Falling in Reverse. Singing along, I keep myself in the zone for what I need to do next.

There's a knock on my "playroom" door. I already have the target strapped to the chair in only his underwear and he's still out cold. His head is dropped to his chest and a steady drip of drool is strung from his mouth to his shirt. I crack open the door to see Dorian and Nova there. She keeps looking up at me and attempting to look over my shoulder. "You swear you're ready for this, little star? You can change your mind at any time, okay?"

She places her hand on my chest. "I know you're trying to look out for me, Rhys, but please, look into my eyes. Deep down, you know we hold the same darkness within us, and I can handle this. Right?"

She's right, there's been little things that have given me a glimpse of the darkness within her, a darkness that called to me.

Stepping back, I open the door more and let her through. Nodding to Dorian, I shut the door and lock it. Turning, I find Nova circling Davide, as if he's a subject to study. Clearing my throat, she looks up at me.

"Do you want to stand and watch or sit?" Looking around the room, she eyes the empty table against the wall. Walking over, she hops on and scoots back until she's leaning against the wall. My phone connects to the Bluetooth speaker and I hand her my phone. "Here you go, DJ Nova." Snorting at the nickname she grabs my phone and begins scrolling. Leaning forward, I kiss her temple then head over to the target.

Hanging just above my head is a retractable hose. Reaching up, I grab a hold of it and pull it down. There's only one temperature setting for the water, and it's set to frozen tundra. Gripping the nozzle, I look over at Nova to check in on her. She hits play on the music, and I can't help but grin at my girl's sense of humor. *Drowning* by *Radio Company* begins blasting through the speaker. Looking back at the target, I push the hose lever to spray him. He jolts awake and gasps, sputtering on the water spraying him in the face. I slowly release the lever and let the hose rise above my head again. Reaching my hand forward, I roughly slap him in the face, "Rise and shine, Davide!" Shaking his head, I watch water droplets fly around. His shackles on his wrist clank around while he tries to move his hands out of the hold. Tsking at him, I kneel down so I can catch his eye. He slowly raises his eyes to meet mine and if looks could kill, this animal would be successful in killing me first. "Yank all you want, you're not getting out. It really sucks when you're held against your will and helpless doesn't it? Do you feel like your victims? Do you feel like your wife, who you abuse every time you've had a bad day, or just cuz you damn well please?" A look of shock comes across his face at my words. "That's right, Davide Arturo, I know all about your extracurriculars. Here's how it's going to go, Davey boy. You give me the answers I'm looking for, and I'll make your death quick. You don't give me the information I want, well, fuck around and find out."

To my left is a table with various cutlery, pliers, nails, hammer and a blow torch. Grabbing my pliers first, I turn back to him, lifting and shaking them in front of his face. There's a quick flash of fear on his face, then he reins it in and goes back to a stoic expression. I tap the tips of his fingers on his left hand with the pliers and let him know, "Alright, let's test this out. I'm going to ask you a question, and if you answer correctly, you get to keep your fingernails. If not," clicking my tongue and shrugging, "well you get the picture."

Bringing the pliers up to my chin and tapping it, I pretend to think aloud, "Hmm, first question, first question, what shall it be?" Thrusting the pliers up in the air in triumph, I exclaim "AHA!" Pointing the pliers towards his face, "Easy question. What is your name?" Pushing the pliers against his lips like a microphone, I await his answer.

He attempts to move his head away, so I push the pliers against his lips harder, pushing past them and clinking them against his teeth. His top lip curls back and he yells, "VAFFANCULO!"

The music immediately stops and I hear Nova jump off the table shouting on a laugh, "I KNOW THAT ONE! It's in one of my favorite movie, *Boondock Saints*."

When Nova walks up and stands next to me, Davide starts shouting, "Hey! Hey, are you going to help me or what?!"

Nova looks at me and raises an eyebrow. Slowly turning her head in the direction of Davide, she retorts, "How about no." She flicks him between his eyebrows and says, "From what I hear you're a piece of shit, and you just told my boyfriend to go fuck himself. Rude. Where are your manners? Your madre and nonna would be so ashamed of your behavior."

He spits down at her feet and shouts, "PORCA PUTTANA!"

Looking down at her feet, she drags the bottom of her right shoe on top of the left, attempting to get rid of the spit. "Okay, fucking eww. Also, I don't know what that means, but I feel like it's not very nice."

"Seemed fitting. I called you a pig whore," he snarls, baring his teeth.

My instinct is to move forward to hit him, but Nova puts her palm against my chest to hold me back. With a move neither of us see coming, she punches him in the face. His head snaps back from the force and his nose starts bleeding again.

"CAZZO!"

Shaking her hand out, she looks at him and says, "Jesus, I know you're Italian, but why bother if we don't have a fucking translator here. The only words from your mouth we want are the answers to his questions, you stupid fuck." Staring at her in awe, she looks back over to me and shrugs, "What? He deserved it."

Gripping the back of her head with my hand, I bring her close to me, "That was the hottest fucking thing I've ever witnessed." Rolling my hips against her so she can feel how hard I am, she responds by grinding her pussy against me.

"Please hurry and get your answers," she whispers. Slamming my lips to hers, I kiss her hard then reluctantly step back. Without hesitating, 'I walk up to Davide, open the pliers and rip out two of his fingernails. He screams immediately from the pain. Pinpricks of blood start pooling at the top of his nail beds.

All of his nails are removed and he still hasn't answered any questions. Becoming frustrated, I throw my pliers back on the table and grab the hammer. Spinning the hammer in my hand, I tilt my head and stare him down. Sweat is pouring down his face and he's slightly panting. "Alright, broken bones or do you want to start talking?"

He tightly closes his lips, refusing to talk. Nodding, I lift the hammer and bring it down hard on his left hand. The sounds of his bones breaking are drowned out by his screams. "What can you tell me about *Amissa Stella*, Davide?" His silence continues so I bring the hammer down and break his other hand. Without missing a beat, I bring the hammer down against his left knee and then the right. He continues screaming from the pain as I turn and toss the hammer on the table.

It's when I pick up the scalpel and turn to him that his eyes go wide and he stammers, "Wh-what are y-you going t-to do with that?!"

Bringing the scalpel to his chest, I begin carving it. He tries to move the best he can, screaming at every rip of his flesh. Blood is pouring from each letter I carve. When I finish, I stand up straight and look at my masterpiece. In big letters covering his entire chest it says ABUSER. Reaching for his head next, he finally starts to talk. "Okay! Okay, I'll tell you! The only important thing you need to know is that they are planning to branch out."

Cutting him off, I ask, "Branch out how?"

"They're not just sticking with manufacturing and distributing regular drugs. They're testing things out to make their own drug. It won't be drugs for just anyone, though. These drugs are only for people that know too much. Before killing them, they want to see if they can wipe their memory. If that doesn't work, then they will kill them."

Holding the scalpel up to his cheek and pressing just enough for blood to pool and slowly drip, I ask, "Is that everything?" There's movement to the right of me and I glance over. Nova kneels and grabs my jeans. Looking down, my mouth has fallen open. "What are you doing, little star?"

Shaking her head, she begins unbuttoning and unzipping my jeans frantically. Talking to my cock instead of me, she says, "Keep going, don't mind me."

Holy shit, I think I'm in love. My jeans and boxer briefs are down just under my balls as she grabs my cock and begins stroking. Grunting at the sensation, I almost lose my balance. "Keep going or I'm going to stop, Rhys."

Letting out a shuddering breath, "Holy fuck! Yes ma'am." Directing my next words to Davide, who is glued to what Nova is doing, I snap my fingers in his face. "Get your eyes off my cock and my girl. What else can you tell me? I know there's more."

I begin carving lines in his face waiting for an answer. Blood is dripping down his face and he screams with every slice I make. I can barely focus on the task at hand while Nova has my cock shoved so far down her throat. I'm sure if I reached down and gripped her throat I could feel my cock there. Unable to stop myself, I start thrusting my hips. She pulls back a bit and brings her hands up and begins a twisting motion with her hands while sucking hard on the crown. Holy fuck, this woman is going to be the death of me. I've had decent head before, but nothing, and I mean nothing, compares to this. My woman is a fucking goddess. Slightly losing my balance from the feeling, I slip and the scalpel jabs into his eye.

The pain doesn't register at first, so all that can be heard is Nova sucking my cock and the squelch of his eye being punctured. At the same time I say, "Oh shit," Davide starts screaming from the pain. Blood mixed with a jelly-like fluid begins pouring out of his eye socket. "Yikes. That does not look good, Mr. Arturo." Making a blech face, he attempts to glare at me with his good eye.

Fuck, I'm gonna cum. Bringing my free hand down to Nova's head, "I'm close, little star. Fuck, I'm so close." She doubles down her effort and begins sucking and stroking faster. The scalpel is shaking in my hand, attempting to cut more. She drops her hands and sucks down my whole cock in one go. Grabbing my hips, she begins pulling me towards her as if she could get my cock any further down her throat. She swallows and it's the most amazing feeling. "F-fuck, I'm cumming. Holy fuuuuuuuck."

Losing my balance, the scalpel stabs Davide in the neck. Grabbing the top of his head, I push myself up and yank the scalpel out. Blood begins spurting out of his neck and he starts gasping and gurgling on the blood. "Oops. I guess playtime is over." Nova whines at my words, not realizing I'm talking about

Davide and not her. She releases my cock and I look down at her just in time to see her stick her tongue out with my cum pooling on her tongue. She wiggles her tongue at me and then closes her mouth and swallows. Oh fuck. *You don't know it yet, but you're gonna be my wife, Nova Skye Hart.* Reaching my hand out to help her up, she grabs it and I pull her up to kiss her. I can taste myself on her, but I can't bring myself to give a fuck. Swiping my tongue around every inch of her mouth, she battles my tongue and finally getting a hold of it, she sucks my tongue like she did my cock. Moaning, I pull back from the kiss and bite her lip. "Fuck, you're perfect. Let's get the fuck out of here, little star."

She furrows her brow and says, "But what about..." but when she turns to look at Davide, she sees that he's dead. "Ohhh, guess I missed that part. Damn."

Kissing the top of her head, I grip her hip to lead her towards the sink to clean up. "You were a little preoccupied, sweetheart."

"It's hard to beat a person who never gives up." ~Babe Ruth

CHAPTER 10
STOLEN DANCE

Nova

As soon as I wake up, I realize a few things all at once. First, I didn't have a single nightmare. Second, I'm pretty sure the reason for that is wrapped tightly around me right now. I could get used to waking up next to this man. Third, apparently watching Rhys work really turns me on. Not only did I suck his cock right there in front of his target while he was torturing him, but he took me home and spent the whole night worshiping my body. The things that man can do with his tongue, fingers and cock should be fucking illegal.

Oh. Oh, and look at that, apparently I am now insatiable as well because I'm so fucking wet thinking about last night. Slowly turning in his arms, I inch my way down his body. He stirs a little and I freeze. Fuck, please don't wake up yet, I want this to be a surprise. I'm glad we fell asleep naked, it's so much easier since I don't have to attempt to remove any of his clothes without waking him. When I reach his cock, I stare at it for a moment. How the fuck is this man so big, that even soft it's intimidating? My fingers gently wrap around the base as I flick the head of his cock with my tongue. I drag my tongue through the drop of pre-come filling his slit. The salty taste bursts on my tongue and I draw lazy circles around the crown, loving how every lick makes his cock harden. I lick him from base to tip, making sure to put a little pressure with the barbell on my tongue.

Rhys lets out a little grunt in his sleep and I freeze, peering up through my eyelashes. It looks like he's still asleep, so I wrap my lips around the head of his cock and start sucking while stroking up and down his shaft with a twist of my wrist. Rhys moans and rolls to his back, and I follow along still with his cock in mouth and hand. Now that I have a better angle, I grip his cock with both hands and begin stroking and twisting in opposite directions while sucking hard. His hands come down to my hair to grip me tight. There's a slight pinch of pain, but it just turns me on more. Rhys' gravelly voice comes from above me, "Mmmm, fuckkkkk. Just like that, little star. Holy fuck, this is the best way to wake up. Fuck, you're amazing."

I smile at the praise and keep going. Flicking my tongue out, I slowly push my barbell against the vein running along his cock. With a groan, Rhys grips my hair tighter and thrusts his hips. Knowing he's close, I push forward and shove his cock all the way back to my throat. Through gritted teeth, Rhys shouts, "HOLY FUCK! Yes, just like that, fuck, sweetheart." His hand goes from my hair down to my throat, giving it a slight squeeze. "Oh fuck, I'm gonna cum. I can feel my cock in your throat. Fuck, that's so fucking hot."

Relaxing my throat as much as I can, I move my head up and down in quick but short movements to hold him in my throat. Spit is pouring out of my mouth, and the only sounds in the room are the suction of his cock down my throat and his moans. Rhys grips my throat tighter, "Fuck, fuck, fuck, mmm, not like this, not like this."

He lets go of my throat and grabs me to pull me on top of him swiftly. I squeal from the movement and we both start laughing. When our eyes meet, he stops laughing and I almost stop breathing from the fire in his eyes. His thumb runs along my jawline. "You're so fucking beautiful."

Thrusting his hips up, his cock grinds against my wet pussy, and we both moan from the feeling. I place my hands on either side of his head and lean down to his neck where I lick up to his ear and bite the lobe. He hisses from the bite and grinds his cock against me again. Sitting up, I reach behind me and grab his cock, bringing it to my entrance. I guide the tip inside and move up and down, barely letting it go in and out. He grips my hip and grits his teeth, "Don't fucking tease me, sweetheart." Just as he starts to thrust up, I drop down to the hilt.

We both moan and shout, "Fuuuuuuuck."

I use my palms on his chest for leverage to bounce on his cock. Chasing the feeling, I bounce as hard and fast as possible, my tits bouncing with the motion. Rhys releases my hip and throat and brings his hand to my tits, gripping and squeezing them tight. With his thumbs he flicks and rubs my nipples until they're erect. "Fuck, just look at you, little star. So fucking perfect. Fuck, you're doing so good, sweetheart, so fucking good. Just like that."

His praise elicits a moan from my lips and I lift until only the tip of his cock is in my entrance and slam myself down. I grind against his cock, my clit rubbing just above his cock. I bring my right hand down to my clit and start rubbing in fast circles. Rhys pushes my hand out of the way and circles my clit in furious circles. "Oh fuck, yes, yes, please don't stop. I'm so close, Rhys."

Biting his lip he tilts his head back and groans, "Fuck, keep saying my name, little star." With his right hand on my nipple, and his left on my clit he pinches both at the same time, "Cum for me, Nova, cum for me right fucking now."

Letting go, I do just as he says and cum so hard, I see those galaxies behind my eyelids he told me about. I keep falling and falling, I don't know which way is up or down, I don't even know if I'm breathing anymore. When I come to, I'm splayed out across his chest panting. "There you are, little star."

Unable to speak, I nod my head against his sweaty chest. I

groan when I realize I missed him cum. "What's wrong, sweet-heart?" he asks while rubbing soothing circles on my back.

With an annoyed growl, I harrumph, "I missed you cumming."

He thrusts his hips up, his cock still inside me, "Yeah, but you can feel my cum, can't you? Trying to drip past my cock?"

Wiggling my hips a little, I nod my head and say, "Mhmm." Quickly flipping us over so I'm on my back, he pulls his cock out and I whine at the loss. He chuckles and playfully slaps my pussy. Letting out an obscene moan, I look down at him with wide eyes. With the biggest smirk, he winks and says, "Like that huh? Noted."

Looking down at my pussy, he groans, "Fuck, I don't think you understand what it does to me, seeing my cum dripping out of you." A concerned look crosses his face and he clicks his tongue, "This won't do."

Bringing his fingers forward, he scoops up the dripping cum and pushes it back inside of me. "Wh-what are you doing?"

At first he doesn't answer, caught up in the moment of scooping his cum up and putting it back inside of me, twisting and scissoring his fingers around. "It's yours, all yours, can't waste it."

Laughing at his words I start to lean forward to push his hand away. At the same time, he pushes up and hovers over me, rubbing his cock on my pussy lips. "How are you hard already? You're 27, not 20, you're not supposed to bounce back that fast anymore!"

Thrusting his hips forward, he slams his cock all the way in my pussy again and groans. "Sweetheart, I'll get this hard for you over and over again when we're in our 80's. This is what you do to me."

His words are meant to be hot and funny, instead they hit me straight in the heart and I start to tear up. When I don't respond, he looks at me and stops moving. Bringing his palms to my face, he caresses my cheeks, "Hey, hey, hey. What's wrong?"

He starts to pull out but I wrap my arms and legs around him tight, holding him as close as possible to stop him. "No, no. Please don't stop. It's nothing, I'm fine."

Still refusing to move, he leans down and licks a fallen tear. "Why are you crying?"

I look away, shaking my head, "I'm sorry, I'm sorry. Please don't be mad., I'll stop, I promise."

Gripping my chin he turns my head towards him. "Hey, I'm not him, Nova. You can cry whenever you want. I mean, I wish you never had to cry, but if you need to, you cry whenever, I'll never be mad at you for it. I just need to know you're okay. It's a little concerning that you're crying while I'm fucking you."

Nodding my head, "I know. I'm sorry. It's just... I know you were being funny with what you said, but when you said, 'when we're in our 80's,' all I could think was, holy fuck, he wants to keep me, he wants to stay for that long?"

Leaning down he takes my lips in a soft and slow kiss. Licking my bottom lip, he pulls back and says, "Forever. I plan on keeping you forever. Soulmates, remember? You're stuck with me, always."

Placing my hands on top of his, I say, " Not stuck. I'll never be stuck with you. I'll be exactly where I want to be." Moving my hand down, I swat at his side, he gets a shocked look on his face and I laugh, "Now, chop, chop and fuck me, cowboy. We have plans with Dor today."

Grimacing at my words, "Uh, little star. Please for the love of fuck, do not talk about him while I'm inside you. If I wasn't already inside *my* pussy," nodding at his words, "that's right, this is *my* pussy. If I wasn't already inside you, those words would've been an instant boner killer. Never again, Nova Skye." Reaching down he slaps my clit and I half squeal half moan. "Got it?"

Breathlessly, I whisper, "Yes. Rhys Alexander."

Groaning at my words, he pulls back to the tip and then slams his hips forward. "Say it again, little star. Keep saying it til we both cum."

Moaning, we get into a rhythm. I scream his name and he

thrusts hard and fast. After only 4 rounds of this, I can feel the tingling start from my toes working their way up. "I'm close, Rhys, I'm so close."

He thrusts faster and brings his hand down to rub my clit. "Keep going, Nova, keep saying my name."

I scratch my nails down his chest and say his name, almost like a chant, "Rhys, Rhys, Rhys."

On the third one, he slams in and grinds his hips in a circle, shouting, "NOW!"

We both cum at the same time and I try to keep my focus the best I can so I don't miss him cumming this time. I feel his cock shooting burst after burst of cum in me. The feeling makes my orgasm extend. We're both shaking, sweating and panting. He wraps his arms behind my shoulders and flips us so I'm on top of him, both of us passing out.

After waking up, we got ready and headed towards the Mt. Emily trails to meet up with Dorian. We promised him we would hang out up there for the day. When we pull into the parking area, we see that he's already there. This is the first time I'm seeing the car he talked about yesterday, it definitely seems fitting for him. Turning to Rhys I ask, "Uh, what kind of car is that? Other than it being… beige-ish… and screaming, I belong to Dorian Alden, I have no idea what it is."

"Yeah, that car was definitely meant for him. It's a '79 Mercedes Benz Station Wagon," he smiles. Humming at his response, I unbuckle and hop out of his truck. Dorian looks over and gets out of his car when he sees us. The corner of his mouth twitches up in a smirk and from the other side of the truck, Rhys clears his throat, "Don't."

Dorian lifts his hands in surrender and laughs a little, "I swear I won't say it again. Lesson learned from the last time. I will say this though," after taking a dramatic bow, he stands, placing his hand over his chest, "I'm much obliged that you both have graced me with your presence… at long last."

Curling my lips in an attempt to keep my laugh in, I shake in silent laughter. I see Rhys rounding the front of his truck rolling his eyes and flipping him off. He starts making funny faces and mimicking sounds, "I would be much obliged if you fucked right off, fat head." Unable to hold my laughter any longer, I lean forward grasping my knees and laugh hysterically. I can hardly breathe and tears are streaming down my face from laughing so hard.

I feel my hands swiped off my knees and in one swift motion, I'm up in the air and over Rhys' shoulder. "Ahhhh! What the fuck, Rhys!" Leaning down, I smack his ass like a drum. In response he smacks my ass harder and squeezes.

"Quit egging him on, Nova Skye."

Letting out a raspberry, I salute the ground as if he can see me, "Sir, yes, sir, Rhys Alexander, sir." My smartass remark earns me another swat to the ass and I laugh in return.

"Keep it up, little star. Please, I beg of you, keep it up. I'll tell Dorian to go ahead of us and fuck you over the hood of my truck."

Biting my lip at the image that pops in my head, I tell him, "I don't think that's the threat you think it is."

Dorian's feet come into view and I look up the best I can. "Uh guys, can we please hang out for a little bit before you get back to your mating rituals?" Rhys grabs my hips and starts pulling me back, and slowly sliding down his body, he groans.

As soon as my feet hit the ground, I wink and twist out of his hold, skipping over to Dorian and looping my arm through his. From behind me, Rhys sighs out and whines, "Dude, you can't just steal my girl, Dori."

Looking over my shoulder I fake pout at his pathetic, pouty face. Dorian stops and turns us. "Technically, I didn't steal her, Reese's Pieces. She came to me. Sounds like a you problem, brother." At that, we turn around and walk down the trail. After walking for a bit, Dorian takes a left off of the trail.

Scrunching my face in confusion, "Uhh, Dor? We're not on the trail anymore. Where are we going? Wait, wait, don't tell me. This is where you guys take me to murder me and dump my body for seeing and hearing far too much, right? Right?" I put on a fake scared face and hold my palms to my face, and quote *Scream*. "No, please don't kill me, Mr. Ghostface, I wanna be in the sequel."

Rhys smacks my ass and laughs as he walks by, "Alright, Scream Queen, let's go."

Dorian nods his head and slightly pulls me with him. There's an opening through the trees and as we walk through, there's a huge, open field. "We come here a lot to hang out and smoke, sometimes we'll camp too. Technically we're not supposed to, but we're cool with the park rangers. As long as we don't fuck anything up, we're allowed to come here whenever we want."

Looking around amazed by the view, I look up at Dorian and tell him, "That's so fucking cool. This place is beautiful." As we get closer to where Rhys is standing, I see that there's a fire pit with a few stumps around the pit, making perfect chairs, and a fallen log that could be used as a bench seat. Dorian reaches into his black cargo pants pocket and pulls out a rainbow Bluetooth speaker, which he places on one of the stumps. Before starting a song, he pulls his tin and a pack of banana daiquiri *Swisher Sweets* out of his other pocket.

"Damn, Dor, those pants really do come in handy. What else you got hiding in those pants?"

Putting my hand to my mouth and laughing when I realize what I just asked, Dorian looks up at me and smiles, "You're lucky you're like family, or I could give a completely different answer."

Rhys growls, walking up behind me and wrapping his arms over my stomach, pulling me back as much as he can to his chest. Leaning my head back against his shoulder, I tilt towards him and look up. I slowly caress the side of his face, lifting on my toes and kissing his jaw. "Simmer down, ghoulie."

Bringing his mouth to my ear he lets out a low growl, "Your ghoulie."

When we walk back to the log, I see that Dorian has a bundle of flowers. He plops down on the log to begin twisting the flowers together into what looks like a flower crown. Rhys sways us back and forth, humming in my ear while we watch Dorian make crowns. Listening to him hum makes this moment so much more peaceful.

When Dorian finishes with the second crown he looks over at me, holds it out and smiles. "For you, Queen SuperNova."

I take the crown and place it on my head, and with a curtsy I respond, "Why, thank you, Prince Dor." He puts his own crown on, then focuses on the tin and *Swisher Sweets* in front of him. After rolling, he lights the blunt and takes a deep inhale.

Holding it out to us, he wheezes, "Watch it, it hits hard." Rhys brings the blunt to his lips and breathes in deep. I reach for the blunt but he holds it out of reach and grips my chin tilting my face up to his and exhales the smoke into my mouth. We pass the smoke back and forth until I take a particularly big hit. I look over to Rhys and he brings his lips down to mine, as I slowly exhale the smoke into his mouth. After blowing the smoke out, he tells me, "I've decided that's the only way I want to smoke from now on, little star."

The high is already hitting because I giggle at his words, and then clap my hand over my mouth as if it will hold the giggles in. When I see him smile at my giggles, I look between him and Dorian, pointing at both of them. "Do. Not. Make. Fun. Of. Me."

Dorian holds his hands up and turns away, starting the music. Rhys leans down and whispers in my ear, "I'm not making fun of you, baby. Just thinking how cute you are, that's all."

Letting out a pathetic growl, I reach over my shoulder and swat him, "I'm not cute."

Kissing me behind the ear, he mumbles, "You are, sweetheart."

The first song starts playing and my eyes light up when I hear *Stolen Dance* by *Milky Chance*. Pulling out of Rhys' arms, I spin around in a circle smiling. I throw my arms up in the air and shout to the sky, "I love this song!" I start dancing in place and thrust grabby hands towards Dorian, "Come on, Prince Dor, dance with the queen."

He walks over and grabs my left hand, placing his other hand on my right shoulder. While the song blares in the background, we dramatically dance around together. Dorian pushes me out into a spin and brings me back to dance and jump in place. We're laughing the whole time and I look over at Rhys who has a huge grin on his face. Shouting over to him, "Come on, King Rhys, dance with us!"

Shaking his head, he tells me, "Sorry, my Queen, this King doesn't dance."

Bringing my hands to my hips and cocking my hip out, I glare at him, "Your Queen has requested a dance. Do you wish to deny me?"

He laughs and slowly walks towards me to take a bow. As he stands, he puts his hand over his heart, "My apologies, my beloved Queen. Please, do me the honor of dancing with me."

"YAY!" I shout, jumping triumphantly with my arms in the air. Running the remaining distance to him, I jump and wrap my arms and legs around him. Rhys catches me easily and holds me tight to him. Nuzzling into his neck, he sways us back and forth. I drop kisses on his neck and move my head back so I can face him, "Thank you, ghoulie." Confusion clouds his eyes as he looks at me, a question about to spill but I cut him off by placing my finger over his lips. "Thank you for showing me that I can really be happy." I peck his lips but when I go to pull back, he grasps the back of my head to deepen the kiss. His tongue slides along my bottom lip, making me open my mouth enough to let his tongue slide in. Flicking and sliding his tongue around my mouth, it's as if he needs to taste every inch of my mouth.

Groaning, he pulls back from the kiss. "You're trouble, Queen Nova." "So are you, King Rhys," I whisper.

"Real friends are the ones you can count on no matter what. The ones who go into the forest to find you and bring you home. And real friends never have to tell you that they're your friends." ~Mindy Kaling

CHAPTER 11
HEATHENS

Rhys

Nova and I have been inseparable for the last week, and I wouldn't have it any other way. She's joined me everyday at work while we pinpoint exactly where Frankie is. You would think in such a small town he wouldn't be able to hide so well, but somehow the little rat has found a great sewer to hide in. The longer it takes to find him, the more frustrated I get.

Thank fuck for Nova, she's been keeping me in check, without her I'm sure I'd be going off the rails. We only left the warehouse a few hours ago, but I'm ready to get back and continue the hunt. Looking down at Nova sprawled across my chest, I groan. I'm already hard just staring at her. Fuck, she's beautiful. Slowly sliding out from under her, I slip out of the bed and head to the bathroom. I turn the water on and hop in before it's even warmed up.The freezing water makes me jolt, but I brace my hands against the wall and let the water sluice over my body I begin running the mission through my head and everything we've found so far, hoping an answer will magically pop up in my head. We need to find this fucker and take him down. Hearing about the nightmares Nova has about him is nothing compared to actually witnessing it. Every night this week I've had to approach her like a timid animal and bring her back from the darkness. Even when everything clicks that it's me in front of her, I still have to talk to her and make sure everything is okay.

I feel her before I see her and lift my head looking over my shoulder. She steps into the shower, looking at me with wide eyes and biting her lip. I fully turn towards her and open my arms, "Come here, little star."

She walks towards me and wraps her arms around my middle and places her chin on my chest. Bringing my palms to either side of her face, I rub my thumbs under her eyes, as if it will erase the deep, dark circles there. Dropping my head, I place a quick kiss on her lips, once, twice. She whimpers at the loss and I smile, "What are you doing awake, sweetheart?"

Giving a half shrug and a sad smile, she says, "Just knew you weren't with me anymore and woke up. I was trying to surprise you, but you caught me." She gives me a mock glare with the words and my smile grows.

"Apologies, I promise to pretend I have no idea you're here next time." Her mock glare becomes a real one and she lifts on her toes and bites my chin. Wincing at the small bite of pain there, I remove my hands from her face and grip her hip with my left and swat her ass with my right. The sound ricochets off the walls along with her yelp.

"Dammit, Rhys!"

Gripping her cheek, I slowly release and rub circles to soothe the sting. In a high pitched, mocking voice I make a goofy face and say, "Dammit, Nova!"

She brings her hand up and slaps my chest. I hold on to the back of her hand that's over my chest and drag it over to my heart. The movement immediately softens her and she smiles at me, shaking her head. Being this close to her and playing around has obviously brought my cock back to life, which she notices immediately. Looking down, she laughs and says, "Good morning to you too."

I start laughing at her words, but my laugh turns into a choked groan with her hand slowly stroking my cock. She looks up at me, mischief blazing through her eyes. "We both have to go to work, ghoulie, so this is going to be fast. Okay?"

Apparently, her taking control has completely stolen my ability to talk so I just nod my head. She stops stroking and removes her hand, shaking her head. A shocked look comes across my face and I look down at my cock and back up to her, "W-wha-" she cuts me off with a serious look on her face.

"Words, Rhys, I need your words."

My cock pulses hard at her words. Well, this is new. Who knew I liked this so much? Nodding my head slowly, I clear my throat, "Y-yes."

She smiles up at me and gives me a quick kiss, once again grabbing my cock and stroking it. Gripping her hip, I place my other hand on the wall bracing myself. On the upstroke, she swipes her thumb over my pre-cum filled slit and I groan again, thrusting my hips towards her. "Fuck, you're doing so good, sweetheart."

At my praise, she pumps my cock faster, her grip gets a little tighter and on every upstroke she twists her wrist. My grip on her hip gets tighter and my hips keep thrusting up. It's as if I've lost control of my body. While stroking still, she pushes me back until I've hit the wall under the shower head. Dropping to her knees, she licks my slit and then shoves my cock down her throat in one swift motion.

"Oh fuck. Oh shit. Jesus, Nova."

I feel her lips turn into a smile around my cock. Grabbing my hips to hold my cock down her throat, she gently bobs her head. She caresses her fingers down my hip, my thigh and then reaches down and grabs a hold of my balls, slowly rubbing and rolling them around. I can feel the tingle up my spine and know that I'm close. Her hand lifts it up, shaking it around on top of her tongue. I grab a hold of her hand and she pulls mine down, placing it on top of her head. She grips the top of my hand, letting me know she wants me to grab on. Getting a good grip on her hair, I pull and she moans, the vibrations hitting my cock just right. "Oh fuck, fuck, I'm so close, little star. Fuck, please don't stop."

She bobs up and down, keeping as much of my cock down her throat as she can while still moaning on my cock. She starts pulling back, running her barbell against the vein on my cock. With just the head in her mouth, she licks around the crown and sucks harder. She places her hand on my cock and does a quick twist stroke, sucking as hard as she can, and it's my undoing. "Fuck, fuck, fuuuuuuuuuck."

Shot after shot of cum hits her tongue and the back of her throat. She sucks on my cock like a fucking straw, trying to get every last drop out. Sagging against the wall, she slowly pulls back, looks up at me and sticks her tongue out showing me my cum and then swallows it. "Fuck, that's hot. I fucking love when you do that." A knowing smile pops up on her face and she slowly starts to get up. I grip her under her arms and pull her the rest of the way up, kissing her hard. Refusing to move our mouths away, I speak against her lips, "We have to go, sweetheart."

Whispering back she says, "I know."

————⋆

Taking Nova to *Swan & Scribe,* I walk her in and bring her to the front desk where Vanessa is. She smiles up at us, "Well, hello there." She looks over to Nova with a smirk on her face to which Nova blushes and laughs, "Shut the fuck up, V."

I lean down and kiss Nova on the temple, "I'll see you in a little bit. Miss you already."

"You too, be safe."

I look over to Vanessa, but before I can say a word, she holds up her hand. "I know, I will keep an eye on her. I'll call if necessary, promise."

Tapping the countertop twice, I tell her, "Thank you." Turning towards Nova, I kiss her again and walk away.

Pulling up to *Vega Altair*, I park my truck and head straight to the conference room. When I walk in, I see everyone already there scoping out as much surveillance of the town as they can. Walking up to Dorian, he looks over at me with a giddy expression on his face and practically vibrating in place. "What's up, Dorian? You find something?"

Nodding his head frantically, he points to the screens. "I think so, I can feel it, Rhys. Today is the day. He was doing so well at sneaking around. Until now. I think he got too comfortable and slipped up."

Pointing to one of the squares, there's a view of the *End of the Road Motel*. "Wait, he went to the same place we picked up Davide? Do you think it's a trap, or just stupidity?"

Dorian rubs his chin and squints at the screen. "Honestly, I think it's stupidity. I mean, you know what they say. Never get high on your own supply, and he definitely gets high on his own supply, constantly. I don't think he's all there anymore."

"Makes sense, anything show him visiting anybody else from *Amissa Stella*?"

Dorian's face gets serious and he takes a deep breath. "I fucked up and didn't even know it, Rhys. I came back here after a shift there, and that motherfucker was right fucking there!"

Whipping my head over in his direction, I ask, "Wait, what do you mean?"

Rubbing his Baphomet tattoo, he lets out a shuddered breath, "His vehicle. I didn't know it at the time, but after watching surveillance I saw the vehicle he was driving. Come to find out the exact same one was parked at *Amissa Stella*. Fuck. I'm sorry, brother. If I had known, you know I would've called you immediately. I just put all this together before you walked in."

Clapping my hand on his shoulder, I give him a little shake. "Hey, it's fine. You have an eye on him now, keep watching, I'm gonna go get all my stuff ready." Walking to the door, I swivel around, "Hey, can one of you get a hold of Vanessa and give her the 911 message to get her and Nova here ASAP?"

A chorus of "Yeah's" echoes around the room.

"Thanks," I shout over my shoulder as I turn around to head to the armory. Filling my duffel with every possible weapon I could fit in it, I zip it up and walk over to the armor wall to grab my vest and boots. After getting the vest strapped and boots laced, I grab the duffel and head to my playroom. Looking around the room, I rack my brain on what else could possibly be helpful to Nova in here. Pulling my phone out, I call Dorian, "What's up, Rhys?"

"Hey man, I'm just wrapping up in the playroom here. Can you grab a Fentanyl syringe for me? I wanna debrief as quickly as possible with everyone and then go pick him up. I can't risk seeing Nova beforehand, I need to keep focus, ya know?"

"Yeah, yeah, of course. I'll go grab it now."

Just before I leave, I realize I need to throw the Bluetooth speaker on the charger. Torture without music is a total buzzkill, can't have that. When I enter the conference room, I'm happy to see everyone is ready to go. With the way they look right now, The Horde is such a fitting name for them. It's as if they're ready for war. Soon, very soon.

Adrenaline pumping through me makes it impossible to sit still. I pace the room while I smoke. Dorian looks like a mad scientist right now, his hair is all over the place, probably running his fingers through it over and over. He claps his hands once and rubs them together. "Alright, we all know the plan? Same as last time. Rhys goes in first, I'll pull in across the street next, and then you guys will slowly go through the parking lot and head to the back side. Ha, back side." Clearing his throat he shakes his head, "Sorry, wrong time. Anyways, stick to the plan. We all know our call names and signals." Spinning in a dramatic circle, he then points to the door, "THUNDERCATS ARE GO!"

Everyone laughs and shakes their heads. As I walk behind Dorian, he suddenly turns around, making me step back, "Down boy. What's up?"

He reaches into his pocket and pulls out his hand out to flip me off, "Fuck you. Also," he then reaches in his other pocket and pulls out the black case, "the sleepy poke you asked for."

Laughing, I lift my hand to poke him in the forehead when the lights shut off and turn back on flashing red. A loud, automated voice repeats, "S - O - S," on a loop.

I look around to see everyone scrambling around. "Dorian, what the fuck is going on? I don't even know about that alarm, what the fuck is that?!"

Dorian rubs his Baphomet, and his eyes are a mix of rage and sorrow. Walking around me, he shouts, "Somebody shut the alarm down, we need to get V on the phone right now!"

At the mention of V, I immediately think of Nova and freeze.

Has something happened to her?

Has time stopped?

Has my breathing stopped?

My heart?

My brain?

My vision?

Searing pain to my cheek and the shock of freezing water has me snapping out of it. Gasping for air, I blink my eyes rapidly, clearing the blurred vision. Shaking my head, I look down and realize I'm on my knees. Looking up in confusion, I find Dorian standing over me. "I'm sorry, but you were losing your shit, and we need your help. *Nova* needs your help." Nodding his head towards the screens, he says, "Come on, we have V on the phone letting us know what happened."

When I reach the table, I grip the edge so tight my knuckles are white. V sounds panicked and dazed. "I-I uh, I'm not sure how long I've been out for. You're going to have to go back at least an hour on the traffic cam footage. The piece of shit walked into the store and I watched Nova turn white as a ghost. He walked right up to the counter with his stupid, smug face. He said all these fucked up things to her, and that if she didn't go with him, then he would kill everyone in the store. She walked out with him and I followed. I tried to stop him, I swear. I jumped on his back and tried digging my fingers in his eyes and scratching his face. He started thrashing around and tossed me off of him. I tried to get back up, but he pointed his gun at me and said if I moved then he would shoot Nova right there. I held my hands up, but he kicked me in the head. When I came to, I sent the SOS right away. I'm sorry, I'm so sorry. Fuck. Harp, can you please come pick me up? I need to be able to help you guys. I can't just wait here and not know what's going on."

Jade jumps up and grabs her things, shouting towards the phone, "I'm on my way, hunny. Go sit down inside."

Trying to focus is proving difficult. "Brother, please," I croak, pleading with Dorian.

"I know. I know, man. I'm trying, I'm looking right now." Looking up at the screen, I see he's rolling through the footage as quickly as he can. Within seconds, I see the doors of *Swan & Scribe* burst open. That piece of shit is shoving Nova. He's fucking touching her.

"THERE!"

We watch as the scene unfolds exactly as V said. My blood is boiling and I can hear my heart pounding in my ears. This motherfucker will die. Shoving my shaking hand into my pocket, I grab my smokes and lighter. Once lit, I blow the smoke in the air and tell everyone, "Listen, I'm hopping in Beauty. Somebody call me and keep me posted on which direction to go. I refuse to fucking waste time and sit here."

Dorian opens his mouth, and I'm sure it's just to argue what I said. Holding my hand up, I shake my head, "No, don't even say it. It is a fucking waste of time to sit here and wait for you to pinpoint their location. If I'm already on the road, it's that much sooner I can get to her. You guys may think you know what he put her through, but you have no fucking clue. I can't let him put her through that again. I'm outta here."

. . .

166

Running to the playroom, I grab my duffel and toss it over my shoulder. As I'm running out to my truck, *Teenage Dirtbag* starts playing. Dorian starts speaking immediately, "He's on the back roads! I'm pretty sure he's heading to the trails! Go, go, go!" Tossing my cigarette out, I hop in my truck and throw my phone on the seat. I peel out and head out of the parking lot. Speeding over to the back roads, I shout, "Dorian, tell The Horde to start calling in distractions, I can't be followed for this!"

In the background I can hear numerous voices shout, "ON IT!" *Fuck, I really hope the deer aren't on the road right now, I do not have time for Bambi's bullshit.*

"Wait, what the fuck?!"

"What?! What do you mean, what the fuck, Dorian?! What's going on?!"

"Don't go the second set of trails, I think he's going up the ATV ones instead. Be careful on that turn!"

"I KNOW WHAT I'M DOING, DORIAN! DAMMIT!" Punching the steering wheel, I gun it towards the first turn.

"Rhys, I can't help you past that point. The last set of cameras are right by that turn. The best I can do is tell you if he hits that turn or follows the curve."

"Yeah, man, I know. I'm going as fast as I can. I'm almost there, what do you see?"

In a low voice I can hear Dorian repeating himself, "Come on, come on, come on. Make the turn, make the- HE TOOK THE TURN! Any second now I'm going to lose visual, the good news is he's not used to the trails like us. He might not realize how long it takes to climb up that hill. Call us if you need us. Bring our SuperNova back."

"You know I fuckin' will."

Hearing the phone beep with the end of the call, I zero in on my target. As soon as I'm down this hill, it's damn near a straight shot. A drop of sweat lands in my eye and I blink it away the best I can, "Son of a bitch!" The turn comes up and I quickly scan for oncoming traffic, punching the gas and making the turn. My tires squeal, dust and smoke flying behind me.

Slightly fishtailing, I correct it and push forward. "I'm almost there, little star. Just hold on a little longer."

Remembering I can't take this kill from her, I check my glove box for the tranquilizing gun. I swipe around the paperwork and napkins in there while keeping my eye on the road. Feeling metal touch my fingertips, I grip it and pull it out. Bingo. Approaching the big hill that leads to the ATV trails, I pop the truck in 4-LO. As I get higher, I scan the area and I don't see anything at first. I'm not sure why, but my gut is screaming at me to look back in a hidden area where people go for target practice. Making sure I'm as far from the cliffside as I can get, I whip my head to the right and check. Catching sight of a car, I yank the wheel to the right, kicking gravel everywhere. Not the best surprise entrance, but it's the best I can do.

Slamming on my brakes behind the parked car, I grab the tranq gun and hop out. I walk around the old Monte Carlo, and the sight that greets me has me seeing fucking red. Frankie has his arm around her neck in a chokehold with a gun held to her temple. She has a black eye already forming and her lip and nose are bleeding. The tears are running down her face, mixing with dust and blood.

He looks up at me and laughs maniacally, "Well, well, well. You must have spread your legs a lot for this one. Exactly how many times did you let him stick his cock anywhere he wanted for him to actually show up here for you?"

Gritting my teeth, I tell him, "Shut. The. Fuck. Up. Let her fucking go. You think you're some sort of badass putting your hands all over her? Why don't you step to me, bitch."

She flinches when he pushes the gun further against her temple. "Looks like I," tapping her head harder with each word, "taught. You. Well."

Silent tears continue falling down her face, all life drained from her eyes. She's checked out. *I never want to see her like this again.* "NOVA! I need you with me." *Come on, little star. I need you out of the way for this.*

"Hate to break it to ya, hero, but she's not here right now.

There's no getting through to her when she's like this. Believe me, if beating her didn't break her of the habit, shouting definitely won't work."

Ignoring him, I crouch down to try and meet her eyes. I take a deep breath and try one more time. "I know you're somewhere in there, little star." At the endearment, the fog starts to lift from her eyes and she blinks once. My voice cracks as I try one last thing, "This life…"

She lets out a breathy whisper, "…and the next." Blinking her eyes rapidly, she looks up and sees me. A voice filled with wonder and emotion she says, "You're here."

"Always, little star."

"Wow, you are a damn good actor, man. I almost believe you *actually* care about this slut. Impressive."

I zero in on his movements, noticing he's about to make a huge mistake for himself. He brings the gun away from her temple and brings his hand to the gun over and over in applause, "Bravo!" Nova notices the movement and immediately dives to the left. His eyes flick to where she dove, "Wha-"

Taking advantage of the opening, I lift the tranq gun and shoot a dart in his neck. "Bullseye, bitch." Luckily the sedative is fast acting, his words are cut off and his eyes roll to the back of his head as he falls backwards. Running towards Nova, I drop to my knees sliding across the gravel and grab a hold of her.

Wrapping her arms around my neck as tight as she can, she sobs against my neck, "I love you, fuck, I love you, I love you, I love you. Thank you."

I've always heard that you find perfection in the imperfect moments, and this is the perfect example of that. This isn't some chick flick where it happens during some cheesy moment. No, this is real, and this is fucking ours. I thought I felt peace and comfort because of her before, but right here, right now, I could die a happy man just from hearing those three words. Slightly pulling back from her, I place my palms on either side of her face. I kiss her tears away, and between each kiss tell her, "I love you, fuck, I love you, I love you, I love you."

Through a half sob, half laugh she says, " You can't just steal my words, ghoulie, you're supposed to say it your own way."

Looking in her beautiful eyes, I whisper, "No, it just means that we love each other the exact same. We won't ever have to wonder if we love the other more, we'll just know that it's the same. Our love will keep growing and we'll be side by side through it all. This life..."

Sniffling, she smiles and says, "and the next."

"Your friends will always have your back no matter how badly things may go." ~Unknown

CHAPTER 12
I WILL FOLLOW YOU INTO THE DARK

NOVA

After Rhys picked me up and sat me in his truck, he loaded Frankie in the back and we headed back to the warehouse. Throughout the whole drive I was glued to his side, neither of us wanting to be separated from the other. The moment we backed into the warehouse, everybody was already there ready to greet us. All the girls took me to the kitchen and cleaned up the blood from my nose and lip. V stayed in the background, probably beating herself up over how things went down. When this weight is lifted, I know we'll have to talk about everything.

As I head into the playroom, I grasp the doorknob and freeze. *You can do this, Nova. It's almost over.* Taking a deep breath, I twist the knob while keeping my head down. Walking in, I turn to shut the door and lock it. Bracing my forehead against the door, I breathe in through my mouth and out through my nose. I turn around and see Rhys watching me. "Are you ready, little star?"

Wiping my sweaty palms against my pants, I force myself to move my feet. As soon as I'm next to Rhys, I see that Frankie is strapped to the chair with duct tape. *Oh fuck. That's not enough.* *He's going to get out. What if he hurts Rhys? He'll make me watch.* *Just like he always said. Make me watch and then rape, torture and kill* *me. I can't breathe.*

"Shh, shh. I'm right here. He can't hurt you ever again. I'm right here, little star. Just breathe for me." The haze is lifting, I can feel his body wrapped around me and I grip the back of his shirt. Twisting it around and digging my hands into his back I pull him against me as much as I can. I can smell his cologne, which slowly makes me calm down. I melt against him as he rubs the back of my head. "There you are, sweetheart. You're doing so good, keep breathing for me. We'll do this at your pace. However you want to do it, okay?" Nodding against his shoulder, I pull back and look up at him. His hands wipe away the tears I didn't know were falling.

I slowly exhale a shaky breath and assure him, "I'm okay. I'm ready."

Nodding his head, he smiles at me, "Is he secure enough for you, or would you like to add more restraints?"

I look over at Frankie and notice the straps around his wrists and ankles, "I… I think he needs more. He's really strong, Rhys. I don't want him to get out."

He turns my chin towards him, "Hey. I can add more, okay? He won't get out of them, I promise." Grabbing a chain and padlock from the table, he walks over to Frankie and wraps the chain around his arms and chest, locking it in place behind his back. Another chain and padlock are wrapped around Frankie's legs multiple times and locked in place. Standing up, he turns to me, "Good?"

I give him a small smile, "Yeah, thank you."

"Anything for you, little star. Tell me where you want me and when you're ready to start, okay?" he says after giving me a slow kiss. I immediately know I need him by me through the whole thing. I turn the volume down on the music a little bit. The music is definitely needed, but I can't have it blasting when I try to tell Frankie everything I need to get off of my chest.

Putting my phone down on the table, I look over at Rhys and hold my arms open. He walks over and embraces me.

"I need you close, is that okay?"

He rubs soothing circles on my back, "Of course that's okay, sweetheart. Whatever you need."

Levitate by Sleep Token begins playing and the calm I needed in this moment washes over me. Raising up on my toes I give Rhys three quick kisses and gently push on his chest. He steps back and moves aside, giving me the space I need to move around. Taking a deep breath to steel myself, I step up to the hanging hose and reach up to pull it down. Holding it with two hands, I aim it at Frankie's face and squeeze the lever spraying him with the water. At first nothing happens, and I look over my shoulder to Rhys, confusion etched on my face. Hearing a choked gasp, I whip my head around, startled. Frankie's shaking his head around, choking and spluttering on the water.

"W-what," cough, "the fuck," cough, cough. Releasing the nozzle, I let go of the hose. I wait for him to register what's going on. He looks up and his eyes narrow, gritting his teeth, "Well, well, well. If it isn't my cum-guzzling gutter slut." Nodding behind me, "Tell me, Nova, how many times did he have to force himself to fuck you, so you could get the help you needed?"

Rhys steps forward and I hold my hand up stopping him. I look over my shoulder and mouth, "Thank you." Turning back to Frankie I say, "Jokes on you, Frankie. He was already coming after you long before we met. Now that he knows of our history, it was just added motivation for him to take you down. I always knew you were a piece of shit, but I had no clue about all the other shit you were up to though. There's so much I need to say to you, but honestly, I don't even know where to begin."

Letting out a deep, demonic laugh he says, "Oh, Nova, Nova, Nova," moving the best he can but the restraints all clank around with his movements, "you realize how pathetic this is right? You need all these restraints and some pussy-whipped motherfucker

173

to take me down. Typical Nova. Can't do a fucking thing on your own. What did I tell you? I told you that you would always be fucking worthless, and nobody would ever truly want you. This guy doesn't love you, you're just easy pussy to fuck. Not even great pussy, just easy."

Growling at his words, I lift my hand up and swiftly slap him across the face, screaming, "SHUT THE FUCK UP! JUST FUCKING SHUT UP!"

A drop of blood pools at the corner of his mouth and he licks it. "That all you got, Sweet Cheeks?"

Flinching at the nickname he gave me long ago, I feel my stomach turn. Fuck, don't throw up, Nova. "I'm not your Sweet Cheeks anymore, Frankie." Walking over to the table, I pick up a scalpel and watch the light reflect off of it. "Keep saying stupid shit, Frankie, and I'll cut your fucking tongue out. I don't need to hear a fucking thing you have to say. For once, you're going to fucking listen to me." Hovering the scalpel over his face, I glare down at him. "Remember, Frankie, if you cry like a little bitch I'll keep going until you stop. Your tears will just turn me on."

Tilting his head back as far as he can, "You fucking bitch! You better make it fucking count. I can't wait to keep my promise to you and fuck you with a knife until you fucking bleed out." Shoving the scalpel into his cheek, it punctures his skin. Blood drips down his face and he screams out. "Ah, fuck! You fucking bitch!"

Gliding the knife down his cheek, the blood continues pouring down. Rolling my eyes at him, "You always said I didn't listen, but honestly it's you who doesn't listen. I told you I would cut your tongue out if you didn't shut the fuck up." Looking back at Rhys, "Handsome, can you please light the blow torch and bring me a pair of pliers?"

His eyes light up and he nods, smiling at me. With the blow torch lit and pliers in his other hand, he walks up to me. I take the pliers and look at Frankie, "I already know what option you're going to pick, but it might be easier if you just stick your tongue out for me."

Rolling his lips in tightly, he shakes his head no. I click my tongue and shrug, "Okay then. Hard way it is." I jab the scalpel against his lips and the spot wells up with blood from the small hole it left behind. He opens his mouth wide, yelling from the pain and I take the opportunity to thrust the pliers in, clamping them around his tongue.

"Ah, ah, ut uh uck. Et ohhhhh!"

Gripping his tongue tighter, I pull it out further. "Aww, what was that? I can't understand you. Such a shame. Remember all the times you just didn't want to hear a fucking thing from me while you tortured me? How does it feel when it's the other way around?"

He attempts to talk again, and I tilt my head towards him. "Huh? What? Oh, I'm so sorry, I can't understand you." Gripping the scalpel tight, I bring it down against his tongue and saw away. The muscle begins splitting apart, blood pouring down his chin, a few spurts hitting my hand. Frankie screams and gurgles on the blood dripping down his throat. As I cut all the way through, I raise the scalpel and grip the tongue with the pliers, causing blood to drip down my hands and wrists. Looking at both, I smile and look back at him. Shaking the hand that holds his tongue towards his face, I tell him, "Now, if you keep up blabbing away, or attempting to, at least, I'll shove your tongue down your throat."

"Can you please torch his tongue to stop the bleeding?" I ask Rhys.

He steps forward and gives me a kiss, "Of course, little star."

Tossing the scalpel and the pliers holding his tongue on the table, I place my hands on the table and take a breath. Frankie screams again when Rhys cauterizes his tongue. The smell of burning flesh hits the air immediately and I crinkle my nose. As gross as the smell is, I can't stop thinking about how good this feels. Frankie gets to feel how I did every time he tortured me. I'm slaying my fucking demon, and apparently that's an aphrodisiac. A slow smile creeps up on my face as an idea forms. The perfect 'fuck you' to Frankie after all the fucked up things he would say to me every time he raped me.

Rhys walks up to the table and puts the torch down on the floor. I look at the table and then look up at him. He looks down at the table too and then at me, confusion written across his face. "What are you thinking, little star?"

Biting my lip, I look away from him. How the fuck do I tell him my plan? Will he be okay with it? A touch to my chin has me looking back to Rhys. He puts his thumb on my bottom lip and gently pulls it from my teeth. Before he pulls back, I flick my tongue and lick the tip of his thumb. His pupils dilate from the move, and he pushes his thumb closer to my mouth. I suck on the tip of it, gently nip at it and pull my head back.

"I need you. Would you… would you be mad if I asked you to fuck me right here, as a big fuck you to him?" I whisper.

He's quiet for a moment and I begin to worry, looking down in embarrassment. I start to step back but he lunges forward and grips my hips tight, "Whoa, where are you going?"

"I just thought that maybe you didn't want to. You didn't say anything."

Smiling at my words, "You short-circuited my brain for a moment there, sweetheart. I'm all caught up now. Where do you want me?"

Already knowing what I want, I grab the table and turn it so it faces Frankie horizontally. I then pull it back so the end of the table is front and center. Pushing some of the weapons back and out of my way, I slowly turn and lean against the table.

Rhys walks up to me, caressing my cheek with the back of his fingers. "Just like this, little star?"

I nod my head and give him a come hither motion with my finger. When he leans down, I bring my mouth to his ear and whisper, "I was going to bend over, but if I do that he's going to think that you can't stand looking at me while we fuck."

His eyes darken and he literally fucking growls at my words. Oh. I thought I was wet before, but I'm fucking soaked now. With a smirk, he leans down and effortlessly lifts me by the hips, placing me on the table. "If you keep throwing me around like that, I'm going to get used to it and expect it all the time."

In a husky voice, he whispers, "Good."

Letting go of my hips, he grabs the hem of my shirt and slowly lifts it off of me. Frankie grumbles loudly, attempting to talk and shout but no longer able to. Cupping both of my breasts, Rhys squeezes them and leans down, kissing the mounds. He mouths my right nipple through the bra and it starts to pebble. Gripping the top, he slowly pulls the cup down until my breast falls out. He licks across my nipple and blows against it, the sensation pebbling it further and I push my chest towards him, needing more. Sucking my nipple into his mouth, he flicks his tongue around. I hold him in place by the back of his head as he sucks and licks my nipple. Releasing it with a pop , he pulls the other cup down to give my breast the same attention as the other one. Reaching behind me, I unclasp my bra and slide the straps off of my arms, tossing it to the floor. He releases my nipple and kisses up my chest and the side of my neck, goose-bumps pebbling my skin along the way. He flicks my earlobe with his tongue, sucking it into his mouth before nipping the skin behind my ear. He tells me, loud enough for Frankie to hear, "You're so fucking beautiful, little star. I need to be inside you now."

Moaning at his words, I whisper, "Please."

He reaches over his head behind him to grab his shirt and tear it over his head while he kicks off his boots. I unbutton and unzip my pants and Rhys steps forward with his pants undone, hanging off of his hips. Wrapping his fingers around the top of my jeans and panties, he slides them down. Putting my hands against the table, I lift my ass so he can rip them off along with my shoes. Standing up, he grabs his pants and underwear and pulls them down to the middle of his thighs. Walking back to the table, he grips my thighs and pulls them apart. Bringing his hands to the back of each thigh, he lifts me so I can wrap my legs around his hips. He brushes his fingers up my thighs, making me shiver at the sensation. His fingers run up until he reaches my hips and squeezes, pulling me towards him until my ass is at the very edge of the table. My body jolts, feeling as if I could fall off.

"Shh, shh. I got you, sweetheart. I'd never let you fall."

He reaches down to grip the base of his cock. I watch as he drags the head of his cock through my slit. Bringing his cock to my entrance, he pushes in so that only the head of his cock slides in.

"Grab my shoulders, sweetheart."

Throwing my hands on his shoulders, I grip tight. As soon as he feels my tight hold, he slams forward, gritting his teeth.

"Mmm, fuck," he growls.

At the same time I shout, "Ohhh."

Holding me as tight as he can, he puts his head down to my shoulder and thrusts fast and hard. The table is scooting back from the force and weapons are falling off the table with a clang to the floor. I grit my teeth to keep them from clacking together with every thrust. I pull him towards me and latch on to his lips. There's nothing sweet about this kiss, it's all teeth and tongues. Primal instincts have kicked in and we're fucking like animals. I feel his hand around my throat and a little squeeze. Our lips are just bouncing against each other now as he roughly tells me, "I need you to cum for me, little star," reaching down with his other hand he circles my clit, "cum for me. Right. Fucking. Now."

The moment he finishes his sentence, he pinches my clit and squeezes my throat, cutting off my air. All at once the tingle shoots up my body into a full on explosion and I shout, "Oh fuck!"

My vision goes black, and my whole body is trembling. I feel a gush between my legs. Oh, good, he's cumming too. When the orgasm slowly fades, I open my eyes. I notice that Rhys is looking down, so I follow his gaze and find him staring down at the soaking wet floor. Still looking down, he says, "That was the hottest fucking thing I've ever seen in my life." He slowly lifts his head and gives me a sexy smirk.

"What was hot?"

"You squirted all over my cock, and the floor, too, as you can see."

Letting out an embarrassing laugh, I say, "Umm, I'm glad you think it's so hot, or I would've died right here on the spot."

I hear a muffled grumble to the left of me and look over. I burst out laughing, "Holy shit! I completely forgot about him."

Grabbing Rhys' face I give him a loud, sloppy kiss. Hopping off of the table, I bend over and grab the hammer that fell. A smack to my ass makes me jump and yelp, "DAMMIT, RHYS!"

He laughs and I spin around while holding the hammer. I point it in his direction, giving him a mock glare, "Watch it, mister."

Turning back towards Frankie, I hold the hammer up and give it a shake. "I know it's not the same as the valve you hit me with, but it'll still hurt just as bad. At least I hope so." Circling around him, I bring the hammer back and swing it forward into his head. There's a slight crunching noise and a spurt of blood comes out. His head shoots forward and he screams. Walking in front of him, I tsk him, "Now, now. I seem to recall when you bashed my head in your exact words were, 'shut the fuck up and stop crying!' So, with that said. SHUT THE FUCK UP AND STOP CRYING!"

Bringing that memory up makes more flash before my eyes, like a horror movie of memories. Bashed in head, black eyes, busted lip, busted ears, being whipped with cords and hangers, raped continuously from him and random objects he would find. Getting angrier and angrier by the images, I lift the hammer and swing it down to his hand. The bones in his hand break as I smash it over and over, but it can't be heard over the sounds of both of us screaming. I step back and look down at his mangled hand, panting from the exertion. Turning away, I toss the hammer on the table and grab a knife and the pliers.

I walk back to Frankie and lean down to pull his basketball shorts down. Lifting the knife, I bring it down hard into his thigh. He screams from the pain, I'm too far gone to bother listening. Yanking the knife out, blood begins pouring from the wound. With the pliers, I grip his cock and stab his cock over and over. Blood drips and squirts, hitting my clothes and his thighs. After multiple stabs, it separates from him and I drop the pliers to the floor. Looking up, I see sweat pouring down his face and he's panting. "LOOK AT ME BITCH!"

Keeping his head down, he slightly shakes it. I place the knife under his chin and as I push up, he immediately brings his head up and glares at me. "I'm free of you. Your hold on me ends now." I thrust the knife forward into his stomach and twist it. Yanking it out, I look down at it and back to his bulging eyes. "I'll be the last thing you see before you die. You always said it would be the other way around." Moving closer, I look him dead in the eye to say, "I win bitch!" On the final word, I shove the knife through the side of his neck. Pushing so hard that it goes out through the other side of his neck. I continue staring into his eyes until I see him fade away and take his final breath. When I release the knife, it's as if I'm coming back to life. I gasp and stumble backwards.

I feel Rhys' arms around me instantly, holding me in place against him. "Hey, hey, hey. Are you okay, little star?"

Gripping tightly to his arms around me, I whisper, "I'm free."

"Do not just slay your demons; dissect them and find what they've been feeding on." ~Unknown

CHAPTER 13
JUST BREATHE

Nova

Opening the door to *Swan & Scribe*, I zero in on my target. First things first, I need to talk to V. I know she's beating herself up over the shit that went down with Frankie. The evidence is written all over her face when she looks up at the chime of the door, and her face goes from a bright and shining smile to one of total defeat. Quickly averting her eyes, she spins in circles, moving her hands around like she's trying to find something to do. Standing on the other side of the counter, I say, "Hey, V."

Without looking my way, in a quiet voice she says, "Hey, Nova girl."

Bringing my hands up I place them on top of the counter, "Listen, cut the shit."

At my words, she whips around, her curly hair bouncing with the motion and her eyes wide, "Excuse me?"

"You heard me, V. Cut the shit. I know you're sitting here blaming yourself over what happened with Frankie, but you need to stop. You know I suck at the whole comforting thing, and I'm just going to be blunt. If you wouldn't have listened to him, a lot of people would've died, including us." Bringing my right hand to my chest, I add, "I don't blame you. So, please, stop blaming yourself. It's making you withdraw and I think that's worse. You said you were really my friend, so be my friend and don't check out."

Her eyes fill with tears and she looks at my face, seeing the bruises that have darkened. Her face starts to crumple.

"Don't. This," waving my hand around my face, "is not your fault either. I'm gonna go sit with The Horde for a bit. Why don't you go take a look at some of the astronomy books you hid."

Narrowing her eyes she whispers, "How do you know about those?"

Rolling my eyes, I throw my hand up, "Don't act innocent, your acting skills aren't up to par."

Gasping, she whisper-shouts, "Rude!"

As soon as I sit down with The Horde I can feel all their eyes on me while I *attempt* to read my book. Rolling my eyes down at the book and letting out an exasperated sigh, I look up at all of them. Knew it. "Seriously, guys. I'm fine, so can you all just get back to your own shit and stop staring me down like I'm going to detonate at any moment?" Looking all of them in the eye while saying this, they still continue to look at me with concern. Closing my book, I set it down in front of me and narrow my eyes at them. "I could leave. I can't exactly enjoy my book with all of you attempting and failing at reading my mind. Listen to me. I am fine. I am fucking free. Do you know how amazing it feels to be able to just breathe?"

Muggz is the first to speak up, "Okay, babes. Just know, if that changes at any time we're here for you. You're doing great now, and I'm so happy to hear that, but it's like grieving in a way." I go to cut her off to disagree about grieving, but she puts her hand up to silence me. "I'm not saying that you are grieving him, but the emotions you go through will be exactly the same. There will be times of happiness and freedom you feel, but there will also be dark, depressing times that drag you down. Just, keep in mind that all of us are here for you."

I clear my throat and nod my head to her, "Thanks guys. Now, everyone get back to your own shit. I want to finish this book before Rhys picks me up."

I'm at the end of my book and I attempt to suppress the smile on my face when I feel Rhys here. It's a good thing I'm looking down at my book or I would look like a psycho to everyone. Fighting my smile is impossible, so my mouth is dancing between a frown and a smile. Kneeling down next to me, he throws his arm over the back of my chair and props his elbow on the table, laying his head on his hand. I lose the fight hiding my smile as he leans in close, brushing his lips against my ear. "How many times have you reread that sentence, little star?" His words aren't even seductive, yet my body reacts immediately. I barely suppress the shiver running through me. Taking a slow and stuttered breath, I close my book and slowly turn my head towards him. He refuses to move back so his lips graze my ear and across my cheek as I turn. Our faces are centimeters away and it's like we're both memorizing each other's faces. His eyes crinkle at the corners while delivering a heartstopping smile. This man will be the end of me, I know it.

Breathlessly, I whisper, "Hi, ghoulie"

Running the backs of his fingers down my cheek he responds, "Hi, sweetheart. You ready to get out of here?" I can see it in his eyes, he has the same questions as everyone else. He wants to give me the space to figure it out in my own head first, but I can see the battle within him to pull it out of me and mend it on his own. Nodding my head I put my book in my backpack and throw it over my shoulder. Before I have it all the way up my arm, Rhys is already sliding it off and throwing it over his shoulder. "I don't know why you even attempt it, little star, I'm going to take it every time."

He's still in my space, so I place my hands on his chest and lightly push. "Yeah, yeah, yeah. Move your ass, Casanova."

Putting his hand over his heart, he fake pouts, "You wound me, sweetheart."

Rolling my eyes at him, "Watch it, I haven't wounded you yet." A bloodied and screaming Frankie flashes before my eyes and I freeze. Knowing Rhys caught it, I clear my throat and paste on a fake smile, "Let's go, ghoul."

He stands there and searches my eyes, shifts his eyes to The Horde and back to me quickly. Nodding his head, he reaches a hand out to me and I take it. Interlacing our fingers, he squeezes my hand and I squeeze in return. Throwing up a peace sign with my right hand I say, "Peace out, bitches."

Walking up to Rhys' truck, he opens the door for me and helps me in. He slowly pulls the seatbelt across my chest and clicks it in place. Dragging his fingertips across my hip from one side to the other, he leans forward and kisses my temple. Holding his lips there I lean into the touch. Slowly withdrawing, he shuts my door and rounds his truck, hopping in on his side. Starting it up, he hands me his phone and says, "Fire it up, DJ Little Star." Scrolling through *Spotify*, I find the song *Follow You* by *Bring Me The Horizon* and click play. He reaches over and puts his hand on my thigh. As we head towards *Vega Altair*, he starts rubbing his thumb back and forth while singing along. I slide my head against the headrest in his direction to watch and listen to him while he sings. I can't stop the smile that forms even if I wanted to. As if the man isn't perfect enough in every way, he has a voice like honey. The kind of voice that even if you've never truly experienced what home is, you just know that it's where you are after the first note he blesses you with.

Rhys parks and turns off the truck, giving my thigh a double squeeze. Reaching down, I attempt to unbuckle my seatbelt when my hand is trapped beneath Rhys'. He shakes his head no at me and places my hand on my thigh. "Keep touching that buckle, or reach for that door and I'm gonna spank your ass, Nova Skye."

A blush rises on my cheeks and I bite my lip, nodding my head at him. He hops out of the truck and rounds the front. *Don't threaten me with a good time, Rhys Alexander.*

As soon as he gets close to my door, I swiftly unbuckle my seatbelt and pull the handle on the door pushing it open. I look up at Rhys, who looks stunned at first, but then his eyes darken and he smirks at me shaking his head. Yanking the door the rest of the way open, he steps into my space. He grabs my legs and quickly twists me until they're dangling between him and the truck. His hands slide up my legs until he grips my hips and pulls me down so I'm standing in front of him. Pinned between his very hard body (and I mean, everything is hard) and the truck, he spins me around until my back is pressed against his chest. I feel his breath fanning the side of my face as his lips brush my ear. "Just remember you were warned."

His hand falls between my shoulder blades and he pushes down. I bend over to lay my upper half on the passenger seat and turn my head to the side. Sliding his fingers down my spine I shiver from the anticipation. The hand gripping my hip slides up under my shirt with a barely there touch. The curtain of hair in front of my face flies out and back towards my face with every panted breath. He circles his hand over my ass and then the touch is gone, I tense up preparing for the strike. "Hands above your head, little star."

Bringing my hands over my head, I lay them on the seat in front of me. SMACK!

"Ungh, mmm." I bite my tongue to distract from the sting on my ass, and clench my thighs. My clit has its own heartbeat from the sensation. I'm not prepared for the second hit either. SMACK!

"Ungh, mmm, fuck." Rhys gives my ass a squeeze and the

sting slowly dissipates. He brushes his hips against my ass. I can feel his bulge, as if it's seeking my pussy out.

I push back against him making him groan, "Fuck, little star. That was meant to be your punishment, not mine." Gripping my hips, he thrusts his hard cock against my ass twice, circling his hips. *Teenage Dirtbag* starts playing on his phone and I feel the loss immediately when he pulls back. Pulling myself up, I slowly turn and face Rhys as he looks at his phone. He looks up at me with a grimace, "I swear to fuck, I'm changing his name in my phone to *Cockblock*."

Giggling at his words, I shake my head and put my hand to his chest. Bringing his hand up fast, he gently covers mine and holds it in place. The happy light in his eyes quickly fades and it morphs into the one I saw earlier, concern over my state of mind. Knowing I have to distract him away from it, I lean up on my toes and kiss him. Nodding my head towards the warehouse I tell him, "Come on, ghoulie. Cockblock is waiting."

He guffaws at the words and sighs, "You are something else, sweetheart. Let's go before he blows up my phone." Pulling me towards him, he shuts the door and we head inside.

When we walked into the conference room, Dorian is sitting down at the table with papers scattered all around. The screens are flickering through various camera angles and locations. Getting closer, I notice him looking at page after page as if they're just blank sheets of paper to toss aside. He doesn't seem to notice us, so Rhys clears his throat while simultaneously knocking on the table over the papers Dorian is reading. His head snaps up and he briefly looks at us unfocused and scrunching his brow. Blinking a few times apparently clears the fog and he smiles, "Oh hey! Good, good, you're here. Lots to talk about."

I look at Rhys to see if he finds this strange, and I notice that he's looking at Dorian with a blank face. *Okayyyy, apparently this is nothing new at all.* "Hey Dor, did you even see what was on all those papers you were flipping through? I've never seen anyone flip through pages so quickly."

As if a lightbulb goes off in his head, his eyes go wide and he says, "Ahhhh, yes, that. I have an eidetic memory and I can read-"

Cutting him off, Rhys steps in waving his hand in a stopping motion and a shake of his head, "He's a genius and reads very fast. You said you had something important, brother. If you dive into that talk with Nova now, we'll be here awhile."

With a bashful look, he gives a quick nod. I put my hand on his arm and he looks up at me. *He really has perfected this golden retriever puppy look, geesh.* "Hey Dor, when you guys don't have work to do, I would love to talk all about that big, beautiful brain of yours."

His eyes light up at my words and he gives me a big, dopey smile. Looking over at Rhys, I tell him, "You two play nice, I'm going to go pillage the fridge for my caffeine fix." As I turn to walk away, I feel his hand at my elbow pulling me back. Turning my head just in time, he swoops in and kisses me. As I pull back, he starts digging into my soul with his eyes again, so I turn away from him and head out of there.

Is it hot in here or what?

Grabbing my collar, I push and pull it quickly to create a whoosh of air to fan me. I head to the fridge and open it, scanning the contents until I see the badass glass bottles of *Coke*. I swipe one and hip-check the door shut. Placing the bottle on the counter, I start the scavenger hunt for a bottle opener. I go from drawer to drawer searching until I find the bottle opener in the back of one. EUREKA! I place it on the bottle cap and pop it off. With a hiss and a small burst of carbonation, I drop the cap on the counter and bring my hand down to put the opener back in the drawer. I lose my grip on the opener and it drops to the floor with a clatter. The noise immediately makes me freeze.

I'm no longer looking at a laminated kitchen floor, I'm

looking at concrete, with weapons littered across the floor. Clutching my chest and falling against the counter, I snap out of it from the bite of pain on my lower back when I smacked the counter.

I look around to make sure I wasn't caught this time. *Snap out of it, Nova. Just like you told everyone else, you're fine. You're fucking fine. You're being such a little-.*

Gasping at the direction my thoughts were going, I realize they weren't my own. I grab my Coke and start chugging it. I crave the burn it leaves behind from the carbonation. Pulling my smokes out of my pocket, I light one up, shoving the pack and lighter back in my pocket and start pacing the kitchen.

This is ridiculous.

I'm fucking fine.

My demon is gone, I can breathe again.

I'm fine.

My feet are moving all on their own and I'm led out of the kitchen and towards the armory. Finding myself in front of the door, I realize it wasn't the armory I was going to at all. Turning the knob, I slowly push the door open, as if the demon is back and ready to jump at me. I shut it behind me and press my back against the door. My own body is fighting itself, I feel myself being pulled further in the room, but another part of me is trying to push as hard as possible against the door. Taking a long drag of my smoke, I toss it to the floor and stomp it out. *Fuck it.* Pushing off of the door, I start walking towards the chair in the middle of the room. As I get closer, I notice the weapons still scattered around. The ones used are still covered in blood, matching the blood spilled and splashed across the concrete. The pungent smell of copper and urine still clings to the air, making me scrunch my nose.

Copper, copper, blood, blood, so much blood.

Why? Why is there- oh.

The events of that day speed through my mind.

Water, awake. Slap, blood. Scalpel, blood.

Blood, blood, blood.

188

Oh my god.

Oh fuck.

Pacing back and forth in front of the chair, I methodically snap the hair tie on my wrist. The sting of the continuous snapping against my skin barely registers. My breath is shaky, the panic rises quickly.

What did I do?

There's so much blood, I'm going to get caught. Fuck, we're going to get caught.

We're all done for.

I have to fix this.

Fix it. Fix it. Fix it.

Spinning on my heel, I scan the room for what I need.

Sink, yes, the sink. Rushing over to the sink, I look in the cupboards below and find various cleaning products and scrubbers. *Yes, perfect.*

Grabbing bleach and a scrubber brush, I start to turn towards the blood.

No, no, no.

I turn back and start piling all of the cleaning products in my arms. Kneeling down, I put everything on the floor, then crawl over to the weapons sprawled across the floor. After finding the duffel bag, I shove everything inside as quickly as possible and toss it on the table with a thud. The weapons already on the table make noise scraping across it. Grabbing those in handfuls and not caring that most of them are sharp, I start throwing everything in the bag as well.

Once it's all picked up, I heave the bag on my shoulder and take it to the sink. I jam in the sink plug and turn the hot water handle on full blast. With the duffle still on my shoulder, I grab handfuls of weapons and toss them in the sink.

I have to clean all of this.

I can't leave a fleck of blood anywhere.

I don't want to go down for this, but I really don't want everyone else in trouble for it.

Shaking my head frantically at the thought, I yank the strap off of my shoulder, tip it upside down and shake the remaining weapons out. I run back to the cleaners and grab the bleach, uncap it and dump it along the table, and the chair itself.

Dropping to my knees, the thud loud even in my ears, I grab the scrubber brush and scrub the floor in the area closest to me. Blood and bleach bubble up together, clinging to the brush, floor and my fingers. The area I'm scrubbing turns to a mix of red, pink and white.

"It's okay. Everything is fine. I'm fine. We're fine. You won't fucking win Frankie. You didn't take me out while alive, and you sure as fuck won't do it in death. Fuck you, fuck you, FUCK YOU!"

Scrubbing, scrubbing, scrubbing.

My lungs are burning from the bleach, but I don't care, this needs to be done.

I'll protect all of us. I can do that. I will do that.

Tossing the brush aside, I jump up and reach for the overhead hose, spraying the area I just scrubbed. Realizing I just touched the hose with my bloody hands, I look up at it.

Shit. I'll take care of that once everything else is clean, it's fine.

Just like everything else.

Fine, it's all fine.

Letting go of the hose, it shoots up in place and I drop back to my knees scrubbing at a new spot. My heart is pounding and I'm panting. Sucking in breaths makes the burn of the bleach more prominent and I begin coughing. My eyes are burning and my vision is blurred.

I can't stop.

Keep going.

Don't stop.

Don't you fucking stop, Nova.

Don't be a pathetic, little bitch.

"Shut up! Shut up! You're gone! You can't hurt me anymore. Just get out of my head!" Dragging myself across the floor and scrubbing furiously along the way, I feel a pressure against my hand. Everything is a blur, I have no idea what it is. "Wha-"

My whole body is engulfed, my senses a total mess. At first I don't realize what's happening. Then, just over the smell of the copper and bleach, I smell it. Home. Sighing and melting against the pressure, it grips me tighter, *he* grips me tighter.

The haze is broken and I can hear him humming *Hey Jude* by *The Beatles* in my ear. Completely back in the moment, I realize I'm sobbing against Rhys' neck. We're holding onto each other as if our life depends on it, and in this moment I really feel like it does. I pull back to look at him and my heart shatters. I've seen a lot of horrible, heartbreaking things in my life, but this... he's... crying.

Bringing my hands up, I go to grip his face, immediately stopping when I see a mix of blood, new and old, mixed with bleach bubbled up and pouring down my hands and wrists. Looking at my hands in horror, my eyes flicker back and forth, connecting the dots. His voice cracks as he begins to speak, "Sw-sweetheart?

"We need to clean your hands, little star. You hurt yourself." I look between him and my hands, furrowing my brow trying to remember how I hurt myself from scrubbing the floor. Scooping me up, he brings me as close to his chest as he can and carries me over to the sink. He places me on the small metal surface connected to the sink, gripping my hips tight and bringing his forehead to mine. "I'm so sorry I wasn't here, sweetheart. Never again. I'm with you every step of the way, okay?"

Nodding against his forehead, I take a deep breath, whispering, "I'm sorry. I just wanted to fix it."

Squinting his eyes and lifting his brow, he looks away and then looks back to me. "What do you mean, sweetheart? There's nothing for you to be sorry for. And what are you trying to fix?"

I look towards the mess and then back to him, "I didn't want us to get in trouble with all of this evidence. It didn't start off that way. I... I was in the kitchen and a noise brought it all back. Then I was here."

Pulling back slightly, he kisses around my face. Forehead, cheeks, nose, chin and finally my lips. "Listen to me, sweetheart. Everything is going to be okay. None of us are going to get in trouble, okay? You're safe. We're safe. Say it with me. Say, I'm safe."

Whispering, I repeat, "I'm safe."

Kiss.

"Now, say we're safe."

"We're safe."

Kiss.

"One more time for me, little star. I'm safe. We're safe."

Breathing in through my nose and slowly letting it out I say, "I'm safe. We're safe."

Kiss.

"Let's get you cleaned up and go home." Yes, home. Home is wherever he is.

"She conquered her demons and wore her scars like wings." ~Atticus

CHAPTER 14
FREE FALLIN'

Rhys

When I saw all the cuts from the knives and chemical burns from the bleach, my heart broke even more for her while I cleaned her up. I knew everything was going to hit her soon, and I was ready to be there for the fall out. I was not prepared at all for it to happen while I was going over information Dorian found. I'll never forgive myself for it, she went through it alone and got hurt. I'll be making up for it for the rest of our lives... wait, rest of our lives? Fuck it, I know she's it for me. Soulmates or not, I don't give a shit that it's "too soon," she's mine and I'm hers. I carried her out of there and stopped by the conference room to give Dorian a heads up we were leaving. The moment he saw her wrapped tightly around me he started to rush over with a panicked look on his face. I gave him a subtle head shake and he froze in place. I let him know I was taking her to our place and knowing that he would want to help, I asked if he would look up how to treat cuts and chemical burns. He nodded his head so fast he looked like a bobble head and ran back to his laptop. The whole drive to my place was torture since I couldn't hold her as I drove. As soon as we got to my place, I ran to her side and scooped her up again. She immediately wrapped around me like a koala again, gripping me tight. The events drained her and it didn't take her long to fall asleep after we laid down on my bed.

Bzzz. Turning my head towards my phone on the nightstand, I contemplate ignoring it. *Bzzz. Bzzz.* Holding back my growl of annoyance, I slowly breathe out through my nose. *Bzzz.* Slowly moving my hand from Nova's back, I reach out and grab my phone. Good thing I put The Horde's numbers and call names in my phone or I would've completely ignored Jade.

> HARP: Dorian told me what happened! Is she okay? What do you guys need?!
>
> HARP: He told me she has cuts and chemical burns. I made something that will help heal the wounds. I'm sure she's sleeping, so I'll let you know when I'm on my way and then when I'm there so I don't have to knock.
>
> HARP: I'm on my way now. When I get there you can tell me what you guys need and I'll go back out and get it. Please tell me she's okay.
>
> HARP: I'm about a minute away, I'll stay in my car until you let me know I can meet you at the door

.

Shit. I'm so glad she has people that care about her and want to help, but damn, I really don't want to wake her up.

ME: Hey sorry. Yeah, she's asleep but I think she'll wake up either way. Hop on out, I'll meet you at the door.

Putting my phone back on the nightstand, I wrap my arm back around her. I sit up, moving as slow and gently as possible. Getting a good hold with my arm under her ass and my other wrapped around her shoulder blades, I press her further against me and slowly stand. She stirs and mumbles something I can't understand. I wait frozen in place for her to settle again. Nuzzling further into my neck, I feel her small breaths but she doesn't move anymore. I head down the hall and to the front door.

Before it's fully open I peek my head through the crack and mouth, 'shh," to Jade. I open the door the rest of the way and step aside for her. She looks at Nova with concern in her eyes, and then holds up a bag. Nodding my head towards the kitchen, she follows me in there and gently places the bag on the counter. She holds up her hands and mimics writing on a piece of paper. Pointing to the drawer behind her, she turns and opens it, pulling out a notebook and a pen. Scribbling something on the paper, she puts the pen down and then turns towards me with a sad smile. She watches Nova for a moment, waves at me and then heads out of the apartment, shutting the door quietly. I look down at the notebook.

Text any of us at any time if you guys need anything. I mixed together a healing salve for her hands. Apply it at least 3 times a day, no bandages so the wounds don't suffocate. Wash your hands before applying. Be prepared for the smell, it's slightly bitter and pungent. It's a mix of turmeric, aloe and coconut oil. There's drinks and smokes in the bag for you both as well.

. . .

Smiling at the note, I head back to my room and slowly lay down with Nova again. As soon as I get comfortable, she stirs and her breathing changes. Knowing she's awake, I gently rub my hands up and down her back. I feel her tongue against my neck and I groan, my dick twitching in my pants. She scrapes her nails along my jawline where my beard has grown in. I haven't shaved since we started our hunt for Frankie, and the way she plays with it makes me think she digs it. Running her nose up my neck, she brings her lips to my ear and whispers, "I need you, Rhys. Take me to the stars and make me feel alive again."

Shit, can't say no to that. Flipping us over so she's on her back, she yelps and lets out a broken laugh. Her smile is so bright, but tears are pooling in her beautiful eyes. Bringing my lips towards her eyes, she flutters them shut and I kiss each eyelid. She opens her eyes and the movement makes the tears fall. As soon as I catch sight of it, I kiss the tears away from each cheek. My heart breaks more and I feel a lump in my throat forming. I hate seeing her like this, it's fucking killing me. With my lips pressed against her cheek, I whisper to her with a crack in my voice, "Please, please don't cry, little star."

She looks at me, more tears threatening to spill and she whispers to me, "Please, Rhys."

Her nails scrape across my beard again and she gives me a half smile. I crash my lips to hers, our mouths swallowing our moans down. Taking advantage of her open mouth, I thrust my tongue forward and slide it against hers. My tongue swirls around her mouth and she captures my tongue and starts sucking on it. Kissing down her jawline, I press my lips to the pulse point in her neck, sucking it once and then flicking my tongue across it. She hisses from the sting and then rolls her hips up moaning. I sit up to straddle her hips and grip the hem of her shirt, lifting it above her belly button. Lowering my head, I lightly nip her hip, making her thrust up again. My tongue traces along the top of her jeans from one hip to the other, and I

196

slowly move up until I'm circling her belly button. She makes the most intoxicating sound and pants, "Stop teasing me, please."

"Mmm, you beg so sweetly, little star." I grip the hem of her shirt and slide it up further, "Lift your arms, baby, careful with your hands." I take her shirt off, making sure not to hurt her hands, "Lift up for me, sweetheart." Lifting herself up slightly, I reach behind her to unclasp her bra and slide it off. Both breasts in my hands, I give them a squeeze and flick my thumbs over her nipples. Her breath hitches, rolling her hips up. She hits her target and my hard cock throbs from the contact. Groaning, I fight the urge to grind my cock against her pussy. Slowly caressing down her ribs and stomach, she yelps and giggles. God, I love that laugh.

She sees the twinkle in my eye, and glaring back she says, "Don't you dare, Rhys Alexander." I laugh, shake my head and unbutton her jeans. I slowly drag the zipper down, the only sound in the room is her panting and the teeth of the zipper spreading apart. Gripping the top of her jeans and panties, I slowly pull them down. Sliding off the bed as I pull, I untie her shoes and toss them away. Grabbing her pant legs, I rip them the rest of the way off of her feet. I let my jacket slide down my arms and fall to the floor. While kicking off my boots, I reach behind me and grab the back of my shirt, yanking it up and off. When I look up, I catch Nova scanning my body while biting her lip. I unbuckle my belt and yank the belt buckle so hard the belt slides through the loops and makes a snapping noise. Her eyes widen and she gasps at the movement. I slowly unbutton and unzip my jeans, hooking my thumbs behind my jeans and boxer briefs I pull them down and kick them off. Placing my hands on top of her ankles, I caress them while slowly spreading her legs apart. Kneeling between her calves, I slide my hands up until I reach her thighs. Squeezing them, I push them further apart and lean down, placing a kiss on each inner thigh. She shivers from the contact and goosebumps break out along her skin. With each kiss I leave, my beard

197

scrapes along her thighs and she moans. I look up to see a fake pouty face.

Confused, I ask her, "What's that look for, sweetheart?"

Putting her hands up, her palms facing me, she wiggles her fingers and rolls her eyes. "Your beard feels fucking amazing on my skin, and all I want to do is grab your hair and pull you towards me but I fucking can't."

I squeeze her thighs and give her a small smile, "I'm sorry, sweetheart. I have something for that and we'll take care of it soon, okay? Until then, be a good girl and keep your hands up."

Her breath hitches the moment I say good girl and I smirk. Gripping her thighs, I spread them further apart and lean down, licking from her entrance to her clit. The moment I reach her clit she thrusts her hips, so I pull my tongue back and tsk at her with my lips still against her. I had plans for my girl, but with her hands bothering her, I need to make this quicker than I would like. Bringing my hand towards her soaked pussy, I drag my middle and ring fingers up and down her slit. Reaching her entrance, I thrust my fingers in and curl them up. My lips wrap around her clit, where I suck hard and then pump my fingers in and out, hitting her g-spot over and over. Her thighs clamp around my ears, drowning out the sound of her moans. I feel her thighs start to tremble and her pussy tightens around my fingers. Knowing she's close, I suck her clit harder, feeling her cum gush past my fingers to my wrist. *Fuck yeah.* Her legs are shaking so hard, they can't decide if they need to be against my ears or away from them. Releasing her clit with a pop, I slowly pull my fingers out and bring them to her lips. Coating her lips I tell her, "Open up for me, sweetheart."

She opens her mouth and I guide my fingers in, closing her lips around my fingers and sucking them clean. Pulling my fingers free, I bring my wrist to my mouth and lick the juices that dripped down it. Sitting down between her legs, I grip her hips and pull her up on my lap. Her legs wrap around my hips and her arms drape over my shoulders. "Hold your arms out over my shoulders to keep your hands safe. I promise I'll make it up to you, but this is going to be quick. Feeling you come apart on my tongue almost made me lose it right then and there." I lift her up by her hips and drag her wet pussy over the head of my cock. The moment my cock pushes in and I pull her down all the way hard and fast. Her head falls to her arm on my shoulder on a scream and I grunt, "Fuck. You feel so fucking good, sweetheart. Just hold on, baby, let me make you feel good." Gripping the globes of her ass, I pick her up and slide her down my cock, thrusting up the best I can. Her pussy clenches tightly around my cock and my thrusts stutter, "Oh fuck. Oh fuck. Just like that, sweetheart." I feel her walls squeeze tighter around my cock. Keeping hold of her ass with one hand, I reach down with my other one to strum her clit fast. Her moans in my ear are driving me to thrust harder. "Fuck, I'm close. Tell me you're close, baby."

"Mmm, so… so close, Rhys. Fuck."

I feel the tingle up my spine and pinch her clit. On a silent scream, I feel her get impossibly tight around me and tremble. Her orgasm tips mine off and I'm gripping her tight against me, thrusting in one last time and my cock lets out spurt after spurt of cum. "Fuck, fuck, fuuuuuuuuck."

After cleaning up, I put on a pair of boxer briefs and put one of my shirts on her. Carrying her to the kitchen, she looks down at the bag on the counter I set her down next to. Tilting her head down to it, she asks, "What's that?"

Pulling the drinks out first, I tell her, "Jade stopped by and brought us drinks and a healing salve for your hands. Speaking of, we need to apply it."

Setting two of our drinks on the counter, I take the rest to the fridge. Walking back to the counter, I see Nova reaching for her drink. Swooping in, I pick it up and crack it open and hand it to her. With a shy look, she puts her head down and whispers, "Thank you."

I tilt her chin up. "You don't have to thank me for taking care of you, little star. I'll happily take care of you. Always." Her breath hitches on the word, always. Her eyes flick back and forth between mine as if she's searching for the truth in my statement. I lean forward and kiss her lips, whispering against them, "This life and the next, soulmate." Hearing *Teenage Dirtbag* scream from my room, I hold up my finger to her and roll my eyes.

Running to the room, I grab my phone and answer it, "Hey man, what's up?"

Dorian's frantic voice starts spouting question after question, "How is SuperNova? Is she okay? Do you guys need anything? I didn't want to bother you in case she was resting. It's very common for people to rest after such a traumatic episode. Did you know that the corticotropin-releasing factor and the hypothalamic-pituitary-adrenal axis system have a lot to do with how people respond to the overload of stress during a traumatic episode? It has negative feedback-"

Shaking my head, I chuckle, "Dor! Please, please. Can I answer your questions? You're doing a panic info bomb on me, take a breath, man." I hear him take a deep breath, the brushing noises against the phone tell me he's most likely nodding his head as if I can see him. "She's doing... the best she can. She just woke up a little bit ago. All of this is going to take some time," letting out a shaky breath and clearing my throat, "just like it's going to take me forever to make up for not being there." My voice cracks on the final word, clearing my throat again I shake my head, cutting off my own breakdown.

"What do you have to make up for? You didn't do anything wrong?"

Letting out a humorless laugh, "Didn't I? I knew the breakdown was coming. I was ready to be there for her through the whole thing, and I wasn't. Not only did she suffer through it all alone, but she's hurt. Her hands are cut and burned and her knees are bruised from the floor. That's on me. Anyways, what's up man?"

Unable to stay away from Nova any longer, I turn and head

towards the kitchen. When I walk in, she looks over and her eyes zero in on my gray sweats hanging low on my hips. Letting her know I caught her, I shake my hips, making my cock dance around. Her eyes go wide and she lets out a gasp. When she lifts her eyes up to mine, I smirk at her and I see the blush creeping up her neck and cheeks.

"So, with all the information we found, I think we need to do some recon. I'm thinking we go to the lake, act like we're just there to hang out and have fun, but also keep an eye on what goes on when I'm not there. See who shows up, who leaves, things like that. Do you think Nova would be up for it? She could relax and enjoy the day while we do that, what do you think?"

Walking up to her, I squeeze myself between her legs. "Why don't you ask her yourself, I know you're dying to talk to her."

"YES!"

I pull the phone from my ear at his shout and look at it with a death glare as if Dorian can see it. Putting the phone on speaker, I grit through my teeth, "Dude. No more yelling."

Dorian lets out a nervous chuckle, "Right, right, sorry. I just really want to talk to SuperNova."

She smiles at his words, "Hi, Prince Dorian."

"You can't see right now, but I am bowing, Queen Super-Nova. How are you doing? Are you doing okay? If you need-"

Cutting him off mid sentence, I tell him, "Dude. You're doing it again."

Clearing his throat he says, "Right. Sorry. Anyways, I just wanted to know if you were feeling up to hang out tomorrow. You should know it won't be a regular hangout, as much as I would like it to be. I was thinking you could hang out and relax at the lake while Rhys and I do some recon watching *Amissa Stella*." While they talk on the phone, I place it on the counter and pull the salve out of the bag. Opening it up the bitter, citrus scent hits me and I pull my head back with a grimace. Sticking my tongue out dramatically, I shake my head like I can shake the smell away. Nova is watching and her whole body is shaking with silent laughter. I mock glare at her and apparently that's the straw that broke the camel's back because she opens her mouth and full-on belly laughs. "What's happening? What's so funny, guys?"

Tears are streaming down her face and she starts waving her hand back and forth as if that will make her laughing stop. Gasping for air, she responds between laughs, "I'm… sorry… Rhys… funny face… I'm dying." She clears her throat and takes a deep breath, wiping her cheeks with the backs of her hands, "Sorry, sorry. Yes, absolutely Dor, I would love to go with you guys. We'll see you tomorrow, but we have to get going. Rhys has to put some… concoction, ha cock. He has to put something Jade made on my hands. Thank you for calling and checking in, Prince Dorian."

Speaking in a posh accent he responds, "Yes, yes, I shall see you tomorrow, milady."

Ending the call, I walk to the sink and wash my hands, humming the A, B, C song to make sure my hands are perfectly clean to touch her wounds. Standing between her legs again, I look at her and she's smiling. "What?"

Her smile gets bigger, "You were humming the alphabet while washing your hands. I don't know why, but for some reason it was really adorable."

I scoop up a dollop of the salve and grasp her wrist, pulling it towards me. Smirking, I tell her, "That's cuz I am adorable."

Rolling her eyes, she lets out an exasperated sigh, "I take it back. Not adorable at all."

Shaking my head, I laugh, "Anyways, heartbreaker. She wrote down what's in it, but I honestly don't know if it will hurt or not. I really, really hope it doesn't. I'm so sorry if it does. Wrap your legs around me and squeeze as tight as you need to." I gently pull her lip from between her teeth, soothing it with my thumb. "Alright, one, two, three."

Gently placing the dollop in the palm of her hand, I slowly

slide it around the palm of her hand to spread it out. At first contact, she jolts and squeezes her legs around me tightly. I go to step away, but she squeezes me trying her best to keep me in place. "No, no, please. It's okay, I'm sorry. I'm okay, I promise. I just, it freaked me out a little, but it's not that bad. It actually feels soothing, please don't stop."

Searching her eyes I see her face is relaxed and she doesn't seem to be putting on a front. Making sure I cover both sides of her hand and all around her fingers, I spread the salve making sure not to miss any of the cuts and burns. I do her other hand and twist the top back on the jar and wash my hands to remove the salve residue.

"Now what do I do? I can't touch anything with this shit all over my hands and I smell like a basket of weird oranges."

Laughing, I shake my head, "It's supposed to help, smartass. I'll help you with whatever you need. I'm guessing you're not ready for bed since you slept already. Do you want to go watch movies in my room until we have to go meet up with Dorian?"

Her eyes light up and she nods her head, "If we switch movies for *Fruits Basket*, you have yourself a goddamn deal."

"Absolutely! Let's go, sweetheart." Picking her up from the counter, we head back to my room and settle in to watch her show.

"Your soulmate is not someone that comes into your life peacefully. It is who comes to questions things, who changes your reality, somebody that makes a before and after in your life. It is not the human being everyone has idealized, but an ordinary person, who manages to revolutionize your world in a second." ~Unknown

CHAPTER 15
FALL IN LOVE WITH YOU

*R*HYS

After a few episodes of *Fruits Basket*, Nova went back to sleep. I've spent more time watching her sleep than the show, just memorizing every inch of her. Her head is back against the couch with her hair laying across the couch seat. Her pouty lips are slightly parted and she's letting out the softest of snores. Knowing my little star, she'd be adamant that she absolutely doesn't snore. I grab my phone from my pocket and see that we have about an hour and a half before we have to meet up with Dorian. Quietly standing, I head to my room and start packing a bag with extra clothes for both of us and towels. After tip-toeing to the kitchen, I reach under the sink and cringe at the creak of the cupboard, muttering under my breath, "Shut. The. Fuck. Up." I pull out a box of garbage bags from the cupboard and a roll of duct tape from a drawer. Back in my room, I pull out a few garbage bags and curse at the noise. I shove the bags and tape in my bag and zip it up. After stowing away the box of garbage bags under my bed, I return to the living room.

My eyes light up and my cock stirs at the sight that greets me. Nova has stretched out a little more and my shirt has ridden up. It's resting at her hips now and my girl's pussy is on full display. Dropping to my knees, I crawl across the floor to her. My stomach now laying between her legs, I lean forward, grazing my beard across her inner thighs. She slightly stirs, spreading her legs further. I flick my tongue out, just barely licking across her folds. With a quiet moan, she lifts her hips towards my face. I part her folds, opening her up to me. Either the little temptress is already awake and pretending she's not, or even in sleep she's ready for me. Smiling at the sight of her already wet for me, I lick a circle around her entrance and up to her clit, giving it a barely-there flick. Tilting my head back, I bring my middle and ring fingers to her entrance. I pump my fingers slow and shallow, my tongue flicking across her clit. Pushing my fingers further in, I alternate between scissoring and come hither motions. Her moans get louder and she rolls her hips against my face. Pumping faster, I flick up with each push in, hitting her g-spot over and over. Licking a circle around her clit, I latch on and start sucking. Nova thrusts her hips upward and her gasping moan turns into a shout of, "Oh fuckkkk, ghoulie!" I laugh against her pussy, making her moan again, and in a sleepy voice says, "Fuck, even when you laugh against my pussy it sets me on fire. Fuck, please don't stop, Rhys."

Lifting my head, I look at her and smile, "Good morning, little star."

"Good morning, Rhys," rolling her hand around and thrusting her hips against my chin, she adds, "pretty sure I said don't stop."

"You bossing me around here, little star?"

Groaning, she throws her head back against the couch, "Nooooooo."

Leaning down, I kiss along each fold and then give her clit a loud and sloppy kiss. "Good, cuz I just found me a diamond in the rough."

Her head shoots up and she glares down at me, fighting a smile, "Don't. You. Dare. Start."

Sitting back on my heels, I place my hand over my heart,

"Me? I would never. I just wanted to tell you that my heat-seeking missile has found its target."

She grabs the pillow on the couch and smacks me in the head with it. Grabbing the pillow from her, I look at it and then down at her. A smirk slowly grows on my face and I'm sure my eyes shine with mischief.

"Rhys Alexander. Don't. You. Dare."

Clearing my throat, I pause for a moment. "This pillow is comfy and all, but I find more comfort inside of you. Also," leaning forward, I slide my hands up the shirt she's wearing and squeeze her tits, "I much prefer these pillows."

Sitting up further, she narrows her eyes at me. Attempting to close her legs, and unable to do so with me between them, she says, "You've been banished. My pussy is now off limits to you." With an exaggerated gasp, I make a pouty face. I nuzzle against her folds and my nose brushes against her clit, making her moan. Her thighs clench around my head when I start talking against her pussy, the vibrations making her moan more.

"I'm sorry, please don't take my pussy away from me."

Rolling her hips against my face, she moans, "Then maybe you should put that mouth to better use than talking nonsense."

Yelling against her pussy, I say, "YES, LITTLE STAR!"

Giggling, she claps her thighs against my head twice. I look up to see her smiling as she says, "The beard and talking combo really does it for me, ghoulie."

"Yeah? Be a good girl for your ghoul and put your hands up. If your hands drop at all, I stop. Do you understand?"

Whimpering at my words, she nods. Realizing she didn't use her words, she breathlessly says, "Yes, Rhys."

"You're such a good fucking girl."

Grasping her hips tightly, I bring my face back down and lick around her entrance. I twirl my tongue around in circles inside of her. Pushing my face forward as much as I can, I suck and lick, moving my head up and down so my nose brushes her clit. Nova writhes beneath me, moaning. "Fuck, Rhys, just like that." I feel her legs graze against my legs. Reaching my hips, she digs her feet in against my boxer briefs, "Off, take them off." I shake my head against her pussy. "I'm gonna, fuck, Rhys, I'm gonna-" Her words are cut of on a silent scream as she cums, continuing to lick and suck as she rides out her orgasm. Sitting up, I grab my underwear and yank them down to my knees. Clumsily lifting each knee to bring them further down, I kick my feet behind me to get them off.

Nova starts laughing at my fumbling and I look up to glare at her, "Laugh it up, chuckles." Her laughing grows louder and I snap. Her eyes are shut so she doesn't see it coming when I lunge forward. Grabbing a hold of her, I flip her over so her chest is against the couch. She squeals from the momentum and keeping her pinned to the couch with my body, I quickly grab her hands before they slam against the couch. Bringing them behind, I tap them against her lower back. The move makes her moan and arch her back, thrusting her ass towards me. *Noted.* "Keep your hands here. Do. Not. Move."

She forgot to use her words, so I release my hold of her hands and slap her ass. "Ahh, fuck." Turning her head over her shoulder she asks, "What was that for?"

Grazing my fingertips across my handprint, I shake my head, "Don't think I forgot how much you love that, first of all. Second of all, I told you to do something and you didn't respond. Do I have to repeat myself, little star?"

Shaking her head she says, "No, I won't move my hands."

Squeezing her ass, I nod and say, "Good girl." A blush blooms across her face and she bites her lip. I act as if I'm taking a picture and make a clicking noise, "Filing that one away for a rainy day." Bringing myself closer to her, I grasp my cock and stroke it. I'm close enough that the tip of my cock and my hand brushes against her with each stroke. She gives a little shake to her hips, and I smack her ass with my left hand.

"Ahh, fuck."

Rubbing the tip of my cock down her crack, I push until my

cock is sliding through her soaked pussy and rub my tip in a circle around her clit. Her ass lifts further and pushes back, my cock sliding back and forth, hitting her clit every time. Feeling close to cumming already, I grip the base of my cock hard and take a deep breath. Bringing my cock to her entrance, I thrust my hips forward until I'm fully seated inside her. She lets out a gasping moan and thrusts backwards, circling her hips. Grasping her wrists with one hand, I get a hold of her hair with the other one. Twisting it around to get a good hold, I pull my hips back so only the tip of my cock is inside her. Gripping her wrists and hair tighter, I yank her head back while thrusting forward. Pistoning my hips faster and faster, I grit my teeth, holding on as long as possible. I have her head pulled back far enough that she's looking up to the ceiling and she shouts, "Fuck! Oh! Fuck! Mmph!" Her pussy clamps down around my cock and she screams, "Rhys!"

Unable to hold on any longer, I thrust forward once more and shout, "Nova!" Spurt after spurt of cum shoots from me and I attempt to push my hips further against her. When I release her hair and wrists, she flops against the couch panting. I pull her close, brushing her hair away from her neck, and slump forward, wrapping my arms around her. Nuzzling my face into her neck, I kiss her just behind her ear and whisper, "I love you, Nova Skye Hart."

Tilting her head against my face, she whispers back, "I love you, Rhys Alexander Slater." Smiling against her neck, I take a deep breath and squeeze her.

"We have to get ready to go, sweetheart."

"Mmm. I had a feeling. I'm starting to think this is our thing before we have to go somewhere." She ends her sentence on a giggle and I start laughing too.

"I think you're right. New rule... no, no, new law. No leaving anywhere until I make you cum. Somebody smack the gavel down, law is set, court adjourned." She wiggles her hips, making me groan at the sensitive tingle that shoots through my cock. "Mmph. Stop it, sweetheart. Sensitive."

"Well get moving, ghoulie. We have to go."

"I didn't say I didn't want to be inside you anymore, just don't wiggle around for a little bit. I'm trying to calculate how to get us to the shower from here without taking my cock from its warm home."

"Ghoulie, get your fucking cock out of me and get your ass to the shower, before I take your warm home to *my* apartment *until the next life.*"

Gasping dramatically, I pull my cock out and jump away from her. "Hurtful, little star, very fucking hurtful." Bending down, I scoop her up into my arms and pick her up. Tilting her head against my shoulder she looks up at me and drags her fingernails across my beard back and forth. Shuddering at the feeling of her scratching my beard, goosebumps pop up across my jawline. Once I step into the bathroom, I set her down on the counter and kiss her forehead. Turning towards the shower, I get the water started and wait for the right temperature. Walking back to Nova, she opens her legs for me and I step in between them. "As much as I love showering with you, sweetheart, we're going to have to take separate showers or we're never going to meet up with Dorian."

With a slight pout she nods, "I know. I'm going first, though." Pressing her lips to mine in a bruising kiss, she pulls back and gives me the shooing motion.

Getting ready to take the last turn for the lake, *Teenage Dirtbag* starts playing on my phone. Rolling my eyes and shaking my head, I chance a glance at Nova, "Sweetheart, can you please answer that? Tell him to chill the fuck out."

Picking up my phone, she laughs, "I'm not going to be mean to him for you, ghoul. Hello, Dor."

"Oh! Hi, SuperNova! Are you... uh... are you guys... busy?"

"DUDE! We've talked about this!"

"No, I distinctly remember our conversation being about me not making lewd comments or gestures. Which I full-heartedly agreed to since I grossed myself out doing it. I was only asking if that was the hold up here, not for details. Retract the claws, beast."

Sighing in exasperation, Nova raises her voice, "CHILDREN!"

Dorian and I both say in a defeated tone, "Sorry."

"Thank you. Dor, we're two seconds away, okay?"

"Ooo, okay! Bye!"

Nova snorts and shakes her head, putting the phone down, "You two are ridiculous sometimes, I swear."

Reaching over, I squeeze her thigh, "Yeahhh, but you love us."

Putting her hand over mine, she rubs it and says, "Yes, ghoul. I love you guys." Pulling into a parking space, I put the truck in park and shut the truck off, turning towards Nova. Copying my movements, she turns and leans against the door smiling at me.

"I'm really glad we have you in our lives, sweetheart."

Winking at me she says, "I'm really glad I have me too."

Lunging forward, I start tickling her, "Oh that's it you little shit!"

Laughing and shouting, she wiggles around trying to get away from me. "Stop, stop! I'm sorry ghoul, I'm sorry! Mercy! Mercy! I'm gonna pee!"

Moving my hands down, I give her a yuck face, "We should probably discuss kinks at some point, babe. Hate to break it to ya, but that is not one of them." Raising her hand to slap me, I quickly grab her wrist, "Watch the hands, sweetheart."

Groaning, she lays her head against the window, "You know how annoying it is that I have to wait to heal to pop you in the chest for your shit?"

I bring her hand towards me and kiss the inside of her wrist, "I know, sweetheart. I'm sorry." Looking over her shoulder, I see Dorian walking towards the truck. "Incoming."

Looking over her shoulder, she laughs, "Time to go, ghoul."

Dropping my duffle on the ground, I kneel down and unzip it to pull a towel out. Kneeling down beside me, she looks in the duffle bag, "Uh, ghoulie? What's with the garbage bags and duct tape? Work stuff?"

"I know you'll want to swim with me, so I brought it so we can protect your hands from the water."

Smiling, she leans over and kisses my cheek, "Thank you."

"Anything for you, sweetheart." Nodding my head towards Dorian at the picnic table, I say, "I think Dor's gonna roll up a blunt, I'll meet you guys over there." Watching her walk away, a smile forms on my face. My cock chubs up and I realize how much of a turn on it is to see her wearing my clothes. Walking up to the picnic table, Dorian's already lit the blunt and I can smell a mix of weed and peach as I take my shirt off. Throwing my leg over the bench, I sit behind Nova and wrap my arms around her waist. Dorian stretches his arm out and hands the blunt to Nova. She leans her head against my shoulder, taking a big puff and holds it. Handing the blunt back to Dorian, she looks up at me and puckers her lips. I bring my mouth to hers so she can exhale the smoke into my mouth.

Dorian takes a drag, and attempts to talk while holding the smoke in. "Okay, so here's what I'm thinking-" exhaling the rest of the smoke, he covers his mouth and starts coughing. He starts again after wiping the tears from his eyes. "Anyways, here," grabbing the blunt from him, I wave my hand for him to continue, "one of their guys always takes a smoke break and walks around the lake. I figure we keep an eye out for anything unusual before he goes for his walk, and then when he does his walk around here, we just keep an ear out if he takes any impor-tant calls."

I scan the area and look back to Dorian, "Do they have their own cameras around here, or just yours?"

With his pointer finger in the air, he makes a circular motion and says, "The cameras here are all mine, all of theirs are on the inside of the building and just over the front doors. They're programmed to scan the area so there are times the camera is pointed in this general direction, but it's too far to accurately pick anything up. If need be though, I can get on my phone and push their camera in the direction I need it to be. Why?"

Handing the blunt back to him, I scratch at my beard, "I'm thinking my next target is going to come to me. Does he follow a smoke schedule or is it random? Cuz I gotta figure out when to have you and Nova head on out."

Nova pulls forward and my hands fall away from her waist. Swiveling around, she glares at me and says, "Excuse the fuck outta me?"

Putting my hands up in the air and off to the side, "Whoa. What did I say?"

"Don't be a fucking cockblock, Rhys. Am I with you or not?"

Gesturing my hands to my cock, I smirk, "I would never cockblock you, sweetheart. It is all yours any time you want it. And of course you're with me, but that has nothing to do with me doing my job."

Rolling her eyes, she lifts from the bench and turns to fully face me. "You know what I mean, Rhys. Everybody we know is a part of this and helps you, so why the fuck can't I? Why was it only allowed with Frankie's bitchass, but I can't help you with anyone else? Do you think I'm fucking weak? Do you think I can't fucking handle it?" Shoving her hand in her pocket angrily, she winces and pulls her cigarettes out. Lighting one, she looks away from me and takes a drag.

I walk towards her to calm her down, "Hey, I don't think you're weak, little star. You're the strongest fucking person I know. I just don't want anything happening to you. This is all new for me, okay? I've only ever had to worry about Dorian and myself. If you want to be a part of this, by all means. I want you with me always. But can't we work on some self defense first? I mean, I even work with Dorian on that shit and he's rarely ever a part of the action."

On an exhale she says, "There's three of us here against the one guy, Rhys. I think I'll be just fine. I actually have an idea that might help lure him in."

An immense feeling of pride feels like it's going to burst

through me at Nova's reaction and how she handled this. Unable to hold back, I step into her space and wrap my arms around her. Wrapping her hand around my neck, she holds the one with her smoke away from me. Bringing my lips to her ear I whisper, "I'm so fucking proud of you, little star. I'm always going to worry about you when it comes to this, but I just really needed to tell you how fucking proud of you I am. You just stood your ground and fought for what you wanted without a trace of fear. Did it feel good, sweetheart?"

She looks at me and searches my eyes, "Both? It felt good to stand up and say what I wanted, but I don't feel so great about the whole yelling and cussing at you thing. I actually feel like a piece of shit for that. I'm sorry."

Bringing my hand up, I brush a strand of hair from her face and run my hand down her cheek. "Thank you for apologizing. I'm not upset I promise, but I understand why you need to clear the air on that. I know you don't want us to treat each other like that."

Lifting on her toes she gently bites my chin, "Could you not read my mind? It's freaky, stay in your own brain lane, ghoul."

Throwing my head back, I laugh at her word choice. "How 'bout we sit back down with the abandoned puppy and you tell us what your plan is?"

Looking over I see Dorian with his arms crossed and a pout on his face, "Would you stop calling me your puppy? You're more animal than I am, ya fucking rabid beast."

"Seriously guys, finish that blunt so you *both* chill the fuck out." Removing herself from my arms, she heads to the picnic table and straddles the bench. Walking over I go to sit behind her and she puts her hand up shaking her head. "No, absolutely not. You go sit with your bestie. Smoke and make up while you listen to my plan. I swear I'm going to do that mom trick I've heard about where they make their kids wear the same shirt until they play nice."

Looking down at her I smirk and say, "Okay, mommy."

"No, absolutely not. You get your mommy kink fix with porn."

Pouting I say, "Okay, mamas." Her pupils dilate and she briefly looks away, clearing her throat. *Bingo*. Walking over to the other side of the table, I plop down next to Dorian, making sure to bump into him. Smirking at Nova, I lick my lower lip slowly. Getting an elbow to the side, I scowl over at Dorian. "Dude, watch it."

"You watch it."

"Anwaysssss. My idea. I'm thinking you guys hide somewhere and I'll be in the lake. When I see the guy, I'll act like I'm struggling to swim and beg for help. Hopefully the dumb shit comes to the rescue and you sneak up on him. Wham, bam, thank you, ma'am." Apparently I make a face at her plan because she pipes up again and says, "Don't make that face at me, Rhys Alexander. It's a good plan. Right, Dor?"

"Uhh," looking between the two of us, he says, "I mean, it is a good plan, but what if something happens? Like if he tries to… do more than just rescue you."

"NOPE! Don't like that. I'm sorry, I love you, Nova, but no way. Not with the image that just popped in my head."

Groaning, she rolls her eyes, "Okayyy, what if we partially keep the plan? What if we make him think that *you're* the attacker, and I need help to get away from you? That way, you're right there and he can't do anything to me."

Nodding my head, "Yes. I like that much better. But if we're going to do this, I need you to listen to me every step of the way. If I sa-" Cut off by the sound of snoring, I narrow my eyes at Nova, who has her head dropped and making snoring noises.

Growling, she snaps her head up and smiles, "Carry on, my green-eyed ghoul."

"Keep it up, sweetheart."

Flicking her eyes down and back up she says, "Oh I could if you'd like me to."

"Eww, guys. It's one thing to see the happy and in love shit, but this, no thank you. You're freaking me out." With a full body shiver, he grimaces.

"Alright, cry baby. Come on, little star. Let's get your hands all covered up."

Dorian jumps up from the bench, "Wait, what am I supposed to do?"

"You could go swim behind a log or some shit, so you're out of sight."

"Have you lost your mind? Do you know the amount of microorganisms that are just breeding in that water?! You know I don't swim in this lake!"

Laughing, I nod, "I know, but your reaction every time is fucking priceless."

Jabbing his finger towards some trees he says, "I'll be over there, asshole." Walking away he mumbles under his breath, "Such a dick."

Turning towards Nova, I see her lift the shirt she's wearing. Inch by inch, her skin is exposed and I can't look away. The sound of a throat clearing gets my attention, I look up to find Nova staring at me with her lips twisted to the side. Sliding her hand up her stomach slowly, she caresses her cleavage and then slowly up her neck. With her pointer finger she points to the corner of her mouth and says, "You have a little something just there, drooly, I mean, ghoulie." Walking up to her, I grip the back of her thighs and pull her up. Wrapping her arms and legs around me, I nuzzle my face into her neck and lightly bite. Clamping her thighs tighter around me, she lets out a small moan, "Rhys, don't distract me. What are you doing?"

Breathing her in, I sigh in contentment, "You really know how to make a guy fall in love with you over and over. Do you know that, little star?"

"I didn't even do anything, ya goof." Holding onto her, I kneel down over the towel and lay her down. Biting her collarbone then kissing it, my mouth brushing her skin with every word spoken, I say, "You don't have to." Letting go of her, I sit back on my heels, "Now, stop distracting me, we need to take care of this target, so I can take you home and zero in on my favorite target."

Shaking her head, she snorts, "You're ridiculous."

Shrugging, I reach into the duffel bag and grab the garbage bags and duct tape, "Maybe, but you're the one who went and fell in love with me, so doesn't that make you just as ridiculous?"

"Ooo, maybe I've just completely lost my mind."

Grabbing her wrist, I pull the first garbage bag over it and up her arm, "Why must you hurt me?"

"Quit your whining and tie me up, big boy."

Throwing my head back, I groan, "You're fucking killing me. Just remember all this shit you're pulling when I get you home tonight." Looking back down at her she's smiling bright and the light breeze is tossing her hair around. "I should've had Dorian cover your hands, at this rate I'll never get the job done." Bringing my attention back to her hands, I wrap the duct tape around her wrist and up her arm. Doing the same to the other hand, I slide down her body and help take her socks and shoes off. Standing up, I stretch my hands out to her and help her up. Kicking my boots off, I bend over and rip my socks off, tossing them in my boots. Taking a deep breath, I wrap my arm around her waist and look at her, "You ready for this?"

Lifting her shoulder, she says, "Ready as I'll ever be. Come on, ghoulie, get me wet." Bending down, I grab hold of her and toss her over my shoulder and smack her ass. Moaning, she turns her head and bites my side.

"Mmm. You asked for it, Nova Skye. Wish granted." Once we're in the water, I slowly slide her down my body and keep a hold of her hips. Brushing my lips against her, she deepens the kiss and wraps her legs around me. Groaning, I lick her bottom lip and push my tongue through her lips. Flicking our tongues and entangling them, she reaches down and brushes her covered hand across my cock.

Panting in each other's mouths, she says, "Put it in, just for a second."

"Hold on to me." Wrapping her other arm around me again, I let go of her hips and pull my shorts down just enough to pull my cock out. Grabbing her shorts, I pull them just below her ass. I blindly aim my cock towards her pussy, the head of my cock catching on her entrance and I push up. Rolling her hips, she guides me the rest of the way in and we both moan. I hold her in place by grabbing her ass, she slowly rolls her hips again, and I squeeze her ass tighter. Shaking my head, "Be a good girl and stay right there, little star. I can barely think as it is, and we still need to pay attention to our surroundings. Can you do that for me, sweetheart?"

With a little whine, she nods her head, "Yes, Rhys."

"Mmm, good fucking girl."

"Don't. Don't say that right now, or I'll have to be a bad girl and not listen."

"Fair enough."

Bringing her hands from my neck, she places them on my chest. Something must catch her eye, because she looks away from me and her eyes slightly widen. Taking a deep breath, she lets out a blood curdling scream and I grimace. *Showtime.* Nova starts thrashing around, my cock falls from her pussy and I pull up both of our shorts. "GET OFF OF ME! HELP! SOMEBODY HELP ME! DON'T TOUCH ME!" Under her breath, she grits her teeth, "Shout. Something. Back."

Whispering, I say, "Please, forgive me. I promise I don't mean it. Fuck, I don't like this. STOP FUCKING MOVING, BITCH! JUST SHUT THE FUCK UP!"

I hear shouting behind me, "HEY! WHAT THE FUCK?!"

The sound of splashing behind me tells me he's closing in. Getting ready to turn, I let go of Nova and start to turn. A kick to my knee makes me stumble, "Shit!"

I watch in slow motion as Nova swims around me towards the target. "Oh, thank you, thank you, thank you! Please, get me out of here, please!"

His hand grips her as he whispers in her ear, and then she's shaking her head in a panic, "What? No. No, just get me out of here please." She looks down and then back up to him. He starts pushing her aside, making his way towards me. He's so tall I can no longer see her behind him, as he closes in he abruptly stops and groans, "What the fuck?!"

Attempting to turn towards her, his body lunges forward over and over. *What the fuck?*

"I SAID NO!!!" Nova's hands come into view behind the guy and I see the glint of metal. Plunging the knife into his back and neck over and over, she keeps shouting, "You stupid fuck, I told you no! Why does nobody ever fucking listen to the word no!"

Blood is pouring from his mouth and wounds, her actions and the pain combined have completely frozen him in place. When he finally slumps face forward into the water, she pulls away from him.

"Stay back, sweetheart. Let me check his pulse." Swimming forward, I press my fingers to his carotid artery and feel the faintest pulsing. Grabbing hold of his hair, I push his head further into the water, his body slightly twitches, the last of his fight retreating. When the twitching stops, I feel for his pulse again and this time it's gone.

Dorian's yelling gets my attention and I look over Nova's shoulder. "Yeesh, good thing that was the right guy, or this would've been real awkward, right?"

"Don't freak Nova out. We both know that was the right guy or you would've come running out causing a scene." Looking to Nova, I search for any sign that this was too much. Finding nothing but calmness, I ask, "You did so well, sweetheart. You good?"

"I should probably be freaking out right now, but it had to be done. He was going to hurt you. We should probably get him loaded up, huh?"

"Yeah, do you want Dor to move my truck down here, and you get our stuff packed up? Or do you want to move the truck and he packs up?"

Looking at me like I just grew two heads, she whispers, "You'd let me drive, Beauty?"

"Of course I would. Dorian's the only one I've ever allowed to, but yes, you can drive her any time."

"Wow, you really do love me."

"Yes, little star, I really do love you. Let's get this taken care of so I can show you how much. Deal?"

Walking backwards with a huge smile on her face, she nods, "Deal." *I want to put that smile on her face every fucking day.*

"I seem to have loved you in numberless forms, numberless times... In life after life, in age after age, forever." ~Tagore

CHAPTER 16
I'D RUN TO YOU

NOVA

When I wake up, I look over and see that Rhys is still asleep. My mind drifts to the events at the lake and our conversations about me helping out. His concern over me makes me love him more, but I can't let his love stop him from getting me prepared. I have a feeling if I didn't bring it up, he would put off the self-defense lessons as long as possible. An idea forms in my mind and I smile. Sliding out from under his arm, I keep looking up to make sure he hasn't woken up. As I roll over, I realize I'm closer to the edge than I thought. Unable to catch myself, I grapple for the edge of the bed, failing and tumbling to the floor with a thud, "Shit." Grabbing the edge of the bed, I pull myself and peer over the bed. *Thank fuck I didn't wake him.* Crawling across the floor, I find his clothes and slip on a pair of shorts and a t-shirt. I crawl my way to the door and look over my shoulder to check he's still asleep. Pulling myself up, I open the door just enough to slip through. Quietly shutting the door behind me, I tiptoe down the hall to the kitchen. I enter the kitchen and find Dorian standing there drinking one of his iced teas. Looking up, he smiles big and opens his mouth to talk.

Putting my hand up, I bring my finger to my lips and quietly say, "Shh. I have a plan, I don't want Rhys waking up yet." With an excited look on his face, he makes a zipping motion over his lips. "Where's a good hiding spot around here? I'm going to get my self-defense training started with a quickness."

Dorian curls his lip up and grimaces, "That is not a good idea, SuperNova. Rhys is not someone you sneak up on, and if he accidentally hurts you because you caught him off guard," hissing through his teeth, he shakes his head, "he will never forgive himself. He's already having a hard enough time with-" Coughing, he puts his head down and mutters, "Shit."

Walking in front of Dorian, I tilt my head dramatically to the side to reach his eyes, "Hard enough time with what, Dor?"

"He knew something from... *that* day would set you off somehow, and he was ready to be there for you. He wanted to be right there to help you through it, so you didn't feel all alone. But-"

"But it didn't happen that way. I wish he didn't feel so responsible about it, but I also know nothing is going to change the way he feels about that day." Standing up straight, I cross my arms, "That was the only plan I had to kick-start the training. Do you have any ideas?"

Chuckling into the bottle of his iced tea, he says, "Oh, I definitely have a plan. But you have to be up for it, and he's going to be apoplectic... times infinity."

Snorting, I shake my head, "I can't believe you just used a fancy ass word and ended it with times infinity. Anyways, what's the plan? Fuck it, tell me on the way there."

Turning to walk away, Dorian grabs me by the crook of my elbow. Looking over my shoulder, I follow his line of sight and see he's staring at my bare feet. Wiggling my toes, I quietly laugh, "Right, shoes would be good. Well, fucky ducky. Wish me luck. Gotta sneak back in there and grab my shoes."

"Good luck."

Walking as quietly as I can down the hall, I reach the door and put my ear to it. Quiet snores filter through the door and I slowly turn the door knob. Opening the door a crack, I slip in and see Rhys still asleep. Spotting my shoes at the end of the bed, I drag my feet across the floor. I pick them up and start walking backwards towards the door. The floor slightly creaks and I hear Rhys grunt and roll over. Freezing in place, I hold my breath. His snores start again and I exhale, turning towards the door I slip through and speed walk to the kitchen. Whisper-shouting I say, "Chop, chop, let's make it snappy, Dor. That was fucking close." After grabbing his keys and drink, we sneak out of the apartment, bursting into laughter, "Hurry, run faster, Dor."

He unlocks the door and hops in, reaching over he unlocks my door for me and pushes the handle down, pushing it open for me. Grabbing the door, I hop in the car. I buckle up and laugh harder. "Let's get this chariot rolling!"

Dorian starts the car and backs out of his parking spot. Looking at the interior, I look over at Dorian and say, "She's beautiful, Dorian."

Scrunching up his face, he looks at me in confusion, "Uhh, Nova. My car wasn't assigned a gender when manufactured. Cars never are."

Shaking my head, I laugh, "You're absolutely correct, Dori-an." Turning the volume knob up, *Heartbroken* by *Jessie Murph, Diplo* and *Polo G* starts playing. Bouncing in my seat, I shout, "I love this song!" Rolling my window down, I stick my head out, the wind blowing my hair around as I sing at the top of my lungs with a smile on my face. Looking over to Dorian, I see him belting out to the song and dancing in his seat. When the song ends, I turn the volume down and ask, "So what's the plan, Dor?"

Briefly looking at me he makes a goofy face, "Hear me out, okay?" Nodding for him to continue, he takes a deep breath, "Okay, just know that if you don't like the plan, I can take you to *Vega Altair* and you can wait for him there. But I was thinking, what if I drop you off at the trails? I'll temporarily turn your location off and of course when Rhys wakes up and finds you gone with your location off, he's going to lose his shit in a panic. He's going to try to get a hold of me, even though I'll be at work unable to pick up the phone. I'll shoot him a quick text, reminding him I'm at work and ask what he needs. When he tells me to turn your location back on, because, let's be serious, that's exactly what he's going to do, I'll turn it back on for him. He'll drive like a bat out of hell to you, only to find you hanging out in the parking lot just vibin'. What do you say, SuperNova?"

An evil laugh slips out of me, "Ohhhh, he's gonna fucking kill you, Dor. I fucking love it though."

He gets a goofy smile on his face and bursts out laughing along with me. "Oh man! It's been nice getting to know you, SuperNova, but today is the day I die for sure! Think of me fondly from time to time. Oh, and definitely smoke a blunt and leave the roach with me." At this point we're laughing so hard we're clutching our stomachs and tears are rolling down our faces. Once we pull into the parking lot, I pull my phone out and turn off the location. Parking the car, he looks over at me, "You're 100% on board with this? It's totally fine if you're not."

I push the door open and give him a sidelong glance. "I promise, I'm totally fine with this. I'd give you a fist bump, but," I say, wiggling my fingers around, "ouch. Air five?"

Laughing, he nods, "Air five."

Putting our hands up we pretend to high five. He looks at the time displayed on the dash and purses his lips. "Hey, I didn't realize how early we ran out of there. I still have a bit of time before my shift starts. Wanna smoke?"

"Pfft, such a silly question. Let's go!"

"I'm gonna leave the car on so we can listen to music. Go ahead and open up the back hatch." Hopping out, I run to the back to do as he asked. As soon as I sit down, I hear the opening notes to *My Girl* by *The Temptations*. Walking around the car, Dorian sits next to me and lights up the blunt. The smell of weed and strawberry fills my nostrils. He blows out the smoke and he hands it over with a smile, "Our lucky day, already pre-rolled sitting in my center console."

I take a puff and holding the smoke in, I say with a heavy voice, "Score." Blowing the smoke up in the air, I hand the blunt back to Dorian. "I love this song. " Passing the blunt back and forth, we hum along and then finish the song together.

Sighing out loud, the high bringing out questions I usually wouldn't voice. "Hey, Dor?"

"Yeah, SuperNova?"

"I know I should ask Rhys first, but I wanna be able to ask you these things too. Do you think you guys would ever give your parents another chance? Like, you see other people happy and having good relationships with their parents, does it ever make you wonder?"

"Honestly? Even if it was an option, which it's not, I don't think I would. I mean, don't get me wrong, I do envy those with good relationships with their family, but it's never made me want to give them another chance. They had plenty of chances when I was a kid that just needed his parents. They chose not to, and I don't need them anymore. They taught me not to need them. As far as Rhys, I really don't think he would. They're as dead to him as my parents actually are."

Whipping my head around, my eyes widen and my mouth drops open. "Wh-what?"

With a sad smile he nods, "Yeahhhhh. Curiosity got the best of me. Ya know, during one of those jealous spells. I wouldn't have reached out, but I just wanted to know, ya know? Long story short, my hunch about them all those years was right. They were on drugs, and I guess the start of their death was an over-dose. The fire completed the process though. Tends to happen when you pass out with a lit cigarette." At the end of his sentence he shrugs as if we're talking about a rainy day.

Looping my arm with his, I lay my head on his shoulder and whisper, "I'm really sorry, Dor. I understand that they were horrible to you, and I wish you never experienced that. But I know their choices still hit you when you least expect it."

Laying his head on top of mine, he says, "Is your story the same, SuperNova?"

Slightly shaking my head, our hair rubs together and I respond, "Yes and no. It all went down after... a family member did some things to me, and my parents chose sides in the whole situation. For my dad, everything was more important than family. His fucking religion came first, the kids at the church came first, his job, yard work, the dog, on and on. He was the prime example of taking things too far with your beliefs. Everything always came back to it. It was the end all, be all, cure all. With my mom, it was basically the same thing, everything else was more important. What started out as a spending addiction, turned into a gambling addiction. She was so obsessed she would take money wherever she could get it. From me, from family, from her friends, her boyfriends after her and my dad split. Although, honestly, neither of them were faithful, so there was probably some crossover there. Anyways, she was so hooked on it that she would make demands of me to follow her rules and curfew, but she was never home. She'd be gone a day at a time, sometimes two or three. She would buy random things as an apology, as if that made up for it, only to turn around and throw it in my face as well as play the victim in the situation. I know other people had it worse with their parents, but things were definitely toxic with mine. I wrote my dad off when they split, and then when I was able to get the fuck out of my mom's house, I wrote her off too. I don't check in or anything, even when jealousy rears its ugly head. I learned long ago that some people just don't deserve extra chances. Especially after proving over and over that they wouldn't actually work on doing better for themselves." *Unravel* by *TK From Ling Tosite Sigure* starts playing. "Oh, that's gotta be my ghoulie. Showtime."

I turn and face Dorian as he answers his phone. "Hey-"

Loud enough to be heard without the speakerphone, Rhys starts screaming. "DORIAN! NOVA IS GONE! HER LOCATION IS OFF! TURN IT THE FUCK ON! WHERE THE FUCK COULD SHE BE?!"

225

"Whoa, whoa, whoa. Are you sure she's actually gone? Or did you just wake up in bed alone and go to the worst case scenario?"

"I'M NOT A FUCKING IDIOT, DORIAN! I LOOKED EVERYWHERE! SHE'S NOT FUCKING HERE! HER SHOES ARE GONE, HER SMOKES ARE GONE, HER PHONE IS GONE! SHE. IS. FUCKING. GONE. HELP ME, MAN! I CAN'T FUCKING LOSE HER! I WILL FUCKING END EVERYONE AND EVERYTHING IF SOMETHING HAPPENED TO HER!"

"Okay, okay. I have to hang up to turn on her location, okay? I have to head into work, so I'll shoot you a text when it's back on."

"HURRY!"

Ending the phone call, Dorian looks at me and blows air out of his mouth. Rubbing his Baphomet tattoo, he looks at me, "Yikes," hitching his thumb over his shoulder, "I better get that location on and head to work. I hope to continue this talk, probably in the afterlife now, heh."

Laughing, I nod, "I'll put in a good word for you. Have a good day at work, Dor. Be careful."

"You too, SuperNova." He shuts the back hatch and starts walking to the driver side.

"Hey, Dor?"

Looking back at me he asks, "Yeah?"

"I'm really glad you and Rhys have had each other all this time. Thanks for letting me into your family."

He clears his throat and nods, "Of course. Now you have me thinking he's really going to kill me, heh. Call if you need anything." Nodding my head, I walk backwards a few steps and then turn around to walk away.

I find a bench to sit on and pull out a cigarette to light one up. My right leg bounces as scenarios popping into my head about how this will play out. Blowing out the smoke from my final drag, I stomp the smoke out before throwing it in the garbage can. The sound of a revving engine and scattered gravel reaches my ears. *Fuck. Showtime.* As if I'm on autopilot, I jump off of the bench and walk to the back of it, crouching down. With the tips of my fingers, I hold onto the slats of the bench and peer through. Beauty comes into view and Rhys skids sideways to park. In an instant, his truck is off and I hear him jump out, door slamming shut. *Shit.*

He comes into view, walking behind his truck. His hair is disheveled and he's panting. His boots pound the pavement as he stomps across the parking lot and he screams, "NOVA!?"

Slowly rising from behind the bench, I let out a small wave when his eyes land on me. He stops all movement and just stares with his mouth agape. "Hiya, ghoulie."

Clenching his jaw, he grits out, "What. The. Fuck?!" Biting my lip, I take a step back and shrug. "Nova Skye Hart, don't you fucking dare." Taking another step back, the change in him is instant. Even from here, I can see my loving and concerned boyfriend has left the fucking building, and in his place is a beast on the hunt. "I'm telling you right fucking now, Nova Skye. If you fucking do it, you better light a fire under that sexy ass and fly like a shooting fucking star." I release the hold I had on my lip and a smile starts to break across my face as I take another step back. With a barely there nod, he says one word that sounds more animal than human, "Run."

Twisting around, I break into a sprint. As soon as I enter the trail, I hear gravel crunch and look over my shoulder. In the distance I see Rhys heading towards me with slow, calculated steps. My pulse picks up in anticipation of what's to come, and I immediately break into a sprint down the trail. I thought I had a good head start, but Rhys is fast and I can now hear him behind me. Quickly looking over my shoulder again, I can see he's not far behind, so I pick up the pace from a sprint to an all out run. *Fuck, knees to chest bitch, knees to chest.*

Rhys calls out in a deep, raspy voice, "Put some pep in your step, little star. Your ghoul is going to fucking devour you."

He sounds closer this time, I chance one last look over my

shoulder, instantly knowing it was a mistake. My feet trip over something. Knowing me, it was my own damn feet. *Fuck, I'm going down.* Falling towards the ground, I throw my hands down in front of me to catch my fall. *So much for these hands healing any time soon.* At the last second before I hit the ground, Rhys' strong arms wrap around my middle pulling me up. He leans forward and whispers in my ear, "I caught myself a shooting star. Did you think you could hide from me? I'll always find you, in this life and the next."

I'm panting, and I can't tell if it's from the run or the anticipation. Breathlessly, I whisper, "How mad are you?"

Bringing his nose to my hair he inhales, and drifts his nose down my neck. When he reaches the junction between my shoulder and my neck, he bites down hard. My body is confused, I clench my thighs from how turned on I am, but hiss from the pain of the bite. With his teeth still latched on to my skin he says, "I'm really fucking mad. Punishment now, conversation later." Rhys pushes me off the trail and towards the trees. Once he's pinned me between himself and a tree, he yanks the shorts I'm wearing down to my ankles. In an instant, my panties are torn from my body and I hiss at the air caressing my body. I look over my shoulder just as Rhys inhales the scent of my arousal on my panties and shoves them in the pocket of his jeans. "Put your hands up on the tree, Nova, and hold on tight." He then kicks each foot, separating them further apart. I hear the zipper of his jeans and a moment later, he's rubbing his cock through my soaked pussy lips. He pulls back and I whimper at the loss of him. He bends down and bites my ass cheek hard, then stands up and smacks me in the same spot, rasping out, "Bend over for me, little star. Give me what's mine." I comply immediately, so turned on and needing him inside me. He smacks my ass one more time and thrusts all the way in to the hilt. Yelling from how deep he is, he covers my mouth with his hand. "Shh, shh, you never know if other people are walking around here. Can you be quiet for me?"

Nodding my head yes, I suck in a deep breath as Rhys

removes his hand from my mouth. Moving his hand down, he wraps it around the front of my throat. Rhys thrusts in hard and fast and with every word he grits out, "You. Are. Mine."

Sweat drips down my forehead, causing bits of hair to stick to my skin. With every panted breath against the tree, my hair fans out and meshes itself with the bark. He pulls out quick and I gasp, "Wait, what are you doing?"

He rips my shoes and pants off then lifts me up against the tree. My ass scrapes against the bark and I hiss at the bite of pain that hits. Wrapping my legs around his hips, he thrusts back inside. I bite my lip to hold in my scream and my eyes close. Rhys demands in a hard voice, "Look at me, Nova!" Immediately looking into his eyes, he says, "Good fucking girl."

Blushing at his praise, he puts one hand on my throat and reaches down with the other to rub his thumb around my clit. His thrusts become erratic, so I know he's getting close. "F-fuck, Nova, fuck, I want you to cum with me. Come on, sweetheart, cum with me." He rubs my clit faster and right as he pinches it, my pussy clamps tightly around his cock and both of us cum at the same time.

"Fuuuuuuuuuuck," we yell out in unison. Both panting, Rhys kisses my forehead, as I drop my legs from his hips he pulls his cock out. Rhys looks at me, swivels his finger around making the turn around motion. Turning away from him, he begins inspecting my back and ass to see what damage the tree did. He kisses my back and ass, and I feel his tongue against my skin.

Goosebumps pop up on my flesh and I shiver, moaning, "What are you doing?"

Grabbing my hip, he spins me around and I see blood across his lips and chin. Before I have a chance to react, he crashes his lips to mine and I can taste my blood on his lips and tongue. Moaning into the kiss, he licks into my mouth and I suck my blood from his tongue. He slowly pulls from the kiss, my teeth gently scraping against his tongue. With his lips still on mine, he whispers in a pained voice, "Did I hurt you?"

229

I look in his eyes to reassure him, "No more than I wanted you to, ghoulie. Promise."

Releasing the breath he was holding, he nods, "Let's get dressed, and then we're going to have a talk about what the fuck just happened this morning."

We pull our clothes on in silence, occasionally looking at each other, as if to make sure we're really still there. I feel pieces of dirt and bark in my hair, so I shake it out. After we finish getting dressed, Rhys extends his elbow to me through which I loop my arm and sidle up as close as I can get to him. We head back to the trail, walk along the path for a bit. Rhys takes a turn off of the trail, and I realize we're heading to the area where we smoked and danced with Dorian. Reaching the logs, he chooses to sit on the fallen log, straddling it. Pointing down to the log, he says, "Sit with me."

Straddling the log in front of him, I take a deep breath and rush out, "Please don't kill Dorian!"

Snorting, he shakes his head, rubbing his fingers through his beard. "I'm not going to kill him... yet. What the fuck were you two doing? Why did you leave like that? Do you know what was going through my head when I woke up and you were just gone? I was losing my fucking mind with every possible fucking scenario of what could've happened."

An ache forms in my chest at his words. I had a feeling he would react this way, but to actually see and hear the result of it, makes me feel awful. Dropping my head, I whisper, "I'm sorry." His fingers grasp my chin and he lifts my head to look at him as I speak. "This morning I told Dorian my plan and he was adamant that it was going to end much worse than this. When he explained why, it made sense, so I asked if he had any suggestions."

Holding his hands up to stop me, he asks, "Wait. What was your plan?"

"I just really want you to teach me self defense. I know you said that you would, but I also feel like it's something you would put off for as long as possible. So I was trying to rush that. I was going to hide in the apartment and then jump out at you. Dorian basically said your fight response would kick in and you would end up hurting me and feeling awful. Like you already have been. Which by the way, you've gotta knock that shit off. You and V both, honestly. Anyways, he came up with this plan instead. We both knew you weren't going to be happy about it, but we figured it would help push you to take action and work on self defense training with me."

Running his fingers through his hair roughly, he nods. His hands grasp my thighs and places them around his hips. Sliding his hands up my thighs, he caresses my sides and wraps his arms around me tightly. Bringing his face down to my neck, I feel him breathing me in, "I was so fucking scared, little star. The thought of losing you, when we just found each other again, I couldn't fucking handle it. I know we always say this life and the next, but I'm not ready to start that journey to the next life yet. I want to enjoy every possible moment we have here in this one. I promise to help you with the training, but you have to understand this isn't a one size fits all deal. This takes time, focus and patience. Everyone has a different learning style with fighting as well. So please, just work with me here okay? And don't ever fucking do this again, please. I'm fucking begging here, and I'm not a begging man." Playing with the ends of his hair, I snort at his words. "Alright, alright. I'm normally not a begging man, but with you I am."

I kiss the side of his jaw and then his lips three times. "I'm sorry, ghoul."

His thumb glides across my bottom lip while he says, "I know, little star." He grabs his phone from his pocket and shakes it towards me, "Now to give Dorian a warning." As the beeping noise for voice recordings comes on, Rhys starts speaking, "Dori, Dori, Dori. Count your days, brother. You're lucky my little star is okay, or you'd be a dead man to me... bitch." The phone does the double beep to signal the recording is complete.

I jab my pointer finger into his shoulder and say, "That was not nice! Message him back right now!"

His head tilts back and forth like he's thinking about it. When his gaze meets mine again, he smiles big and shakes his head, tossing his hair about. "Nah."

"Rhys Alexander Slater! Message him back right now, and tell him you didn't mean it. He was so nervous about how you would react, you're going to make him feel worse."

"Pfft. Good."

"Fine, think of it this way. He did it for me. And I know how you feel about making sure I get the things I want and need. That's all he was trying to do, Rhys. Please." Pouting at him, I attempt Dorian's puppy eyes.

His eyes narrow at me and he says, "Stop trying to channel your inner Dori pup." Messing with his phone again, it beeps and he starts talking, "Queen Nova has requested I take back what I said," growling, he continues, "fine, fine, I take it back. Just don't do this shit again, dude. Keep your head on a swivel, Dor." With a double beep, the message is sent. "Better?"

Kissing his lips, I say, "Better. Thank you. I love you, ghoulie."

Deepening our kiss, our tongues fight for dominance but his wins as usual. "I love you too, little star. This life…"

"And the next." Dorian's ringtone starts playing and Rhys unlocks his phone to check the message. As he reads, his brow furrows further and further. "What is it? What's wrong?" Turning his phone towards me, I lean forward and start reading.

> D: Our client found out about the job you have in Lawrence and they want in. Unclear if they are willing to cooperate or if they'll take from you.

What the fuck does that mean? Looking up at Rhys, the only word that comes out of my mouth is, "Huh?"

His thumbs hover over his phone while he bites his lip. Reaching forward, I pull his lip from his teeth and ask, "Rhys, what does that text mean?"

Scratching his beard he says, "It's code. When something serious is happening, we say there's a job in Lawrence. He specified that it was *my* job, so that means they know I'm the one who has been taking their guys out. That last part basically means he doesn't know if they're going to back off or if they're going to start a war with me. Fuck. We gotta go, sweetheart. We gotta check out this information and stay ten steps ahead of them." As we head back to the trail he takes a deep breath and letting it out he asks, "You ready for this, little star? This could be the beginning of the end."

Stopping immediately, I turn to him, "I love you, Rhys. I'm not going anywhere. This life and the next, right?"

"Always, little star."

"I don't know how it is you are so familiar to me - or why it feels less like I am getting to know you and more as though I am remembering who you are. How every smile, every whisper brings me closer to the impossible conclusion that I have known you before, I have loved you before - in another time, a different place - some other existence." ~Lang Leav

CHAPTER 17
'TIL OUR LAST DAY

Rhys

Ever since Dorian dropped the bomb of *Amissa Stella* knowing about me, we've all been on edge. We've been working late every night trying to get as much information as possible. If I'm being honest, I give zero fucks about them knowing anything about me, bring it the fuck on. My cause for concern are the possibilities of what could happen to Nova and Dorian, hell, I'm even worried about The Horde. I haven't known them for long, but they're looking out for my girl and my brother, so they're good in my book. While The Horde is scrolling on their laptops for information we pulled on different staff from the asylum, Nova and I are helping Dorian with mapping out stops they've made. He's really embracing the part of a string theory guy, while we watch surveillance and tell him who makes stops and where. Nova is able to help pinpoint locations here in town, but I have to help him with the places out in Pendleton and Tri-Cities. Giving him the final location, he drags his finger across the map and rubs his chin. Turning to us, his eyes light up, "I have an idea!"

"What's the idea, Dor?"

He runs his fingers through his hair, which makes it stick up in disarray, "Hear me out, hear me out. Road trip!"

Nova looks back at me in confusion and then we both look at him, "Uh, we're kinda in the middle of a shit sandwich here, Dor. What makes you think this is a good time for a road trip?" I question.

Rolling his eyes, he tilts his head back and speaks to the ceiling, "I'm pretty sure I just asked you to hear me out, I wasn't finished yet." Bringing his head back down to look at us, he continues, "Do you see these areas here," pointing to the map at Pendleton and Tri-Cities, he adds, "I say we go scope out these places. We get to have an adventure, but we're working at the same time. We can find out for sure what they're doing out there, or at least get some sort of idea. What if they're branching out to these areas? This is shit we definitely need to know. Right?" Clasping his hands together he starts bouncing on his toes.

Nova shrugs, "I'm here for whatever you guys need, but a road trip definitely sounds amazing," searching my eyes, she asks, "what do you think, ghoulie?"

I think about the idea and give a slight nod, "Yeah, I think it's definitely worth looking into. But if we do this, we're not going naked. I'm bringing my bag of goodies with me just in case. We need to be extra vigilant after your info bomb. I'm not risking anything happening to you guys. Deal?" In unison, Nova and Dorian both nod with big smiles, "DEAL!"

———————⋆

Filling up my duffle in the armory, I head back to the conference room. "Alright, like I said, anything unusual happens or any emergencies, there needs to be three of you making calls. Figure out now what three are calling and who is calling each of us.

Also, don't forget to send us pings if any of these people are in the same locations as us, or at least near those locations." Everyone nods in the affirmative and Dorian taps the table. We say our goodbyes and I reach my hand out to Nova as she walks up. Bringing her hand up to my lips, I kiss it and we head out to Beauty. Once we get to the truck Dorian rounds the front and hops in on the passenger side. Opening my door, I pick Nova up and she yelps. Setting her down in the middle, I look at her and smile, "Eventually that won't surprise you anymore."

Laughing as she sticks her tongue out at me, I walk to the back of my truck and pop open the back window. I throw the duffle bag in and walk back to the driver side door. Once I start the truck, I hand my phone to Nova. She unlocks it and immediately picks out *Iron Hearts* by *Pocomota* and *Kaydro*. Grabbing my phone back from her, I pocket it and ask, "Song stuck in your head or something? That was a quick pick for you."

"Been on a loop in my head all day, might as well listen to the real deal. Sounds much better here than in my head."

"I'm sure you sang it beautifully in your head, sweetheart."

Snorting, she shakes her head, "Ghoul, just cuz you're blessed with that honey-smooth voice doesn't mean the rest of us are. My sound range is more on par with drowning kittens."

Dorian grabs our attention with his sad voice piping in, "Aww, that's awful, why would you say that, SuperNova? That's all I can picture now. Poor kitties."

Laying her head on his shoulder, she pats his arm, "Sorry, Dor. My voice sounds like nails on a chalkboard, better?" His head against hers in response and he nods.

Growling, I reach over and push his head off of hers. "Yeah, that's enough of that." Dorian rolls his lips, holding back his laugh.

Nova apparently doesn't give a shit about holding back and bursts out laughing. "Ghoulie, ghoulie, ghoulie. Of all people, I'm sure we can all agree, Dorian is the *last* person you should be worried about."

Gritting my teeth, I start driving out of the parking lot. "I'm not worried, but I don't have to like it either." *Great, even I hear the pout in my tone. Three, two, one.*

Leaning her head on my shoulder, she lays her palm against my thigh and starts cooing at me, "Aww, my ghoulie has his pouty voice. Don't be sad, ghoulie, you know I love you da mostest."

"Question, little star."

"Answer, ghoulie."

"How's that ass of yours feeling?"

I can feel her side glance as she says, "Umm, weird question, but my ass feels fine. Why?"

"Keep it up and it won't."

She squeezes my thigh and moves around in her seat as Dorian bursts out, "Oh, gross. Please tell me it won't be like this the whole road trip? Maybe we should take mine or Nova's car. Have some... space from each other."

"Jesus, Dorian. Look behind you. You would think that big ass brain of yours, that stores endless amounts of information, would remember that I put a full seat in the back. And before you start info dumping all over us, it has seatbelts and every-thing." Out of the corner of my eye I see him shaking his head mocking me. "Hit him for me, little star."

"Hit him back for me, SuperNova."

Crossing her arms, she says, "Oh no, I may be *literally* in the middle of you two, but I'm not going to get *in* the middle of this shit. You two can hash that shit out when we get to your place to pack. Hell, you guys can go at it all over again when we stop at my place to pack." Curling my lip at the words *my place*, I continue to mine and Dorian's apartment. She doesn't know it yet but it's her place too, we'll be fixing that fucking soon.

With all of our bags loaded, Nova and I hop in the front seat, and Dorian jumps in the back. "Next time, will you please let me help with the bags?"

She wiggles her fingers around, "I told you, whatever that

shit is Jade made, my hands and fingers are all better. And shouldn't we be discussing how your injuries are? How's the leg?"

"Pfft, work hazards are a part of the game, sweetheart. I'm fine. Back to you. Injured or not, you're not carrying your own shit anymore. We've been over this, get used to it."

"Agree to disagree. Phone please, DJ Little Star is officially on the job." Aiming grabby hands at me, I laugh and hand her my phone. She smiles big and looks back at Dorian. "You ready for this, Dor? I don't know if you've heard this song before, but it's definitely a song for us to jam to."

Looking in the rearview mirror, I see Dorian sit up with a dopey smile on his face, "Oooo, let's hear it!" As we leave the apartment, the song starts and she maxes out the volume and immediately starts dancing and singing along. Looking at my phone, I see it's a song called *Ecstasy (slowed down)* by *SUICI-DAL-IDOL*. I can't help the smile on my face as I watch her. She's in her own world, belting out the words, and I chance a glance in the mirror and see Dorian dancing in his seat, bobbing his head to the beat. The words are hot as fuck, and all I can think about is doing the things they sing about to my little star. The thought must cross her mind, too, as I continuously catch her staring over at me blushing at some of the words. *Noted.*

Hitting the construction over the pass, I turn down the music and call out to Dorian. "So are we thinking Tri-Cities first, then turn around and hit Pendleton? Or do you want to do it the other way around?"

"I was actually thinking we hit all the stops in Pendleton, then Tri-Cities and then when we're heading back hit Tollgate. What do you think?"

"Yeah, especially going through Tollgate, I think Nova will love it." I reach over and squeeze her thigh. She brings her hand down on top of mine and starts rubbing her thumb across my knuckles. "One of the locations is a food stop, right? I'm thinking we hit that first and get some grub while we scope shit out. Sound good?"

Dorian pipes in first, "Sounds good to me."

Nova nods and says, "Yeah, I'm good with whatever." Dorian types the restaurant into his maps app and it directs me to the location.

When we pull into the parking lot, I see that it's an Italian restaurant. "Is this just them missing home, or are we thinking they actually own this little slice of Italiano home? I'm telling ya right now, if they own it, we're not eating or drinking anything. Look it up, Dor." Pulling my hand from Nova's thigh, I reach up and start playing with her hair. She unbuckles and lays down with her head in my lap looking up at me, I start playing with her hair again.

After a few minutes, Dorian speaks up nervously, "I'm not finding any connections, but, maybe we shouldn't risk it. Let's go pick up food elsewhere and then come back here and make it look like we're trying to figure out directions or some shit."

"Dammit, Dor, I just got comfy. Ugh," Nova moans as she pulls herself up, sliding back over to her side and buckling up. After getting our food, we went back to the restaurant for a bit and there was zero activity. Finding dead ends at the rest of the locations, we hit the road for Tri-Cities.

As we get closer to Tri-Cities, I notice Nova isn't as lively with her dancing and singing. Turning the music down, I reach over and rub her thigh, "Hey. What's going on in that head of yours, little star?" Giving her time to find the words, I reach into the glove box and grab Dorian's strawberry *Swisher Sweets* and toss them back to him. I grab her smokes and a lighter, lighting one up and handing it to her. With a sad smile, she takes it and rolls down her window. Lighting up one of my own, I roll down my window and take a drag.

"Okay, so, I'm obviously new to all of this. But is it normal to just not find anything like that? Or does it seem too easy, which automatically makes it shady?" Taking a puff of her cigarette, she flicks the ash out the window and continues, "Also! How the fuck are the cops not looking for *any* of you? There's no manhunts, there's no news broadcasts or articles. Like how the fuck is that possible? Aren't you guys fucking scared that means there's some huge investigation they're keeping under wraps, and then they're gonna fucking pounce and take us all out? Fuck, they're not even going to get the bad guys, cuz they're probably paying them off. Holyyyy shit, is that what's happening here?"

Seeing an off-road area to pull into ahead, I pull into the gravel lot under a transmission tower. I park the truck and face Nova. "Hey, hey, hey. Come here."

Waving my hands towards myself, she unbuckles and slides across the seat to me. She's panting and has tears in her eyes, gripping her face, I pull her towards me and kiss her forehead. "I need you to listen to me. Can you do that for me, little star?" Sniffling, a tear falls down her cheek. Kissing it away, I whisper in a pained voice, "Don't cry, please don't cry. Everything will be okay. When it comes to the *Amissa Stella* people, hell, even people like Dor and me, we fly way under the radar. We don't do anything out in the open, and we're not well known. So if something happens, it's not something that people take notice of, other than our core group. So please, I beg of you, don't cry and don't worry. The police will *never* come for us. Okay?"

Draping his arms over the back of the seat, Dorian leans in. "I'd give you the statistical probabilities but I know it gives Reese's Pieces hives. I really don't want to deal with his whining over his informational overload hay fever, so just know that we're safe... from the police."

Moving my hand from her face I flip him off, "Get fucked, brainiac."

Shaking her head she lets out a watery laugh, "You two are seriously ridiculous, but thank you. I love you both very much.

Even when you drive me crazy with your brotherly bullshit. I'm sorry for my freak out and holding up the trip."

Grabbing her hands, I lift them to my mouth and kiss them three times. "Don't apologize, sweetheart. You haven't ruined anything. Now get your sexy ass back to your seat. The sooner we're done scoping places out, the sooner we can run around on some adventures."

Looking over my shoulder I still see Dorian with his arms crossed on the back of the seat, resting his head atop of them. Reaching back, I palm his forehead and push him backwards, "Buckle up, buttercup."

Falling back on his ass, he scowls at me, "Dick."

"Prick."

Parking across the street from a warehouse, I look back at Dorian. "Hey man, why don't you give The Horde a call and ask them to pull up traffic cam footage around here and see if we can get any information there. I'm starting to think we just gave ourselves a freebie road trip, cuz we're not finding shit."

"On it."

Nova lights up a smoke and hands it to me, then lights one of her own. "Make sure you don't throw that butt out of the window when you're done, sweetheart."

Raspberrying in my direction, she rolls her eyes, "Why thank you, Captain Obvious, I'll be sure not to do something so stupid."

"Alright, red-ass, I see what you're doing."

With a look of confusion, she lifts a brow at me, "Red-ass? Don't you mean smartass?"

"Ohhhh, no, no, little star. I meant red-ass, cuz that's the shade your ass will be if you keep it up. I love the way you try to subtly beg as if I won't notice." A blush spreads across her cheeks and she looks away, biting her lip. Sliding towards her, I push her hair behind her ear and whisper, "You blush so beautifully, little star." Her whole body shudders at my words and she takes a deep inhale off her cigarette.

"Uh guys, could we maybe keep the foreplay to a minimum? Side note, just got off the phone with Rader. They're all looking into surveillance, they'll give us a call if they find anything, or a quick text if there's nothing of importance."

"Sounds good. Shoot them a quick text and tell them to be ready to wipe traffic cam footage if they do find something. I have an idea." Scratching my beard, Dorian and Nova catch the glint in my eyes.

"Ohhh, I'm picking up what you're putting down, my friend. It rhymes with shma-shmoom doesn't it?"

Nova whips her head in my direction with a shocked look and a peal of laughter, says, "Holy shit! I knew you were packin, ghoulie, but had no clue you were packin' that!"

"Oh, eww, SuperNova. Whyyy?"

Shrugging, she looks over her shoulder at Dorian, "Sorry, not sorry."

Dorian's phone rings and he answers, "What's the word?...Fuck, okay. You guys know what to do. Yeah, thank you. Bye. Welp, time for a light show."

"Fuck yeah. Let's go."

Dorian goes through my duffle bag, grabbing everything we need and putting it at the top of the bag. Nova and I put our smokes out in the ashtray and hop out. Opening the window and tailgate, Dorian shoves my duffle towards me. I toss it over my shoulder and Dorian crawls out of the truck. Keeping an eye out, we head towards the warehouse. "Alright, Dor, hold on to all of this and we'll start placing the C4 at different points of the building."

Nova puts her hand on my arm and tilts her head, "Umm, excuse me, wanna tell me how C4 was added to your *Mary Poppins* bag?"

Behind Nova, Dorian speaks up and says, "Just a… cookbook creation. That's all."

Nova looks over her shoulder at Dorian and snorts, "Yeah, okay."

Dorian hands over the first block of C4. Placing it against the building, he holds on to the remaining bricks of C4 and permacord holding it together. Placing it in a wave pattern in three sections on each side of the building, we drag the remaining piece of permacord and walk with it as far as it will go. Reaching the end of it, we drop it and run back to the truck. Grabbing the remote for the anti-handling detonator I start a countdown. "3, 2, 1, bombs away, bitches." Clicking the button, I slowly drive down the road. The first explosion goes off and we're close enough that it jolts the truck. Seeing that it worked, I speed down the road away from the warehouse.

"Alright, boys. It's officially adventure time, and I have an idea for the first one. Is there a mall around here, ghoul?"

"Yeah, there's a mall here, sweetheart. What do you have in mind?"

With a cheshire grin she says, "Oh you'll see."

Once we get to the mall, I hop out and run to Nova's side to open her door. Kissing her lips, I step back and reach my hand out for her. "Uh, guys, little help here?"

I look back to see Dorian giving puppy dog eyes to be let out. "Dude, just climb over the seat and hop out. Watch the upholstery though." Rolling his eyes, he huffs and starts clumsily climbing over the seat. Hopping out, he shuts the door and follows behind us. As soon as we walk through the doors, Nova pulls me towards the light up map. After a quick search, she finds what she's looking for and pulls me along again. When we stop in front of the anime store, her eyes light up and she smiles wide. I look up and there's a huge wall of adult onesies.

She shuffles through them until she jumps and claps her hands, "Yay!" Grabbing a hold of one, she hands it over to me.

Getting on her toes, she lifts up for a kiss. Against my lips she says, "For my ghoulie." She steps back and I look down at the onesie, and sure enough, it's a *Tokyo Ghoul* onesie. "Start your hunt, Dor. Find one you like." Pulling down another one, I see that she picked out a *Kit The Cat Kigurumi* onesie. Dorian scratches at his chin while searching and smiles big when he finds what he wants. Pulling it down, he holds it up like kids do when they show off their Christmas presents.

When I see that it's the *No Face Man* from *Spirited Away*, I laugh, "Awesome." Dorian and Nova loop arms and start skipping to the register. "After we pay, would it be okay if we hopped in a changing room real quick and put these on?"

The cashier laughs and nods, "Yeah, that's fine. That'll be $77.97, please."

Nova starts reaching into her pocket and I swoop in. "Sneaky bringing your wallet here. Not happening though. Here ya go." Handing my card over to the cashier, they swipe it through the machine. After the approval beep, they hand me the printed receipt, "Thanks."

"No problem, have a great night."

Piling into an open changing room we all pull on our onesies. Looking at each other, we all burst out laughing. "Holy shit. Best idea ever, sweetheart." Pulling our hoods on in unison we walk out and wave at the cashier on the way out.

Nova releases my hand and runs over to an out of place shopping cart. She looks over at Dorian and waves frantically, "Come on, Dor!" She animatedly points to the cart, herself and him. Laughing, he holds on to the shopping cart as she climbs in. *Oh fuck.*

"Dorian, if she gets hurt I'm kicking your ass."

She rolls her eyes and says, "Booooo, don't be a fun sucker, ghoulie. Leave him alone." Sitting down, she holds onto the sides of the cart, while Dorian pushes the cart and carefully gets it off of the curb. Once he hits the parking lot she shouts, "Hold up, Dor." She whispers something to him and he nervously looks over at me.

"What the fuck are you two up to?"

Nova giggles, "Ohhhhh nothing, ghoulie." Standing up in the cart, she does a surfer pose and yells, "SURFS UP, DUDE!" Dorian pushes the cart through the parking lot while they yell and laugh.

Fucking A, these two will be the death of me. Parking the cart next to the truck, I walk up to it and hold my arms out to Nova. "Come here." Standing up, she wraps her arms around my neck. I grab a hold of her and lift her out of the cart. "Legs, Nova." She wraps her legs around my waist and I carry her to the passenger side. "Come on Dor, you first."

He climbs over the seat and falls over to the other side. "Oww."

"Smooth, real smooth." Placing Nova on the seat, I buckle her in and drop a kiss on her shoulder. Once I'm in, I look to her and Dorian, "Where to next?"

"Ooo, ooo, let's go to that lake off of Tollgate!"

"Fuck yeah, sounds good. Ready, sweetheart?" Making one last stop in town, we hit the road and head towards the lake. Dorian and Nova jam out the whole time. Finding an open spot where there aren't any campers, I back the truck up to an opening that faces the lake. I keep the truck running so we can listen to music. *Stargazing* by *The Neighbourhood* starts playing, and the timing is perfect. Dorian starts rolling a blunt on the seat while Nova and I sit on the tailgate. Wrapping an arm around her, she lays her head on my shoulder. She looks up at me, her hair tickling my face. "I love you, Rhys. Thank you for everything."

Dropping a kiss to her temple, I say, "I love you too, Nova. Nothing for you to thank me for, though."

In a soft voice she says, "Yes there is. You make me happy. I feel seen with you, loved and protected. Things I never thought were possible. I almost let this slip through my fingers, I'm glad I didn't."

"You may think that, but we both know we were inevitable. This life and the next, remember, little star?"

"Always." The smell of weed and peaches fills the air and Dorian starts knee crawling across the back of the truck. Sitting behind us, he takes a few hits and passes the blunt to Nova. She takes a big hit and connects our lips to blow the smoke into my mouth. *Iris* by *The Goo Goo Dolls* starts playing and I hand the blunt off to Dorian to finish. Hopping off the tailgate, I hold my hand out to Nova. I pull her down and bring her close to me. My arms wrap around her waist, she places her hands on my chest and I start swaying back and forth with her.

She smiles big and then looks up at me, "This night is perfect, ghoulie."

"Perfect." When the song ends, we walk back to the truck and see Dorian putting his phone away with a goofy smile.

"I'll send it to you guys, had to capture the moment. Anyways, I set out all the sleeping bags and pillows. Please, for the love of all the Gods, do not bone next to me."

"Ooof, I don't know if I can promise that, brother."

Nova smacks my chest, "Eww, no. Not happening, ghoul. Don't worry, Dor, I wouldn't do that to you."

Opening the driver side door, I shut the truck off and shut the door. Walking to the back of the truck I look in and see the two of them getting situated. "We leaving the back open or shut?"

Dorian and Nova both respond, "Shut!" Laughing, I nod and hop in the back of the truck. Pulling the tailgate and window shut, I kick my boots off and crawl over to mine and Nova's connected sleeping bags. We bunch up our onesies to use as pillows and go to bed.

The next morning, I wake up to scrambling and Dorian's frantic words, "Shit, shit, shit. Guys! We gotta go, like right now."

Nova snuggles in closer to me and I groan, groggily saying, "What's going on, Dor?"

"We overslept, I'm gonna need you guys to drop me off at work."

"Shit. Alright, man."

I lean down and kiss the top of her head, lightly shaking her. "Come on, sweetheart. We have to get Dorian to work."

With a cute growl, she shakes her head against me. She jolts up when I smack her ass, "Dammit, ghoul!"

Shrugging, I smirk, "Got you to get up though, didn't it?" Scowling at me, she unzips the sleeping bag and crawls towards the tailgate to slide her shoes on. Crawling up behind her, I bite her ass and she yelps. I put my boots on and open the window and tailgate. Jumping out, I turn and grab a hold of Nova to help her out. Opening the door, I pick her up and place her on the seat. I buckle her in, grab her left hand and kiss her left finger three times. I run over to my side and hop in, starting the truck. As soon as the time pops up, I realize Dorian wasn't fucking around about us oversleeping.

We pull up in front of *Amissa Stella* with 15 minutes to spare. "Look at that, Dor. Got you here with time to kill."

"Thank fuck for that. I'm gonna head in now. Hopefully starting early will get me outta here early. Please don't forget that you have to pick me up at the end of my shift." Nova moves aside for Dorian to get out.

She looks up at him and says, "Don't worry, Dor. I'll make sure we're here right on time to pick you up. Have a good day, please be careful."

"Of course. Have a good day guys." Hugging Nova goodbye, he waves at me and smiles. Waiting until he walks inside, I pull away and hit the road. I bring Nova's hand up to my lips to kiss it. Dropping her hand to my thigh, I keep hold of it there.

"What's the plan, ghoul?" At the end of her sentence, she squeezes my thigh and my cock starts to harden.

I shift in my seat and laugh, "Uh, I have a few ideas."

"Perfect, me too."

Moving her hand out from under mine, she unbuckles her seatbelt and I whip my head over, "What the fuck are you doing?" Her finger comes up to her lips to shush me as she

247

crawls across the seat. Lying on her stomach, she starts unzipping my pants. "Oh shit."

My cock hardens further, as she pulls the waistband of my underwear down enough to pull my cock out. She starts slowly pumping my cock, making my hips jerk and I slightly swerve. "Shit, shit." Correcting the truck, I bring my hand down and rub the back of her head. She licks around the tip of my cock, and runs her tongue through the slit. "Mmm, fuck, I love you."

Kissing the length of my cock she says, "I love you, too." The vibration of her voice against my cock makes it twitch. Her tongue glides against my cock before she puts her mouth around the head of my cock and starts sucking. She pushes her head forward until her nose brushes against me, my cock hits the back of her throat and she slightly gags. The feeling makes me groan. With her tongue licking the underside of my cock side to side, she sucks harder and bobs her head. Running my fingers through her hair, I warn her, "Fuck, I'm not gonna last long, sweetheart. I'm so fucking close." My words seem to spur her on because she sucks harder and faster. Bringing the tip of my cock to the back of her throat again, she does small bobs of her head and swallows around my cock. Sweat drips down my temple and I feel the tingle running up my spine. Gripping the steering wheel tight, I press my left foot down hard against the floor of the truck, "I'm cumming, little star, oh fuck, I'm cumming." Spurt after spurt of cum shoots down her throat. Slowly sliding back, she sucks the tip of my cock trying to get every last drop. After one last spurt on her tongue, she releases my cock with a pop. Looking up at me, she sticks her tongue out, showing me the last bit of cum there. Swallowing it down, I groan. "I fucking love when you do that." Tucking my softening cock away in my underwear, she buttons and zips my pants back up and slides over to her side again. Once we get to my apartment, I hop out and slam my door shut. Running to her side, I open the door and grab a hold of her. Tossing her over my shoulder, I shut the door and start running to the apartment.

Nova laughs and smacks my ass, "Rhys, slow down."

"No can do, sweetheart." As soon as the door is shut, I walk her over to the glass coffee table in the living room. I slide her down my body, laying her down on top of the coffee table.

"What are you doing, ghoul?"

"Don't distract me, little star. It's my turn. Be a good girl and let me love you." At my words, she squeezes her legs together. Grabbing her shoes, I throw them behind me and lean down to unzip and unbutton her pants, pulling them down slowly. Walking to the other side of the table, I pull her shirt off and discard it to the floor. I then grab the center of her bra with both hands and tear it apart.

Gasping, she looks at me bewildered, "What the fuck, Rhys?!"

"It was in my way, now it's not, problem solved." Bending down, I grip her breasts and squeeze them together. A slap to the side of her breast makes her gasp turn into a moan. Dropping a kiss on her lips, I walk to the end of the table and kneel down on the floor. I grab her calves and pull her towards me. Throwing her legs over my shoulders, I grip her thighs, pulling until her ass is hanging off of the edge of the table. Her hands reach out as if to catch herself and I click my tongue. "Hands up, little star. Grip the edge of the table." Throwing her hands back she grabs the edge of the table. "Good girl."

Moaning at my words, she wiggles a little. Grazing my beard along her inner thighs, she shivers as goosebumps pop up across her flesh. I lick her thighs where goosebumps have popped up. Bringing my nose down, I run it along her folds and nudge her clit. She's already soaked and I groan at the taste of her. Bringing my hand to her pussy, I spread her open and lick from her entrance to her clit. Reaching up, I press two fingers to her lips, "Open up, sweetheart." Once she opens her mouth, I push the two fingers inside, "Suck."

Wrapping her lips around my fingers, she sucks and licks my fingers clean. Pulling my fingers free with a pop, I bring them down to her pussy and pump them in and out of her. My lips come down on her clit, my tongue flicking against it. Curling my

249

fingers up, I hit her g-spot, each time her hips thrust up and her moans become louder. Hitting the spot over and over, I feel her start to tighten around my fingers. Her thighs start to tremble, and I let go of her clit and slowly pull my fingers out. She whines at the loss of me and I smack my hand down against her pussy. Moaning louder, she wiggles closer to me. "Do. Not. Cum."

Pushing my fingers back in and latching onto her clit, I start all over again. I bring her to the edge over and over again. Her whole body is shaking and she's panting. I grab her under her ass and stand up with her. Gripping my beard, she pulls me towards her and starts kissing me, tasting herself on my lips. Licking my bottom lip, she pushes forward and deepens the kiss. My hands squeeze her ass andI groan into the kiss, sucking her tongue into my mouth. Fumbling with the doorknob on my door, I kick it open and toss her on the bed, making her yelp and then giggle.

Reaching behind me, I pull my shirt over my head and toss it down. While kicking my boots off, I start unbuttoning and unzipping my pants. Ripping my pants and underwear down, I start kicking them off of my feet. At the end of the bed, I look Nova up and down. My cock hardens and I bring my hand down to stroke it. She lifts up on her elbows and watches me while biting her lip. I smirk when she makes the come hither gesture. Dropping to the bed, I crawl over her, dragging my hands up her legs as I go. Apparently I'm taking too long because she sits up gripping my beard and pulls me towards her.

Biting down on my lip, she demands, "Stop teasing me and put your fucking cock in me, ghoul!" I get in between her legs and bring her right one up and over my shoulder. Turning my head, I kiss her calf. Gripping my cock with one hand, I guide it to her entrance. Running it up and down her soaked slit, I bring it back down and push in. With every thrust forward, I tighten my grip on her throat. Gurgling out moans with every squeeze, she pants, "Kiss me, kiss me, please fucking kiss me." Growling,

I bring my lips to hers and kiss her roughly. Nipping and sucking at her lips, I shove my tongue in and tangle our tongues together. I feel Nova's pussy tighten around my cock before she shouts into my mouth, "I-I'm cumming, fuck, I'm cumming!" Thrusting harder and faster, sweat dripping down our bodies, my hips start to stutter. Pushing through it, I continue pumping my cock in and out of her. Right as I'm about to cum, I thrust forward as hard as I can, setting Nova off again. Her whole body is convulsing as she screams my name out. Both of us are breathing hard into each other's mouths. Sliding her leg from my shoulder, it falls to the bed with a thud.

I rest my weight on my arms, pressing my body against hers. "I live here now."

Turning her face, she kisses my beard, "As much as I love you and I love this, we need to set an alarm to get Dorian."

"I regret to inform you that Rhys can't come to the phone right now. Please leave a message after the beep. BEEEEEEEP!"

Pulling my beard she laughs, "Rhys Alexander! Just do it. I know you don't want him staying there any longer than he has to."

Grumbling into her neck I say, "Evil woman."

"You love it."

Biting her neck and making her moan, I let go and whisper in her ear, "Only cuz I love *you*."

"I love you too, ghoulie. Now quit stalling."

I get up to grab my phone from my pants and set the alarm, leaving it on the nightstand. "There. Happy?"

Patting the bed aggressively, she says, "Yes, now get your ass in bed. You're my pillow." Jumping over her, I lay down and open my arms, letting her snuggle in across my chest as I grip her tightly to me.

Waking up a few hours later, we stumble around and get dressed. I bend forward and point to my back. "Hop on, sweetheart." Once she jumps on my back, I reach behind me and grab

251

her ass to hoist her up. Wrapping herself around me, I walk us to the kitchen and open the fridge. Grabbing one of her *Monsters*, I put it above my head so she can grab it. I shut the fridge with my foot after I get a *Cherry Coke* for myself and head towards the door. Getting situated in the truck, we head towards *Amissa Stella*.

"How much longer do you think he has to work there for?"

Scratching my beard and thinking about it, an answer doesn't form. "Honestly, I don't have a fucking clue. Hopefully sooner rather than later. He doesn't want to be there any longer and none of us want him there any longer either."

Nova gives a full body shudder, "I couldn't imagine. I don't know how he does it. I would lose my mind being there around those sick fucks."

I bring her hand to my mouth and kiss her knuckles, "Me too, little star, me too." Pulling into the parking lot, I find a parking spot and we wait. I look at the time to see that we made it ten minutes early. Looking over at Nova, I give her a cocky smirk.

"What?"

"Wanna make out?"

"Kinda. You think Dorian wants to?"

Rearing my head back, I grit my teeth, "What the fuck did you just say?"

Her serious face cracks and she bursts out laughing, "Oh my god you should see your fucking face! Priceless. God, that was gross to say, but totally fucking worth it for that reaction."

Scowling, I cross my arms over my chest, "Not. Cool." Unbuckling her seatbelt, she slides over and puckers her lips. Leaning in to kiss me, I keep dodging them, "Nope, don't want a kiss anymore." She stops trying and starts to move back to her side. Grabbing a hold of her, I drop kisses all over her face. "I thought you didn't want a kiss anymore, ya big baby?"

"I lied. I always want your kisses. Now kiss me back."

A knock on the top of the truck gets our attention and we

look up. "Oh cool, he got out early. Let's blow this popsicle stand."

"When death takes my hand I will hold you with the other and promise to find you in every lifetime." ~Commitment

CHAPTER 18
TAKE ME BACK TO EDEN

Nova

Rhys, Dorian and I pull into the parking lot of *Vega Altair*. By the looks of the empty lot, we've arrived before The Horde. Rhys parks the truck and turns it off. As he pulls the keys from the ignition, a smile forms on my face. Slowly reaching down, I place my hand over the button to release my seatbelt. Just as my thumb touches it, in a sharp tone, I hear, "Don't. You. Dare." Biting my lip to hold back a laugh, I start to push the button down. My hand is ripped from my seatbelt and brought to Rhys' mouth. After a quick bite to my hand, I pull my hand away from him and hold it to my chest.

"Umm, excuse you," I say.

Narrowing his eyes he huffs, "No, no, excuse you. I told you to stop touching that thing. Have you already forgotten what happened the last time you tried that?"

My heart flutters and my pussy pulsates. Clenching my thighs, I glare at him, "Damn it, ghoul!"

Dorian props his arms up on the back of the seat and looks between us, "Uh, what's happening here? Can we go inside now?"

Rhys and I answer in unison, "Nothing."

He looks between the two of us again, realization dawning, "Oh, eww. Let me the fuck out, right now. You two are insatiable, honestly."

Rhys guffaws and shakes his head. Reaching over, he unbuckles my seatbelt. Hopping out, he leaves his door open for Dorian. Rushing around the truck, he gets to my side and yanks the door open quickly. Dramatically throwing his arm out, he slightly bows his head, "Milady."

Rolling my eyes, I clear my throat and put on a posh accent, "Why, thank you kind sir."

With a big smile, he grabs a hold of me and pulls me from the truck. Slowly sliding me down his body, I run my hands down his chest. Looking into each other's eyes, we both move in for a kiss. A throat clears and we pull back and look over at Dorian.

With his hand holding on to the strap of his messenger bag, he slightly pulls it away from his shoulder, "Guys, seriously. *Work. Amissa Stella.* Let's go, please."

Dodging Rhys' arm, I squeeze between him and the door and walk over to Dorian, looping my arm around his. "Sorry, Dor." When we walk up to the doors, Dorian places his hand against a black box. A whirring sound starts and a bright, green light flashes underneath his hand. When it expands, a handprint grows in size and then shrinks to fit the size of his hand.

There's a double beep and an automated voice says, "Please continue with the retinal scan." There's a clicking noise and the automated voice says, "Please keep eyes open until you hear approved or denied." Dorian leans forward, with his eyes to the retinal scan. There's a clicking noise and the automated voice says, "Approved," with that the doors make a clicking noise and then buzzes. Dorian opens the door, letting me go through first.

I look at the scanners and him with amazement, "That is so fucking cool."

He smiles over at me, "If you want, we can get you set up in the system, as well."

My eyes widened, "Really?! That would be amazing. Thanks, Dor."

Nodding his head at me, he looks over at Rhys walking up. He starts shuffling inside, pulling the door with him. "Don't you fucking dare, Dori!"

Slamming the door shut, he stands there waving and I gasp. Rhys reaches the door and slams his fist against it, "Hardy, har, fucking har, Dori. Now open up." Dorian continues standing there, his body shaking in silent laughter. Rhys looks over to me and lifts a brow, "A little help here, little star."

"Oh, no, no. Nice try, Reese's Pieces, don't rope your girl-friend into this. This is payback, bitch."

"Remember this next training session." Dorian whips his head in my direction with a panicked look on his face and mouths 'fuck'.

Walking up to him, I pat his shoulder, "I would suggest running, in three, two-" Before I even say one, he's already taking off in a full on run with his messenger bag smacking against his hip. Laughing, I turn my attention back to Rhys. Grabbing the door handle, I push the door open and he grabs a hold of it.

Slipping in, the door shuts behind him and he grabs a hold of my ass, pulling me close. Bringing his mouth down, he kisses my forehead, cheeks, nose and then finally my lips. Lingering against my lips he says, "You always save me, my little star. I love you."

Kissing him again, I say, "I love you, too, ghoulie. Now let's go see where Dorian ran off to."

After finding Dorian, he got all skittish and grabbed a hold of me. Pulling me with him, he took care of getting my hand and retina scans completed. We're now back in the conference room and I see Rhys sitting on the edge of the table watching surveillance footage on the screens. Walking in front of him, I step back between his legs and rest against him. Wrapping his arms around me, he brushes my hair to the side and places a kiss behind my ear. Nuzzling further into me, he sighs, "I missed you, little star."

Melting into his embrace, I lay my head on his shoulder and turn towards his face, "I wasn't gone that long, ghoul, but I missed you too. We're fucking ridiculous, I swear."

"You guys really are cute, but very ridiculous."

Shooting my eyes in Dorian's direction, I glare, "Bite your tongue, heathen."

Sticking his tongue out, he shakes his head back and forth, "Mlehhh."

Rhys squeezes my hips, "Alright, you two. I cannot believe you're making me be the voice of reason here. We have work to do, let's get to it."

Dorian puts his tongue back in his mouth and nods, "Of course. And yeah, you being the adult here is really weird." He gives his body a full shake, "Gross. Anyways, I think our focus should be on the higher ups, so to speak. Don't get me wrong, we still need to take out the ones on the bottom of the totem pole, but we also need to look into what the big wigs are up to. We'll watch surveillance and follow their patterns. I also think during one of my shifts I need to sneak in some of our own cams and bugs."

Looking over my shoulder, Rhys nods his head with his jaw clenched.

"What's wrong?"

Releasing a breath, he shakes his head, "It's a great idea, that will help us out a lot, but I'm really worried about you, Dor. I know we've worked on training, bud, but what if there's more than one of them? I think we should go over what your exact plan is here."

Before he starts, I turn towards Rhys and start pushing on his thighs, "Scootch, please." Putting his hands behind him, he starts sliding back on the table. Opening his legs further, I hop up on the table. Settling in, Rhys scoots forward, pressing his body to mine. Closing his thighs around mine, he brings his arms around me and rests his hands on my thighs. Nodding my head, I bring my hand out to Dorian, "Okay, sorry, please continue."

Clapping his hands together, he starts, "Okay, so I'm thinking it should be pretty easy since I'm the janitor. I'll carry a few cams in one pocket, bugs in the other. While changing out garbage bags, I can place the bugs on the edge of the trash cans that curl over at the top. The cams will be a little more tricky. I won't know a good spot until I'm actually in the room I'm planting it. I'll definitely need to keep an eye and ear out for people so I don't get caught."

My vision starts to blur and my head pounds, rubbing at my temples I lean further against Rhys. Taking a deep breath, I open my eyes and see Dorian checking out surveillance again. Pulling Rhys' hands off of my thighs, I hop off of the table. "I'm gonna go get a drink from the kitchen, do you guys want anything? And, before you say no, I'm thinking we need a smoke session, so you're going to want a drink."

Dorian snaps his fingers and shoots a finger gun my way, "I like the way you think, SuperNova. I'll roll a blunt now, and I think I'll go with one of my iced teas. Any flavor is fine, please and thank you."

With an overly exaggerated wink and a thumbs up, I tell him, "I gotchu, Dor." Rhys leans against his elbow on the table and swings his legs back and forth over the edge. "I'll take whatever you bring me, sweetheart. There's also a surprise in the fridge for you."

My eyes light up and I gasp, "A surprise?! For me?!" Turning away from them quickly I run to the kitchen, the sounds of their laughter trailing behind me.

Running straight to the fridge, I rip open the door and see rows of my *Monster*. A crazy smile appears on my face and I let out a silly laugh, "Yayyyyy!" Grabbing a Monster, I pop it open and take a sip. Setting it on the counter, I search the fridge for an iced tea and *Cherry Coke*. Pulling them both out, I kick the fridge shut and hold the two drinks in one hand. With my free hand, I pick up my *Monster* and head back to the conference room. I sway a little as I walk through the door. Bracing myself against the door, I take a deep breath and then push towards the table. Putting the drinks down on the table, I see that Rhys is still on the table rubbing his temples. Brushing my fingers through his hair, I lean in and kiss his temple. "Drinks are on the table, you two. Before we smoke that blunt, I think we should order some food and call The Horde so they can take over for the day. Sound good?"

Rhys grabs my hand and pulls me in between his legs. Wrapping his arms around me, he nuzzles into my neck, whispering, "Sounds good, little star." Looking over my shoulder, I see Dorian frozen. His eyes are wide open, the blunt to his lips and the flame of the lighter just in front of the blunt.

"Dor, you're going to burn yourself. How about Rhys and I make the phone calls at the same time, that way we can smoke sooner."

Turning my head towards Rhys, I let him know, "You can order our food, I'll call The Horde."

He looks at me with a half smile, "Why am I not surprised?"

Shrugging, I pull my phone out of my pocket and call V. While the phone is still ringing, I shake it in Rhys' direction and mouth, 'food'. Making a face at me, he grabs his phone from his pocket and makes his call. There's a click on the other end of the line and then V's voice, "*Swan & Scribe*, this is Vanessa, how may I help you?"

"Hey, V," stepping back from Rhys I walk to the other side of the table so our conversations don't clash.

"What's up, Nova girl?"

Rubbing my forehead, I lean against the table, "Hey, the guys and I are at the warehouse and we're starting to hit a wall. Rhys is ordering us food right now and we're going to smoke, but we need to take a knee here. I'm calling in reinforcements for the *Amissa Stella* hunt." I hear V's laughter on the other end of the phone and pull it away from my ear, bringing it back, I ask, "Uh, what's so funny?"

Through laughter, she says, "I just didn't realize we needed an announcement that we're needed so you can go *take*," more laughter," a, a, kneeeee."

At this point she's wheeze-laughing but I roll my eyes and a chuckle escapes me. "V! Get it together, ya perv! That is not what I meant, and you fucking know it! When you get yourself under control, can you please contact the rest of The Horde?"

Through peals of laughter she shouts, "YUP! BYE!"

Ending the call, I pocket my phone and walk back over to Rhys and Dorian. They're both looking at me with their heads tilted. Waving my hand and shaking my head, "Nothing, just V and her dirty mind twisting my words. Anyways, what's the update on food?"

"I went with pizza. I almost went with burgers and fries, but I know how you feel about cold fries. That okay?"

Walking up to him, I go to give him a kiss on the cheek, but he turns his head and captures my lips. Smiling against his lips, I say, "Perfect. Thank you, ghoul."

Behind me, Dorian clears his throat, "I'm lighting this bitch up, quit sucking face so we can start sucking on this blunt." Snorting at his words, Rhys and I burst out laughing. With an exasperated sigh, Dorian rolls his eyes and looks up to the ceiling shaking his head. "You guys are honestly the worst sometimes." Bringing his head back down, he has a smile on his face, bringing the blunt to his lips, he lights it and puffs twice then blows the smoke out. Taking another hit, he holds the smoke in and starts shaking on the cough he's holding in. Handing the blunt to Rhys, he turns his head and coughs out a stream of smoke. Bringing his fist to his chest, he pounds and rubs his chest in circles.

Walking along the table, I place my hands on it and climb up. I have my head pressed against Rhys' back as I lie back on the table. Feeling his body move away, I tilt my head back as far as I can and see him grabbing the chair at the end of the table and sitting down. He reaches forward with grabby hands and I stretch my arms above me. With the blunt in his mouth, he grabs my hands and pulls me until my head is at the edge of the table. Letting go of my hands, I let them drop so they hang over the table. He purses his lips and takes a drag off of the blunt, the smell of strawberry and weed floats through my nostrils. I'm mesmerized by the flare of the cherry when he inhales. With the smoke in his lungs, he brings his arm back, handing the blunt to Dorian. Grabbing both sides of my face, he leans down until our lips seal together. Slowly blowing the smoke into my mouth I start inhaling it. Rhys pulls from my mouth and leans back as I blow the smoke out. Making our rounds with the blunt, Dorian puts it out just in time for a buzzer to go off. The screens pull up the video feed for the camera outside the doors.

Dorian and Rhys turn into kids on Christmas morning, their faces lighting up and they shout, "FOOD!" making me start giggling uncontrollably. Rolling off of the table, I barely catch myself in time. Holding my stomach, I try to take breaths in between laughs.

Pointing towards the door, I laugh, "Food... Getting... Food."

I feel arms wrap around me as we walk towards the door, "Not without me, little star. Can't be too careful." Walking to meet the delivery guy is next to impossible with Rhys holding on to me from behind. We're practically waddling our legs with our bodies swaying side to side, laughter pouring from both of us the whole way. Reaching the door, Rhys lets go of me and pushes the door open. Clearing his throat, he greets the delivery guy, "Hey man, thanks."

After we've grabbed the stack of pizzas, the delivery guy waves and says, "Enjoy."

Rhys steps back in and I shut the door behind him. Getting back to the conference room, he puts the stack of pizzas on the table and lays everything out, opening them all to reveal what he ordered. My eyes light up when I see a cheese pizza, a pepperoni pizza, a meat lover's and a chicken and bacon pizza with garlic parmesan sauce. Bouncing on my toes, I start clapping, "It's a good thing I know you guys like this stuff too, or I'd think you ordered all of this just for me." I sit down and grab a slice of cheese pizza.

Dorian runs over and grabs a slice of pepperoni, stacking a meat lover's slice on top. Opening his mouth wide, he takes a huge bite of the two slices together and groans, "Mmmm, it's so good, sooooo goooood. Get in my belly."

Rhys pulls out the chair next to me and grabs my legs, pulling them onto his lap. Grabbing a slice of meat lover's, he sits back and takes a big bite. "Fuck yeah. Got my girl, got my best friend, smoked a good blunt and now I'm gonna devour this fucking peeeeza pieee."

Laughing, I take a bite of my pizza. Barely getting the words out with my mouth full I tell him, "Eet uh goo thing I ov oo sho much."

Snapping his head in my direction, he barks out a laugh, "Wanna run that by me again there, sweetheart?"

Narrowing my eyes at him, I obnoxiously chew my food and swallow it. Enunciating my words, I say, "I. Said. It's. A. Good. Thing. I. Love. You. So. Much. Happy? Did ya catch it now?"

Putting one hand up, he says, "Hey, don't blame me for not understanding pizza mouth language. And why is it a good thing you love me so much? I mean I know why, but why are you saying that?"

"Cuz you were being a goof. Finish your peeeeza pieee, ghoulie."

"Okay," shrugging his shoulders he shoves the rest of the pizza in his mouth. The camera feed from out front is still displayed on the screen and we see The Horde all pulling up and parking. Dorian keeps a close eye on their approach and shoves the remainder of his pizza sandwich in his mouth. When the group gets close enough, he hits a button on his phone and the doors open for them. The Horde all walk through the door, greeting us. Everyone grabs a slice of pizza and takes a seat at the table. Rhys taps my ankle when I'm taking a sip of my *Monster*. Looking up at him, he nods his head towards the door. Scrunching my brows, I tilt my head in response. His eyes shift between the door and me and he nods his head to the door twice. Dropping my legs from his lap, I stand up.

Following suit, Rhys stands and addresses everyone, "Dori, you fill them in on everything before we all head out. Nova and I are gonna go walk the high off so I can drive us home."

Everyone chuckles and Fish laughs, "Walk, right." Flipping him off, Rhys grabs my hand and interlaces our fingers, pulling me out of the conference room.

Walking through the door of the armory, Rhys shuts the door and locks it. At the click of the lock, I look down at it and then back up to him. I feel the heat in my cheeks and I smile, "What are ya doing, ghoul?"

Breaking out the sexy smirk that makes me weak in the knees, he nods behind me. "Hop up on the ammo island, little star."

Turning around, I walk up to it and climb up. Dangling my legs over the edge, I rock my feet back and forth with my hands in my lap. "Now what?"

Ignoring my question, he slides his coat off of his shoulders, letting it fall to the floor. Reaching over his head, he pulls his shirt off. Biting my lip, my eyes are glued to the tattoo covering his chest. As much as I love our accidentally matching tattoos, I really love this one. Rhys prowls towards me with a wicked glint in his eyes. Walking behind me, I start to turn my head to look at him and he 'tsks' at me. Rolling my eyes, I look in front of me again. His hands and shirt come into my field of vision, and I see that he's rolled the shirt up a few times. Bringing the shirt over my eyes, he wraps it around my head, gently knotting it at the back. Bringing his lips to my ear, he whispers, "Is it too tight? Pulling your hair?"

Shaking my head no, I whisper back, "It's perfect. Plus you already know I don't mind my hair being pulled."

Growling in my ear, he says, "Careful. Only my hands will have the pleasure of pulling your hair. Not even my shirt gets to do that." Placing a kiss behind my ear, I whine at the loss of him when he pulls away. I hear a drawer open behind me and things being shuffled around. The drawer slams shut behind me and he says in a low command, "Give me your hands, little star." Shivering at his words and tone, I move my hands behind my back for him. Grabbing my wrists with one hand, he pulls until I fall back against him. "Such a good fucking girl."

Clapping my thighs together, I let out a breathless, "Fuck." I feel hard plastic around one wrist and hear a zipping noise as it clasps around my wrist. Doing the same to the other wrist, he begins rubbing circles above the zip tie cuffs.

"Move your wrists a little for me, sweetheart. How do they feel?"

Slightly moving my wrists, I feel the bite of the plastic against my wrists, but it's not too much to handle. "They're good, I'm okay."

Wrapping his arms around me he pulls me further back, my ass and legs sliding across the island. Once my shoes hit the island, they start scraping against the countertop, leaving a squeak in its wake. My feet pass over the edge and drop to the floor. Running his hands over my breasts, he slowly slides down over my stomach until he reaches the hem of my shirt. Slowly lifting it up, his knuckles caress my skin on the way up. A little shiver overtakes me at the tickling sensation and the anticipation of what's to come, other than me. When the shirt is over my breasts, he lets go and grabs my bra in the center. Pulling it down, my breasts fall out of the cups and the air hits my exposed nipples, which start to tighten. Twisting my shirt in his hands, he pulls forward and my upper body hits the countertop. I hiss at the feeling of my nipples grazing the cold wood. Bringing his hands to the front of me, he unbuttons and unzips my jeans. Running his thumbs under my panties, he slowly pulls my jeans and panties down. He runs his fingertips against the backs of my calves and up to my thighs, squeezing the globes of my ass. Feeling his lips on my ass, he kisses each cheek and then leaves a bite behind. I jolt as I feel his hand slap

264

down hard on my left cheek. My surprised gasp turns into a moan. I hear the clink of Rhys' belt and then his zipper. Grabbing my hips, he pulls them back to further expose my pussy to him.

I feel the head of his cock dragging through my soaked slit and he groans, "Fuck, little star. Always so soaked for me." Panting at his words, I push my ass further back. Another slap to my ass has me pushing against the island. "Be a good girl and stay there. I promise to make it up to you, but this has to be fast." The head of his cock pushes through my entrance and he thrusts forward, in one stroke he's fully inside of me.

"Fuck, Rhys."

Grabbing my hips, he squeezes, "Say it again, little star." With every thrust in he hits my g-spot, making me moan.

"Rhys. Fuck, Rhys." Grabbing a hold of my hair, he twists it around his hand and pulls back while thrusting inside of me. "Oh, fuck. Yes. Oh, please, Rhys."

Fucking me harder, through gritted teeth he asks, "Please what? What do you need, little star?"

With every thrust my teeth clack together and I shout, "Make me cum, please. Please make me cum, ghoul." He pushes between my shoulder blades, laying me across the counter again.

Pressing himself over my back, he whispers in my ear, "I fucking love it when you beg me, sweetheart. It sounds so sweet coming from your lips."

Pulling back until just the tip of his cock is in me, he thrusts all the way into the hilt and swivels his hips. He brings his hand down to rub my clit in fast circles and I feel the tingle start in my toes, shooting up my legs. My heart is racing and my stomach tightens. "Fuck, I-I'm cumming, Rhys, fuck I'm cumming."

My pussy tightens around his cock and he groans, pinching my clit. I fall apart and feel my pussy soaking his cock and my thighs. "Holy, holy fucking shit, little star."

His hips stutter and lose their rhythm. Pushing further into me, he freezes and I feel his cock pulsing, my pussy milking every last bit of cum from him. Leaning over me, every pant of breath floats through my hair. There's a pound on the door and we both jolt, his cock pulling free from me.

"GUYS! Now that you have COME down from your high, get your asses home and *sleep*!"

Both of us start laughing, "Holy fucking shit! If he showed up before you made me cum, I might've had to kill your best friend, ghoulie."

"Fuck, you and me both, little star. If he did, I definitely would've followed through on changing his contact name to Cockblock."

We clean ourselves up, get dressed and walk back to the conference room hand in hand to say our goodbyes. Walking into the conference room, they all erupt in boisterous cheers. When the cheers die down, I laugh, shaking my head, "Well, we were going to be nice and say our goodbyes, but on that note," lifting my hands up, I flip them the double bird and start walking backwards, "get fucked, bitches."

Turning away I hear a shout of, "I THINK Y'ALL DID THAT ENOUGH FOR ALL OF US!"

After getting to my apartment, Rhys and I decided to lay on the couch together watching *Fruits Basket*. After watching a few episodes, we pull ourselves from the couch and walk to my room. On the way there, I make a stop in my bathroom and grab my Bluetooth speaker. Turning it on while heading to my room, I put it down on my nightstand. I pull my phone out and scroll through my music. Pausing at *Mind Over Matter* by *PVRIS*, my thumb hovers over the choice. Snapping out of it, I click the song and it starts playing through my speaker. I walk over to my dresser and grab my wooden box. I turn to see Rhys stripping out of his clothes and freeze. His shirt is already off, and I watch as he shimmies out of his jeans. Just as they pass his knees, he must feel my eyes on him because he looks up and smirks. "Like what you see, little star?" The words register too late and he adds, "I'll take that as a yes."

Shaking my head, I then nod, "Mhmm."

Chuckling, he pulls his jeans over his feet and tosses them across the room. Flopping down on my bed in just his black boxer briefs, he spreads his legs, interlocking his fingers and places his hands behind his head. Blinking a few times, I walk over to the bed and put the wooden box down next to him. He looks down at it and back up to me, "What's that?"

Nodding towards it, I say, "Open it up, ghoulie."

As he opens it, I start pulling my clothes off. His eyes light up when he opens the box "Fuck ye-" His words die on his tongue as he looks up and sees me in just my bra and panties. Looking me up and down, he clears his throat, "As I was saying, fuck yeah." Biting my lip, I slightly blush at his appraisal.

Rubbing my temples, I look at him and point to the box, "Light it up, ghoul."

He lights the joint with a lighter and takes a puff, blowing the smoke out in my direction. "As you wish, little star." I pick up the box to carry it over to the dresser and swap it for my ashtray. Walking back to the bed, I set it on the nightstand and drop my knees to my bed. Crawling over to Rhys, I turn over and lay my head on his stomach with my legs dangling off of the edge of the bed. Running his fingers through my hair, he softly says, "That can't be comfy, sweetheart. Come lay between my legs."

I sit up and then flip myself over so I can crawl in between his legs. Lying on my stomach, my breasts squish between me and his hips. Bringing my hands up to his stomach, I prop my chin against my hands and look up at him. Looking back at me, he smiles, "It's getting harder and harder to decide which view I like best with you."

Wiggling a little, I feel his cock slightly harden and I snicker, "Mmm, I can tell it's getting harder."

Handing me the joint, he shakes his head on a laugh, "Behave, little star. We're supposed to be *resting*. You're going to crumble the last bit of control I have here." Sucking on the joint, I inhale the smoke. Holding it in, I slowly start blowing it out in his direction. This moment reminds me of my conversation with

Dorian, and yet again my lack of filter while smoking rears its ugly head.

"Can I ask you a question, Rhys?"

Grabbing the joint from my outstretched hand, his eyes soften, "You can ask me anything you want, Nova."

Biting my lip, I look away, "You say that now."

I feel his fingers on my chin and he turns my head in his direction. "Hey, I promise, you can ask me anything. What's going through that mind of yours, sweetheart?"

Releasing the breath I was holding, I say, "Do you ever think about finding your parents again? Talking to them? Maybe even forgiving them?"

There's a slight click in his jaw and he takes a drag from the joint. Slowly blowing out the smoke, he looks down at me and hands me the joint. "I don't need to find my parents, I know exactly where they are. Their location never changes. Just like the way they are never changes. And no, I don't plan on ever speaking to them or forgiving them. That ship sailed long ago. They made their choices and I've made mine. They didn't want me and I don't want them. Why? Are you thinking about that with your own parents? It's okay if you are. Just because I feel the way I do, doesn't mean you have to feel the same. You're free now, sweetheart. You can feel whatever it is you need to feel."

Stretching over Rhys and the bed, I tap ashes onto the ashtray, take a hit and then hand the joint back to him. Blowing out my smoke, he takes smoke in and then curls his finger at me. Leaning in, he presses his lips to mine and exhales. Inhaling the smoke, I grab the joint from him and put it out in the ashtray. I blow out the smoke away and lay down next to him. Rolling my head towards him, I sigh, "Sometimes I get curious. The curiosity usually hits after I get jealous of an interaction I've seen with a kid and their parent. But no, I don't think I'd ever choose to talk to them again, and I've never been good at the whole forgiveness thing. I'd honestly prefer forgetting all about it if I could. Looking back, there aren't many happy or fun memories, so maybe it's just better to forget. I mean, don't get me wrong, there were times where things were happy or fun, but I second guess it now, ya know? Like I can't trust what my mind is telling me. Does that make sense?"

He brings his hand to my hip and starts rubbing circles along it with his thumb. "It makes perfect sense, sweetheart. Anytime you need to talk about this, I'm here. Or if you ever change your mind and decide it's an avenue you want to pursue, then I'm with you every step of the way."

Closing the distance, I kiss his lips three times, and whisper, "I love you, ghoul."

"I love you too, little star." *Take Me Back To Eden* by *Sleep Token* starts playing and we both smile at each other.

Sighing, I say, "I really love this song."

Nodding his head, he starts playing with my hair, "Me, too." Humming the song together, my favorite part starts, and Rhys leans in looking into my eyes and starts singing along.

Whispering, I say, "I love when you sing, ghoulie." Bringing my hand to his shoulder, I start pushing until he's laying on his back. I turn towards him and throw my leg over him, straddling his hips. While he sings, I start tracing the constellation tattoos across his chest and ribs. There's constellations everywhere, intermixed with blue and green watercolors. All V's talks about astronomy, I recognize a few of them. Tracing the Gemini tattoo over his heart, I smile, "I love how this whole piece came together. Especially this Gemini one that happens to be over your heart. Your tattoos really scream that your past self picked them out. Almost like a message for you, a reminder. How else do you explain our matching tattoos? Then you have this one, with my zodiac over your heart and our favorite colors blended together." Placing his hand over mine and cradling it to his heart, I look up at him.

"I love that there's so many connections to us with my tattoos. Although I'd really like to kick my past self's ass for not tattooing coordinates or some shit so I could find you faster."

Sleep starts to overtake me, I feel my eyelids drooping and

slowly blinking. Before darkness consumes me, I whisper, "I wish I would've found you sooner, too."

"If there's one thing I am sure of, I am sure that you have always belonged with me."
~Akif Kichloo

CHAPTER 19
WORK SONG

Nova

Engulfed by darkness, I feel like I'm suffocating, bound in place. The panic sets in and my heart starts racing. Where am I? What's happening? I can't tell if my eyes are open or shut, I try to open my mouth to scream for help, but nothing comes out. I can hear the pounding of my heart in my ears and nothing else. It's quiet...too quiet. Trying to move my limbs it's as if my whole body is frozen, pinned in place by concrete. Counting to three, I give it my all, I have to move, I need to see, I need to scream. One, two, three! "HELPPPPPPP!"

The darkness is lifted and my limbs are no longer bound, I'm free to scream. Blinking away the blurred vision, I see Rhys in front of me, panic-stricken and gripping my body. His words don't register at first, squinting my eyes, I concentrate on his mouth moving. "NOVA! NOVA, I'M RIGHT HERE! YOU'RE SAFE! IT WAS JUST A NIGHTMARE!"

Taking a deep breath, I nod my head. Releasing the breath, I croak, "Rhys."

"There you are, little star. I'm here, you're safe. It was just a nightmare. Come here." He pulls me towards him as he lays on his back and brings me to his chest. Rubbing circles on my back, he starts whispering, "Shh, shh. It's okay, you're okay." Taking deep breaths, I sink further against him. The last of my fear and anxiety leaves me as Rhys starts singing *Mine* by *Sleep Token*.

Inhaling his scent, I place a kiss over his heart, "Thank you, ghoulie."

"Of course, sweetheart. Do you want to talk about it? That was a bad one."

"Not much I can really say. It wasn't anything or anyone in particular. I just couldn't see or move."

Tracing the constellations on his chest, an idea forms in my mind. "Rhys?"

Moving his hand from my back, he brings it to my hair and starts playing with it, "Yeah?"

"I-I have an idea. It might seem crazy, at least to other people, and you don't have to do it if you don't want to, I'll just do it on my own-"

Rhys gives my hair a slight tug, "Sweetheart, you're rambling. You know you never have to be nervous with anything you want to say or do. Not with me."

Taking a deep breath, I quickly say, "Iwantmatchingtattoos."

Rhys' chest shakes beneath me as he laughs, "It's a good thing I'm now fluent in the language of Nova. What matching tattoo do you have in mind, little star?" I reach down to his side and give him a slight pinch. Hissing from the pain, he brings his hand down smacking my ass and growls, "Ouch, what was that for?"

"You laughed at me. Rude."

"Fair enough."

Patting my ass like a bongo drum, he adds, "what's the matching tattoo?"

"I figured since we say, this life and the next, maybe we could tattoo *every life* on our left ring fingers. Is that okay? Would you want to do that with me?"

"Look at me, Nova." I place both hands on his chest and placing my chin on top, I stare into his eyes. "You haven't figured it out yet, have you?" Looking away for a moment, and then back to him, I tilt my head in question. "I've been thinking I want to get a tattoo with you as well. As for what you haven't figured out yet, little star...I'd do anything you asked of me. Even the things you can't voice, I'd do it for you. I'd risk it all for you. Even if it kills me to be without all I need to take in everything that you are, I would do that for you. You need the eyes that see everything you are? I'll cut them out and drop them at your feet. You want my ears that listen to your beautiful voice? They're yours. You want my hands that get to touch and caress every inch of you? Take them. You want my heart that beats for you and you alone? I'll carve my beating heart from my chest and lay it in your hands. All of me belongs to you, little star."

My eyes well up with tears at his words and for a moment I'm speechless. *I don't feel worthy of such an offering.* As the first tear falls, he's already there catching it with his thumb and bringing it to his mouth to lick away. "I'd do it all for you too, ghoulie."

Lifting up, I reach behind me and grab his cock. I love how it starts to harden after a few strokes. Rhys groans and I look up to him. He sits up and captures my lips roughly. I continue stroking his cock as our teeth clack together and our tongues intertwine. Swallowing each grunt and groan he lets out with my strokes, I suck his tongue hard, lightly scraping it with my teeth. I look between us and lift myself, sliding my soaked pussy across his cock, the head notched at my entrance. I place my hands on his chest and drop down all the way, moaning at the feel of his cock stretching me.

Rhys growls from my pussy squeezing his cock and I start bouncing up and down. He brings his hands to my hips, gripping them tight and helping guide my movements. Dropping back down, I start circling my hips and my clit rubs against his pelvic bone.

Panting, I yell, "Oh, fuck." He releases his hold on my hip

and grips the front of my throat, pulling me down towards him. Planting his feet firmly on the bed, he starts thrusting up at a punishing pace. "Ohhhh, fuck, fuck, just like that, Rhys." I grab his face to pull him closer. We slam together, the movements of his thrusting making the kiss all tongue and teeth. Our mouths are wide open against each other as we pant, moan and groan into each other's mouths. Sliding his hand from my hip, he caresses and squeezes my ass. I whine at the loss of his hand and then shout into his mouth when I feel the sting of his hand slapping against me.

He pulls back from me and brings his finger to my mouth. "Suck." Wrapping my lips around his finger, I suck and lick all around his finger. His hand glides down and starts circling his finger around my asshole. Yelping at the surprise, he chuckles. "Shh, shh. I'll be gentle, I promise."

Whispering to him, I let him know, "I trust you."

"Be a good girl and rub your clit for me." With one hand on his chest, I start rubbing my clit in slow circles with my fingers.

As he thrusts his cock back in, the tip of his finger breeches my hole and I gasp, "Oh fuck!" With every movement of his thrusts, his finger slides further in.

My pussy squeezes tightly around his cock, making him grunt and grits his teeth, "Fuck, little star. Tell me you're close. Cum with me, sweetheart. Rub your clit faster." He wraps his lips around my nipple, licking and sucking softly at first. On his last thrust in with his cock and finger, he bites down on my nipple and my orgasm tears through me. My eyes squeeze tightly shut, my head lifting on its own as I shout to the ceiling. Galaxies burst behind my eyelids and my whole body is on fire. I drop back down to his chest, we're both panting, soaked in sweat and cum. "Holy, holy fucking shit, little star."

Unable to form words, I let out a, "Hmmm." Minutes or hours pass by, I'm not sure which and I feel Rhys rubbing my back in circles and I whisper, "I love you, ghoulie."

"I love you too, little star."

. . .

After taking our shower, which we only left due to the glacial temps making us shout and jump out, we headed to my room to get dressed. Once we're in the kitchen, Rhys goes through my fridge and freezer. I hop up on the counter and watch him pull out a package of sausage. Smirking, I gasp to get his attention. He turns to look at me and I wipe my mouth drastically as if I'm drooling. "Mmm, I'm so ready to choke that thick sausage down."

Rhys gets a horrified look on his face and places the sausage to his chest. Shaking his head he says, "No, nope, uh-uh. If you're going to drool and choke on any sausage it will be mine." Ripping the freezer door open, he throws the roll of sausage in and slams the door shut.

"Dramatic much, ghoulie?"

"We're going and getting breakfast burritos, you blasphemous woman." I jump from the counter to follow him to the bedroom. As I'm getting dressed, I turn around to find Rhys staring with a thoughtful look on his face.

"What?"

Blinking his eyes as if he's coming out of a trance, he shakes his head, "Uhh, nothing. I-I was just picturing you in my clothes." Nodding, I plop down on the bed to put my shoes on so we can leave

Once we're in the truck, I grab my phone from my pocket and pull up my text thread with Dorian. Without looking up, I tell Rhys, "You're gonna have to be temporary DJ. I'm texting Dor and inviting him to breakfast burritos and ink therapy."

"Fantastic idea. I know for a fact if he heard about our plans without an invite, we would for sure be dealt with pouty puppy eyes." Snorting at his comment, I type out a message.

> ME: Hey Dor! Rhys and I are planning on getting breakfast burritos and then getting some ink therapy. You in?

While I wait for Dorian's response, I hear the beginning of *Alkaline* by *Sleep Token* playing. I smile over at Rhys and find him already looking at me. "I love this song, ghoulie."

"You know what I love?"

Tapping my finger on my chin, pretending to think, I say, "Hmmm, the options are endless here."

Rolling his eyes, he pokes my side making me yelp, "No, smartass. I love you."

Wiping my hand across my forehead and flicking away non-existent sweat, I say, "Phewww, thank fuck for that, cuz I love you, ghoulie." *Hey Ya* by *Outkast* starts playing on my phone, and I know it's Dorian texting me back. Breaking the moment between us, I look away and check the text.

> PRINCE DOR: Indubitably! I'll be ready and waiting for you guys to come pick me up. I'm so excited.

> ME: Fuck yeah! I'll text you when we're getting ready to pull into the complex. Signing off, Prince Dorian.

> PRINCE DOR: 10-4, Queen SuperNova.

Laughing at his response, I pocket my phone and look at Rhys again, "Dor's in. Now, let's go get those breakfast burritos, since you denied me of my morning sausage."

He holds his finger up in the air, "Pause. I did not deny you your morning sausage. You can have mine any time you want. I just cut short your drool session over the *wrong* sausage."

Through my fake cough, I say, "Cry baby."

His eyes darken as he whips his head in my direction. Slowly turning his attention back to the road, he growls, "Keep it up, little star. I'll make you the cry baby while you choke on my cock."

Mocking him, I silently mouth his words back to him while shaking my head back and forth. I stick my tongue out and add, "Your threats are not what you think they are, ghoulie."

"You say that now. Just wait." When we pull up to the drive-thru at the little Greek shop, I do a little happy dance. Rhys orders our breakfast burritos, turning to me when he's finished. He's smiling at my dance and I shrug, "What? I fucking love their breakfast burritos."

His smile widens, "That's my girl."

With the breakfast burritos between us, Rhys headed towards his and Dorian's apartment. As we get closer, I pull out my phone and text Dorian.

ME: Prince Dorian, breakfast burritos acquired. Closing in on your location now, good sir.

PRINCE DOR: Running.

We both start laughing at the sight of Dorian. He has a dopey grin on his face and he's bouncing on his feet. "Oh my god, he's really living up to that puppy persona." Once we've pulled up, I grab the food and slide over to wait for Dorian.

Dorian pokes his head in as the door opens, "Hey guys!"

"Hey, Dor!"

Hopping in, he closes the door and smiles at us, "Thanks for the invite, guys!"

I talk into the bag as I shuffle through the bag to hand out burritos,, "Of course. We can't go on an adventure without Prince Dorian. That's just a crime."

287

Reaching in front of me, Rhys says, "Hey man, our DJ is busy, can you pick a song?"

There's no response, so I look over at Dorian and find him with his mouth agape and his eyes wide. I wave my hands in front of his eyes and I say, "Earth to Dorian! Anybody home?"

He opens and shuts his mouth a few times and then says, "Is everything okay? You never let me pick the music. Breakfast burritos, ink therapy and now this? Are you guys leaving me?" The look on his face breaks my heart, he truly believes we're leaving him.

"Dor, nothing is wrong, and we're not going anywhere."

I pat Rhys on his stomach, "Tell him, ghoul."

"You're stuck with us, Dori. I mean, obviously there will come a time that Nova and I get our own place to grow our family, but we'll never leave you behind, Dorian."

His eyes light up and he shouts, "A FAMILY?! You guys are gonna grow a family?! When?! Soon? Oh, please tell me soon. I can't wait to be Uncle Dor." He's jumping in his seat and has the biggest smile on his face.

"Whoa, whoa, whoa. Let's slow down here. Last I checked, I'll be the one carrying these semen demons, and I would like to wait a bit, if that's quite alright with you two. Push back the date on Mission Hijack Nova's Uterus, please." They both laugh and I look between the two of them, "What the fuck is so funny about that?"

Between laughs, Rhys says, "You... Called... Our... Babies... Semen Demons!"

Dorian adds in, "And... And... Mission... Hijack... Nova's... Uterus!"

Rolling my eyes, I grab a container of their burritos and slam them down in their laps, "Laugh it up, assholes. Eat your damn food. Maybe I'll just go get ink therapy by *myself* and get *something else*."

Rhys immediately stops laughing and I look over at him. The look on his face is priceless and I bite my tongue to keep from laughing. In the most defeated voice ever, he says, "What do you mean something else?"

Shrugging, I open the container for my burrito, pick it up and take a big bite. Looking at him again, he's staring at his burrito pouting. Finishing my bite, I push the bottom of his burrito up towards his face. "Stop pouting and eat your burrito. I was just joking, ghoulie."

Grumbling, he says, "Worst joke ever," and takes a giant bite of his burrito.

A bell jingles above us as we walk in to Stellar Ink. Behind the counter we find a short and stocky guy covered in tattoos with a spider web tattoo on his bald head. He greets us with a friendly smile, "Hey folks, what can I do ya for?"

Blech, I hate when people say it like that. Rhys waves his thumb between the two of us and says, "We're just looking for two words in script on our ring fingers, and this guy over here," he scrunches his brows as he gestures to Dorian, "well, I'm not sure what he's getting."

Dorian steps between Rhys and I to chime in, "Sun and moon over my heart."

Looking over my shoulder, I look up at Dorian, "Aww, Dor. That's sweet. Any particular reason?"

Shrugging he gives a half smile, "Just felt right."

Standing from his seat, the guy taps the counter twice, "Alright, who's getting stabbed first?"

Lifting my hand, I excitedly say, "Ooo, me, I'll go first."

Turning around he waves his hand in the air, "Follow me."

Letting go of Rhys' hand, I round the counter and follow the guy to a room in the back. Rhys is hot on my tail, his boots tapping the linoleum. Looking behind me I see Dorian standing there twisting his hands. "Dor, let's get a move on, I need ya."

His eyes light up and he speed walks to catch up to us. The man holds up a notepad and a pen and says, "Do you want to write down the words you want, or do you want me to do it in a specific style of script?"

Turning to Rhys, I ask, "Can you write it, please? I want it in your handwriting."

Smiling wide, he nods, "Absolutely, I want mine with your handwriting, too." Walking over to the guy, Rhys takes his time writing down *every life*. Once he's finished, I step up and do the same.

The guy shakes his head and starts to open his mouth, "Please don't say what everyone else says. We're paying for your beautiful work, not your differing opinions on the matter."

With a half nod he chuckles, "Damn, alright then. You got yourself a firecracker there, pal."

Putting his arm around my waist, he squeezes my waist, "That's my shooting star right there."

Within 20 minutes my tattoo is finished and it's Rhys' turn. He plops down on the seat and looks up at me, pouting, "Hold my hand, little star. I don't know if I'll survive this."

Rolling my eyes, I walk to the wall and lean against it crossing my arms. "Nice try, ghoulie. If that was the case you wouldn't have made it through your half sleeve or chest piece."

"Hurtful, sweetheart, very hurtful." Wrapping up Rhys' tattoo, the artist works on a design for Dorian. He immediately loves the design of the sun and moon intertwined. Pulling his shirt off reveals all kinds of artwork on his arms and chest.

"Wow, Dor, I didn't realize you had more than just your Baphomet. Cool."

He lights up at the praise and smiles big, "Thanks, SuperNova."

After leaving the tattoo shop, we all agreed that we would head to *Swan & Scribe* to see what everyone was up to. During the whole drive there, Rhys held my hand and kept kissing close to my tattoo. Walking through the doors, V looks up and smiles. "Well, well, well, look who decided to grace us with their presence." Nodding towards the back of the store she adds, "The Horde is back there. I have a few books to put away and then I'll join you guys."

"Are you actually putting books away, or are those books for," bringing my hands up I do air quotes, "V's 'secret stash' of books?"

Pointing her nose up in the air, she sniffs, "I don't know what you're talking about."

Shaking my head, I laugh and pull Rhys along. Rounding the corner we see everyone sitting around the table. Looking up they all greet us and wave. Letting go of my hand, Rhys walks ahead and pulls out my chair for me, dramatically showcasing the chair, "Milady."

With a little curtsy, I walk over to the chair and sit down, "Why thank you, your majesty."

All the guys pipe up with, "Eww," "You guys are gross."

The girls step in telling them all, "Shut up."

Everyone starts talking in hushed voices and trying to discuss findings on *Amissa Stella* in code. Leaning against the wall, I start rubbing my temples. I feel so tired. Shaking my head, I stand up and Rhys' hand falls from my thigh.

Looking up at me, he asks, "Hey, what's wrong?"

Putting on my best smile I say, "I'm just feeling really tired. I'm gonna go splash my face with ice cold water and then go get a *Monster*. Do you or Dor want anything?"

They both shake their heads and say, "No, thank you."

Snorting, I nod, "I don't think I'll ever get used to you guys doing that. Alright, I'll be back soon."

I step past Rhys and he twists in his chair, grabbing my elbow, "Hey, do you want me to go with you?"

Patting his head, I shake my head, "No, no, I'll be fine. I love you."

Squeezing my arm, he says, "I love you."

Heading to the bathrooms, I see V heading my way. "Hey, are you okay, Nova girl?"

"Yeah, just feeling tired. Gonna go attempt to wake myself up. I'll see ya back at the table."

"Okay, sounds good. Maybe ask them for two *Monster's.*"

"Jokes on you, V. That was the plan all along."

Grabbing the handle to the bathroom door, I take a deep breath and shake my head. Walking in, I head straight for the sinks and turn on the cold water tap. Waiting for it to get cold enough, I grip the edge of the counter and hang my head. "Holy fuck balls, I'm tired." Pushing up from the counter, I run my right hand under the water. Feeling that it's cold enough, I dip my head and start splashing my face with the water. Splash. Wipe. Splash. Wipe.

The sound of the door squeaking open alerts me to another presence. Quickly rubbing the water from my eyes, I blink to see who just walked in. My heart starts pounding and I clench my fists, seeing the person in front of me is not who I would expect to find in here.

First off, it's a man. He's wearing all black; boots, cargo jeans, and a hoodie with the hood drawn up. Even his eyes and hair are black to match. "What the fuck are you doing in here? Do you not understand what the signs on the door mean? This is the *ladies'* room. I'd say only pussy allowed in here, but that would just mean I agree your pussy ass belongs in here. GET THE FUCK OUT!" Without a word he starts walking towards me.

———————✦·

Rhys

As the conversation continues, my mind keeps wandering to Nova and wondering if she's okay. Rubbing my eyes roughly as if it will wake me up, I start to wonder if maybe we caught some sort of bug. My heart starts pounding and I grip my chest. *Something's wrong.*

I start to let everyone know when V and Jade exchange a look of fear.

"You guys feel it, too?"

From beside me, Dorian speaks up, "So do I. Guys we need to fan out and scope shit out. Now. Don't make a scene though."

V stands up and lets us know, "I'm going to go pull the fire alarm. Maybe a group of us should work on getting everyone out first." Everyone agrees and follows after V.

"I'm gonna go find Nova."

The sound of the alarm starts and lights are flashing. Groups of people start heading to the front with questions of, "Is there a fire?" "I wonder what's going on?"

When I get closer to the bathroom I notice a man in all black not heading towards the front of the store. *Red light.* Walking up behind him, I tap his shoulder, "Hey man, we're supposed to be exiting the building."

Swiveling around, recognition crosses his face and he sneers, "You."

Showtime. Before I get the words out, he's already reaching inside of his jacket. *Fuck that.* In one swift motion, I headbutt him in the face and bring my leg behind him as I shove him. He topples over my leg and falls back, the knife he was reaching for falling to the floor with him. Lunging for the knife at the same time, he kicks out at me and his foot lands on my knee just right. The pain drops me to the floor and I attempt to grab the knife again. He's closer to it, so I grab a hold of his legs and start pulling him back from it. Kicking back, he gets me in the eye, "SON OF A BITCH!"

Ignoring the screaming pain in my face and knee, I try to jump over him to grab the knife. The burning pain in my leg tells me I'm too late. I look down to see there's a slice through my jeans and blood is pouring from the wound, covering my hip to the top of my thigh. "You're gonna wish you didn't fucking do that."

Getting a hold of the arm that has the knife, I pull and twist as hard as I can, the snap tells me his arm is broken. Looking down the evidence is clear by the awkward angle his arm is in.

"Motherfucker! I'll fucking kill you!"

Dropping down to my knees, I grimace at the searing pain shooting from my hip to knee. Gritting my teeth, I reach down and wrap my hands around his throat, "Not if I kill you first."

With his arm broken, he's only able to grab and scratch at my hands with his right hand. Holding on to his neck with my left hand as tight as possible, I take my right hand and snatch the knife out of his hand. Gripping the handle tight, I shove it into the side of his neck. He gasps and gurgles on the blood pouring from the wound. Eyes wide, he attempts to claw at me. As he gets weaker, his hand drops and the light dims in his eyes. With one last gurgled breath, he's gone.

"Piece of shit." Looking around I don't hear or see anyone else, they must have gotten everybody out of here. Attempting to stand, my wounds don't allow it and I tumble to the floor. "Fuck!" With the knife still gripped in my right hand, I start crawling across the floor, dragging my injured leg behind me. *I have to get to Nova. Please tell me I'm not too late.*

Once I've reached the bathroom door, I bring my hand up and grasp the handle as best as I can. The blood on my hand makes me slip right off. "Son of a bitch, come on!"

Wiping the blood on my pant leg, I reach up again and grip the handle tight. With as much strength as I can muster I pull myself up, losing my balance with my weight swinging the door open. Releasing the handle, I throw my body towards the wall and hang on to the door frame. "Nova! Please tell me you're in here, baby!" Stepping forward with my left foot, I drag my right along. Rounding the wall, I see a man on top of Nova.

"MOTHERFUCKER!"

Attempting to run towards them I fall, slamming my knees to the floor. "Fuck! Get the fuck off of her!"

With panted breaths, I hear Nova force the words out, "Ghoulie… please… get… him… off… me!"

Scooting forward, I shove the man and he topples over. When he hits the floor on his side, I see that he's dead and has a knife sticking out of his neck. "That's my fucking girl. Looks like we're starting to kill these fuckers the same. Are you alright, little star?"

Taking a deep breath she nods, looking up at me she smiles, "Fuck, I love you."

"I love you, too." I reach for her, but she rolls away from me and jumps up. She walks to the door, and I look over my shoulder, "Nova?"

I hear the click of the door lock and see her walk around the wall with a smirk on her face. "I know now isn't really the time, but I need you inside me right now, ghoulie."

As she walks towards me, she unbuttons and unzips her pants. Pulling them down to her ankles, she starts kicking them off. "Let me ride you, ghoulie."

Rolling over to my back, I unbuckle my belt. Working on the button and zipper next, Nova looks down and sees the blood from my leg. Dropping to her knees next to me, she gasps, "Oh fuck! You're hurt, Rhys! We have to fix this!"

Grunting, I pull my pants and underwear down. "I don't fucking think so, little star. Get over here and ride my cock. I fucking need you, too."

Shaking her head, a tear falls from her eye, "But, you're hurt. We have to get you help."

She's close enough to me that I grab a hold of her and drop her to my lap. "First ride, then I'll get bandaged up."

Nodding her head, she grabs my cock and brings it to her pussy. Wiping the fallen tear, I softly say, "That's it, little star. Be a good girl and sit on my cock."

Moaning at my words, she drops down on my cock. She's moving slowly, so I grip her hips and pull her down. I groan from the pain in my leg, but keep moving her up and down, encouraging her to move. "That's it, just like that, sweetheart. You take me so fucking well."

Placing her hands on my chest, she looks me in the eyes, "I love you, I love you so fucking much. I was so scared I wouldn't see you again."

Bringing my fingers to her clit, I start rubbing in fast circles, "Shh, shh, it's okay. I'm not going anywhere. I'm right here." Her pussy squeezes my cock and I can already tell she's close.

Her hips falter and she pants, "Oh, oh my fucking God!"

Growling, I grit my teeth, "No, not a God. I'm your fucking ghoul and I'm going to consume every fucking inch of you, little star. Now cum for me. Cum all over my cock."

Gasping, her movements falter, and she starts falling towards my chest. Ignoring the pain, I thrust up hard and she moans, "Fuuuuuuck!" When the last drop of cum shoots up, I drop my hips down and flop my legs out. Breathing hard, she kisses my chest, "Okay, now we have to get you all fixed up."

The blood loss has me drifting in and out of consciousness. Whispering, I say, "I might need some help, with my pants cuz-" *Darkness.*

"It's easy to recognize our soulmate. When we meet them and find true love, after a time you can't exist without that person, you'd rather die than lose them." ~Glen Rambharack

CHAPTER 20
PRIVATE FEARS IN PUBLIC PLACES

1 WEEK AGO

Rhys

Pulling into the parking lot, I find a parking spot and we wait. We made it ten minutes early and I give Nova a cocky smirk Her eyes meet mine as she laughs, "What?"

"Wanna make out?"

"Kinda. You think Dorian wants to?"

Rearing my head back, I grit my teeth, "What the fuck did you just say?"

Her serious face cracks and she bursts out laughing, "Oh my god you should see your fucking face! Priceless. God that was gross to say, but totally fucking worth it for that reaction."

Scowling, I cross my arms over my chest, "Not. Cool." She slides over and puckers her lips. She leans in a few times to kiss me but I keep dodging her, "Nope, don't want a kiss anymore." She stops trying and starts to move back to her side but I pull her to me and kiss all over her face.

"I thought you didn't want a kiss anymore, ya big baby?"

"I lied. I always want your kisses. Now kiss me back."

A knock on the top of the truck gets our attention and we look up.

"Oh cool, he got out early. Let's blow this popsicle stand." I look around but don't see Dorian. "What the hell is taking him so long to get in? He can't really believe he's going to jump out and scare us after already knocking on the truck."

Nova huffs, "Oh, this is ridiculous. I'm gonna scare him before he even tries to scare us." She quietly pushes the door open, slides out of the seat and hits the pavement without a sound. Looking over at me, she smirks and brings her finger to her mouth to shush me. With a wink my way, she tiptoes to the back of the truck. She shouts out, "Gotch-" the end of the word dying on her lips. What the hell? My heart starts pounding with the continued silence. Hopping out of the truck, I head to the back to see what's going on.

Before rounding the corner, there's sudden movement and instant pain to my head. "What the fuck?!" The sight in front of me makes me sick to my stomach. Ignoring the wet feeling running down my face and the throb in my head, my vision zeroes in on a man with his arm around her throat and a gun to her head. There's a second man with a gun, the same motherfucker that just slammed it against my temple. "Let. Her. Fucking. Go," I demand. The dead man holding Nova around the throat must be squeezing tighter, because her eyes bulge as she attempts a gasp and claws at his arm.

The second guy raises his gun to my face and in a heavily Italian accent states, "Walk faster, Rhys Slater." Looking at Nova again, she attempts a nod. Fuck, only for you, little star. Turning around, I feel the gun shoved against my back and my steps falter from the aggressive punch of the gun.

"Watch it." He presses the gun harder and I growl in annoyance.

I start to turn towards the entrance of the asylum but the guy behind me tsks, "Nice try, take a left." Following his directions, we head to the left. He's guided us to the back of the asylum, and stops at the basement bulkhead doors. Pushing me forward again, he says, "Grab the padlock, SLOWLY, drop it at your feet and kick it away." The padlock is unlocked and dangling from the latch. I feel the throb in my head increase as I bend down to pick it up. Pulling it free, I start to stand and the guy barks, "DROP IT! Then kick it away." Dropping it to the ground, I kick it with my boot and it scrapes across the pavement a few feet away. *"Open the doors. Slowly."* Looking over my shoulder at Nova, I see the guy still has a hold of her around her throat and the gun to her head. These motherfuckers will die slowly and painfully.

"Sweetheart, you okay?"

The guy behind me pushes me again, *"QUIT STALLING! Open the fucking doors."*

I bend down and grumble under my breath, *"Bet your bitchasses wouldn't be so tough without your fucking guns."* Grabbing hold of the bottom of the doors, I rip them open, the wood slamming against the ground and bouncing slightly. Daylight makes the top of the stairs easy to see, but the rest are plunged into darkness.

"Move your ass, bastardo."

"Oh, meatball, at least be clever with your insults." Shaking my head, I take my first step, *"Amateur."* Taking the steps slowly as to not miss any, I notice a small light just ahead of us. A clicking noise draws my attention, and then I see a bright circle of light on the floor beside my feet.

"Don't fucking move. You try anything and my friend is gonna blow your pretty little whore's brains all over the place. Got it?"

"You're gonna regret calling her a whore." My body jostles back and forth as he shakes me by my coat.

"I. Said. Got. It?"

I pull my shoulder away from him and grit out, *"Yeah. Got it!"* The sound of his shoes against the floor click as he walks. Something flicks and the sound of buzzing above starts as row after row of fluorescent lights illuminate the basement. The glare of the bright lights make my eyes squeeze shut and slowly open them so they can adjust. This room looks like their own version of my playroom. The glaring difference, instead of one chair there's over a dozen of them,each one has vital monitors on rolling carts beside them. Hanging on the side of the cart is some sort of headband contraption. Fuck, that's not good.

Nova

The pressure around my neck has lessened, but the gun to my head has not. This piece of shit is pushing hard enough that there will definitely be bruising. Beads of sweat are popping up across my forehead and a lone drip falls down my spine making me shiver. Pushing us towards the chairs, I watch as the other guy twists Rhys around by his jacket and shoves him down into the chair. Rhys grips the armrests and leans forward and the fucker in front of him backhands Rhys in the face. I throw my body forward to scream, "DON'T FUCKING TOUCH HIM!"

The arm around my neck tightens and I scratch at his arm to release me. Bringing his mouth to my ear, his hot breath pants against my skin and hair, making my stomach roil. "Shut your whore mouth." As he shoves me towards the chair next to Rhys, I trip and stumble, only being caught by the arm around my neck. My head is pounding and I gurgle from the pressure on my neck. Once he releases my neck, I rub at it and gasp for air. Sucking in as much as I can, I feel my body flying as I'm shoved against the chair. The force of the push has me bent over at an awkward angle over the chair. I try to push myself off the chair so I can turn but feel a hand pushing against my back, holding me in place. "Mmmm, perfect position for a whore like you. Maybe we should play a little before the big event."

As I struggle against the pressure of the hand, I hear Rhys yell, "Get the fuck away from her! Don't you fucking dare! You pay attention to me. Come on, you-" His words are cut off by a grunt. I see him facing me and there's blood running down his face. The fucker must have pistol whipped him again. Keeping my eyes on Rhys, there's a clicking noise behind me that grabs his attention. Looking towards it, his eyes widen and he shakes his head frantically, "Don't! Don't you fucking do it, motherfucker!" Tears well up in my eyes and my heart races. Please, please no. I can't go through this again. Feeling a tug on the back of my jeans, I let out a yelp when there's a piercing pain on my lower back. The sounds of shredding are behind me and I feel the cold bite of air against my skin as my back, ass and legs are exposed. He jostles me around as he cuts and pulls at my jeans. Rhys is screaming but I don't understand the words coming out of his mouth. Drifting away from the horrors surrounding me, I come to again with a stinging against my cheek. Blinking away the tears, I look ahead and see that I'm now sitting and strapped to the chair. There's a chill in the air hitting my exposed skin. Looking down I see that I'm only in my bra and panties. The man in front of me has his black hair in disarray and a disgusting grin on his face. He's smiling so big I notice the yellow stains on his crooked teeth. Rolling my head to the left, I see Rhys looking at me with a pained look on his face. I realize his mouth is moving and he's speaking to me.

Squeezing my eyes shut, I open them again and noises filter in. The buzzing from the lights are loud and Rhys keeps repeating himself, "Look at me, little star. Right here, come on, sweetheart. Just look at me. There you are. Hi, baby. Keep looking at me." A punch to his face has his head smacking the back of the chair and he whips his head in the direction of the man that just punched him. "SON OF A BITCH! Why don't the both of you focus on me? Stop being pussies and take on a man. Leave her be! I'll kill you, I'll fucking kill all of you!"

The tears continue to fall and I croak out, "Ghoulie."

Immediately looking at me, his eyes soften, "Hey, little star. I'm right here."

Sniffling, I plead with him, "Please stop fighting them, ghoul.

They're going to do this their way. So please, please let's just focus on each other to get through this. I need you."

The tears well up in his eyes, and he nods, "Okay, sweetheart. *Whatever you need, I'm here every step of the way. I love you."*

Sobbing, I reply, "I-I love you, too, ghoulie."

"Enough of your sappy bullshit! Shut the fuck up!" *Gritting my teeth, I hold back my retort.* Just ignore him, Nova. His words don't matter. He's not here. You and Rhys aren't here. Anywhere but here. *Hissing from the bite of pain to the center of my chest, I feel my blood trickling down my sternum and stomach. Cold hands grip at my mounds, grabbing hold of the bra and ripping it from me. My nipples harden from the chill and I squeeze my eyes shut.* This sick fuck is going to think it's because of him and not the cold air. I'm gonna be sick.

"Nova!" *My eyes shoot open at the sound of Rhys' voice.*

"You stay with me, little star. Keep those pretty blues on me, sweetheart." *Nodding my head, I keep my focus on Rhys as my pussy is now being exposed to the sick motherfucker in front of me.*

"Aww, there it is. Look at that pretty little whore cunt. Come look at this whore's cunt, Alonzo." *In my peripheral, I see Alonzo walking towards us and stopping in front of me. My face contorts while looking at Rhys.*

He mouths, 'I love you', and I mouth it back.

Rough and calloused hands grope at my mounds aggressively. Grunting, I hear the man that tore my clothes from me say, "Oh fuck yeah. Look at these fucking whore tits. Fucking perfect. I can't wait to get my dick in between them." *Rhys is torn between looking at them in a fit of rage and looking back to me quickly softening his gaze. My hand is continuously nudged, and I realize it's Alonzo brushing his hard cock against my hand, practically humping it. Squeezing the armrest the best I can, it only eggs him on to hump harder against my hand.* "Oh fuck yeah, you little fucking whore. Come on, open those fingers. I know you wanna brush those fingers across my cock. Come on, whore."

The tapping of shoes on the floor echoes across the room and a booming voice yells, "Che cazzo state facendo, idioti?!" *Both men jump away and turn towards the man that just entered.*

In voices that sound more like little boys than men, they both say, "Scusa, capo."

"Unbelievable! The two of you had one fucking job, and this most certainly wasn't it. What if mia figlia found you two doing this?! Get the fuck outta here, I'll call you if I need you." Both men scurry off and the third man comes into view. He looks much older than the other two, with black hair slicked back and a touch of gray at the temples. His olive toned skin is mostly unblemished, other than very fine wrinkles next to his eyes. He adjusts his black tie and steps forward, slightly bowing his head. "Apologies. They were not supposed to touch you in such a way. Let me find a cover for you, my dear." Curling my lip at his words, I roll my head to face Rhys. The feel of fabric covers me, and I look down to see a blue hospital gown laid across my body. "Again, I apologize for the behavior of those idiots."

"Hey! Get the fuck away from her." He steps away from me and goes to stand in front of Rhys. "Don't pretend you're not the monster you are. We both know you join those sick fucks to torture, rape and beat women. Your favorites are family members. Isn't that right... Adriano Cifarelli?"

Adriano smiles down at Rhys, "Ahhh, so you do know who I am? Good, good. I love it when my experiments and I know of each other, it makes it so much more fun, Rhys Slater." Tilting his head to the side, he pauses and then speaks again, "You don't seem surprised that I know your name. Interesting, very interesting. And yes, you are correct. I do love my playtime with women, but unfortunately I cannot do that here. I do not want mia figlia - oh scusa - my daughter, sorry, I do not want her witnessing such horrors. She would be very upset with me."

"You don't give a shit about the other women in your family or your men's family. Why the fuck does your daughter's opinion matter so much to you?"

His face turns bright red as it contorts in anger, "BECAUSE THOSE WOMEN ARE FILTHY, USELESS WHORES!" Clearing his throat, his face slides back to a smile and he adjusts his tie again. Slightly shaking his head, he continues, "My daughter is nothing like them. She is clean and pure. Untouched by the depravity of this world.

294

She is my perfect angel, my best creation. Now, let's talk about my next best creation. I'm not sure how much you have found out while torturing my men, but I'll let you in on the secret. After all, it will die with the both of you. I've been working on a new drug, Dimenticare. In small doses, a person can get high and simply forget. It'll be a hit with the junkies that got hooked on other drugs to forget the horrors they've experienced in life. Now, in high doses, little piss ants like you that annoy me simply forget everything. Less blood on my hands if I can just make people forget what they know about me and this place." Looking over to me, he tuts, "Poor, sweet, Nova. I am very sorry for the things that Frankie did to you. Even I knew that you didn't fall under the umbrella of women that deserved that kind of abuse. You remind me so much of my angel. It pains me to bring you into this, but it must be done. A little payback for Rhys, but to also keep you from trying anything if I free you." Looking over his shoulder, he shouts, "I know you two are still lurking in the shadows! Get over here and help me!" The pounding of their shoes closes in and I see them towering behind Adriano. Snapping his fingers with both hands, he points at both of us and barks out, "Alonzo, strap Rhys up. Aldo, strap Nova up. Keep your hands only on her head." Aldo steps up to the cart next to me. Grabbing the weird headband, he turns towards me and places it on my head. When I start shaking my head, he presses down harder, the metal of the headband biting into my skin. Pulling away from me, he turns to the cart and grabs a small plastic container and pulls out a black mouth guard. Looking over to Rhys, our panicked faces mirror each other. My cheek is nudged with rubber and I whip my head towards Aldo.

Without a thought, I spit in his face. My spit lands across his eyes and he snaps them shut. "You bitch!" He angrily wipes my spit down his face, and his other hand crosses over his body, winding up to hit me. Mid swing, his wrist is caught before he backhands me. "It counts as her head, boss."

Ripping the mouth guard out of his hand, he pushes him aside, "Give me that you bumbling idiota. Now, Nova, can we please not continue this way? That was your one free shot, I'll give you that. Anymore and we're going to have a problem, my dear."

Bringing the mouth guard to my mouth, I roll my lips inward.

Nudging it a few times, he tilts his head. Reluctantly, I open my mouth a little and he shoves the mouth guard in. Two loud thuds to the floor grab my attention. I see Rhys' boots tossed aside, scrunch my brows in confusion and then look back to Rhys. He shrugs his shoulders the best he can and then growls as his mouth guard is shoved aggressively into his mouth. Yelling through the mouth guard with a muffled, "Hey!" Alonzo looks over at me and smirks. "HUHK WHOO!"

Bringing his hand up to his ear and cupping it, he tilts his head, "What was that? Couldn't quite catch it."

Adriano walks over to him and smacks him on the back of the head, "Enough." Glaring in my direction as if I hit him, he rubs the back of his head. Adriano walks to the cart next to me and starts turning the machines on. Snapping his fingers, he looks at Alonzo, "Pay attention. Follow my lead." A quick grimace pops up on his face, quickly morphing to a straight face. He turns to the cart next to Rhys and turns the machines on as well. Adriano grabs a wire and connects it to one of the monitors before attaching the finger clip at the end of the wire to my pointer finger. The sound of my heartbeat beeps through the machine. Grabbing the blood pressure cuff connected to it, he lifts my arm by the wrist and wraps it around my bicep, connecting that to the machine as well. Strapping it in place, he pushes a button and it starts squeezing my arm tightly. After a continuous pulse of pressure, the machine beeps, and with a hiss of air, the cuff releases its vice grip on my arm. Turning the cart to face Alonzo, he points to the machine. "Watch where I turn the knob to." Turning the knob, an obnoxious, grinding click starts. Rhys starts grunting and speaking through his mouthguard. I look in his direction to see his eyes bulge out and him nodding his head at me. "This is only the beginning, you two." A jolting pain shoots through my whole body, stretching my body out tight as I shake through it. I lose sight of Rhys as my eyes roll to the back of my head. Opening my eyes slowly, I see Rhys trying to open his as well. Drool drips around our mouth guards and we're both panting. My head pounds and every muscle aches, even my heart is hurting. The shocks and pain continue. How long have we been here? Time feels non-existent now. Has it been minutes, hours, days? My vision is blurred, and I attempt to blink it away, but even the act of blinking is *exhausting.* Please, please let me see Rhys one more time. Just one more time, please. *I feel a pricking sensation in my arm, the pain and exhaustion has such a stronghold I can't even pull away.* Darkness.

Dorian

Leaning against the reception desk, I drum my fingers and continue to cross and uncross my ankles. What is taking them so long? *Standing up straight, I lift the flap of my messenger bag and dig around for my phone. I pull it out and check the time.* Hmm, fifteen minutes late. *Pulling up surveillance on my phone, I check the parking lot and see Rhys' K5. Smiling wide, I shake my head and whisper, "You dirty dogs." Heading for the entrance, I push open one of the doors and jog down the steps. Keeping my head down to avoid an eyeful, I follow the sidewalk and check my peripheral for Rhys' truck. When his truck comes into view, I blindly reach my hands out. When I feel the hood of his truck, I start drumming my hands against it. With nothing but silence, I risk looking up at the windshield. Empty. I squint and again, no Rhys and Nova. Slightly raising my voice, I walk towards the back of the truck, "If I find the two of you mid-coitus, I will lose my mind." Reaching the back of the truck, I take a deep breath, "Better cover all your bits, I'm opening the window!" Pushing the button on the window, it slowly starts popping open. Pulling it the rest of the way*

297

up, I shout, "Gotch- what the fuck?" Where the fuck are they? "I swear, if you knuckleheads lost track of time down at the lake and forgot about me, there will be hell to pay." I look down to open my messenger bag and I notice blood drops on the ground. "What the fuck?" Looking around the parking lot, I don't see or hear anything. My heart starts to race and my palms feel sweaty. Bracing myself against the tailgate, I grip it tight and my vision starts to blur. Deep breaths, Dorian. Keep your shit together. Letting go of the tailgate, I shakily shut the window. Walking with a quick stride around the truck, I stop and take a deep breath. Don't be suspicious, Dorian. Slowing down my pace, I walk up to the driver's side door and open it. Climbing in, I pull my bag over my head and put it down next to me. With shaking hands, I open my bag and dig through it for my phone. I pull up the surveillance footage and rewind it to half an hour ago. Watching closely, I see Rhys pull into his parking spot. Bringing the phone closer to my face, I look all around the footage to see if anything grabs my attention. THERE! Behind his truck, I see two guys walking up and crouching behind it. They pound on the truck and moments later, Nova's door opens and she slides out of the truck. "Get back in the truck, Nova, please get back in the truck." Watching the scene unfold I feel sick to my stomach. No, no, please no. "FUCK!" Punching the steering wheel, I grimace and whisper, "Sorry, Reese's Pieces." Tears well up in my eyes. KNOCK KNOCK! Gasping, I drop my phone to the floor and look over. My eyes widen at who I see. Quickly schooling my expression, I paste on a fake smile and grip the handle to lower the window. Clearing my throat, I say, "H-hello, Mr. Cifarelli, sir. How are you?"

With a bright smile, he says, "Hello, Dorian, my boy." Looking around the truck he grabs hold of the door. "This isn't your usual mode of transportation. Is this new?"

With a nervous chuckle, I say, "Oh, no, no. I had to get a ride to work today. My friend was going to pick me up, but he must have decided to just leave it here for me to get myself home." With another nervous laugh, I rub the back of my neck. "He must have got caught up with his girlfriend." Dumbass. Don't word shit like that.

There's a twinkle in his eyes with my words and he smiles brightly and nods, "Ah, yes. Young love. Are you doing alright, Dorian? You look awfully pale and sweaty, I hope you're not coming down with the flu."

Waving my shaky hands, "Oh no, nothing like that, sir. I wouldn't dream of coming to work and spreading my germs, I promise. I just, uh, I skipped out on lunch today, that's all."

"Ah, yes. Well, you go get yourself fed," tapping the truck, he adds, "I must be going now. I have a very important meeting to attend to."

My mouth feels like sandpaper and I lick my lips, "Oh, yes, of course. Have a wonderful day, Mr. Cifarelli."

Stepping back from the truck, with a sinister voice he says, "Enjoy your freedom, my dear boy."

Shoving my hand in my messenger bag, I feel around for my keys. Once I grip cold metal, I wrap my fingers tightly around them, the bite of the metal cutting into my fingers. I shuffle through until I find the spare key Rhys gave me. I attempt to put the key in the ignition but my hands are so shaky they just clatter to the floor. Leaning down to grab them, I remember I dropped my phone as well. I look around, to make sure Mr. Cifarelli is out of sight, pick my phone up and see that it's still playing surveillance. Taking another deep breath, I reach down for the keys and get them in the ignition. Starting the truck, I pull out of the parking spot. Continuously checking the rear view and side mirrors for any sign of being followed, I head in the direction of Swan & Scribe. "Stay calm, Dorian. Just stay fucking calm. Rhys and Nova need you. Focus, focus, focus." A sob creeps up my throat and I growl out, "No, not now. Later. Save them now. Cry later. I'm coming to get you guys, I promise."

"Your love is like the stars; it guides me through the darkest of nights." ~Unknown

CHAPTER 21
I MISS YOU

1 WEEK AGO…

*D*ORIAN

*My whole body feels like it's vibrating. Once I pull up to Swan &
Scribe, I toss the keys and my phone in my messenger bag. Throwing
the strap over my shoulder, I run shaky fingers through my hair. My
sweaty hands slip off on my first try at grabbing the door handle.
Wiping my hand down on my pants, I grab the handle again and grip
it tight. I jump down from the truck and land on slightly wobbly legs. I
rub my beard and slightly pull on the ends. The bite of pain brings me
back to the task at hand.* Keep moving Dorian, they need your
help. One foot in front of the other. *Opening the door, the jingle of
the bell above me gives away my entrance. V lifts her head to greet me,
the friendly greeting dying on her lips the moment she sees me. The
book in her hand slips and falls to the floor. She stands in front of me
gripping my arms. In a panicked whisper, eyes wide she asks, "What is
it, Dorian? What happened?"*

*Swallowing the lump in my throat, a hoarse whisper comes out
when I say, "Where's The Horde?" Squeezing my arms once, she let's
go and takes a step back.*

"Come on, they're in their usual spot." Nodding my head, I follow behind her and count my steps as if it will keep me focused on the task in front of me. 947, 948, 949. The scraping of chairs on the floor and a gasp brings my attention away from my feet. Looking up, I find everyone looking at me.

Jade has her hands clasped over her mouth and a tear falls down her cheek, "Please, please no."

At her words, everybody looks to her, and a chorus of, "what?", "huh?", "what's going on?" echoes in the small space.

She grips the edge of the table, "We need to go somewhere more private. Now."

Vanessa steps forward, throwing her thumb back over her shoulder, "I-I have to go get someone to watch the store. I can't boot everyone like we did the day of the attack here. P-People will get suspicious. Everyone head up to one of the book nook rooms, I'll be up there as soon as I can." Running a hand through her curls, she takes a shaky breath and turns to walk away.

Taking the lead, Viking walks ahead of everyone and waves his arm, "Let's get a move on, guys."

Jade steps up beside me and loops her arm around mine, in a soft voice she says, "Come on, Eagle. We're in this together." My throat is thick with the emotion I'm trying to suppress, so I nod my head, and wave my other arm in front of me. Following everyone, she whispers, "One foot in front of the other."

Everyone is spread out around the room, some standing and some sitting. Minutes after getting as settled as we can, Vanessa comes barging through the door. As soon as she slams it shut, her first word is, "Spill."

Rubbing my Baphomet tattoo, wishing it would take away the ache in my chest, I take a deep breath and whisper, "They're gone."

There's a collective gasp in the room, followed by the group saying, "WHAT?!"

Words fail me in this moment, and Jade steps in saying what I'm struggling to. "Not like that, guys. What Dorian is trying to say is

Nova and Rhys have been taken." Putting her hands up to stop everyone from stepping in and cutting off her words, she continues. "They were taken when they went to pick Dorian up from work. Unfortunately, that's all I can see. I-I can't explain it, there's darkness there and I can't find my way to them."

Clearing my throat, I find my voice, "We need to get to Vega Altair. I can show you guys the surveillance footage I saw. It's... it's tough to watch, but we need all hands on deck here. Maybe some of you can see things in the footage that I couldn't pick up on. The goal here is to save them, but we have to be careful and smart about this. I thought for sure I was going to be next. On my way out, Mr. Cifarelli stopped to talk to me. We already knew that he knew about Rhys, but the way he was talking, I really think he suspects me of something too. I can't be sure, but... but some of the things he said and how he said them really had the alarms blaring in my head."

Mrs. Valour steps forward and throws her hands up, "Well, what the fuck are we all doing just standing here? Let's fucking go!" Filing out of the room, we all head down the stairs and out of the book store.

Walking towards Rhys' truck, Fish calls out, and I turn to look at him. "Hey, Eagle? You need one of us to drive for you?"

Gripping the keys tight, I hold them to my chest as if I'm protecting them, "N-no, thank you. Rhys doesn't let anyone but...h-he doesn't let anyone drive Beauty except for me and Nova. Thank you, though."

Nodding his head, he says, "Yeah, man, sure. We'll be right behind you." With a quick wave, I turn and run to the truck. As I'm closing the door, the passenger side door opens up, and I shoot my head up. Vanessa and Jade hop into the truck, looking ahead and not acknowledging my questioning look.

Before I can ask, Jade says, "We may not be able to drive for you, but we can keep you company. Let's get a move on it, hun." Starting the truck, my hand freezes on the gear shift. "Why aren't you guys more upset about this?"

Vanessa speaks up first and quietly says, "It doesn't feel real, yet."

Jade lets out a small laugh, "I may only see darkness right now, but that's only because we need to bring the light to them. We'll find them, I know it."

. . .

Pulling into **Vega Altair**, *I pull the keys from the ignition and put them in my pocket. My hands are still clammy so I rub them on my pants before sliding out. Walking towards the warehouse, I faintly hear my name being called. I look over my shoulder and see Vanessa holding my messenger bag up in the air. With a sheepish smile, I nod and grab it from her, "Heh, thanks, can't believe I forgot that." The sound of car doors closing grabs my attention and I look up. Seeing the rest of The Horde here, I decide to head towards the doors to let everyone in. Getting to the scanners, I lean forward and place my eyes in front of the retinal scanner. A loud beep with a flash of red light goes off, the automated voice announces, "Access denied." Scrunching my brows, I stand up straight and scratch my head. Starting to lean forward again, I feel a hand on my arm and look up at the concerned face of Vanessa.*

Patting my arm twice, she gives me a sad smile, "I'll scan us in, Dorian."

Stepping back, I wave my hand towards the scanners, "Oh, yeah, of course. Thanks." After scanning us all in, Vanessa guides me to the conference room. Walking in, my eyes immediately focus on the **Cherry Coke** *can that Rhys sliced and twisted, making what he called a 'work of art'. Freezing in place, I stare at it and memories flash before my eyes. Sucking in a breath, I stand up tall and pull my shoulders back. Something clicks in my brain, pushing the sorrows and worry to the back of my mind. Clearing my throat, I walk up to the table and place my messenger bag down. Reaching in, I grab my phone and pull up the surveillance footage. My phone connects to the screens and I rewind to the right spot and look around at everyone.*

"Alright, I'm starting it up right before everything happens. Let's see if there's any information we find here that's useful."

We reviewed the footage over and over, and we discovered something when we watched the footage from after I left. Shortly after, one of the employees was seen walking out of the building looking at his phone. Walking to the spot Rhys' truck was parked in, he looked at his phone, the parking spot and the area surrounding it a few times. When he brought the phone to his ear, we zoomed in to attempt to read his lips. I paused, rewound and play it again, squinting my eyes to focus on his mouth. "There. Is it just me or is he saying black K5?" Rewinding it again, everyone looks closely, and everyone nods in the affirmative. "You guys thinking what I'm thinking?"

Muggzy speaks up first, "That this guy is being sent out to follow you?"

"I thought so, too. Good, I can't wait for a meeting." Watching the footage a little longer, I see the man jump into an old, beat up Lincoln Continental. Without a word, I head for the door, ignoring everyone's questions. Finding my way to the armory, I grab one of Rhys' empty duffle bags and toss it on the ammo island. This is not my realm, so I spin in a circle to try and figure out what I need to grab. Closing my eyes, I take a deep breath. Think like Rhys. What would Rhys grab? A knock on the door and the click of boots on the floor catch my attention. Opening my eyes, I turn to see Viking leaning against the door frame with his arms crossed.

"What's the plan here, Eagle?"

Spinning my finger in a circle, I shrug, "Weapons. Bag. Go."

With a heavy sigh, he uncrosses his arms and walks up to the ammo island, placing his hands flat against the surface. "Listen man, I don't mean this as a dig, but I'm not gonna bullshit you either. You're not him-" Opening my mouth to respond he puts his hands up to stop me. "Just hear me out. You're not him, and that's okay. You both have your own strengths and training, in completely different things. You're great at what you do, and Rhys is great at what he does. I understand he's done some training with you, but we have to be smart about this. You can't just go out there unprepared and hope to achieve the same things he does."

I walk around the room and start grabbing various knives from one wall and tossing them into the bag. Opening and closing the various drawers in the ammo island, I find different types of zip ties and grab a few of each, tossing them in the bag with the knives. "Listen, Viking. I understand what you're saying, but I'm not going to sit around with my thumb up my ass doing nothing. I'm going to do everything I can to find Rhys and Nova. I'm not going to just do the tech shit. I'm doing all of it. I'm not fucking quitting until I find them, and if that means taking over for Rhys for a bit, then so fucking be it. Nothing and no one will stop me."

"Dorian, slow down. I'm not stopping you, I just need you to use that big brain of yours and be smart about this. You also need to accept all of our help. You're not alone in this."

Scoffing at his words, I shake my head, "Not alone? I'm not alone?! Were you there? Did you let your best friends get fucking kidnapped?! NO! NO THE FUCK YOU DIDN'T!" Beating my fist against my chest with every word, I grit out, "I. Did. Me. It was ME!"

Viking stands in front of the wall with bulletproof vests. He tosses one my way and I fumble a bit trying to catch it. "Put that on. I'm going with you, and don't fucking argue. I really don't feel like getting in a brawl with Rhys after we rescue them. You know he'll be pissed if I just let you go do this on your own. Also, you do realize this will for sure let Cifarelli know you're a part of all of this, right?"

Grabbing my hair by the roots, I give a slight tug and nod, "Yeah, but he can't throw all his cards down on the table and announce that he knows. I'll be fine. I'll just have to be a little extra careful while I'm there. Especially when I go plant those cameras and bugs. I knew I should've fucking done that today." Growling in frustration, I zip up the bag and go to pick it up. Viking slaps my hand away and I look at him annoyed, "What the-"

Pointing at me he demands, "Put the fucking vest on, I got this."

After we stopped in the conference room to get everyone on board with the plan, we headed out to drive around town. Fifteen minutes into the drive, we noticed the Lincoln Continental tailing us. As I check the rear view mirror again, my eyes clash with Viking's in the back of the truck, "So where do you think would be a good place to lead him to?" Bringing my attention back to the road, I await his response.

"Hit the back roads, we'll lead him to the trails. We'll need the seclusion to get a hold of him. You're going to hop out first since he's *following you. I say you take the trail, I'll keep an eye out as he follows you and then I'll sneak out of the truck and walk up behind him."*

Raising a brow, I question, "How exactly are you going to sneak up behind this guy? You're called Viking, not Ninja."

Scoffing at my words he says, "That was the dumbest thing I think I've ever heard come out of your mouth. Ninja's aren't the only ones that can be quiet and stealthy. You've just lost your genius card."

"Keep it, the card was useless to me anyhow. Couldn't even get a discount breakfast at the diner like the senior citizens." The sound of a zipper catches my attention, "What are you doing?"

"Just pay attention to the road."

Hitting the back roads, I check the mirrors again and see that the guy has backed off a little more now that he's the only one behind us. Taking the final turn, we start to climb the hill, as we're halfway up I notice that he's just hit the incline. I speed up a bit more, dust and rocks fly behind the truck. When we reach the top of the hill, the parking area is empty. Finding a spot, I quickly park and shut the truck off. "Alright, I'm gonna jump out now and stand by the head of the trail. When he's close enough and I know he's seen me, I'll start walking down the trail. You think maybe we should be on the phone with each other? Keep each other posted, but also make it look like I'm preoccupied with my call?"

"Good thinking. Not card worthy thinking, but it's good."

"Hardy har fucking ha-" Clearing my throat, I stop my sentence when I realize I was about to use one of Rhys' lines.

"You good, Eagle?"

Quickly looking in the mirror and meeting Viking's eyes, I smile and nod my head, "Wha- yeah, I'm good. Hopping out now, call my phone when I hit the trail opening." Hopping out, I speed walk to the trail, my shoes crunching against the gravel below me. At the head of the trail, I put my hands in my pockets, and rock back and forth. My phone rings and when the call connects, I can hear the car pulling up. Moving my feet forward, I nod my head, "I know you have to be quiet on the other end of the line, but this feels really weird. It's one thing to talk to yourself when you're all alone, but to have an audience creeps me out. Please tell me the deadline is closing in, or no don't tell me, you can't talk. Ugh." The sound of gravel behind me answers my question, so I continue walking forward. A twig snaps in the distance and with great effort I don't freeze at the noise. Viking's end of the line is so silent, I check to make sure the call hasn't disconnected. Weird, still connected. How the hell is he so quiet? A grunt and a muffled shout echoes behind me. I turn to see Viking has one hand clasped over the guy's mouth and his arm wrapped around his throat tightly. Walking towards them, I notice his widened eyes start to roll back, his eyelids fluttering until they slowly close. Falling limp in Viking's arms, he lets go and the guy falls down to the ground with a thud, dirt billowing up around him. "Holy shit, I think you were more quiet than a ninja. How did you do that? I didn't even hear you on the other end of the line." He grabs a hold of the guy's feet and starts dragging him back down the trail.

Looking over his shoulder he smirks, "This is the time I should say, if I told you I'd have to kill you." Leaving it at that, he continues dragging him across the trail and parking lot. "Run ahead and open the tailgate for me."

When he reaches the back of the truck, I clear my throat, "You're really not going to tell me how you're that quiet, are you?"

"Nope. Grab his arms, help me throw him back here."

Leaning down, I grab a hold of him under his armpits. "On three, we lift. One, two, three." On three, we both lift him up and plop him down in the back of the truck. Sitting on the tailgate, Viking swings his legs up and knee-walks through the back of the truck. "I got it back here, get us to the warehouse." Nodding, I shut the tailgate and window with a click.

After backing into the warehouse and shutting the bay door, I start working on autopilot. The sound of the door clicking shut brings me out of the trance and I'm frozen against the door. With a shaky breath, I attempt to step forward and fail to do so. Don't be a pussy, Dorian. Fucking move. With the final restraint secured, Viking looks over his shoulder, "You good? You don't have to stay here for this."

His words give me the motivation I need to move away from the door. Scratching at my beard, I nod my head, "I do need to be here for this. I already told you, I'm here every step of the way, I'm doing everything that needs to be done to get them back."

With a quick nod he says, "Stay here, I'll be right back." While he leaves the room, I turn towards the table and start to empty everything from the duffle bag. Viking comes in carrying tequila, salt and a bag of lemons. He puts everything down and looks at me. "What?"

Waving towards the items, I ask, "Is this your idea of torture? Wine, dine and sixty-nine him? What the fuck is this?"

"Watch and learn, kid," he scoffs.

"I'm not a kid," I grumble under my breath. Dragging the table closer to the chair the guy is in, he turns towards him, rears back and smacks him across the face. The guy's head swings to the right from the momentum and groans from the pain.

"What the fuck?"

Smacking him in the face again, in a gruff voice Viking says, "Wake up, bitch."

Snapping his head up, his eyes widen, "What the fuck?" He moves the best he can, but the restraints tighten against him. "Let me go, what the fuck is this?" Looking over Viking's shoulder, he narrows his eyes at me, "You."

There's a crack when he tweaks the guy's nose and he shouts, "Don't look at him, look at me! Don't play stupid, you know why you're here and what we want to know. Start talking."

Gritting his teeth he says, "I'm not te-"

His words are cut off when Viking punches him in the jaw. "Don't bother finishing that sentence. That's not what I want to hear." Turning to the table, he slides a knife closer to the edge of the table. He picks up the knife, pulls out a lemon and slices it.

"What the fuck is this, a fucking cooking show?"

"Don't worry, the cooking will come with time." After opening the bottle of tequila and flicking open the salt, he turns towards the guy, wielding the knife dripping with lemon juice. Bringing his empty hand behind him, he grabs hold of the table and drags it closer. "Ready to talk?"

"Fuck. You."

Clicking his tongue, he tilts his head, "Rather not." He pours a little tequila on the blade. With a quick swipe of the knife, he slices a half inch cut across the guy's cheek and he hisses. Picking up the salt and a lemon wedge, he brings them both towards the cut, squeezes the lemon and shakes a dash of salt on top of it.

"Ahh! Fuck, fuck, fuck! Fuck you!"

"We're talking in circles here. Move on to the subject that matters. Tell us what we want to know." Rolling his lips in, he shakes his head vehemently. Viking shrugs and places the tip of the knife at the very corner of the guy's left eye. Squeezing his eyes shut as if it will keep the knife out, sweat drips down his forehead, a drop landing on the knife tip. Dragging the knife down a little, blood bubbles up at the site and slowly drips down his cheek. He picks up the salt and puts a dash of it in his palm. Placing his finger on the guy's eyelid, he pushes it up while pulling under his eye with his thumb. When the salt hits his eye, the guy starts screaming at the top of his lungs. Letting go of him, Viking grabs a lemon wedge, opens his eye again and drips the lemon juice in his eye as well. My stomach rolls and I turn away from the sight before me. Placing my hands against my stomach, I take a deep breath in from my nose and hold it, slowly letting it out. A hand gripping my shoulder makes me jump and I turn to find Viking standing there. Lowering his voice he says, "There's no shame in you needing to leave. You don't have to stay for this." From behind Viking, we hear the man laughing hard. Viking turns to look at him and I tilt my head in question. Did Viking already break this guy?

"Yeah, you should probably leave, pretty boy. I have nothing to tell you about Rhys and Nova.*" My heartbeat pounds in my head and I see red at his words. Blindly reaching out, weapons clatter against the table and I grab a hold of a random knife. Yelling , I charge at the guy and stab him in the thigh. Our screams echo throughout the room. Blood pours around the knife in his thigh. I watch the blood soak through his jeans and coat the knife while I twist it back and forth.*

"You don't get to say their fucking names. The only thing I want to hear from you is what we want to know, or we can stick with listening to the music of your screams. Pick. Now." Keeping his mouth shut, Viking and I work side by side leaving slices across his skin and adding

salt and lemon. Blood is dripping and pouring from various wounds and he has his head tilted back, panting through his greeted teeth.

Between labored breaths he says, "Okay. Okay. I'll. Tell. You." Dropping his head,he paints on an evil smile, blood coating his teeth and gums. "By the time you find them, it'll be too late. The fucked up part is it will be planned perfectly. They'll either die just before you reach them, or you'll find them as they take their final fucking breaths." Viking slightly pushes me to the side and thrusts a bowie knife in the guy's chest. Grunting, the guy looks down at his chest and wheezes. Sucking in a breath, he coughs and specks of blood shoot from his mouth. Twisting the knife, Viking yanks his hand down and cuts through until he hits the guy's navel. The specks of blood turn into spurts. The nausea hits again and I clasp my hand over my mouth. His eyes roll to the back of his head and a gurgling breath leaves him. Turning, I make a run for it to the sink and fall forward, vomiting the contents of my stomach. Spitting a few times, I turn the water on and wash it down the drain. Slapping the tap off, I lay my head on my arms. The clap of Viking's boots on the floor hit my ears.

Looking down between my arms, I see his boots to the side of me. "Hey, I can take care of all this. Why don't you head home, take a breather and do your brainiac thing. I'm not even gonna attempt to tell you to get some rest, cuz I know you won't do it. Sound good?" Nodding my head against my arms, I slowly stand up and push off of the sink. Swaying a little, Viking grabs a hold of my shoulder. "Got it?"

Wiping the back of my hand across my mouth, I grimace at the sight and smell of my vomit. "I got it, thanks. Keep me posted if you guys find anything, okay?" Nodding his head, he slowly releases my shoulder and I head out of the playroom.

I stomp up the steps to my door and unlock it. Dragging my feet across the threshold, I slam the door shut behind me and drop my bag to the floor. Heading to the kitchen, I open a cabinet and pull out a tall boiling pot and a box of matches. Carrying them to the bathroom, I put the boiling pot in the shower. I throw my shoes in the shower. I pull all my *clothes off my body and toss them along with the socks into the boiling pot. Throwing a lit match down, the flames slowly start eating through the clothes. I grab a random bottle of liquor from the top of the fridge and bring it back to the bathroom. Twisting the cap off, I pour some over the flames, making them blaze above the top of the pot. Taking a drink, I grimace from the burn as it goes down and watch the flames burn my bloody clothes. Waiting for the clothes to completely burn, I start washing the blood off of my shoes. Making the water as hot as possible, I let the water splash over the shoes and scrape the blood with my fingernails. I hiss from the heat of the water and watch as my hands start to turn pink. The water goes from red to a light pink color and I'm still scraping blood from the shoes. I pull the handheld shower head down to spray the pot of flames, it hisses as it extinguishes. Smoke billows in the air and I cough from accidentally inhaling some of it. After making sure all the flames are out, I place the pot on the counter and turn to fix the temperature of the water.*

I step under the water and let it run over my head. Bracing my hands on the wall, I drop my head and shut my eyes. The surveillance images pop up in my head and I draw in a sharp inhale, remembering how scared Nova looked when they grabbed her. Her eyes were continuously checking where Rhys was, I knew all her fear was placed on what would happen to Rhys. My body jolts at the memory of them slamming the butt of the gun on Rhys' head. As if a movie is playing in my head, the surveillance images are mixed in with memories we all made together. The memory of meeting my best friend, my brother in middle school. How we saved each other. Making flower crowns and dancing around with Nova, jamming to music. Sobs wrack my body, my hands slip from the wall as I fall into a heap to the floor. Curling into a ball, I wrap my arms around my legs as my body shakes from the sobs. The tears and snot wash away from my face with every pelt of the water from above. Struggling to breathe from the sobs, I hiccup, "I'm. Sorry. I'm. Sorry. I'm. I'm. I'm. So. S-s-sorryyyyy."

Flashes of Rhys from the time we met until now flash through my mind, and a grown Rhys leans down with a smile and says, "I need you, brother." He turns to ash and flies away and then I'm dancing around being silly with Nova.

She throws her head back and laughs, then looks back to me with a single tear rolling down her cheek. "Please save him, Prince Dorian."

Nodding my head, I speak against my bicep, "I will, I will, I promise. Oh, how I miss you both. I will save you both.*"*

"The stars will guide you home." ~Unknown

CHAPTER 22
HYPNOSIS

Nova

SOMETHING FEELS OFF WHEN I WALK THROUGH THE DOORS OF *SWAN & Scribe*. The first thing I notice is that V isn't behind the front counter. I go further into the store, where I can see people sitting at tables or walking around. Their faces seem blurred and I can't make sense of what they're saying. Rubbing my eyes, I look around at everyone again and they all stay the same. *What the fuck is going on?* Making my way towards the back, I turn the corner and see V, Dorian and The Horde all sitting around the table talking. Clearing my throat to get their attention, nobody stops or even looks in my direction. "Sup, fuckers."

Still no reaction from them.

What the fuck?

Walking closer to the table, I stand at the corner and put my hands down, "Hello?! What's up, guys?" I clap my hands obnoxiously, "Hellooooo!" A wave of dizziness hits me and I slump down to catch myself on the table. The sound of boots on the floor captures my attention and I turn my head. Looking over I see Rhys, his face lights up and he gasps.

We run towards each other and meet in an embrace. "Oh, little star, thank fuck."

I squeeze him tighter and a sob escapes me, "What is happening, ghoul? Something's wrong. They won't talk to me or look at me. A-and the people up front, th-they look and sound weird."

Nodding his head against my shoulder, he says, "I know, I know. I feel like I've been wandering around this place like a ghost. Nobody has a clue that I'm here. Let's go outside for some air, see if that helps us figure out what the fuck is happening." My vision blurs and I feel dizzy when we pass the doors on our way out. I can hear *F U In My Head* by *Cloudy June* playing and I'm no longer standing outside of *Swan & Scribe* with Rhys. We're now laying in his bed listening to music. Jolting upright, I look down at Rhys who has his eyes closed, singing along to the song. I shake his shoulder, making his eyes open, "I've been waiting for you, little star."

Scrunching my brows in confusion, I shake my head, "Waiting for me? Ghoulie, what the fuck is going on? Why aren't you more freaked out about this?"

"Because you're here. Believe me, the times that you're not are when I have my freak outs. But when I see you, everything is better. Now," opening his arms, he wiggles his fingers, "come cuddle with me, sweetheart. We don't know how long we have this moment for." I lay down and snuggle my face into his neck, placing my hand over his heart. I take a deep breath and wait for his breaths and heartbeat to calm me. Only this time there's nothing there. I can't feel his breath against my hair or his heart beating against my hand. When I open my eyes, the sight before me is terrifying. *No, no, no.* I'm on my back and Frankie is above me with his hands wrapped around my throat. I've been here before, but there's no way it's happening now. Frankie's dead.

Squeezing my eyes shut, I repeatedly say, "This isn't real, this isn't real, you're not real, it's just a nightmare." Darkness and silence surround me. *Is this what it feels like to die?*

Rhys

I walk into my playroom and immediately freeze. "Who the fuck are you, and what the fuck are you doing in here?!" Stomping my feet across the floor, the sound of my boots hitting the floor echoes around the room. I go closer and see that the person in the chair is Nova. My Nova. "WHAT THE FUCK ARE YOU DOING?!" I close the distance and spin him to face me. "I'll fucking kill y-" My words die on my lips when I see that the man has no face. "What the fuck?!" I look at the man again and his face flickers from a blank face to Frankie's face. A loud buzzing comes over the Bluetooth speaker and then *Where Is My Mind* by *PIXIES* starts playing. With an unamused chuckle, I shake my head, "Figures. GREAT SONG CHOICE, BRAIN!"

The sound of Nova's panicked voice gets my attention, "Ghoulie! Get me the fuck out of these restraints!"

I slam my shoulder against the guy standing there in order to get to her, "Out of my way, flicker face." When our shoulders connect, his face flickers again and changes to Cifarelli's face. "Fucking creepy." Tucking a strand of Nova's hair behind her ear, I slide my hand down the side of her neck and whisper, "Hi, sweetheart." As soon as her restraints are off, she wraps her arms around my neck, pulling me towards her.

"What's happening, ghoulie? I fucking hate this."

I wrap my arms around her and rub the back of her head. "I know, sweetheart, I know. It would be really fucking great if all this bullshit was done and over with so we could have a moment that we know is real." Something heavy slams into the back of my head and I fall forward. Nova disappears from my arms as I'm falling. Bringing my hands out in front of me to catch my fall, the floor never comes and I continue to go down, down, down.

Nova

How can someone feel like they're awake yet not? I feel like I'm caught in between the two. My body feels heavy and only dark-ness surrounds me. My mouth feels like sandpaper and I want to shout out, search for Rhys, but I can't tell if my mouth is even moving. *Am I forming words, is there any sound coming out?* There's an incessant beeping noise in my ear. No, not just one, there's two different beeping sounds. *What is that?* I'm not sure which way is up or down or what is real or not anymore. There are moments when I feel like I'm watching a movie of mine and Rhys' life. A constant reel of memories plays in my mind. Sometimes there's bits and pieces that I can't quite figure out if they are from this life or another, or just dreams playing in my head. A chill takes over my body, and I'm suddenly aware of my stomach rolling. Light pierces through my blurred vision and I'm not sure if I want to attempt to shut my eyes against it or blink it away. The double beeping grows louder and in the fog of my mind I realize it's the sound of heart monitors. My face feels wet and I'm not sure if it's tears or drool, maybe both. A murmured voice gets louder. I still have no control over my body, but this is the most present I've been. My head rolls to the side, unable to stop it and the sight in front of me makes me want to scream. Rhys is laying in a bed next to me and he's facing me. The pain and confusion on his face shatters my heart. Attempting to speak, the only sound that escapes my sandpaper mouth is a crackle. A voice with a heavy Italian accent fills my ears and I want to run far away from it.

"Ah, those tears you shed, my dear. Bellissima." Rhys' face grows red and tense and a long, drawn out crackle escapes his throat.

Rhys

The strength of my mind and body has been taken from me, and with this dense fog on my brain, I feel like this is the worst thing possible. This doesn't happen to me, I can fight anything and anyone, but my years of training haven't prepared me for this. My vision clears and I realize that losing my mind and body isn't the worst thing, the sight before me is. My little star is strapped down to the bed next to mine and there are tears and drool falling down her face. I vaguely remember images of us and those closest to us playing in my mind, or was it real? My sole focus is on her and I want to touch her, talk to her… save her. A voice with a heavy Italian accent speaks and I will myself to just move so I can kill him. "Ah, those tears you shed, my dear. Bellissima." His words piss me off, and I fight as hard as I can to move, to yell out. Along with my mind and body, I realize my voice has been stolen from me as well. Instead of yelling at the piece of shit, the only noise that escapes my Sahara mouth is crackles and grunts. "Wonderful, the once conquering hero is awake as well. The three of us have so much to talk about." Finding himself funny, he chuckles and waves his hands. I realize I'm seeing triple and he only waved one hand. "Apologies. What I mean to say, is that I will be chatting with you two while you try as hard as you can to piece it all together. Now, let's see if you two are ready to pay attention."

He walks over to Nova and caresses her cheek. A wheezing whine escapes her and I again attempt to yell. Our combined sounds make him laugh more and he nods. "Oh yes, you two are definitely ready to pay attention. I thought you both should know, a few days ago our little Dorian discovered your disappearance." With a fake sorrowful look, he shakes his head, "He was just beside himself. He tried very hard to hide it, especially when I confronted him in your truck, Rhys." I don't even know if my body is showing a reaction on the outside, but internally the heart monitors show that both Nova and I are panicking. The beeping grows faster and louder with the pounding of our hearts at the news. Watching the monitors his disgusting smile grows and his eyes darken. "He's so worried about the two of you, I don't think he even realizes I have him *exactly* where I want him. You both seem to think you're so fucking sneaky, but I'll always be ten steps ahead of you. You know the saying, keep your friends close, but your enemies closer? You thought that tactic would work in your favor with him working here, but in reality, it's working out so much better for me. I have all of you right where I want you, and poor, sniveling Dorian will be doing his damndest to find you. Little does he know you're both right underneath his fucking nose. I have to say, it was a close call though. If he had come searching for you two any sooner, it's quite possible he would have run right into my men taking you. Now, I know things are foggy, so I'll give you a little time to come back to your senses. I haven't given you enough Dimenti-care yet to wipe your memory, so I'm going to need you to answer some questions for me soon. Usually, I know you'd fight it and tell me to go fuck myself. But let's just skip all that and you tell me what I want to know. Maybe, just maybe, for your cooperation, I'll let your precious amore go." With his hands clasped in front of him and his smug smile, he takes a few steps back. "Don't go anywhere, you two. I shall return, very soon." Turning to leave, he opens the door and steps out. After shutting it, I hear the sound of the lock clicking. Rolling my head towards Nova, I see her attempting to mouth something to me.

———⋆

Nova

I refuse to stare at that old bastard while he spoke to us. Keeping my eyes on Rhys the whole time is helping bring my awareness back. As soon as the door shuts and locks, his head turns to look at me. There's so many things I want to say to him, but I know the words won't come out. *Now would be a great time for us to be able to read each other's minds.* Breathing in slowly, I let it out and try to form words. A crackle falls from my mouth on the first word, "G-houl."

Rhys is stronger than me, and it shows when his response seems to come easier to him. In a low, gruff voice he says, "Little star." Opening my mouth again, he tilts his head as if shaking it no. "S-ave. Y-our. V-oice." The grimace on his face and his panted words tell me talking is harder for him than I thought it was. "I. Love. You. Too." Squeezing his eyes shut, he blows out a breath and beads of sweat fall from his temple. "I," clearing his throat a few times, he continues, "I need you to listen to me, little star. We both know we can't trust these people, no matter what they say. I need you to remember that with whatever comes next. They're going to do whatever they can to get us to talk. I need you to remember that I love you with everything I have, sweetheart. This is only the beginning-" His words are cut off by the sound of the lock clicking. He looks at me, waiting for me to acknowledge his words quickly. Sniffling, I nod my head the best I can and smile at him. His smile is cut short by the door opening, and his soft, loving face morphs into Rhys the Beast.

I look towards the door and I see Adriano standing there

smiling down at me. "Aww, there, there, my dear, don't cry. Although, the shine of your tears really does bring out the beauty of your eyes." My stomach rolls again and I know it's from his words and not from the drugs he gave us.

"Hey! Cryptkeeper! Look at me, not her!" His smile grows as he continues to look at me and ignores Rhys. Putting his hands behind his back, he slowly turns towards Rhys.

"I may not want to hurt her because she reminds me of my daughter, but if you continue running your mouth with your nonsense, I shall forget all about that and focus all my anger on her. So what's it to be, my boy?" Rolling my head towards Rhys, I see his jaw clenched and a pulse ticking along it, reluctantly nodding to agree. The sound of a clap makes me move my head and look at Adriano again, who's rubbing his hands together with a gleam in his eyes. Behind him is a rolling table, which he brings in front of him. Reaching behind him he pulls out a small dagger. The blade is curved to match the gold Italian horn dangling from his necklace. Twisting his wrist back and forth, he looks at the blade and then makes a show of carefully placing it on the table.

"Family heirloom. Quite poetic don't you think? To use a family heirloom on the very person that threatens to harm my family. Let's start simple, shall we? How many are a part of your operation, other than Dorian and Nova?"

Rhys grimaces at his words and rolls his head towards me with a panicked look. Looking back at Adriano, he says, "Thanks to you, she now knows more than she did before. Her and Dorian only had an idea of what I do for a living, not who I was going after. So thanks for dropping that bombshell on my girl-friend." Even with the slight fog still hanging onto me from the sedation, I realize the game he's playing with this guy.

Knowing I need to make it believable, I force the words out with a slight rasp, "How could you? You know what I've been through, how could you keep this from me? Bring more danger to my life, when I thought I was finally free of it all."

"I'm so sorr-"

Before he can finish his sentence, Adriano cuts him off, "My, my. Secrets are never good for relationships, my dear boy. Not with your spouse or with friends. Why did you hide this from them?"

"I thought it would keep them safe. Fat lot of good that fucking did. I'm sorry, sweetheart, I really am. I thought it was the right thing to do." Letting out a fake sniffle, I roll my head so I'm looking at the ceiling.

"YOU SON OF A BITCH! I'LL FUCKING KILL YOU!" The sound of his pain and anger has me quickly turning my head back in his direction. Tears spring to my eyes and I swallow the bile creeping up my throat. He's pressing the tip of his blade into Rhys' arm, blood falling around the blade and down his arm, dripping to the floor. The flesh of his arm surrounds the blade as if holding it in place, Adriano pulls back hard and his flesh reluctantly lets go.

"Now, how much do you know about my operation?"

"Do your men not give you enough of an ego boost? Is that what this is? You just want to hear me tell you that I only know what *you* already fucking told me. Which is the fucking truth. Abuse and kill innocent people, check. Manufacture and distribute drugs, check. Working on creating your own drug, check. The. Fucking. End. That's all I fucking know. Happy now?"

Nodding his head, "As long as it's the truth, then yes, this would make me very happy."

Tapping his finger against his chin, he tilts his head, "Hmm. How to see if you're telling the truth? Hmm, hmm, hmm." Clicking his tongue, he drops his hand and walks over to me. Pointing his blade at me, he pushes it close to my arm.

"DON'T YOU FUCKING TOUCH HER! I ANSWERED YOUR QUESTIONS! WHAT HAPPENED TO NOT WANTING TO HURT HER CUZ SHE REMINDS YOU OF YOUR DAUGHTER!?"

He drops the blade and turns towards Rhys, "So soon you have forgotten. She may *remind* me of my daughter, but she is *not* my daughter. I will do whatever is necessary to get to the truth. Now, please, be polite and stop interrupting me." Pressing the tip of his blade to my arm I wince and gasp from the sting. The tip of the blade is sharp enough to leave a shallow cut along my arm as it glides down. Slowly dragging it down my arm, he asks again, "Is that everything you know, Rhys? Are you telling me the truth?"

"YES! THAT'S ALL I KNOW! PLEASE, PLEASE STOP HURTING HER! I SWEAR, THAT'S ALL I KNOW!" When he pulls the blade away, I can hear my blood dripping to the floor, like the sound of water dripping from a faucet. Our heart monitors both beeping rapidly to match our racing heartbeats.

"Very good. I believe you." Pulling a handkerchief from his pocket he starts wiping the blood from my arm and leans forward, whispering, "Very sorry, my dear."

Rhys

Watching him as he steps away from Nova, I glare at him while he approaches. "Can we just skip you hurting her from now on, and you just realize I will tell you what you want to know? I know you don't give a shit about innocent people when you believe they've wronged you, but I can assure you, Nova has never wronged you and she is the very definition of innocent."

Tilting his head, he lifts his brow, "You do realize that things would go much smoother if you just listened to me and answered my questions. You aren't running this show, I am. You'd do well to stop giving me orders, Rhys." Stepping backwards, he points his knife back and forth between Nova and I. "Get comfortable, you two. I shall return *very* soon." He walks to the door and opens it to step through but before the door closes, he pokes his head through with a smile, "Behave."

I release the breath I was holding when I hear the lock click. I turn towards Nova and our eyes connect, "Are you okay, little star? Does it hurt?"

Looking down at her arm and then back at me, she shrugs the best she can, her restraints jangling with the movement. "I'm okay, ghoulie. Just feels like an annoying papercut."

"I love you, little star. Thank you for-" Pausing, I look around the room the best I can and squint. Clearing my throat, I look at Nova again, "Thank you for being so understanding about me lying to you and Dorian. I know it upsets you, and I'm really sorry about that."

Narrowing her eyes at me, she opens her mouth but stops. A look of concentration crosses her features, "Even if you think it's protecting me, don't lie to me again, Rhys." Whispering under her breath, she adds, "If we ever get out of here."

"Hey, look at me, sweetheart." Turning towards me, a tear falls from her eye, sliding over the bridge of her nose and down her face. The sight breaks my heart and I wish I could reach out and wipe her tears. "We're going to get out of here. Say it, sweetheart."

Taking a deep breath, she says, "But what if-"

Shaking my head no, I lower my voice and growl, "Say. It. Nova."

In a defeated voice, she says, "We're getting out of here."

The lock clicks and the door opens, revealing Adriano and his goons following behind. "Oh, look, sweetheart, the three stooges are here, it's our lucky day." Adriano chuckles at my words while the other two grit their teeth. The sound of Nova's laughter catches my attention and I roll my head towards her.

"I couldn't help it, they reminded me of angry bull dogs."

Looking towards the guys, I start laughing, "Oh, shit, you're right."

"YOU AND YOUR WHORE NEED TO SHUT THE FUCK UP!"

Adriano holds his hand up, "Settle, Aldo. Go stand by Nova. Alonzo, you go stand by Rhys." Aldo stomps his feet as he walks up to Nova and glares down at her. Alonzo and Adriano walk up to me and I grit my teeth. "Alright Alonzo, hold on to him tight." My eyes widen when I see the syringe in Adriano's hand.

Nova and I both start chanting, "No, no, no." Stabbing the needle into my arm, my teeth grind together at the feel of the needle. He presses down on the plunger until the syringe is empty, then drops the syringe on the metal table and picks up the other one.

Walking towards Nova, he directs Aldo, "Grab a hold of her. Tight enough so I don't fuck up the poke, but not enough to harm her." Wincing, I watch as he pushes the plunger down. Needing Nova to be the last thing I see, I look away from the syringe being pulled out of her arm, and look at her beautiful face. I'm fighting the fog, and I can tell she is fighting just as hard.

My eyes slowly blink shut and the last thing I hear is Adriano's warped voice say, "Sweet dreams."

"Your soulmate will be the stranger you recognize." ~R.H. Sin

325

CHAPTER 23
EVEN WHEN I'M NOT WITH YOU

DORIAN

A loud bang startles me awake. Jerking my head up, I swat away the papers that are stuck to my face. The light is harsh so I squint my eyes open and see Vanessa standing in front of me on the other side of the table. "Figured I'd find you here." She pushes a drink towards me and says, "Iced green tea. I had them add some fancy energy shot to it. How long have you been here for, Dorian?" Tilting her head, she waits for my answer. Pushing my hair out of my face, I look around the room as if the answer will present itself.

"Umm, awhile? I'm not quite sure."

Sighing, she shakes her head, "I had a feeling. Everyone else will be here soon to help out. You really should get some rest, Dorian. Don't you have a shift at that awful place in about," she looks at her phone screen, "eight hours? If you were going to bed right now, that would give you enough sleep, but we both know you won't be."

I put my arms out towards the papers on the table and then point to my face, "You just woke me up. I slept, I'm good to go."

Rolling her eyes, she jabs her finger towards the drink,

"Drink it. We both know that was a mini cat nap for you." The drink starts to slip from my hands with the condensation. Placing it back down on the table, I lean forward and wrap my lips around the straw, gulping half of it down. "Better?"

Crossing her arms, she narrows her eyes at me, "Be a lot better without the attitude. But sure, better."

With a sad smile, I put up my hand, "I apologize, I don't mean to take it out on you. I'm just really upset and my brain is not working the way it usually does, which really pisses me off. I know I'm missing something, feels like having a word on the tip of your tongue and not quite being able to grasp it. "

She places her hand on my forearm and squeezes. "I know it'll come to you. There's a lot going on, and lack of sleep doesn't help. Haven't seen you smoke either. So your body and mind are all out of whack," she said.

Scoffing, I shake my head, "I haven't smoked, and honestly I shouldn't be eating, drinking or sleeping either. If Rhys and Nova don't get that luxury, why should I?"

She steps back and pulls a chair out to sit. "Listen, the smoking part is obvious. But we don't know about the food, drinks or sleep. Let's just work together to save them. That's all we can do. What have you found so far?" As soon as I open my mouth to tell her, the security system beeps and surveillance footage pops up on the screens. The Horde have arrived, so I open the security app on my phone and buzz them in.

Putting my phone on the table, I look up at Vanessa, "I'll just wait for them to get in here, so I can tell everyone at the same time." Nodding her head, she picks up her coffee that I just noticed she brought for herself. "I hope everyone brought their own refreshments or they're going to feel excluded from our little drink and think sesh."

Giving me a sad smile, she follows a drop of condensation with her finger. "You talk like him sometimes. He'd get a kick out of that, huh?"

Scratching my beard, I laugh, "God, I did say one of his cheesy rhymes. He would definitely love that shit." Groaning, I shake my head, "I'm taking it to my grave, I'll deny it if you ever tell him."

"Ha, deny it all you want. All I have to do is tell Nova girl first, and she'll tell him for me. We both know he'll believe her."

Throwing my head back, I chuckle, "You're right. SuperNova could pull a prank on him and say I did it, and he would for sure come after me for it. Trouble, the both of them."

"Oh, absofuckinlutely."

The Horde files in and looks at the both of us slightly laughing. Sitting around the table, Fish stares me down, "Secrets don't make friends, guys. What's so funny?"

"Noth-"

Cutting me off, Vanessa says, "Dorian was talking like Rhys and then we started talking about how much trouble those two are."

I give her a mock glare, "Traitor." Sticking her tongue out at me, I roll my eyes and look towards The Horde. "Alright, Vanessa asked me what I've found so far, and I figured I would wait for everyone to be here so I only have to say it once. Honestly, I don't have a whole hell of a lot. Most of what I'm finding are things we already knew. There's something I'm missing and I'm hoping it comes to me sooner rather than later. Until then, I want that surveillance of the capture running on a loop. Fresh eyes are helpful as well, so I'm going to pass these papers around the table and I want everyone to take a look and see if anything jumps out at them." Shuffling the papers together, I smack them down on the table to straighten the pile. Sliding them over to Viking, he grabs a page and starts passing the rest down.

Turning towards the screens, I grab the remote and hit play on the surveillance footage. Spreading my legs, I lean forward to rest my elbows on my knees while I watch it play through. My anxiety peaks when that tip of the tongue feeling is pounding away at my brain. Biting my thumbnail, I stand up and walk closer to the screens. I start muttering, "What is it, what is it, what is it?" A hand clasps my shoulder tightly, making me startle, "Geez, don't do that."

Viking steps next to me with a laugh, "Sorry, Eagle. You're talking to yourself over here. What's up?"

Raising my hand, I point at the screens and shake my finger at them. "I'm missing something, I just know it. It's been bothering me this whole time, but when I watch this it sets me off even more." Grabbing my hair by the roots, I slightly tug. "Any other time I'd have this figured out after a day, fucking two tops. And please don't feed me the same lines Vanessa already did. I know there's a lot going on, but it still pisses me off."

"Alright, how about this... I'm sure you already have this footage memorized, but watch it through once more. Then, I'm going to ask you questions about the footage and we'll go from there. Sound good?"

Lifting the remote, I rewind the footage and start it from the beginning. Pressing play, I nod, "Sounds good." As I watch the footage closely, I'm repeating every move that's made in my head. When it ends, I hit pause on the remote and look over at Viking.

"Okay, turn towards me and close your eyes." Lifting a brow at him in question, he rolls his eyes and crosses his arms, "Don't make it weird, just do it." Sighing, I turn towards him, he grabs the remote from my hands and waves towards my face.

Groaning, I close my eyes, "Okay. Eyes closed. Now what?"

"What's the first thing that happens, Eagle?"

Breathing in from my nose, I slowly release the breath through my mouth and see the scene play out in my mind. "Two guys walk up behind Rhys' truck."

"Which direction are they coming from?"

"They walked up from the direction of the lake."

"Good. What happens next?"

"The taller guy slaps his hand on the top of Rhys' truck."

"Good. Keep going, play it out."

Rubbing at my Baphomet, I continue, "Nova opens her door

329

and hops out. She's smiling and saying something to Rhys. She starts slowly walking along the side of the truck. When she gets to the back, she starts to talk but she's cut off when the shorter man grabs her. He has a gun to her head and is holding her. Rhys walks towards the back of the truck and the taller guy pistol whips him." My breathing increases and my heart is racing. I can feel the lump in my throat, swallowing hard and clearing my throat, I continue with a slight crack in my voice. "W-words are exchanged. Rhys is pushed forward to walk beside his truck and a gun is at his back. And then... and th-"

"And then what, Dorian. What happens after they start walking?"

Gasping, a light bulb shines bright in my head. Opening my eyes, I reach forward, "Holy fuck, and then! Give me the remote! I got it! I fucking got it! Holy fucking shit, I can't fucking believe I didn't think of this sooner."

Viking hands the remote over with a smile, "Take it away, Eagle."

Grabbing the remote, I zoom out of the footage and follow the direction they're going. Clicking buttons, I switch cameras when necessary. The Horde comes up behind us and I vaguely hear murmurs of, "What is it? What did you find?"

Putting my hand up, "Shh, shh, hold on, hold on. Wait for it, wait for it." The footage plays out and we watch as they have Rhys open up the basement bulkhead doors. Watching them follow the steps down I stop the footage. "Holy fucking shit! Unfuckinbelievable! They've been right fucking there this whole fucking time. We could've saved them a fucking week ago!" Turning, I shove through the group and throw the remote as hard as I can. Bouncing off of the table, the shattered pieces fly out like a bomb blew them up. "FUCK!"

Stomping over to my filing cabinets filled with various gadgets, I start ripping drawers open and shuffling through. A hand at my back stills me, "Dorian, hun, please take a breath. Let us help you. What are you looking for?" Jade's hand on my back and her calm tone soothes me.

Nodding my head, I look at her over my shoulder, "Yes, thank you. I apologize."

"It's okay. Now let us help you," she says with a smile.

Extending my hand towards the cabinets, "I need to put together a kit of sorts. I need a button camera, a few other discreet cameras, bugs and Bluetooth earbuds."

Bending down, Jade picks up a small tote. Standing up, she pushes it towards me and then the drawers, "Okay, put them all in here and you can come sit down with us. Let us know what the plan is, okay?" With a tight-lipped smile, I nod and start grabbing everything I need. Putting it all in the tote, Jade carries it to the table and sits down. Shutting all of the drawers, I walk over and sit down.

Looking around the table, all eyes are on me. With a nervous chuckle, I rub the back of my neck, "Okay, this is what I'm thinking. I never got around to placing those cameras and bugs. During my shift today, I'm going to set all those up." Lifting the button camera up, I show it to them, "This button camera is going to clip over one of the buttons on my jumpsuit. This way you guys will be able to see everything that I do. Also, if I stumble on something important, we'll have footage of it." Putting the button camera back in the tote, I pick up the Bluetooth earbuds and twist them in my fingers. "These, I will wear while I'm on a call with you guys. This way, not only will you see what I see, but you'll be able to hear everything. I'm sure you guys want to know how everything is going, so these things will help with that. Before you ask, no, I won't get caught or in trouble for having these. The janitors are allowed to listen to music while they work. I'm thinking as an extra precaution, one of you here will have music at the ready. If I hear or see something, or someone that you guys can't, I'll tip you off by humming. The moment I start humming, start playing the music so they play through the earbuds. If need be, I'll act like my phone has the voice assistant set up, and when I say music, stop, well you know what to do." Slapping my hands down on the table, I then wave them towards the group, "So, any questions?"

Mrs. Valour sits forward and rests her elbows on the table, "How do you plan on pulling this off without getting caught? You have to be very careful how you place these cameras and bugs. Do you know how you're going to do that sneakily?"

Picking up the button camera, I start flipping it around in my fingers quickly. When I open my hand, the camera is gone, "Just a little sleight of hand." Wiggling my fingers, I add, "One hand will be holding a rag to clean with, and the other will be leaving things behind quickly. I promise I can do this. If worse comes to worst, you guys will see and hear everything, and we know *Amissa Stella* is where they hold people. So you'll all know where to find all of us." I look around the table and everyone has horri-fied looks on their faces. Putting my hands up to placate them, I roll my eyes, "Guys, that's the worst-case scenario, which I highly doubt will happen. It'll be okay."

With an exaggerated throat clearing, Vanessa leans forward. Shaking her phone at me with the time on display she says, "6 hours. You have 6 hours to get your rest before you do this. Go."

"B-but, there's things to do, I can't just-"

"You can and you will. There's nothing else for you to do right now, Dorian. You did it, you cracked the mystery that was eating away at you. Now you rest. You need to be clear-headed and focused for this plan."

At her no nonsense look, I sigh, "Okay, okay. Geez, you're scary sometimes, do you know that?"

With a smile, she tilts her head and narrows her eyes, "Oh, I know. I can get a whole hell of a lot scarier if you keep stalling. Move it, Alden."

Scooting my chair back quickly, I stand up, "Okay, okay, geez. Somebody get a fire extinguisher and put her fire out before she burns us all."

When I wake up, I run to the bathroom and grab a jumpsuit and a pair of boots from the standing locker there. Pulling my shoes off, I toss them in the locker and slam the door shut. I pull my jumpsuit on, button it up and slip my boots on. Turning the sink on, I run my hands through the water and start combing my wet fingers through my hair. After taming my wild locks, I grab a few paper towels and dry my hands off. I head to the conference room and the conversations cease at my arrival. I walk over to the table and grab the button camera first, clipping it on the top button of my jumpsuit. The remaining cameras go in my right pocket and the bugs go in the left. Picking up the Bluetooth headphones I wrap the plastic part around my ear and shove the buds in my ears. "Alright, I'm heading in now. After I park, I'll call you guys so you're with me every step of the way. Sound good?"

Viking stands up, "Wait. I think we're all in agreement that we'd be more comfortable if you took some sort of protection with you."

Grimacing, I stick my tongue out, "Eww, I don't plan on fucking them. Condoms are not necessary. This is a mission, not missionary."

"Not what I meant, mini Rhys," he snorts.

Putting my hand on my chest like I'm offended, I gasp, "I can crack jokes too, ya know. That's not just a Reese's Pieces thing, geez." Bending down, I grab my messenger back from under the table and throw it over my shoulder. I pick my phone up and make sure to put it in my bag before leaving.

Pointing my thumb towards the door, I tilt my head, "I'm outta here. Please have the music ready to go if need be. Might also be good to silence your devices and set security up for silent alarms only. Just to be on the safe side."

As I walk towards the door, everyone shouts out, "Be safe." I put my hand up and continue walking out the door. The first song that plays on the radio after I've started my car is *With You Till The End* by *Tommee Profitt.* Humming along to the song as I drive, some of the words capture my attention. My eyes start to water thinking of Rhys and Nova and I sniffle. "Get it together, Dorian. You had your moment, now is not the time." Tapping my thumbs on the steering wheel as I drive, I focus on the task ahead. Once I pull into the parking lot, I park my car and unbuckle. After I've turned off my car, I shove my keys in my bag and grab my phone. I call Viking and hear the beep of the call connecting in the earbuds.

After a few rings, Viking answers the phone, "Ready?"

"Yup. Okay, I'm going to turn the button camera on, let me know if it connects." Pushing the button camera against my chest to activate it, I wait for Viking's answer. "Anddddd, there it is. Good to go. We're going quiet on our end. Be safe, Eagle."

Locking my phone, I slide it in my breast pocket and button it closed. I hop out of my car, throwing my bag over my shoulder as I head towards the entrance. Walking through the doors, I nod my head and smile at the receptionist. When I reach the staff room, I put my hand in my left pocket and grab hold of one of the bugs. I sit down at the computer used to clock in, look around and double check that I'm the only one there. Unsure if there's any cameras in the room, I grab the mouse and slightly lift it from the mousepad. Pretending to move it around, I pick it up and shake it, "Damn thing is out of sync." Shaking it again, I drop it to the floor and kick it with my foot under the desk. "Dammit, today is not my day." I bend down to grab the mouse and slide the bottom piece off. Flicking the tiny switch on the bug, I place it inside. After I've slid the plastic piece back in place, I dodge the desk and sit up. Putting the mouse down on the mousepad, I move it around, "Finally, geez."

I clock in, push the chair back and walk over to my locker. Throwing my bag inside, I head to the janitor's room. I grab my cart first, roll it over to the shelves and start filling the cart with various cleaners and rags. Kneeling down, I act like I'm checking the bottom shelf for something. I feel around for one of the bugs with adhesive tape in my pocket. Scraping the paper layer off, I pull the bug out and slide it on the metal wheel cover. I reach into my other pocket to pull the paper layer off the adhesive on a camera and slap it on the side of the cart over a screw. I brace my hand on the edge of the cart and the shelf, and push myself up. Grabbing the handle of the cart, I pull it behind me and head towards the door. Making sure nobody is standing there, I pull the cart hard enough to roll it past me. I shut the door and push the cart around the main floor to clean the usual areas. I look around to make sure I'm in the clear, bend down and start shuffling through cleaning items in the bottom of the cart. Tilting my head inside the cart, I whisper, "Somebody check the cameras and make sure I'm clear to head to the basement." Grabbing a rag, I stand up and spray dust cleaner into it. As I wait for their answer, I make my way towards the elevators, dusting every door knob and picture along the way.

"Clear."

Turning the corner, I push forward and stop in front of the elevator. Wiping the doors down first, I then wipe the buttons and push the button to go down. Rocking on my heels, I hear the beep of the elevator hitting my current floor and the doors open. Pushing the cart in, I stand behind the cart and grab a bug out of my pocket. I move towards the buttons display and start wiping it down, pushing against the button for the basement floor. The elevator jolts as it makes its descent and I lock my knees. While cleaning the buttons I decide the wall case holding pamphlets will be the best place for the bug. I pretend to rearrange the pamphlets so I can drop the bug in the bottom of the case. The elevator bounces and beeps when it reaches the basement. Pushing the cart towards the doors, I wait for them to open all the way and walk out. Not knowing where to go first, I turn right and walk down the hall until I reach the double doors. I press my ear against the door, listening for any sign of people inside. Since I don't hear anything, I leave the cart behind and walk through. My mouth drops and I freeze when I look around the room. There's rows of chairs with machinery for taking vitals next to each chair. Whispering to myself in disbelief, "What the fuck? This is like movie shit. Shit like this just doesn't happen for real." Pulling a bug out of my pocket, I remove the adhesive paper from it, flip the switch and bend down. I reach beneath one of the carts and stick the bug on the bottom of it. Standing up straight, my eyes catch on another machine in the cart.

I look closer and realize that it's an ECT machine and I stumble back. "No, no, no. Please, no."

In my earbud I hear Viking grit out, "Is that what I fucking think it is, Eagle?"

Breathlessly, I respond, "Yeah, yeah it is."

"Fuck. Get the fuck outta there."

"Not yet, I have to find them. Remember, if I find anything of importance I'll need some of you to start researching it immediately."

"We're on it, Eagle. Now move your ass."

Huffing in annoyance, I roll my eyes, "I swear, I'm surrounded by bossholes. All of you." Walking back into the hall, I bend down and grab the handle for the broom and the bristle head piece. As I twist the pieces together, I carry the broom down the hall and lean it against the wall at the midpoint of the hallway. I continue down the hall and realize there's only one door this way. Stopping in front of it, I rub the rag around the knob and see a lock. Scrunching my brows in confusion, I stare at it. *Why is there a lock on the outside of a door?* Flipping the lock, I turn the door knob and quietly push the door open. I place my back against the door to look down the hall, listening for any sounds. Not hearing anything in the hall, I notice beeping from the room behind me. Sidestepping into the room, I grab the door and quietly close it. I spin around to take everything in and my jaw drops. My voice breaks, "Oh, fuck."

In the earbud, I faintly hear Viking say, "Fuck." Murmured gasps in the background hit my ears. I stand frozen in place as I stare at Rhys and Nova strapped to beds. They both have those same vitals machines next to their beds showing their heart rate and blood pressure. Other than some bruising and cuts, they look almost peaceful lying there. Wincing, I clap my hand over my ear at Viking's shout, "EAGLE!"

"W-what? Fuck, are you trying to burst my eardrum?"

"If that's what it fucking takes, then yes. Focus. You're no good to them if you get caught too. Search the room. There's gotta be something in there that can help us help them. Get a move on it."

Nodding my head, I wipe the sweat from my brow. "Y-yeah, of course." Turning away from them, I look around the room. Besides them, the room is sparse. Finding another wall case with pamphlets, I pull out a bug and flip the switch, tossing it in the case. As I make my way towards the other end of the room, I notice a double-door fridge. With the clear glass around it, I can see various vials and syringes inside. Quickly walking over to it, I open the fridge and make sure the button camera captures the names on each vial. "Pay close attention to the names on these vials, guys. I need someone to start looking all of this up now."

"Affirmative."

Looking at the labels, I notice there's only two different drugs. The left side of the fridge is filled with vials labeled *Dimenticare*. Part of the label has lost its adhesive and is rolled back. Noticing lettering behind the first label, I reach forward and peel it further back. *Midazolam*. "You guys seeing this?"

"Got it. Unfuckinbelievable. What else is in there, Eagle?"

I push against the label the best I can to put it back in place and I reach to the back of the fridge to pick up the last vial. Putting it in my pocket, I shut the door, and open the right side of the fridge. Making sure the camera catches the labels on this half of the vials, I look and see that these ones are labeled, *Flumazenil*. Pulling a vial from the back, I pocket that one as well. Shutting the door, I turn and walk over to Rhys. Leaning down, I whisper, "I've got you, brother. I promise I'll be back." Standing up straight, I stare down at him with a sad smile. Turning to Nova, I walk over and place a kiss on the top of her head. "I'm

so sorry, SuperNova. I promise I'm coming back for you guys."
Walking backwards, I take a deep breath and stare at my best
friends.

"EAGLE! MAYDAY, MAYDAY! ABORT! Two goons heading
straight for the elevator. Get the fuck outta there now!"

"Shit! Start the music now." Spinning around, I run to the
door and rip it open. Shutting it, I start to move down the hall.

"LOCK! GET THE LOCK!"

"Fuck, right."

Heading back to the door, I flip the lock and run down the
hall grabbing the broom as I go. Passing the elevators I hear the
beep of it reaching the basement floor. *Fuck, fuck, fuck.* Sliding
towards the cart, I put my head down and start sweeping and
humming to *The Summoning* by *Sleep Token*. Muttering under my
breath, I shake my head, "Fucking smartasses." Movement
catches my eye and I look up to two very angry looking men
with their mouths moving. *Oh, I recognize you fuckers.* Pulling one
of my earbuds out, I lift a brow, "What's up?"

"What the fuck are you doing down here?"

Lifting the broom, I slightly shake it, "Uh, my job? Why?"

Throwing a thumb back towards the elevator, the shorter
man shakes his head, "No. The basement floor is for night shift.
Get a move on."

Nodding my head, I twist the broom apart, "Yeah, man, no
problem." Putting the pieces of the broom on the bottom
shelving of the cart, I pull the rag from my shoulder and toss it
in the top part of the cart. Pushing the cart towards the men, I
give them a mock salute and smile, "Have a great day." I hit the
upturned arrow button and wait for the elevator. With a beep,
the doors open and I push the cart inside. When I press the
button to go up, I notice the two men standing there staring at
me. Pushing the button, I smile again and wave. The doors shut
on their angry faces and I fall against the back of the elevator,
releasing the breath I was holding. "Fuck."

"Too close, Eagle. Way too fucking close."

"You're fucking telling me. You guys have from now until the time I get there to decide if you're all in or not. I'll be working all night on what I found. I'm getting them outta here tomorrow. End of."

"We don't need that long to think about it. We're in."

"Friendship isn't about who you've known the longest, it's about who walked into your life, said, 'I'm here for you,' and proved it." ~Unknown

CHAPTER 24
CARRY YOU

DORIAN

"4H-imidazo 1, 5-a 1, check. 4 benzodiazepine, check. Substituted by a methyl, check. 2-fluorophenyl, check. Chloro groups at positions 1, check, 6, check and 8, check. It's exactly the same. All of it."

"DORIAN!"

Jumping from the loud shout in my ear, I turn and look over at Vanessa. Holding my chest as if it will slow my pounding heart, I narrow my eyes at her. "What?"

Sitting down next to me, she props her elbow on the table and rests her head on her hand. "I've been calling your name for a while. What the fuck are you yammering about over here? You're speaking gibberish."

"Oh. It's not gibberish. Those are just all the chemical-"

Holding up her hand to stop me, she asks, "You're about to do that thing Rhys always stops you from doing, aren't you?"

"No?"

Lifting a brow at me, I look up at the ceiling and blow air through my pursed lips. "Okay, maybe. Probably. Yes, yes I was."

"Okay, well Dorian, you have to remember, not everyone has that big ol' brain. So can you explain it to me, wait," looking over her shoulder she yells out, "You guys come here and listen to what Dorian found." Looking back to me, she smiles and waves her hand forward as everyone approaches, "Okay, sorry. Now, please explain this to us like we're learning for the very first time… since we are."

Curving my lips to the side, I look away and think about it. After a moment, I nod my head, "Yeah, yeah I can do that. So the non-gibberish I was speaking about was basically what makes the drug that has Rhys and Nova sedated. All this time we thought they were making their own drug to sell to people, but it's just a front. This isn't their own drug, it's literally a benzodi-azepine. More specifically, it's called Midazolam. I was checking to see if maybe they added their own thing to these vials, but they didn't. They didn't even bother to remove the original label from it, they just glued their own over the top of it. I don't know where they're getting a hold of all these drugs, because there's no way they could get away with this much from one location. Anyways, that's something to tackle another time."

Mrs. Valour leans forward and asks, "Soooo, this is a good thing, right?"

Quickly nodding, I sit up straighter and turn so I'm facing everyone. "Yes! This is a very good thing. This means I know exactly what to give them to bring them out of the sedation. I was able to hack into the hospital's system and see exactly what they administer, how much and how frequently."

Pausing, I furrow my brows when a complication hits me. Viking steps forward and waves his hand in front of my face. Leaning back, I look up at him. "What's up?"

Shaking my head, I blow out a breath, "I just realized there's only one way to pull this off, and it's not going to be easy." Leaning forward, I place my elbows on my knees and rub my hands over my face.

"Well, spit it out. We'll figure out a solution together."

"For starters. I have to keep everyone that goes down there

away from them. I need to be able to go down there and administer the drugs without interruption. Not only that, but I'll most likely have to administer it more than once throughout my shift, and I have to make sure nobody finds them coming out of sedation. Shit, I'll probably have to bring the Midazolam with me so I can inject them with it if they interrupt. My other issue is I'll have to take them out of the bulkhead doors, not up and out through the front doors. Which means whoever is coming to help, will have to park out there and see if there's a padlock on there. If so, you'll have to use bolt cutters to break the lock so we can get out. Other than that, smooth sailing, am I right?" With a nervous chuckle, I laugh at my poor attempt at a joke. Leaning back against the table, I look at everyone, "We need to go over every possible scenario so we're ready for anything. Let's all head to the armory and start packing bags. You guys might need more than just bolt cutters with you. While we're packing up, we can all decide who's going and who's staying."

Jade steps up and smiles, "Oh we already discussed that while you were working on the formula of the drugs."

Clapping my hands together, I nod, "Amazing. What did you guys decide?"

Pointing to each person as she talks she says, "So, we were thinking that Viking, Fish, Rader and Muggzy will be there to take care of the bulkhead doors and be back up if shit goes down. Mrs. Valour and I will be there if Nova needs to be calmed down or helped in any way, since Rhys won't be in any condition to help with that. Vanessa, Mrs. Muggzy, Sable and Lady Sable will stay here and keep an eye on surveillance at the asylum," pausing for a moment she looks up for a moment and then quickly looks back to me. "OH! Also, we figured you would be using your Bluetooth earbuds again, so they will also be ready to play music if necessary. I think that's everything, right guys?"

Everyone looks at each other and nods. "Alright, awesome. To the armory we go. Remember, no such thing as too much or unnecessary for this. Pack as much as possible, honestly."

Pulling up to *Amissa Stella*, I park and shut my car off. I toss my keys in my messenger bag, unbuckle and then grab the steering wheel, gripping it tight. Closing my eyes, I take deep breaths and prepare myself for what's ahead.

"Eagle? You good?"

Clearing my throat, I nod my head. "Y-yeah. I'm good. Everybody in position?"

Murmurs are heard from everyone and then I hear Viking again, "Yeah, we're all ready, Eagle. Keep your head on a swivel."

"10-4, good buddy. Heh, that's what you guys say right?"

"Sure, bud. Over and out." Sliding my messenger bag over my head, I grip my pockets and feel for the cases of syringes I'll need. Patting both cases, I open my door and hop out, readjusting the strap on my bag. Hyper-aware of everything, I can hear the scraping of my work boots against the sidewalk and my bag smacking my left leg with every step as I walk to the entrance.

After clocking in, I head to the janitor's room and start loading up the cleaning cart. Vanessa's voice hits my earbuds, "Eagle? Clear your throat if you can hear me?"

Holding my throat, I act like I'm cracking my neck and clear my throat.

"Good, good. So, everything seems clear right now. Might be a good chance to go administer the first dose to them. Clear your throat again for yes, or give a heavy sigh for no."

Quickly thinking about everybody's usual movements at this time, I agree it's a good time to move forward and clear my throat again.

"Alright, start heading that way, we'll let you know if we see any obstacles."

Grabbing hold of the cart, I pull it towards the door and walk out, pulling at the collar of my jumpsuit to fan myself.

Walking by reception, I smile and wave at the receptionist. "How's that garbage can doing? Need me to empty it for you yet?" The older woman furrows her heavily painted-on eyebrows, looks under her desk and back at me, shaking her head no. Nodding, I smile, "Alright, I'll be sure to check in with you a little later." When she looks back down as a silent dismissal to me, I continue walking towards the elevators. When I approach the elevators, I push the down button and rock on my heels while I wait for the car to arrive. The display lights up and beeps as the doors open for me. I push the cart in, lean down and push the B button. Leaning back against the wall, I wipe the sweat from my brow and take a shaky breath.

"Keep calm, Eagle, all is clear."

I nod my head and grab hold of the cart at the jolt of the elevator. With the beep meaning we've hit our destination, the doors open and I push the cart out.

Viking speaks up and says, "Cameras, guys. Split up keeping an eye out for Eagle and an eye out for us. We're gonna go take care of the doors. Parking now. Jade, Mrs. Valour, hold the phone."

A shuffling noise goes through my earbuds and I faintly hear doors shutting. Mrs. Muggzy comes through as she says, "Hey, Eagle, remember we don't have eyes down there. Keep us as posted as you possibly can while we keep an eye out on the elevator, okay?"

Taking a deep breath, I slowly blow it out and whisper, "Okay." After flipping the lock on the door, I grab the handle and push my way through the door. I shut the door quietly and turn to look at Rhys and Nova. Walking up to Rhys first, I grab the tiny sheet over him and wipe the line of drool falling from the corner of his mouth. Dropping the sheet, I turn and walk over to Nova. Leaning down, I brush hair from her face and

344

place a kiss on the top of her head. Picking up her sheet, I wipe drool and tears from her face and whisper, "Our little secret, SuperNova. I kept my promise, I'm back for you guys."

I pull the case of syringes out of my pocket, unzip it and look at the note inside.

-*Inject initial dose of 0.2 mg (2 mL) IV over 15 seconds.*
-*Assess after 45 seconds.*
-*Inject second dose of 0.2 mg (2 mL) IV.*
-*Repeat dose at 60 second intervals as needed (up to a maximum of 4 additional times) to a maximum total dose of 1 mg (10 mL).*

Pulling out the first syringe filled to 10 mL, I lightly push on the plunger and let a stream shoot out of the needle. Figuring it might take Nova a little longer to come out of sedation due to her size, I turn to her first. There's a blood pressure cuff still around her arm, so I push the button on the vitals machine to start doing a blood pressure reading. Grabbing a hold of her forearm, I watch for her veins to protrude far enough out. *Bingo.* Bringing the syringe down, I puncture the needle into the vein, push 2 mL into it and start counting to forty-five in my head. Flicking my eyes between her arm and her face, I get to forty-five and only see the smallest of changes in her breathing. Pushing the button for another reading, I wait for her veins and then push the needle in again, pushing the plunger down and releasing another 2 mL. Pulling the needle out, I notice the movement of her eyes behind her eyelids and a slight scrunch to her brow. After sixty seconds, I continue the process of pushing another 2 mL. A low whimper falls from her lips and her head moves side to side.

"Shh, shh, shh. SuperNova, it's me Dor. You're okay, every-thing's okay. Shh, shh, shh. I'm right here, I have to help Rhys and I'll be right back, I promise." Placing the syringe down on the metal rolling table, I walk over to Rhys. Pulling the second syringe out I start the process of injecting him. After the second dose he's already starting to come to. "Heyyyy, Reese's Pieces, it's me, Dori. I'm gonna get you and SuperNova outta here, okay? I just gotta give you guys a little more and we can get the fuck outta here." Waiting the allotted time, I give him another dose and then walk back to Nova. I give her another dose, making her eyes open and she blinks away the tears falling from her eyes.

In a cracked and groggy voice, she questions, "Dor?"

"Hey, SuperNova. Yeah, it's me, Dor. I'm right here. Take deep breaths."

Jade

"Eagle? You there?" Looking down at the phone, I gasp and look over at Mrs. Valour.

"What? What's wrong?"

Shaking the phone in front of her face, I whisper, "Call ended. I'm going to try calling him back. Grab your phone and call everyone at V.A.E. Also, go see if the others are on their way back to the truck yet, I have a really bad feeling." Grabbing her phone, she starts punching away at the screen and brings it to her ear. She crawls over the front seat, looks out the window and starts waving frantically.

"Hey! The call disconnected on Eagle's end. Harp is trying to call him now and I'm trying to wave everybody else back to the truck. Are you guys seeing anything on the cameras?"

Growling in frustration at my phone, I hang up my attempt

to call Dorian and try again. Mrs. Valour looks back to me, "Anything?"

I shake my head with a sad smile, "You?"

"No, they're not seeing anything on the cameras at all. Fuck, I really wish we had cameras where he's at. I don't like this."

A wave of nausea hits me and there's a ringing in my ears. Scrunching my eyes closed, I take a deep breath, "I'm really not liking this either. Have they seen you waving them down yet?"

"Noooo, fuck. Wait. YES! Come on, come on, come on." Both truck doors open and everyone starts piling in. Rader crawls over the seat and sits with us, looking between the two of us.

"What's going on, guys?"

Viking, Muggzy and Fish slide in and turn towards us as well. "We got a problem, guys. The call disconnected and I can't reach Dorian. We didn't hear anything suspicious before the call cut out, it just disconnected. They're not seeing anything going on with the cameras on the main floor, but I have a bad feeling. What do we do?"

Punching the steering wheel, Viking shouts, "Fuck! Fuck! Fuck!"

Mrs. Valour puts her phone on speaker and Vanessa speaks up, "Okay, everybody stay calm. Easier said than done, I know, but we all need to take a breath and focus here. I know this is fucking scary, but Dorian is smart. If something was wrong, he's smart enough to be able to get a message to us somehow. He may not have the training that most of you do, but we all know he will fight like hell to save those two. We planned for everything, remember? So everyone just take a minute, take a fucking breath, and remember what our plan was for this exact scenario."

"Swan is right. Muggzy, what did we say was the plan for this?"

"In the event of lost communication, we give Eagle ten minutes to figure out a solution on his own. If we do not hear back from him within that time frame," racking the slide of her gun, she checks the chamber and snaps the slide back in place, "we go in. Fish and Rader go in through the front entrance, Viking and I go through the bulkhead doors."

Fish looks over to me, "How long has it been, Harp?"

Looking down at the phone, I check the call log and see that seven minutes have passed. "Seven minutes. Right before the ten mark I'm calling him again. Ten on the dot, you guys move in."

At the nine minute mark, I call him again. After three rings, Dorian's frantic and hushed voice answers, "I'm sorry, I'm sorry, I'm sorry."

Pulling the phone from my ear, I glare at it and put it on speaker, "What the actual fuck, Eagle?! Where are you? What's happening? Is everything okay?"

"Whoa, whoa, whoa. I said I was sorry. I'm still here with Rhys and Nova. I'm just waiting for them to wake up as much as possible. I don't want to risk it by leaving and coming back later. So I'm waiting here with them and when I think they're good enough to get moving, we're heading to you guys."

Releasing the breath I was holding, I press my hand over my heart, "Are you sure everything's okay? I just have this awful feeling. Why did the call disconnect? Why did it take you so long to answer?"

"Everything is f-ine. Ahem. Fine. I accidentally fumbled my phone and dropped it while getting the case out of my pocket and it ended the call. I was so focused on pulling them from sedation I didn't even think to call you guys right back. Now, is everyone listening?"

Looking up at everyone they all nod and a chorus of, "Yeah's," come from Mrs. Valour's phone.

"Okay, good, good. We're remembering all of the plans for every scenario, right?"

"Yes, Eagle, we were just talking about one of them when *you* disappeared on us. Why? What's up?" There's a pause on his end of the line and I look at my phone making sure the call didn't disconnect again. "Eagle?"

"I'm here. I just... there's one scenario we didn't go over. I know we should've discussed it before we left, but honestly I didn't want any arguments from anyone. I needed all hands on deck for this mission, so I... waited to bring it up. Don't be mad, please don't be mad."

"SPIT IT OUT, EAGLE!" Viking shouts out.

"Okay, okay, geez, don't go having a coronary on me. We have enough obstacles as is without a man down."

"EAGLE!"

"Alright, alright. No excuses, no arguments, our only concern is Rhys and Nova. We all do *whatever* we can to get them the fuck out of here safely. Even if that means leaving me behind."

A chorus of, "WHAT?!" is shouted throughout the truck.

"Guys, please! We made plans for all kinds of scenarios, even agreed that anything could happen to any one of us. So just, agree to this, okay? Rhys and Nova are our number one priority. If you guys can't agree to that, then get the fuck out of here and I'll figure it out on my own."

Rader shouts out, "We're not fucking leaving, Eagle! Everybody just calm the fuck down. Nobody wants to say it, but we all thought of this possibility. We're all here until the very end. So just agree with Eagle so we can get a move on with the rescue mission."

One by one everyone agrees and Dorian lets out a sigh of relief, "Good, good. Thank you, thank you so much you guys. Really."

The sadness of that scenario happening overtakes me and I quietly ask, "You know Rhys and Nova will be very upset with everyone if we have to follow through with this plan, right? Not to mention, even coming out of sedation they're going to fight as hard as they can to interfere. What's the plan then?"

"I already thought of that. Even coming out of sedation, you know Rhys will have some of his strength back. I know it will be difficult to be prepared for a firefight along with getting Rhys, but I think Viking, Fish and Muggzy should be the ones to get a hold of him. As for Nova, you and Mrs. Valour just need to be there to guide her to the truck and try to calm her down like we talked about earlier. I'm going to pocket my phone now and keep an eye on them. I'll let you know when we're on the move."

———★

Shuffling is heard over the phone and Dorian starts speaking. "Alright. No macho, brave badassery from either of you. I know you're still feeling groggy and out of it, but are you good to go? Or do you need a little more time? Try to stand, see how it feels." Slight groaning can be heard in the background as we listen closely. "Okay, good, good. Now sit back down for a minute and take a few deep breaths. Try and kick your legs back and forth, move your arms around, get that blood flowing. Also, Reese's Pieces, I gotta say, uh, heh, I promise I'm only slightly glad you're still groggy for what I'm about to say. I'm not the only one that's driven Beauty."

Rhys' gravelly voice is heard next, "What. The. Fuck. Dori?"

"Hey, hey, listen. It's not like I could do this all by myself, okay. The Horde is helping us all out, so Viking drove Beauty here. Geesh, don't shoot the messenger, it was necessary."

"Ghoulie, be nice to Dor. You know he wouldn't have done it if he didn't have any other choice."

"Thank you, SuperNova. Always the angelic voice of reason. Now, I know you don't like taking orders Rhys, but I need you to listen and actually do what I say. Nope, not a word, listen to me. If I say run, you two fucking run. If I say duck, you duck. Dodge right, dodge left, whatever the case, just fucking do it. We need to be ready for anything, and I'm sorry to say but you guys aren't at 100%, so you have to listen and try with all your might to do what I say. Deal?"

"Deal," Rhys grumbles.

Quietly agreeing, Nova says, "Deal, Dor."

"Alright, try standing up, see how it feels."

"Good? Well, good enough?"

"Perfect. Alright, guys we're heading that way. Everybody ready?"

Looking around at everyone, we all nod, "Yeah, Eagle, we're ready." Viking, Muggzy and Fish hop out first. Rader crawls over the front seat and jumps out behind them.

The back of the truck opens up and Viking pokes his head in. "Stay right here. Sit on the tailgate so you're ready to jump out or slide back in. Keep an ear out if we need you."

Viking and Mrs. Valour share a look, "Be safe, dear."

Viking nods and walks away. "Alright we're about to head through the doors to the main part of the basement."

"Okay, we're all ready, be careful."

A tap, tap, tap is heard as they walk across the basement floor. "Alright, getting ready to climb the steps and open the bulkhead doors."

There's a loud squeak, followed by two loud thumps. A gunshot fires off as Dorian screams out, "RUUUUUUUUU-UNNNNN! GO! GO! GO! NOWWWWW!" My heart is pounding out of my chest and I feel like I'm going to be sick. Mrs. Valour and I jump down from the tailgate and peek around the back of the truck. More gunshots are heard and we see the three of them running towards us. Dorian continues shouting at Rhys and Nova to run. Two men ascend from the basement stairs with their guns pointed towards them. More men appear from each side of the building with their guns raised and they start shooting towards all of us as well.

Viking shouts, "EVERYBODY DOWN! COME ON YOU GUYS, RUN TO US! LET'S GO, LET'S GO, LET'S GO!" Rhys and Nova are running towards us the best that they can, continuously looking behind them.

Dorian shouts at them, "Don't look back, just keep moving forward, you can do thi-" With a groaning gasp, Dorian's words are cut off and he freezes. Holding his sternum, he looks down and blood starts pooling around his hands and pouring from his mouth.

"Oh Gods! DORIAN!" Rhys and Nova stop and turn to look

at Dorian. Slowly, it registers what's happened and they both shout.

"DOR!"

"DORI!"

Dorian drops to his knees and coughs, splattering blood across his chin, "Go! Please!" Shooting a panicked look in our direction, "GET THEM!" Coughing, more blood flies from his mouth. "FOLLOW. THE. PLAN!" Falling forward, he shoots a hand forward to catch himself.

Mrs. Valour and I run to Nova and grab a hold of her, "Come on, hunny, we have to go."

"NO! NO! DOR! WE HAVE TO SAVE HIM! WHAT ARE YOU DOING?! NO! DOR!" Grabbing her tightly, we pull her back to the truck as she sobs and screams. Viking, Muggzy and Fish grab Rhys and start pulling him back.

"GET THE FUCK OFF OF ME! WHAT THE FUCK IS WRONG WITH YOU?! DORIAN! DORIAN!" Rhys pulls away from them the best he can, throwing punches but barely connecting his hits. "WHAT THE FUCK?! GET OFF OF ME! YOU MOTHERFUCKERS! LET GO! DORIAN! GET UP, DORIAN! GET THE FUCK UP NOW!"

"Muggzy, Fish, you're gonna have to get in the back with him so I can drive. Rader, shoot anyone you can. Let's fucking go!"

"Rhys, you have to calm down. Nova is back here, too. I know you don't want to hurt her, so please, calm down." They get Rhys shoved into the truck on his stomach and Muggzy sits on his legs while Fish grips both of his wrists tightly behind his back.

Nova continues sobbing and screaming, "DORIAN! NO! WE CAN'T JUST LEAVE HIM! DORIAN!"

Rhys thrashes around underneath Muggzy and Fish, "You're all dead to me. ALL OF YOU! I'll never forgive you."

He's banging his head on the truck floor and Nova looks over to him. "L-let m-me g-go. H-e needs meeee." She's let go and crawls over to lay down next to Rhys and runs her fingers through his hair, "G-ghoulie, please stop hitting your head. P-please. I'm sorry, I'm so sorry, I love you. I'm so sorry, ghoulie."

Rolling his head, he looks at her and his voice cracks, "My brother."

"A friend knows the song in my heart, and sings it to me when my memory fails." ~Donna Roberts

CHAPTER 25
POSSIBILITY

Nova

WHEN I WAKE UP, I FEEL THE TEARS FALLING DOWN MY FACE THAT I shed in my sleep. As quietly as I can, I sniffle and wipe the tears away. Reaching my hand out for Rhys, I'm met with cold, empty sheets. *Oh, no, no, no. Please tell me this isn't happening.* Jolting up, I frantically search the room hoping he's still here and this isn't another drug induced dream. I yank the sheets aside and jump out of the bed. I'm running to the door when I hear a thud in the closet. Turning around, I walk to the closet and see Rhys sitting on the floor with an open shoe box. All around him are pictures and knick knacks. Hearing my approach, Rhys looks over his shoulder at me with a sad smile, his voice cracking, "H-i, little star." Until this moment, I didn't think my heart could break any further. I was wrong. The sight of his red rimmed tear-filled eyes shatters my heart more.

"Hi, ghoulie. What's all this?"

Clearing his throat, he looks around at the box and everything around him. "Just some stuff Dorian and I collected over the years. I was searching for something important, but got lost in all the memories. Did I wake you?" Lowering myself to the floor, I kneel behind Rhys and wrap my arms around his shoulders. Snuggling into his neck, I place a kiss behind his ear.

"You didn't wake me, ghoul. I think we have enough time, would you like to show me some of this stuff? I'd love to see if you'd let me." He interlaces our fingers and kisses the top of my hand.

"I'd love to show you, sweetheart. Can I ask you something first?" I move everything on the floor and put it back in the box, pushing it aside. I move closer to him, throw my leg over his and straddle him.

With one hand on his shoulder, I run my fingers through his hair and whisper, "You can ask me anything, Rhys."

Brushing his lips against mine, he speaks against them, "I've wanted to say it all morning. Will it upset you if I do?" Shaking my head no, our lips rub together and I pull back. The question makes the ache in my chest worse, and I feel the tears pooling in my eyes. Breathing in through my nose, I blink and a tear falls. Rhys reaches up and wipes it away with his thumb, adding a kiss to my cheek where it first fell. "I guess that answers that. I'm sorry, little star."

Whipping my head towards him, I start shaking my head and grab hold of his face with both hands. "No, no, no. I'm sorry. You didn't upset me. I was just thinking how you wouldn't be able to say it if it wasn't for Dor, ya know? But, yes, you can say it. I know you'll feel bad or maybe feel like it looks like it's not something important to you if you don't. It's okay, ghoulie, I promise."

Pulling me tight against him, he leaves a trail of kisses along my neck and brings his lips to my ear and whispers, "Happy birthday, Nova Skye."

Scratching my nails against the back of his head, more tears fall and my voice cracks, "Thank you, ghoulie." Wiping the tears away on my sleeve, I turn in his lap. I grab the shoe box and slide it between our legs. Resting my back to his front, I lay my head on his shoulder. "Okay, walk me down Dori and Reese's

Pieces memory lane." With a small laugh, Rhys sniffles and I feel him nod his head against mine. With one arm wrapped around my waist, he reaches around me with the other and pulls a picture out of the shoe box.

Looking down at the picture, I gasp, "Awww, oh my god. Look at you two. You both had shaggy, skater boy hair. Your styles certainly never changed either." Scrunching my brows at Dorian's glasses, I roll my head and look up at Rhys. "I didn't know Dorian wore glasses. How did I not know this?"

Rhys snorts and a small smile appears on his face. "He doesn't actually need them. Dorian did the whole 'I wear glasses just-because thing', long before other people did. He just liked the way they looked. Big, grandpa glasses were his favorite to rock." Rhys shakes his head and then puts the picture down. Shuffling through the box, a pair of glasses are revealed and he picks them up. "See? Put those bad boys on. No prescription." Grabbing the glasses from him, I slide them on my face.

Sliding a little down my nose, I look up at Rhys and put on a grandpa voice, "Hiya, sonny boy. Do these make my peepers look real nice?" Laughing, he pushes them up the bridge of my nose. When he removes his hand, they slide back down a little and he laughs again.

"Cute as always, grandpappy." Pulling the glasses off, I fold the arms in and place them down beside our legs. Bringing my attention back to the box he's shuffling through, he picks up a small box and brings it up to his face. "Damn, there it is." Putting it down beside us, I look down at the box and try to read what it says on top.

Looking back up to Rhys, I question, "What is it, ghoul?"

Dropping a kiss to the top of my head, he says, "A present for you. I'll give it to you later on today."

"For me? That's strange. Can't I see it now?"

Putting the picture back in the shoe box, he closes it and pushes it away. "Later, I promise. We have a few things we have to do before we meet up with *them*." Grabbing the glasses, I slide them in my hoodie pocket. I stand up, looking down at Rhys and holding my hand out to help him up. Grabbing my offered hand, he stands up and drops a kiss on my forehead.

"I wish you weren't so upset with them, Rhys. You heard what they said, and we both know they wouldn't lie about something like that."

He walks out of the closet and grumbles, "I just need time." Walking to the door, he stops with his hand holding the knob, "I'm gonna go take a shower."

I lean against the wall, laying my head there and watch as he walks out of the room. Pushing myself off the wall, I turn to shut the light off in the closet. Our anime onesies catch my attention and I walk up to them. Holding the sleeve of mine, I caress the fabric and the memories from that night come rushing in. Pulling my hand away, I lift it to my face and look at my *every life* tattoo on my left ring finger. Thinking about the sun and moon tattoo Dorian got that night, I whisper, "You were always the sun, Dorian." Grabbing both onesies, I shut the light off and walk out of the closet. I toss them down on the bed and head to the bathroom to check on Rhys.

I can hear Rhys' soft cries in the shower. Quickly pulling my hoodie off, I toss it to the floor and walk up to the shower. Slowly peeling the curtain back, I peek my head in and see Rhys sitting on the shower floor with his knees up to his chest. His arms are resting on his knees with his face pressed against them. "Oh, ghoulie."

When I step in the shower, he lifts his head with tears falling down his face. He drops his legs down to make room for me and I lower myself on top of him and hold him tight to me. Wrapping his arms around my waist, he nuzzles into my neck and cries. With one arm wrapped around his back, I start running my fingers through his hair with my free hand. "Shh, shh. I'm right here, I'm right here. I'm so sorry, Rhys."

He takes a deep breath and kisses my neck, and between every kiss he says, "Promise me. Please, please. Promise me." I feel his cock harden beneath me and I pull my fingers from his hair to reach down. Stroking his cock twice, I slightly lift and aim his cock towards my entrance. Once I've slid his cock inside me, he groans and I rest my ass against his thighs.

Placing my hands on either side of his face, I search his eyes and ask, "Promise you what, Rhys? What do you need?" He grips my hips tightly and starts lifting me up and down on his cock.

"Promise, promise me you won't leave. Please, Nova, you can't fucking leave. I won't fucking survive it. I already lost my brother, please don't make me lose you, too. I can't do it, I won't do it."

Caressing his tears away with my thumbs, I lean forward and kiss his lips three times. "I'm not going anywhere. Do you hear me, Rhys Alexander? I'm not going anywhere. You're stuck with me. Got it?" When he doesn't respond right away, I press my forehead against his, and slightly raise my voice. "Rhys, do you hear me?! I'm not going anywhere."

Nodding his head, he rubs our foreheads together and whispers, "I got it, little star. I love you so fucking much." Rhys starts lifting me up and down and thrusting the best he can as he continues chanting, "I love you, I love you." I crash my lips to his, suck on his bottom lip and slowly release it with a pop. Bringing his mouth back to mine, we pant and moan into each other's mouths. I feel the tingle up my spine, my pussy grips his cock tight and I grab hold of him as tight as I can. Just as I start to fall apart, Rhys grunts and groans, "Fuck. Fuuuuuck, I love you."

Feeling his cock pumping inside me, I moan, "I fucking love you, too." Placing my one hand on the wall and the other on his shoulder, I stand on shaky legs. Rhys holds his hands up ready to catch me if necessary. Standing up, he reaches behind him and slaps at the handle to shut the water off. I wrap a towel around myself and hand one back to Rhys. As we walk into the room, I hear his gruff voice behind me, "What's this?"

Looking back at him, I follow the direction he's looking and turn towards the bed. Walking up to the bed, I run my fingers over the onesies. "I just... I was thinking we could wear ours there, and I'd wear my flower crown. I think I want to bring his onesie and flower crown to the service. Is... is that okay? You don't have to wear yours if you don't want to."

Feeling his arms wrap around me, he places his chin on my shoulder. "I think it's the perfect idea, little star. He would love it." Placing a kiss on my shoulder, he walks to his dresser and pulls out a pair of black boxer briefs. I watch the water drip down his body as he rubs it away with his towel. Dropping it, he slides his boxer briefs up and starts shuffling in the drawer again.

Grabbing a pair of underwear and a bra for me, he walks up and hands them to me. "Thanks, ghoulie." After getting dressed, I walk over to the night stand, grab my phone and drop it in my onesie pocket. Rhys walks up to the closet and looks over his shoulder at me.

Tilting his head towards the closet, "The things I want to bring to his service are in here. Are you okay with going into his room by yourself to get his things?"

Swallowing the lump in my throat, I nod and give him a smile, "Of course. Meet at the door?" He nods in return and walks into the closet. Walking up to the dresser, I pick up my flower crown and gently place it on my head. The flowers are all dead so there's a slight crunch when it slides on my head and I wince. Slowly walking down the hall, I stop in front of his door and freeze when I catch my hand ready to knock. Shaking my hand out, I drop it down and grab the door knob. I take a deep breath and push the door open. The scent of weed, strawberries and incense hits me all at once. I rub over my heart in circles as if that will take the ache away. Walking up to his closet, I open the door and step inside. There's an explosion of color with all of his clothes and only a small section of dark clothing. Heading to the back of the closet I immediately spot his onesie and pull it down. Pulling the hanger away, I hang it up and then hug the onesie against me.

I walk out of the closet, close the door behind me and immediately catch sight of his flower crown hanging above his dresser.

Walking over, my phone starts to ring and I pull it out of my onesie pocket. Jade's name lights up on the screen and I accept the call, "Hey, Jade."

"Hi, hunny. I just wanted to call and let you know that everyone is heading over to *Vega Altair*. You guys can meet us there whenever you're ready and we'll buzz you in, okay?"

"Yeah, yeah of course. We're just taking care of a few things and then we'll be heading that way, too. See you soon." Ending the call, I pocket my phone, fold up Dorian's onesie and place it on his bed. Turning towards the dresser, I carefully pull his flower crown down and place it on top of the onesie. Scooping them both up, I walk out of his room and shut his door.

I look up to see Rhys waiting by the door with his hands in his pockets. "Ready, sweetheart?"

"Mhmm, let's go."

Rhys

The Horde is already here when we pull into the parking lot. Shutting the truck off, I thump my head against the headrest and groan. "You knew they'd be here, Rhys. They loved him, too."

Roughly rubbing my hand down my face, I scratch at my beard and turn my head in Nova's direction.

In a sharper tone than I meant to, I say, "I know." Narrowing her eyes at me, I clear my throat and soften my voice, "I'm sorry. I know. Let's do this." Unbuckling, I shove my keys in my pocket and hop out of the truck. Walking quickly to Nova's side, I open her door and reach around her to unbuckle her seatbelt. Helping her out of the truck, I grab her hand and shut the door. She squeezes my hand as we walk to the doors and I squeeze in return, rubbing my thumb over her hand. Right before we reach the doors, it buzzes to allow us entry and I grab the door handle, opening the door for us. Keeping my head down, we head to the conference room. I hear Nova's gasp, I look up and my eyes widen at the sight before us. A hurricane of emotions hits me and it makes me sick to my stomach. None of The Horde are wearing black for his service, they're all in various arrays of bright colors. Part of it warms my heart, because it shows that they knew him well, they knew Dorian was all about his bright colors. Hell, he was the bright color in our lives. Along with the warmth in my heart, the ache of grief hits me. Remembering that they left him behind to die alone makes anger the winning emotion in this moment. "Unfuckinbelievable. Wearing these colors for him doesn't fucking bring him back. It doesn't erase what you all fucking did."

Nova whips her head towards me and hisses, "Rhys. Please."

Shaking my head, I put my hands up and start walking backwards, "I need... I... Fuck, I need a minute." Spinning around, I march out of the conference room and head to my playroom. Pushing the door open, I walk up to the table in the middle of the room and start pushing it back towards the wall. The legs of the table scrape and squeal against the floor. Pushing it up against the wall with a clang, I hop up on the table and lean against the wall.

I pull out Dorian's matching leather entwined bracelet from my pocket. Looking at it, I notice the bright blue shade of the leather straps are slightly faded. Pulling my sleeves up, I look down at my wrist and see the matching bracelet Dorian made for me. Instead of blue, mine is a bright yellow with faded patches as well. The memory of the bracelets washes over me and I close my eyes, reliving it.

It was the summer before our freshman year and we were running around to get away from our parents. We always heard stories of the girls having friendship bracelets and wondered why guy friends couldn't do the same thing. With a badass flair, of course. We decided we were going to make our own and have them made of leather to match our style. I dyed the leather of Dorian's my favorite color and he did the same for mine. Opening my eyes, I twist the bracelet around and then put it back in my pocket. Feeling the box I showed Nova earlier, I pull it out and put it between my legs on the table. Looking at the note written in sharpie on top, I snort and run my fingers over it. *For when the stars align.* "You son of a bitch. I know you wrote this after we met Nova." Pulling the top off, I place it down and pull out the folded paper inside. Opening the note, I start reading it to myself.

HIYA REESE'S PIECES! Now, before you question the note on the box, I totally wrote it BEFORE you and Nova met. So, ha! Insert massive pause here for dramatic effect. Okay, okay, you're right. I wrote this note and the one on the box AFTER you guys met. BUT, the present inside is still the same one I bought when we were looking for these gifts. I know we were supposed to leave the presents alone, but I figured I had to get this sized properly. Do you remember how long we would pester each other to find out what we bought. I'm really hoping the gift you picked for whoever my future girl is, will be as perfect as this gift for Nova. Seriously, I swear this is the same gift I bought all those years ago. You're probably wondering why I'm repeating myself, but you'll understand when you look at it. Please let me be there when you give this to her. I know some moments are meant to be for just the two of you, but I really would love to see the way her face lights up when you give it

Folding the note up, I put it down next to the box and pick it up. I peel back the tissue paper to reveal a silver band with a star in the middle and a bright blue stone in the center. A half laugh, half sob escapes my throat looking at it. "No fucking way. She's gonna love it, Dori." I swipe away my fallen tears.

The sound of footsteps echoing grabs my attention and I look up quickly. Sighing, I smile, "Hi, little star." She smiles in return and walks towards me. Putting the note in the box, I close it and put it in my pocket. Stepping between my legs, she drops her hands on my thighs and squeezes.

"Was it what you expected?"

"More. So much more," I croak.

Squeezing my thighs again she nods, "Good. Are you ready to come back to the conference room so we can start planning?"

"As ready as I'll ever be." Grimacing, I add, "I need to apologize to everyone, huh?"

With a sad smile she places a kiss on my lips and pulls back. "They understand, but yes, it would be nice if you apologized. I know what's going on with you, but they don't. Maybe try to explain to help them better understand."

Furrowing my brows, I look up at her, "How do you know what's going on with me? I can barely comprehend it." She pulls me by the hands and I slide off the table. Entwining our fingers, we start walking towards the door.

"Cuz I know you, ghoulie. There's a lot of emotions hitting you all at once. With them, anger comes through as a defense mechanism. Anger is easier to deal with than grief. With me, I see it all. I get to see the sorrow of it all. I know you don't really blame them, it just feels easier to do so."

Stopping in place, I look down to the floor and sigh. "You're right. I don't. It's so much easier admitting that to you, though."

Squeezing my hand she starts pulling, "I know. Let's go. I'm with you every step of the way."

Everyone turns their attention to us when we walk through the door. I rub and squeeze the back of my neck with a nervous chuckle. Clearing my throat, I look up at everyone, "Listen. I'm... I'm sorry for how I reacted and what I've said to you guys. I'm not handling this very well, I don't know how to navigate this, so I lashed out. I understand that if you had any other choice you would've tried harder to save Dorian. I know him, and I know he had to have told you guys to focus on getting us out of there no matter what. I should be more appreciative for all you guys did when you saved us. You saved my girl. It just might take me some time to wrap my head around my best friend being gone. So, if you could maybe be a little patient with me, I'll work on it."

Everyone smiles and nods and a chorus of, "Of course," and "Yeah," are heard from them.

Clapping my hands together, I nod, "Alright, enough of the rom-com, let's start making plans for these sons of bitches and then go give my brother the service he deserves."

"HERE, HERE!"

———————⭐

Nova

Walking to the back of Rhys' truck, he opens it up and starts pulling out pallets. The Horde walks up and everyone starts grabbing a pallet to carry. After all of the pallets are out, I reach in and pull out the gas can in there. Spaced out in a single file line behind us, we lead the way to our favorite spot. Walking past the logs, Rhys throws his pile down in the makeshift fire pit. I dump a bit of gasoline on the pallet and while everyone takes turns dropping theirs down, I add more gasoline. I walk away from the fire pit and put the gas can down next to one of the sitting logs. Viking steps up to the fire pit and pulls out a matchbook. Flipping the cover over, he rips one match out, strikes it and then lights all of the matches. Tossing all the lit matches onto the fire pit, the pallets are engulfed in flames immediately. Pulling my smokes out of my pocket, I light one up and inhale the smoke. As I slowly blow it out, I look around at everyone. "Whoever wants to go first, go ahead. It's okay if you didn't bring anything to throw in. If you can, maybe just a few words, or a memory of Dor."

After everyone shares, Rhys and I are left. Laughs and tears fell from all of us with every memory and item shared. Looking over at Rhys, I reach out and rub his leg. Looking over at me, he smiles, "You can go first, little star."

With a sniffle, I stand up and stare at the fire. Lifting the dead flower crown, I take a deep breath. "As you can see, I have one that matches. The first time Rhys and Dorian brought me here he made us both flower crowns," my voice breaks on the final word and I clear my throat, attempting to push down a sob. "We smoked, we danced and he was Prince Dorian. He was the sunshine in our l-lives." Bringing the crown to my lips, the dead flowers scratch me as I place a kiss on one. Tossing it in the fire, more tears fall from my eyes. "This," holding up the onesie and then hugging it to me, "is his onesie. Obviously you can see Rhys and I wearing ours. During that trip that took us to Pendleton and Tri-Cities, we picked up these onesies. We wore them everywhere. We gave zero fucks about the looks and whispers." Holding up my hand, I wiggle my ring finger, "We even went to the tattoo shop wearing these onesies. We listened to music and watched the stars that night. Who knew… who knew everything would fall apart the next… the n-ext d-ay." Throwing the onesie in, I watch the flames surround it, and the sob I held back escapes my throat. Bringing my hands up over my mouth, I hold my breath in an attempt to stop. I feel Rhys' hand on my shoulder and I turn towards him and collapse into his arms. Holding me tight, he starts rocking us back and forth. Kissing the top of my head, he places his chin there and starts talking.

"Long story short, Dorian and I made ourselves boy friendship bracelets. This is the one I made for my best friend, my brother. We have a lifetime of memories, and if I could, I would tattoo them all on me and carry him with me until my last day. I… I l-ove you, Dori. I'll make those motherfuckers pay for taking you away from us."

One by one, everyone walks by squeezing our shoulders. "We'll meet you guys in the parking lot. Give you a moment."

After everyone leaves, Rhys brings his lips to my ear and whispers, "I have a present for you, little star. Keep in mind, this isn't what you think it is. Believe me, the real deal *will* happen, just not like this. For now, just know that this is a birthday present from me and Dori."

Pulling back, I blink away the tears and tilt my head. "What do you mean a present from both of you?"

"Along with the bracelets we made for each other, we made a plan. We knew we were going to be in each other's lives forever, and that meant that when we found the one, they would be integrated into our lives. They wouldn't just be with us, but they would be best friends with our best friend." Huffing out a laugh, he adds, "Which most definitely happened when you fell into our lives. Anyways, we decided we would get a gift for that person, and we would give it to them as a present from both of us. I gotta say, Dorian picked real fucking well. Opening that box today blew my fucking mind. With that said," letting go of me he drops down to one knee and I gasp.

"Ghoul?"

Holding his hand up, he smiles, "I told you, it's not that. Believe me, you'll get that proposal. This is just a birthday present, sweetheart."

He pulls the box out from his pocket and opens it up. Pulling back the tissue paper, he lifts it towards me and I look down. "Holy fucking shit. He really bought this before you guys met me?!"

"I know, I know. I thought the same thing, I can't even fucking believe it." Pulling the ring out, he puts the box down next to him and reaches up. Bringing my shaking hand towards him, he grabs hold and kisses my ring finger over my tattoo before sliding the ring on. It's a perfect fit.

"How?"

Letting go of my hand, he closes the box and pockets it again. "Note says he had it sized. I don't have a clue how he pulled that part off."

Throwing my arms around Rhys, I pull him tightly against me. "It's perfect. Thank you, ghoulie."

Looking over to the fire, I smile, "Thank you, Dor."

I sneak a look at Rhys and see him looking up at the sky as a tear falls down his cheek.

Wiping it away, he looks down at me, "Time to go. Sun's going down, Dorian must be ready for bed."

Looking at the sunset, I smile and whisper, "Goodnight, Dorian."

"When tomorrow starts without me, and I'm not there to see, if the sun should rise and find your eyes filled with tears for me, I wish so much you wouldn't cry the way you did today, while thinking of the many things we didn't get to say. I know how much you love me, as much as I love you and each time that you think of me, I know you'll miss me too. But when tomorrow starts without me, please try to understand, that an angel came and called my name and took me by the hand. He said my place was ready, in heaven far above. And that I'd have to leave behind all those I dearly love. ~David Romano

EPILOGUE

Epilogue BURN OUT THE STARS
6 MONTHS LATER...
Nova

LOOKING AROUND THE ROOM, I MEET THE EYES OF EVERYONE SITTING around the table. "Everyone clear on the plan?" They all look at each other and nod. Rhys stands tall with his arms crossed over his chest and nods as well. I pick up the remote and point it at the screens. "Alright, let's do this." Pressing a button, a message appears on the screen in big bold letters. *Do you wish to delete all files? Yes or No.* Moving the arrow over to yes, I hit the button and a loading bar appears on the screen as thousands of pictures and files start exploding in the background.

Tilting his head towards the door, Rhys clears his throat,

"Let's head to the armory." Once we're in the armory, everyone grabs their own duffle bag and fills them with everything we'll need. All bags are filled to the point that they're almost impossible to zip shut. One by one, everyone walks to the wall of bulletproof vests, grabbing their own and putting it on. Putting the duffle straps over our shoulders, we all look at each other.

I step forward and say, "For Dorian." Around the circle everyone steps forward and says the same. As we all walk out of the armory, I freeze when I remember there's one last thing I'll need for this mission.

Rhys stops and turns towards me, "What's wrong, sweetheart?"

"Nothing, I just remembered I need to grab something. You guys go on ahead, I'll be right out."

"You sure?"

Waving my hand I reassure him, "Yeah, yeah I'm sure. I'll be right out, I promise." He places a kiss on my forehead and heads out with The Horde. Walking as fast as I can with the duffle slapping against my thigh, I head to the conference room. Next to the screens is a big, framed photo of Dorian. Running my finger down the picture frame, I smile, "Hi, Dor. We need you with us." Pulling it off the nail, I press the picture against my chest and head outside. The Horde is already loaded up in the van with it running. Rhys is leaning against the front of his truck and pushes off of it when he sees me. Walking up to me, he pulls the duffle off of my shoulder and carries it as we walk together.

Throwing it in the back he looks at the frame and then to me. "What you got there, little star?"

"Our best friend."

With a sad smile, he shuts the back of the truck and guides me to my door. Opening it for me, he picks me up and puts me in my seat. Grabbing the seatbelt, he pauses, "Watch out, Dori." I lift the frame above me with a small laugh as Rhys buckles me in. With the click of the buckle, he slides his hand to my thigh and squeezes. Kissing me three times, he steps back and shuts my door. Getting to his side, he opens his door and looks back at The Horde. "We ready?!"

Viking honks the horn twice and nods at Rhys. Hopping in, Rhys shuts his door and starts the truck. Pulling out of the parking lot, he takes a deep breath and starts tapping the steering wheel. *Burn Out The Stars* by *Bryce Savage* starts playing on the radio and he starts singing along. Looking over at me during parts of the song, he reaches over and places his hand on my thigh. Holding on to Dorian's picture with my right hand, I drop my left on top of Rhys' and rub back and forth. Getting closer to *Amissa Stella*, he stops singing and says, "Hey, little star?"

Looking over at him, "Yeah, ghoulie?"

Glancing over with a sad smile, "This life."

I pull the picture frame away from my chest and look down at Dorian's smiling face. In a tearful voice, I respond, "and..."

"Sometimes the hardest part isn't letting go, but rather, learning to start over." ~Nicole Sobon

... THE NEXT

The story doesn't end here....

NEXT LIFE is coming SPRING 2024

Domestic Violence Helpline & Resources

NATIONAL DOMESTIC VIOLENCE HOTLINE

1-800-799-7233 | 1-800-787-3224

LOVE IS RESPECT
NATIONAL TEEN DATING ABUSE HELPLINE

1-866-331-9474 | 1-866-331-8453

RAPE, ABUSE, INCEST NATIONAL NETWORK

800-656-HOPE (4673) | RAINN.ORG

NATIONAL SEXUAL ASSAULT HOTLINE

1-800-656-4673

Substance Abuse
Helpline & Resources

SAMHSA NATIONAL HELPLINE

1-800-662-4357

AMERICAN ADDICTION CENTERS

313-217-4572

OVERDOSE HOTLINE

FOR IMMEDIATE EMERGENCIES, CALL 911.
POISON CONTROL 1-800-222-1222

DRUGFREE.ORG

855-378-4373

DRUGABUSE.COM

888-969-7116

NATIONAL SUICIDE PREVENTION

1-800-273-8255

ACKNOWLEDGMENTS

To Dean Winchester and the creators of Supernatural. If anyone knows me, they know my love for Dean and all things Supernatural. He was a huge inspiration for the character of Rhys. In this book, Rhys says, "I'm the thing that monsters have nightmares about." Side note, acknowledgement needs to go to the creators of Buffy the Vampire Slayer as well. While researching, I discovered it is a quote from that show as well. I would like to also mention that Dean's chick-flick comment is mentioned in this story as well. It is a line I use quite often with my friends in real life and I couldn't imagine not having it in the story.

There is a shower scene in the story that involves Nova. Nova is a morph between myself and Emma Stone. This scene is a nod to the funny shower scene Emma Stone does in the movie The Easy A.

There is a scene in here as a nod to the ever brilliant, Dr. Spencer Reid in Criminal Minds. Just think, magic trick. If you know, you know.

To The Horde. Yes, The Horde truly exists. These are my people, my found family. Thank you for all of the love and support, ideas and suggestions for the book with your characters. Alright, enough, enough, NO CHICK FLICK MOMENTS!

To my badass and ever so patient (with me haha) editor, Vanessa. Thank you for being a fucking rockstar through this whole process. This book literally wouldn't have happened without you. Thank you for helping me make a lifelong dream come true. Yuck, it's getting mushy again.

Thank you to all of my beta and ARC readers. Your support, feedback and REACTIONS really fueled my fire in the home-stretch. Thank you for helping polish something that is so near and dear to my heart.

Printed in Great Britain
by Amazon